Immaculate Deception

Tenisha Jackson

ISBN-13 978-1-105-04736-7

Printed in the United States of America

10 9 8 7 6 5 4 3 2 1

This is a work of fiction. Any resemblance or similarities to actual events, real people, living or dead, or to real locales are intended to give the novel a sense of reality. Any similarity in other names, characters, or places, and incidents is entirely coincidental.

First Edition: The Diamond Life Series

tenishajackson50@yahoo.com

Cover Design & Illustrations by Oddball Designs

Immaculate Deception

Acknowledgements

First of all, thank you, Jesus, for giving me this opportunity. Hold up, excuse me while I get my praise on...okay I'm back. Thank you, Jesus, for helping me to realize that there is no life without you. Thank you for showing me that if I give you just a little of my time each day that you can make miracles happen.

I would like to thank my mom, Horazine, my brothers, Tony and Jeremy that are always supportive. It has been a struggle, but we did it. I would like to thank my close friend, Aundral Simon, my lifelong friend. You have been there through the thick and the thin; I couldn't have done this without you. Linda Flask Brooks, thank you, my sister from another mother, thank you for all your support, thank you for being a sister and thank you for helping me keep a level head through all of the madness. Chicks, I love y'all, thank you for everything you have done for me.

To my loving friends and family who always got my back, I love you. (Deshun Smith Images) Cuz, you up next, the world's best photographer. Andy Roach, my dear friend, thanks for all the support and love, Burton Brooks, Tanisha Clay, Andrea Hargrave, Romeo, Adu Blay, Kaili Thomas, Broderick Disro. Thanks for being there at clutch time, Andre P. "Big Homie", I love you.

Thank you to my friend and editor Shelia Lipsey. Okay, I think that's it...Oh no, I especially can't forget Jared Allman; thank you so much for being my friend, for pushing me to get this book published and helping me to expose my book to the world. We about to do it big baby, with our future business ventures....Let's Go!

Diamond Life... to the Next Life

This book is dedicated to my family
Zine, Tony, Julie, Jeremy, and Pettie
I love y'all

Prologue

I looked at myself in the mirror and tears welled up in my eyes. The anguish and the pain I had faced in the past year stared back at me. My once beautiful body was now covered in burn marks, cuts, and scrapes.

This scar on my neck, I hate it. It seems like it's the first thing people notice when they look at me, but I try not to let it bother me. I'm so thankful my face did not scar. I only have a small mark on the side of my face from where I had reconstructive surgery on my jaw line. The scars on my body, I can hide, but if my face was fucked up, I don't know what I would do. But anyway, I'm not focusing on the scars or burn marks today, because today is Valentine's Day. Me and my baby are celebrating the love we have for one another.

Texas and I have decided what happened in the past is over. We can't change the past. What we are focusing on now is our future together. I told him that I would, as long as he continues to go to counseling. He has just completed a twelve-step program, so that's a start. I had the cast removed from my leg that I had been toting around for two months. So tonight is going to be special, because I have a little surprise in store for my baby. Ever since the cast was removed, I've been practicing this striptease that I'm going to perform for him tonight. I even got my girl, Tangerine, who dances at Platinum Paradise, to come over and teach me some of her sexy stripper moves. After my boo gets a peek of me winding and gyrating my ass, he'll be ready to plunge all eleven inches of his beefy dick inside me. I'm so excited; this is the first time in months we've had a romantic evening, and I'm hoping the special night I have planned helps spark some of the magic we once shared. I'm doing everything in my power to make sure this evening goes as planned.

Texas and I have been through so much. From the baby momma drama to the mental and physical abuse. But I feel this relationship is worth fighting for. My girls are always asking how I can still go on, considering everything I've been through. I tell them because of love. If you truly love somebody, you'll accept the good, the bad, and the ugly. You'll do anything to make them happy. Plus, I can't do without the lifestyle Texas has accustomed me to. See he's a professional football player, been in the league almost ten years and he is still good; I'm talkin' ESPN sports highlights every Sunday. So from since the first day I met him money ain't never been a problem. We live in a two million dollar home in the Governor's Club at Brentwood. We have a beach home in Charleston, South Carolina, and we own a cottage in Aspen. If you ever lay eyes on him, you would know God himself sent one of his angels down in the form of a man. Standing six five and two hundred and forty pounds with a rich mahogany skin tone and major swag, that's killin' Jay-Z, LeBron and Obama put together, everything about my man is top notch. If you had the chance to receive some of his good lovin', you'll be saying the same shit. Because a man like Texas Reynolds, you'll do almost anything to keep.

Anyway, tonight I have everything laid out. First, we're having dinner at Ruth's Chris Steak House, and afterwards I reserved us the master suite at Loews Vanderbilt Hotel, which is right next door. That's when I'ma surprise my boo with my dance, and after that it's gonna go down.

We arrived at dinner and Texas was just as excited as I was. We both missed the closeness that we once shared and it seems as if we are beginning to bond again.

"Rae, you know I love you," Texas said and grabbed my hand and kissed it. "Without you there is no me."

"And no me without you." I smiled and planted a soft kiss on his juicy lips.

Our entrées were served. We held hands as I led us in a silent prayer. Then I picked up my knife to cut a bite of my filet but quickly dropped it back down on the plate. My fingers went numb. Texas' gaze caught my anxiety. It was the nerves in my hand, they had been badly fractured.

"Babe, you okay?" he asked

"Yeah, Bay." I winced and flashed him a smile faker than a three-dollar bill. I played it off, grabbed my glass with my other hand, and took a sip of champagne. Truth was the nerves were so fractured in my right hand that I would often times have severe nerve spasms that would paralyze my hand for a few seconds, sometimes minutes. But I acted like it was nothing because I'm not going to let anything ruin this evening– no thoughts, no memories, nothing from the past.

After feasting on a delicious dinner of salad, filet mignon, asparagus spears, and a bottle of Perrier Jouet Fleur, we were good and toasted when we left the restaurant. I blindfolded Texas and we walked next door to the Loews Vanderbilt.

"Baby, where we goin'?" Texas kept trying to make me tell him what my plans were.

"Tex, I told you, it's a surprise. You're just gonna have to wait and see." I smiled and grabbed his hand and led him to the elevator.

He was grinning from ear to ear. "Baby, c'mon tell me where we going," he pleaded and pulled me close to him.

"Texas, be patient! Why you think you always gotta know everything?" As soon as the elevator doors opened, I grabbed his hand and led him up to the penthouse suite.

"Relax, baby, I got this."

When I entered the room, I was blown away. It was laid out. The hotel staff had really surprised me. Candles were lit around the room emitting a sweet fragrance. Red rose petals had been placed on the bed in the shape of a heart. The fireplace was lit, with the logs making the room warm and cozy. The curtains were pulled back displaying an intoxicating view of the city. Everything was perfect just as I'd planned.

I removed the blindfold and right away, his eyes lit up like stars against a midnight sky.

"Ahhh, baby, this is so nice."

He picked me up and swung me around then he quickly put me down. "Hold on, baby, let me take this burner out." He pulled his gun from underneath his shirt and placed it underneath the pillow. He wrapped his arms around my waist and picked me up from the ground. He held me for a minute and kissed me before gently laying me down on the bed. His lips touched mine and he snaked his tongue into my mouth. We greedily kissed each other like our lives depended on it. My body unwound as he planted soft, delicate kisses on my neck. A mild tingle rushed through me. My back arched as he slid his slick tongue down my neck. He unleashed my firm titties from my low cut dress and sucked on each of my puffy nipples like a melting ice cream cone.

"Oooooh, baaaaby," I murmured. "Let me feel that dick." I unbuttoned his pants, but before I could pull out his dick, he had dug his fingers into my creamy wetness. "Mmmm," I moaned in ecstasy as I slowly rotated my hips and sucked his fingers inside me.

"Damn, baby you so wet," he whispered. He tried to take off my thong, but couldn't get it over my phat ass.

He smacked me on the ass. "Take that shit off," he insisted and gently gripped me on one of my ass cheeks. He stood up and quickly undressed. His thick pole poked through the slit in his boxers. I pulled down his boxers and slowly stroked my hand down the shaft of his thick, juicy, slab and watched as a small amount of precum oozed out.

My mouth watered. *Mmmm, ain't nothing in the world better than a fat, vein-poppin' dick.* Then I remembered my dance. *Damn! Damn! Damn!* I couldn't wait to slide my simmering pussy on his eleven inches and swallow every inch of him inside me. But I had to be patient first; I really wanted to do my dance that I had worked so hard on. I reluctantly got up to go get in the shower. Texas sat up and grabbed my hand.

"Hold on, mama…where you going?"

"Baby, I'm about to take a shower." I teasingly smiled at him.

"A shower?" He shook his head. "Nah, ma." He pulled me close and nuzzled his head into my belly, softly kissing me on exposed skin. "You can take a shower later."

"No, baby, I'm about to take a shower now." I leaned down and playfully kissed him on the lips. "Plus, I don't wanna ruin the surprise I got for you."

"Dang, Rae, you gon' leave me hanging like this." We both looked down at his swollen head.

A slight smirk adorned my lips. "Baby, be patient; I'ma take care of that later." *Believe me, boo, I wanna tackle that big muthafucka right now.*

He grabbed my wrist. "Man, c'mon on; quit playin'. Lemme get some right fast." He softly kissed me on the stomach.

"No, Tex. If we do it now it'll ruin the surprise I have planned for you." I tried to pull away but his grip around my wrist was so tight. "Boy, let me go." I giggled and he finally unleashed his grip but not before slapping me on my ass.

"Ouch!" I screamed and playfully punched him in the arm, and sashayed off to the shower.

We both got in the shower and bathed each other like we always do. Texas continued trying to make love to me but I wouldn't let him. I wanted to do my dance first. I had worked so hard on this dance I had the ideal song, "Adore You" by Prince, and had the perfect lingerie outfit that accentuated my nice, round ass and slim waistline.

Texas got out the shower first, and I stayed in. I let the warm water stream down my body as I reflected on memories from the past and hoped for a better relationship in the future. After I got out the shower and dried off, Texas peeked in the door as I had my leg on the toilet lathering it with lotion.

"Ooooh, look at that ass," he teased while grabbing onto his hardness.

"Shut the door, boy."

We laughed.

"Hey, baby. I gotta go get something out the car. I'll be right back."

"What you gotta get outta the car? Your pajamas and everything is in the suitcase I brought here earlier."

"Well, I gotta get my phone and some other stuff."

What other stuff? "'Kay. When you come back, I'll be ready," I replied anxiously.

"You betta. If not, I'ma catch a case, 'cause ya' ass gon' get raped."

We both laughed.

He shut the door and I finished getting ready for my striptease debut. I'm so excited. Everything is going as planned and Texas seems like he's getting back to himself.

The steam from the shower had fogged up the mirror. I took my hand and ran it across the glass. Water bubbles cascaded the mirror and it fogged back up. I opened the door to let some steam out, and then flossed and brushed my teeth. I washed my face with my Shiseido skin care line and some of the cleanser got in my eye.

"Damn!" My eye started stinging. I splashed it with cold water and held a towel to it until it stopped watering.

While I had the towel to my eye, I was retracing my dance moves in my head. When I put the towel down and looked in the mirror, my heart skipped a beat. Texas was standing right behind me. I grabbed my chest.

"Baby…. you scared the shit outta me!" I let out a sigh of relief. "I didn't know you were standing behind me." I smiled at him through the reflection in the mirror but the stone cold expression on his face didn't budge.

"I see you found the pajamas I packed for you." He didn't respond. I looked in his eyes. They were different. I sensed something was wrong.

I turned around. "Baby, what's the ma–"

His iron fist met the side of my jaw, crushing my reconstructed jaw line. *What the fuck!*

He grabbed a chunk of my hair and rammed my head directly into the mirror. Glass shattered everywhere, blood gushed from my forehead, and a tidal wave of pain and terror exploded in my head.

God, please, no this can't be happening again. I stumbled back woozily. Grabbing the towel rack to steady myself, I swung at him but missed. His fist landed directly on the rim of my nose. *Plop!* I fell into the tub. The back of my head collided with the concrete wall, and my eyes rolled into their sockets. I blacked out.

"Uhhhh," I moaned, with my mouth hanging open. My eyes fluttered opened, and the grim fate of my reality began to crystallize. My blurry eyes met his. *Nooooo!* He stood over me celebrating the present state I was in.

"Ple….stop," I muttered, as my jaw dangled on its hinges and blood flowed into my mouth.

"Bitch, I'ma kill you!" he snarled through clinched teeth. He snatched me out the tub by my hair, and drug my body through crumpled shards of broken glass into the bedroom. I stumbled to my feet and swung at him. My ring scratched the side of his face. He slugged me in the temple and I collapsed on the bed. He jumped on top of me. His knuckles pounded my face repeatedly. "You, bitch!" He grabbed my neck and started choking me. I tried to fight him off but it was just like hitting a concrete wall.

"I…can't…bre…" My eyes watered as his hands locked around my neck like the jaws of a pit-bull. I tugged and scratched at his hands, trying to pry them off my neck, but the more I pulled, the tighter he squeezed.

"Die, bitch, die!" He seethed and jolted his arms back and forth like he was trying to rip my neck off. I looked up at him and saw pure evil in his eyes. Veins pulsed outta his head as he choked the life out of me. I knew he wasn't going to stop until I was dead.

I stretched my hand across the bed to grab the gun that was under the pillow but I couldn't reach it.

"Noooo....Ple... nooo." Sweat from his forehead dripped on my face as my lungs desperately struggled for air. I kicked and squirmed as he tightened his grip with all his power. I faded in and out of consciousness. I reached for the gun again, but I didn't feel it. My eyes connected with his; I caught a glance of death. At that very second I felt the tip of the gun. I nestled the gun into the palm of my hand and aimed it at him. He immediately loosened his grip and went for the gun. We recklessly tussled over the gun and fell to the floor.

"Ugghhh," I grunted as he landed on top of me, knocking the wind from my lungs, but my grip on the gun was secure. He squeezed my throat with one hand, and he reached for the gun with the other. Suddenly my fingers began to tingle then they went numb. With no trouble the gun was pulled from my hand. My heart stopped.

Boom! Boom! *Oh, my God, this can't be happening*!

Chapter 1

It all began last summer. I had just gotten home from a long and rigorous spring semester which included being on line for Theta Sigma. The pledging system at a HBCU meant hazing, all kinds of drama, paying a shitload of money, and making the Pledges feel like trash. Then after the process is over and we're inducted into the sorority, you realize it wasn't all that it's cracked up to be.

Well, I was glad to be home in Memphis. I was looking forward to spending time with my mom and brother. I had made plans to do nothing; I wanted to sit home and chill because I had to be back in Nashville in two weeks to start summer school. While at home, I wasn't going to any clubs or bars. I had partied like a rock star when I crossed over into my sorority. Plus, I didn't care for the club scene in Memphis anyway; it was different from the club scene in Nashville. In Memphis clubs there's always a group of women looking at your outfit up and down, hating on the latest styles and trendy wear you picked up from college. And I had become accustomed to a different type of man. Guys in Memphis didn't mind splurging on a chick, but it was always something in return. Brothas in Nashville didn't care about the return. They spent money just because they breathed another breath. *And that's what up.* No pun intended but them Nashville cats got it like that. If it's something they like they don't hesitate to show how much they appreciate it.

While I was home chilling, I got a call from my homegirl, Sasha.

"Hello," I answered.

"Girl, what's up?"

"Nothin'. What up wit' you?" I asked nonchalantly

"Broad, just chillin' and getting ready for the summer." Sasha is my best friend, and we go to State together, we hadn't had a chance to hook up since being back home, so I was glad to hear from her.

"Yea, I feel ya," I said.

"Look, chick… check it, you know that Kevin Harris is having his annual Millionaire Baller's party tomorrow night.

"Who is Kevin Harris?"

"A rich ass nigga." We both laughed. "Nah, forreal; he this big time sports agent that represent a lot of them NFL players. This party is for all of the rookies that just signed million dollar contracts with his sports agency, "It's About the Game.""

"Mmmhum," I murmured indifferently.

"They said the one last year was so live. LeBron, Paul Pierce, all of the superstars was there, but the one this year supposed to be even better. I already got my outfit lined up. I'm about to go to the mall with Mimi and help her find something to wear."

There was a silence on the phone. I guess Sau was waiting on me to pronounce my excitement about this party and profess that I was going, but that wasn't going to happen.

"Broad, you going?"

"Going where?"

"Bitch, to the party," she screamed

"Noooo, ma'am. You know that ain't my scene. I definitely don't feel like dealing with all the hoopla." Ever since the Tennessee Tyrants won the Super Bowl, chicks be jocking them niggas like flies on shit. "Sau, you know it's the same set up every time we go to one of them events. Hoe's will have begged, borrowed and stole to come out in their hottest gear trying to come up on a baller."

The last NFL party I went to with Sasha, chick's was standing in line just to speak to one of them dudes, while them cats stood back and programmed number after number into their cell phones and decided which girl he might give the privilege to fuck him for the night. It blew my mind. You would think a chick wouldn't want to talk to a man after seeing him get another woman's number, but I guess it don't matter when you on a paper chase.

"Besides, most of them niggas got the big head anyway, thinking they all that. They won't even buy you a drink. Chicks be sending them drinks and these cats are making millions."

"Girl, whatever. I ain't studdin' that shit you talking 'bout. I just wanna get out and kick it. We can at least kick it in the M one time."

"Girl, I don't know. I'll think about it, but I doubt very seriously that I'll go."

"Aiight, chick. You gon' fall off. I'ma go get me one them rich ass ballers. I'll holla at you tomorrow. Hopefully, you'll have changed your mind."

A small part of me did want to go out and enjoy my new body. I had been on a diet the entire semester and lost weight. Well, not really a diet. I just changed my eating habits and started working out. I went from weighing one hundred eighty pounds to one hundred forty pounds, which complemented my five-five frame very well. I was determined to lose weight by my birthday. I was in the best shape of my life. It's amazing how much losing weight can enhance your appearance.

I had gone to a couple of NFL parties in the past and I didn't like them at all. None of the NFL guys even looked my way. I was not the type of woman they were interested in. I don't know if it was because I was too dark or too chunky. But it didn't matter to me; my rich mocha complexion and doe-shaped eyes have always been my best asset. You know after a black man gets some money, no matter what his profession, he wants everything but a black woman. That's why I give mad props to Obama because he has a black wife that he adores in front of the world.

For example, my cousin, Mimi, is black and Philipino with slanted eyes and silky, jet black hair that hangs pass her bra strap. She doesn't have a bangin' body, but she has a beautiful, golden complexion. And for her twenty-first birthday, my uncle got her some ditties-a bubbly set of 36C's. At first I thought they was too much for her small frame but they grew on her and that bitch keep all type of men in her face: white, black, Mexican you name it. At any rate, she stay running to them NFL parties, and I don't know why because she damn near got killed fucking with one of them NFL dudes. She called herself dating this cat that plays for the Tyrants. He was fine as hell, but he was married. Actually, all he used to do was fuck her. He spent a li'l money on her, bought her a used Honda Accord, and paid her tuition a couple times, but it wasn't really worth all the bullshit this guy had her doing. He was one of them freaky ass dudes, and he used to want Mimi to dress up in costumes and meet him at different locations in Nashville to have sex. The places were places that they could possibly get caught. One time they decided to meet at Centennial Park and perform their little voyeurism sexcapade. Him and Mimi got busy on one of the swing sets, but little did they know his wife had gotten wind of his infidelities and put a tracking device on his phone. While Mimi was riding this dude's dick on the swing set, wifey pulls up and does a sneak attack and tasers Mimi on one of her ass cheeks, and then she tasered the dude on his dick. Then the wife made that guy leave Mimi laid out, right there in the park.

I remember when I went and picked her up, she climbed in my truck smelling like outdoors and musty pussy.

"I'ma get that bitch….that bitch gon' get fucked up', she screamed behind sobs and tears. "Take me to the police station. I'ma press charges on that raggedy ass bitch!"

"Girl, settle yo' ass down," I demanded and rolled down the window.

"Naw, fuck that, Rae. I'ma get that bitch."

"Mimi, you can't do a damn thing to that lady, you over here fuckin' her husband!"

"So…. I don't give a fuck. He don't even want her fat ass. He said he can't stand the sight of her."

"Mimi, at the end of the day that's his wife. He don't give a damn about you," I protested.

"Shut the fuck up, Rae," she screamed. "He does. That bitch just mad he don't want her no more. He love this young pussy I got. He's in love with me."

After she screamed on me, I didn't waste another breath on her ignorant ass. Mimi has always been the type that love other women's men. Why? I don't know but she my family, and I still love her. I finally calmed her down and took her home.

My freshman year of college, instead of putting on the freshman fifteen, I put on the freshman thirty. I was already somewhat plump upon entering college. I was always a thick girl weighing about one hundred and sixty pounds, and the extra pounds I put on made me super thick. In other words, I was fat. I was self-conscious about my weight, because virtually every girl at State had a perfect body. I know that wasn't exactly true, but it was that way to me because I seemed to be so much bigger than everyone else.

While I was on line for Theta Sigma, we was on lock down. We couldn't do anything. We weren't allowed to go to any parties, nor could we be seen in the Campus Center or socializing with anyone that was not in the sorority. Since I couldn't do nothing but go to class, I started working out every day, and by the end of the semester, I had amazingly dropped forty pounds. Now I ain't gonna lie, my weight loss put me over the top and did a lot for my self-esteem. Even so, that groupie shit wasn't my thing.

The club scene in Nashville had become so monopolized by the NFL players. Most of the dudes that wasn't professional athletes, or just some other paid ass nigga, might as well not even come out 'cause they definitely wasn't gon' get any action because every girl in the club was focused on the ball players. Chicks wouldn't even give the regular guys a chance. It was so bad that if a guy approached a woman, the first question she asked was, 'What do you do?' Women wanted to know his profession before they asked his name. If a guy didn't say that he played ball, the chick would quickly move on. It was the same scene in Memphis when it came to the Memphis Grizzlies. I guess it was because the Tyrants had just won the Super Bowl, the Grizzlies had won the championship, and they were on everyone's mind. All I knew was I didn't like those type of parties. I didn't like the set-up or the hype, so I stopped going.

♣

Early Friday morning, my brother and I decided to meet at Ed Rice Running Trail to work out. My brother shot a couple hoops while I ran a few laps around the track. It was a pleasant morning. The air was crisp and meek, and the sun was just beginning to rise. After we worked out, we walked around the track.

"Rae, you done slimmed on down. You look good. You need to keep it up, keep working out so you won't blow back up. That's what a man like, a woman with a nice, firm body and flat abs."

"Thanks." I blushed as a smile stretched across my face. "Awww, don't worry. I love my new body. I'ma definitely keep it up. That's why I'm over here now, because I'm not trying to get back big." It really made me feel good when my brother told me I looked good. He has always been very judgmental, and he will not hesitate to let me know if I needed to lose a few pounds.

"You going out this weekend?" he asked.

"Nah, I'ma probably chill at the crib, but then again, I don't know. I'm thinkin' about going to this party with Sasha tomorrow night."

"Ahhh, forreal, what party?"

"Some millionaire baller party where all the invited guests supposed to be millionaires. She said some big-time sports agent throwing it downtown at the Fed Ex Forum."

My brother looked at me and shook his head as if he was disappointed in what I had just said.

"What?"

"Nothin."

"Well, why you shake your head?" I enquired.

"You and Sasha need to sit y'all asses down," he remarked as he stretched his calves.

"Why you say that?"

"Rae, them niggas ain't thankin' about y'all. To them cats y'all ain't nothin' but a number. Them dudes just trying to fuck. You done seen how many chicks be running up behind them ball playas. Bitches a do any and everything to get one of them niggas on they team and them niggas know what's up. They especially don't won't no gal hanging out in the club all night."

"It ain't even like that; I'm not studdin' no ball playas. I know how it go. I don't even really know any of them cats. I'm just going cause Sasha asked me to, and I don't really have nothing else to do."

"Mmm-hum, whateva." He turned up his lips. "You ain't gotta lie to me. I know Sasha done talked you into goin' to that shit in hopes that y'all gon' find a baller and get married and live happily ever after. "Puu-huh" he chuckled, "Girl, please," he mocked in a high-pitched voice. "I'm just saying that NFL, NBA, I'ma meet me a rich man, is a fantasy. Let Sasha go to that shit. She can go out and kick it and fuck off. Sasha gon' be straight regardless, her momma and daddy paid. Yo' ass is broke, and need to stay focused on your grind and get yo' butt into medical school. You can lose all the weight you want, have on the baddest gear, it don't matter because them guys meet top model chicks all day long. It ain't about that, it's about focusing on yourself. Get ya' mind right, get yo' own dough, and worry about them niggas later," he said as he bounced the basketball.

"I hear ya, Jay."

"Good, then keep on listening. Get some credentials behind you so that when God do send you that special person you'll have more to offer than a pretty face and big booty."

I love talking to my brother. He's gon' keep it real and I appreciate that about him. He's one of the main reasons I decided to leave Memphis and go off to college and pursue a degree in biology. My brother has always motivated me to be the best I can be. Being that I was somewhat chubby and dark-skinned, society had led me to believe I wasn't pretty. My brother was the one who encouraged me to lose weight and help me realize that black is beautiful and it doesn't matter how the world views me. It's about how I view myself. He often reminded me that if a man can't accept me for who I am then that ain't the man for me. I guess he was so real with me because he had played plenty women over the years until he met his match, Champagne.

My brother is a successful investment banker, handsome, six feet even, very nicely built, with a smooth, chocolate complexion, and a neat, low haircut. He's what you call a metrosexual; he loves women and pussy but he's neat and clean just like a gay man. My brother stays in the latest fashion. All his suits are tailor made and he gets manis and pedis more than me. This boggles my mind, because the chick he has been dating for about two years is just the opposite. Champagne; she's not that cute and she definitely not a professional woman. As a matter of fact, she from the hood and is bonified ghetto. She never has a job. She got two kids and her momma has custody of them, but my brother loves the heck out of her. I guess it's because she ain't studdin' his ass. She is the kinda broad that never calls him and he be blowing her up. She's always in the club, and he pays all her bills and he keep her pockets fat. He has caught her cheating plenty of times, but he is still with her. I guess because the broad be putting it down. Word on the street is she be giving niggas good head. I can't figure it out for the life of me why my brother is still with her.

Last summer when I was home from school, I pulled into the parking garage at Dillard's in the Oak Court Mall. I heard a lot of commotion; security guards were screaming and chasing this woman. I looked up and noticed this chick run right in front of my truck with a handful of shopping bags. Low and behold it was Champagne. It was bad enough she was being chased through the parking lot by mall security. What really through me for a loop was she had her kids sitting in the car, and I swear it was damn near a hundred degrees outside. That shit had me so heated. That trifling ass bitch was in the mall stealing while her kids sat outside in a hot ass car. I told Jay about it. He swore he was gon' leave her. He didn't do jack shit. As a matter fact, right after I told him that, he let her move into his crib. My momma told me, 'Rae, stay out of them people's relationship. It's just something about that girl your brother likes.' My momma was right, and to this day I don't get involved in other people's relationships because folks gotta find out on they own.

♣

I got up the next day and went back to the track. Whenever I run, I always feel renewed. Whatever problems I have, I run them off. I went back to the house, took a shower, and decided to go to the mall. On my way to the mall, I was cruising and listening to K-107. The Mega Jam and D.J. Calibri was on having an interview with three NFL players from Memphis.

"What's up, fellas? Are y'all glad to be back in the M-town?"

"Yea, mane, we glad to be here," one of them answered in his thick Memphis accent.

"I miss Memphis and all the beautiful women here," another one responded.

"So how has the good life been treating you guys?" asked Calibre.

"Well, you know it's a lot of hard work and a whole lot comes with the glamorous life, mostly work and a little play," the first NFL player stated.

"You know what they say… the NFL stands for Not For Long," the announcer joked.

They all laughed. "Ahhhh, there you go," one of the ball players added. "Nah, it's all good though. I'm just thankful to be given the opportunity to play in this league. A *bleep* ain't complaining about nothing."

"Yeah, I know you're not with that fat contract you just signed. Now you a part of the MBC, The Millionaire Baller's Club," the announcer cracked. "Look, let me ask you quickly before we take a station break. What's the MBC?"

"Basically it's an organization founded by one of our former colleagues, and what the organization does is donate money to different youth groups. We also help to build community centers in neighborhoods that offer programs to keep at risk youth off the streets. In fact, all the proceeds from tonight's event will be donated to our charities."

"Alright then, that's what's up-giving back to the community. Y'all ready to kick it tonight?"

"You know it, we poppin' bottles all night."

"Yea, fa show," the other two said.

"I'm trying to find my wife tonight so I need to see Memphis' finest, baby."

"Thanks for stopping by the station and showing K-107, the Mega JAM some love."

I had made up my mind not to go to the party but after listening to the interview, I was tempted to go and look for an outfit for the party. However, the conversation I had with my brother about professional athletes was in the back of my mind. By the time the interview was gone off, I found myself near the mall, so I decided to go in and do some window-shopping.

I went in nearly every store but I didn't see anything I liked. Except, I did try on this bangin' Marc Jacobs skirt in Dillard's. It had an array of colors in it. It was a cute pencil skirt that hung off my waist. It had been marked down but with the strange combination of colors I didn't possibly know what type of top I would wear with it, so I didn't even purchase it. I walked down the mall and went into this store call Hot Gear. It's one of those stores owned by one them foreigners. They have li'l cheap clothes, but sometimes you can go in there in the summer and find some cute halters and tanks. So I decided to go in. As soon as I walked in, I saw this cute, yellow halter-top made like a strapless bustier. It looked cute on the hanger but you know how, that cheap shit is; it will be cute on the hanger but as soon as you put it on it will look bo-bo. I tried it on. Surprisingly, it was cute on me and fit me very well. It revealed my belly button. I was loving how flat my stomach was and how the yellow complimented my chocolate skin tone very nicely. *OMG this will match perfectly with that Marc Jacobs skirt*. I quickly ran back to Dillard's and purchased the skirt. I was so excited because I had found a cute little summer outfit for the low low.

Shopping all day had worn me out. I went home and slept for a couple of hours. When I woke up, it was a little after seven. I was hungry and decided to raid the refrigerator. My mom was sitting at the kitchen table clipping coupons.

"Hey, Momma." I gave her a peck on the cheek.

"Hey, baby. You've been sleep for quite some time."

"Yeah, I know. I was tired." I took a long swig from the bottled water. "Momma, what did you cook?"

"Nothing, I'm tired. You gotta go for what you know tonight."

"Dang, Momma, you don't ever cook for me when I'm at home."

She immediately jumped up like she was feeling guilty. I didn't really want her to cook, but most mothers love feeling needed, especially when their kids grow up.

"I would've cooked but I thought you was gon' be running the streets like you always do when you come home."

"Momma, I don't be running the streets," I protested, "Momma, don't worry about cookin'; I'll go get us some take out."

"Nah, you go get you something to eat. I already ate. I went to the Chinese buffet on my lunch break and got me a plate. It's in the refrigerator if you want it."

"Nah, you know I don't really care for Chinese food." My mom goes to the Chinese buffet and gets carryout and stuffs her carryout box like a can of biscuits.

"Alright, well I'm fixin' to go get me something to eat."

My mother has worked two jobs for as long as I can remember. She left my daddy when my brother and I were young. Momma said he was a raging alcoholic. She said he was a very good man but whenever he drank he would act a donkey, which was often. He would become violent and he used to beat the shit out of her. She said he used to get up in the morning and start drinking, and he would drink for days until he was sick, and couldn't do nothing. She said she realized that she couldn't raise children in a home with an alcoholic, so she left.

Being raised without a father didn't affect me much because I always figured that I couldn't miss what I never had. My momma is a

11

strong woman who stepped up to the plate and took care of her business and raised her two kids by herself and with the help of the good Lord. We always had a roof over our heads and a place to live. We never missed a meal and our lights wasn't never turned off. My momma held it down, so when she told me she was tired I knew she wasn't lying.

Just as I was walking out the door, the house phone rang and my momma screamed from the back room.

"Rae, telephone."

"Who is it?"

"It's Sasha."

"Tell her I'ma call her back."

"She said it's important and for you to come to the phone."

"Tell her to call me on my cell phone," I yelled as I was walking out the door.

"Okay."

As soon as I got in my truck my phone rang. "What up, chick?" I answered as I backed out the driveway.

"Girl, nothing. What's up wit' you?"

"About to go and get something to eat."

"So are you going to the party?"

"Nah, girl. I told you I wasn't going to that party."

"Rae, come on. I mean what you gon' do tonight?"

"Nothing...I thought Mimi was going."

"She was, but she got the pink eye."

"The pink eye? How she get the pink eye?"

"From that girl that be putting her eyelashes on. You know that chick be doing lashes out of her house,

"Aww, I thought Mimi went to a salon to get her eyelashes done."

"Nah, you know how Mimi always trying to save a dolla'. She been going to this girl that live in Maxie Homes and letting her do them. I'm sure that girl don't properly sanitize her utensils. One of her customers must've had pinkeye and she gave it to Mimi."

"Mimi so stupid," I scoffed. "She let a chick that live in the projects put her lashes on. She don't even need to wear fake eyelashes anyway; her eyelashes are already long."

"Not anymore. She gotta wear them now. That glue done took out all her lashes, her eyelashes ball-headed." We both laughed. The image of Mimi without her eyelashes popped in my head. "But anyway, girl," Sasha interrupted, trying to get back to the conversation at hand. "Are you going to the party or not?"

I paused for a minute and sighed into the phone. "I don't know," I replied indifferently.

"Girl, come on," she pleaded. "We can make this a girls' night out. You off work for a while; we don't have school, so let's go out one little time while we're at home."

Sasha is so spoiled; she always gotta have her way. She is the type of person that will keep on nagging me until I finally give in.

"Aiight...I guess I'll go. What time are you going to meet me there?"

"About eleven."

"Broad, that's too early. You know we have to get there good and late when everybody is drunk and has sweated out their hair, and looks hot and musty. Then we'll come through like a breath of fresh air."

"Well, I'll see you there at twelve."

"Kay."

I changed my mind about going to get something to eat. I really didn't want to eat heavy because I didn't want to have that full feeling, plus I didn't want my stomach to be sticking out, so I went back in the house and made me a turkey sandwich. After I finished eating, I went to the liquor store and debated on what to buy. I grabbed a bottle of Kendall Jackson Chardonnay and went back to the house and started getting ready for the party. I poured a glass of wine and ran a nice hot bubble bath. While my water was running, I tried on the outfit I purchased at the mall earlier. I climbed in my steaming bubble bath, closed my eyes, and relaxed as I sipped on my wine. Meditating, I was so at peace with myself at that moment. Everything in my life was perfect. I was about to enter my last year of college, and go to med school. I was in the best shape of my life and I had accomplished my goal of becoming a member of a Greek organization.

After I got out the tub, I rubbed my favorite lotion *Body* by Victoria's Secret all over my skin. While applying the lotion, I looked at myself naked in the mirror, and I was impressed with how bangin' my body was. My abs were nice and chiseled and my ass was plump and round. My Victoria's Secret wonder bra had my titties sitting up perky and firm. I put my bustier on, and then I slid on my silk skirt. The skirt hung gently on my petite waistline and clung flawlessly to my every curve. I had on a thong but I had to take it off because the skirt hung so low you could see it. My hair was cut in long layers, so I threw a few hot rollers in my hair then wrapped it up so my curls wouldn't be tight. I applied my make-up and slipped on my Lanvin ankle strap stilettos. I unwrapped my hair, and ran my fingers threw my long, thick layers; my hair flowed loosely down my back like silk.

I looked at myself in the mirror. *Baadow.* Everything looked just right. I very seldom have moments when everything is perfect. Something is always wrong. Either my hair won't act right, or my make-up looks funny, or I will have a pimple on my face. It is always something, but tonight nothing was wrong. I looked at myself in the mirror and said, "Tonight I'm going to have a good night." Little did I know that this night would lead to my demise.

Chapter 2

When I arrived at Club Crème, I called Sasha. "What's up, momma, where you at?"

"It'll probably be about fifteen minutes before I leave the house."

Fifteen minutes means forty-five minutes for Sasha. I know her like the back of my hands. She's one of those people that takes forever to get ready. Sasha really isn't working with anything in the ass department, but the rest of her makes up for it. Her mocha chocolate complexion, smoke gray eyes, and long legs is what sets her apart. She keeps a head full of Bohemian weave streaming down the center of her back. If you didn't know her you would think she was from the islands or Brazil. She does a lot of modeling for hair products. She's been on perm boxes and weave packages. We first met in high school, and became friends but we didn't really get cool until we came to college.

Sasha comes from a wealthy family. Her father is a big time contractor that has constructed exclusive housing developments throughout middle Tennessee, Georgia, Arkansas and Mississippi and her mother oversees the real estate aspect of the company. Basically, her dad builds houses, her mom sells them, and they are paid. When the recession hit, instead of them losing, they gained. They bought so many foreclosed properties and sold them, it was damn near highway robbery.

I knew Sasha would be at least another hour so I called her back and told her that I was going into the party, and to call my phone when she arrived. As I walked up to the door I couldn't help but notice the fleet of top of the line vehicles parked in front of the club. There were Hummers, Benzes, and Ranges. I even saw one or two Lambos. I knew I was walking into a millionaire baller's party.

I walked up to the door and showed my ID to the security guard.

"How much?" I asked.

"Fifty," he said. *Fifty dollars for a party. See, this the shit I be talking about.* If it wasn't for all the big bodies parked out front I probably would've turned around and left. When I walked in, I immediately went to the bathroom. I made sure there weren't any flaws in my outfit. I applied a little more Sephora lip-gloss and proceeded into the party.

It was so crowded that I had to walk sideways to get through the crowd. I found a spot near the bar, and that's when my ex-boyfriend, Reginald, walked up.

"What up, Rae? Damn, you done lost a lot of weight." He turned his lips up and shot me a skeptical stare. "You ain't on that shit now...is ya'?"

"Boy, don't play with me." *Crazy a*ss insinuating *I'm on drugs.*

"Girl, I'm just playin'. Mane, you look good as fuck." His eyes roamed up and down my shapely frame. "And you still got that ass." I shook my head and blushed with a modest smile. "I ain't gon' lie, Rae; you look good."

I smiled. "Thanks, Reggie" I wasn't used to being a size six, so I still hadn't gotten used to my new body.

"What chu' want to drink?" he asked me.

"Ummm, some wine. Get me a glass of Moscato."

"Aiight, I'll be right back."

I dated Reginald in high school. I was so in love with him. I thought we would be together forever. I went away to college in Nashville and Reginald stayed in Memphis. While I was away at college, Reginald started dating someone else, so we broke off our relationship but we still remained friends.

Our breakup really didn't faze me. When I first went to college I was amazed at how different college life was. I was so overwhelmed with my new life as a college student that I stopped thinking about Reginald my first day on campus.

There were black people from all over the United States. People were different from what I was accustomed to coming from Memphis. Black people at State were cultured in the arts, languages, theatre, politics, you name it. Many of the girls in my dorm had gone to private schools and prestigious performing arts schools. Brothas and sistas were outspoken and knowledgeable about many facets of the world. And the men, the men, the men. There was a plethora of top-notch brothas from all over the country, every shape, color, you name it. There were the athletes, the frat boys, and the intellectual smart brothers. Then there were the thug niggas that always kept it one hundred. I had never been around black men from up top. The northern cats hailed from New Yiddy, Ohio, Detroit and the Chi. They were so charming and their swag was to die for. To see one of them brothas walking across campus in a Yankee fitted, slightly saggin', timbed out, just made my kitty-kat turn flips, and they loved to hear a southern girl talk. The west coast brothas in their Dickies and white tee's were laid back, chilled, and easy going. And my soldiers from the dirty-dirty were the coolest and the realest of them all. My freshman year in college was definitely like living in a different world.

Reggie returned and handed me my drink. "They didn't have Moscato so I brought you a Long Island."

"A Long Island Tea?" I asked confused. *How can you go from a glass of Moscato to a Long Island Tea?*

"Yeah, I didn't know what else to get."

"Reggie, you could've gotten me anything besides a Long Island Tea. Why didn't you get me another type of wine? I can't drink this; a Long Island Tea is too strong for me."

"Awww…come on now," he turned up his lips. "Don't start actin' bougie. I know you done lost a li'l weight but don't front, and please don't act like you don't get yo' drink on." He took a sip of his Hennessey and Sprite. "Just sip on it. After you get through dancing and walking around this hot ass club, you'll be done sweated that shit up outta ya."

"Mmm-hum, if you say so," I replied and rolled my eyes at him.

"Look, I see my nigga. I'ma go holla at 'em. I'll be right back," he said. As soon as he walked off, I took a sip of the drink and grimaced. Ugh, I quickly put it down. It tasted like the bartender poured straight grain alcohol in it. I wasn't trying to be one of those folks that I've seen in the bathroom passed out over the toilet, and the bathroom attendant is trying to sober them up. As I was walking around absorbing the vibe, my cell phone rang. It was Sasha.

"Hello."

"Chick, where are you?"

"I'm in the club," I shouted, closing my other ear and screaming over the music.

"Alright. I'm on my way in. Meet me at the door."

"Kay." By the time I made it to the door, Sasha was walking in.

"What's up, diva?" She smiled and eyed my outfit.

"Hey, girl."

"You look cute," she complimented. "Where did you get that outfit?"

"Aww, thanks girl, I pieced this li'l outfit together."

"Chick, I like your 'fit too." Sasha had on a fitted, mint green, Gucci dress with a low cleavage and a pair of Cavalli stilettos sandals. I know her outfit cost a fortune; my outfit was only a couple hundred dollars. However, my outfit was just as cute. We both was killing. I've learned it's not about how much you spend, it's about how you look in what you have on and how well you put your outfit together. But one thing is for certain, and two things for sure, that hair and make-up always has to be on point.

"So, what's up girl? Where the money at?" Sasha asked, as she darted her eyes around the club and peeped out the scene.

"Girl, you know I don't know any of those ballplayers."

"I told you, if you see a man and he's big, and has a thick neck, then it's likely he plays ball."

"Girl, you so crazy." We chuckled and gave each other a high-five.

"C'mon, chick. Let's go mingle," Sasha remarked confidently as she slightly tussled her hair off her shoulder and checked her outfit to make sure everything was perfect.

"Aiight, chick; you get in front."

We walked back to the bar and each of us got a Washington apple martini. Sasha sipped hers down like it was Kool-Aid and then ordered two more. While we were standing there, this little, short dude with a receding hairline walked up and whispered in Sasha's ear. He told Sasha that his friend wanted to meet her.

"Who is your friend?" she asked with two martini glasses in her hand.

"He's standing over there by the D.J booth."

"Why can't he come over here?"

"He's kinda shy."

"Shy...Nigga please." I could tell she was slightly buzzed. She looked down at the guy. She towered over him by at least four feet then she took a sip of her drink.

"Look, boo, tell yo' boy if he can't come over here and talk to me then we can't meet." That's how Sasha is. She always plays hard to get. Her motto is: "I know what my stock is." She knows her self-worth and she won't even look at a man that can't provide her with the lifestyle she is accustomed to or better. Sasha can pull some Grade A brothas with her looks and pizzazz, but her problem is keeping them. I don't know what she does but it seems like when she first meets them, she'll have a cat wrapped around her fingers then all of a sudden the tables turn. Its reversed and she's the one chasing after them, and sad, depressed, and crying.

"Aiight," little buddy answered and walked away.

The next minute, a sexy, light-skinned brotha with a manicured goatee was walking straight toward us. He was sporting some tinted Cartier frames. I peeped out the Louie loafers he had on and the matching custom fitted Zac Posen blazer and slacks. He was too metrosexual for my taste but he looked like he had just stepped outta a GQ magazine.

"Hello," he said and then extended his hand for Sasha and me to shake. "I'm Pace."

"Pace?" Sasha replied, nonchalantly. "That's your name? Pace?" she asked rolling her eyes and taking a sip of her third martini. Every time she meets a guy she's kinda digging, she brings out her divatude. She starts turning up her nose and acting nonchalant like the guy is beneath her. For some reason, men love this because they start pursuing her even more. This confirms my theory that men love a challenge.

A light smile curved his lips. "Relax, ma. I'm Santana Pace the third, but I go by Pace."

Sasha reluctantly extended her hand and offered him a half smile. "I'm Sasha, and this is my girl, Rae."

"You ladies look lovely tonight."

"Thank you," we each told him, though his eyes were fixed on Sasha.

"What are y'all drinking?"

"You can get me another Washington apple martini," Sasha answered and flung her hair off her shoulder. I could tell she was feeling dude by the way she was acting.

"And I'd like a bottled water, please." His friend went and placed our orders from the bar.

"Pace, are you from Memphis?" Sasha asked.

"No, I'm from Chicago. I went to the University of Memphis Law School. I love the ethnicity in Memphis so I decided to stay and practice here."

"What about you?" he asked.

"Well, I'm from Memphis but I attend graduate school in Nashville. I also do a little modeling on the side."

"Mmm-hum, quite impressive." Li'l buddy came back with our drinks.

"This is my assistant, K-Rob."

"Hi, nice to meet you." We both shook his hand. Then Yo Gotti's "Five Star Chick" came on. "Aw, that's my joint right there," Sasha squealed and threw her hands in the air.

"C'mon, Rae, let's dance."

"Girl, I'm good. It's too hot. I'ma chill a minute."

She grabbed Pace's hand and they headed to the dance floor with Sasha bobbing her head up and down. Truth be told, I knew if I went to that dance floor, Li'l Buddy was gon' follow and I was not about to dance with him.

I walked to the bathroom. I was not about to stand there and entertain the do-boy, Pace's assistant, better known as the nigga that's always sitting on the passenger side of his best friend's ride. Uhhhh, no, somehow I always ended up with the broke ass friend or his assistant. But not tonight; I was looking too good. I would kick it by myself before I ended up spending my entire night with someone I was not interested in. I went and touched up my make-up and then left out of the bathroom. Walking from the bathroom, I passed by the VIP section.

The VIP section was on an elevated platform with a velvet rope wrapped around it. The club's decor was cream and the VIP section was cream with maroon backdrop and accents. When you walked up the stairs to the VIP section, you was on stage. It was lights, camera, action. Just about everybody's eyes in the club were glued to the VIP section. This was understandable because that's where the money was. It was all types of ballers and shot callers up there. Every nigga was suited. Cats in Memphis gon' do it! Brothas was out in they finest whips, gear, and bitches. I noticed Triple Six Mafia up there poppin' bottles and then my eyes skated to the other side of the VIP and saw Yo Gotti, another local celebrity and his entourage. T.O. and Ochocinco was up there looking like new money. It look like just about every one of the Grizzles was up there. But I wasn't trying to be staring up there, because the hoes that was up there amongst the riches was looking down on the people that wasn't like they was standing in the food stamp line.

Each guy had at least two chicks a piece. I ain't gon' lie, I was a little envious of the chicks that was up in VIP campaigning and doing it big with all them rich, sexy ass ballers. Every time a bottle was ordered it had a sparkler attached to the cork. It was just a little something so cats could floss and see who was poppin' the most bottles. I got color blind from all the sparklers that were blazing in the air. Everywhere I looked I saw a sparkler; it was like the fourth of July. They was poppin' bottles one after another, dancing just having a grandiose of a time. What really threw me for a loop was it was a line of groupies gathered around the entrance to the VIP section. They was hoping and praying that they would be recognized by one of the heavy weights that was in the VIP section doing it big.

It ain't no way I woulda been huddled around that rope, and let people see me trying to get in VIP. Them chicks was standing around that rope like they was giving away a million dollars. *Guurl, please!* Females were flirting with the security guard, pushing their titties together, licking their lips, anything to try to seduce the security guard into letting them in, but he was not going. If you wasn't a guest of one of the millionaires then your name had to be on the invite list. If not, they were charging a stack to get in, and I knew I wasn't about to pay that. Even if I had it, I still wouldn't pay it. It ain't that serious.

I walked back by the dance floor and laughed to myself as I watched Sasha on the dance floor working Pace. She was on them drinks and acting a damn fool, grinding her ass all on his crotch, straight working him out. I was on my third drink for the night, and I had a nice little buzz flowing. I drank the last bit of my martini and sat the empty glass on the edge of the bar. I glanced around the club and noticed everyone was having a good time, engaged in conversation, dancing, and having fun. But I was standing there by myself with no one to talk to. I felt kind of awkward, like people were staring at me so I pulled out my cell phone and acted like I was dialing a number or checking my messages. When I looked up, I noticed this guy in the VIP section staring in my direction. I didn't know if he was looking at me or at someone standing behind me, so I quickly glanced back down at my phone and pretended like I was texting. When my gaze rose again our eyes locked, the corners of his mouth widened. A shy smile escaped my lips and I coolly glanced at my cell phone as if I had just received a text. He was at least six-four or six-five with a body cut like a precious jewel. His chiseled arms and biceps bulged through his black Lux T. From a distance, he resembled the model Tyson Beckford, but I didn't wanna stare, so I glanced around the club and inconspicuously stole another peek at him.

Then I noticed he was walking out the VIP section and coming in my direction. *Ohmigod.* My heartbeat pounded loudly in my eardrum. *Please, please don't let him come over here. What am I going to say?* I played with my cell phone again, only this time when I looked back up he was standing right next to me revealing a million dollar smile. The man was hands down absolutely gorgeous. Our eyes immediately connected.

"Hello, beautiful."

"Hi," I replied nervously, as I tussled my hair to get my swoop bang out of my eye.

"Are you having a good time tonight?" he asked, flashing his arctic white teeth.

I gently nodded my head while calmly suppressing my nervousness. "Yeah, what about you?"

"It's okay." Our gaze momentarily locked again. His skin tone was smooth caramel that glistens like a warm honey bun. He had deep set Chinese eyes. It looked like he mighta had on some eyeliner but I know he didn't. That's just how tight his eyes were and he had full, well-defined lips. I peeped out his gear. He had on a white tee and some deep blue Tru Religions and some Prada high-tops. *Damn, why this nigga ain't dress up; everybody else in here suited and booted.*

His eyes gradually scoped my entire body. "Yellow." He eyed my outfit and smiled. "It's your color," he complimented.

"Thank you," I replied with a reserved smile. I sucked my stomach in a little. I'm a pro at that shit. I can hold a full conversation and hold my stomach in at the same time without anyone being able to tell.

"Can I get you something to drink?"

"Oh no, thank you, I'm good. I've had enough to drink tonight."

"C'mon," he insisted. "Let me get you one more drink."

"No, really, I can't. If I drink anything else I'll be drunk and won't be able to drive home."

"I won't let you get drunk." He looked me in the eyes and smiled. "Don't worry, I got you." When he spoke those words, my heart fluttered and a secure feeling rushed over me. I knew if I had another drink I'd be slizzard. But the way he looked me in my eyes when he told me he would take care of me, I believed him.

"Okay," *I might as well.*

He grabbed my hand; the scent of his cologne trailed him as he led me to the VIP section. The posh VIP section was set up like a lounge with round about sectionals and coffee tables placed in front of each sofa. As soon as we sat down a cocktail girl walked over with a bottle of champagne and poured us each a glass.

"What kinda champagne is this?"

"It's Ace of Spades. One of my homeys bought it for me."

"Ahhh, that was nice of him." *Damn, I done ran into another do boy.*

"Yeah...so what's your name?" he asked changing the subject.

"Raechel."

"Raay-chaaal," the corners of his mouth widened. "I like that name," he said and took a sip of champagne. His smile alone made my stomach do somersaults.

"But everybody calls me Rae." I leaned back onto the sofa and crossed one leg over the other. I killed the glass of champagne to take the edge off; dude was so sexy he was making me nervous.

"Are you from Memphis, Rae?"

"Yea, I'm from here, but right now I live in Nashville."

His expression brightened. "Forreal? I live in Nashville, too."

"Oh, okay, cool," I replied, taken aback by his response. "Are you from Nashville?"

"Nah, I'm from Houston," he replied.

"Why did you move to Nashville?" I inquired.

"My job moved me there."

"What kind of work do you do?"

"Uhhh,... I work at an elementary school, I'ma janitor."

A janitor, I would meet a fuckin' janitor outta all these rich ass men in here...just my luck! "So what brought you to Memphis?" I asked

"I came down for the weekend to visit my boy, plus I got family down here." He took a sip from the glass and then placed it on the table. I looked at his wrist and noticed the cheap watch he had on, but on the same wrist he had on a bracelet that was made out of thread with different colors in it.

"I like your little bracelet."

"Oh, thank you. My grandmother gave this to me before she died last year. I rarely take it off."

"Ahhh, I'm sorry. How did she die?"

"She had breast cancer."

"Dang, I'm sorry. Were y'all close?"

"Yeah, we were. She helped raise me."

I touched the bracelet on his wrist. "It's beautiful. May I see it?"

He took off the bracelet and tied it around my wrist. I had on my signature Tiffany bracelet but I liked the humbleness of the threaded bracelet on my arm; it was so innocent.

"So, what's your name?" I asked as I admired the bracelet on my wrist.

"Jarron."

"Ahhh, okay,"

"Rae, you didn't tell me why you moved to Nashville."

"You didn't ask." When his look caught mine, his eyes twinkled and I instantly felt vulnerable. I knew this dude wasn't no big time baller, but he still carried himself like one. He had major swag; he was laid back and well-spoken. He acted like the world revolved around him and his interactions with me were so calm and confident. He wasn't doing much, like trying to be cool or a big baller... he just was.

I smiled as I sat my glass back on the table. "I go to State."

"Really?" he asked with interest. "What's your major?"

"I'm a biology major; I'm tryin' to get into somebody's medical school," I said apprehensively.

"Ahhh, really....that's what's up. I'm sure you'll get in somewhere."

"Yeah, I hope so." He stood up and my gaze rose up his gigantic frame towering over me.

Tenisha Jackson

He grabbed my arm. "C'mon, let's dance."

"Huh." I was a bit hesitant because I was caught off guard by the invitation, but I was cool with it, because I love to dance.

He led me to the dance floor. *Dang, dude keeps grabbing my hand.* But I didn't trip. As a matter of fact, I liked the fact that he was taking control. When we got on the dance floor, my song was on, "Freak It like You Want It." The D.J was doing his thang. He was mixin' old skool and new skool. He was bumpin' everything from Biggie to Gucci Mane. Jarron just stood there and gently rocked from side to side, as I bounced my ass on him, and shook my hair like a video hoe. I saw Sasha and Pace, and went over and started dancing beside them. Me and Sasha started showing out. When we get together on the dance floor, we are a force to be reckoned with. We were jammin'.

"Girl, dude got it going on," Sasha whispered in my ear.

"He alright." It was clear Sasha had met a major playa and I was stuck with this ordinary Joe. But I wasn't trippin' because the dude was cool and he had mad sex appeal.

The D.J started playing reggae. That was time for Sasha and me to make a bathroom run because our hair was drenched and sticking to our faces. Before I left I whispered in his ear, "Hey, I'll be right back; we're going to the ladies' room."

"Aiight, come to the VIP when you finish. I wanna talk to you."

"How are we gonna get in; we don't have any wrist bands?" He grabbed my hand and pulled me close.

"Relax." He looked at me with a partial smile. "I got you. I told you I'ma take care of you. Just come over there."

"But."

He wrapped his arms around me and whispered in my ear, "Shhhhh."

I smiled at him and me and Sasha sauntered off to the ladies room.

"Rae, please tell me you gave dude yo' number?" Sasha asked.

"Nah, he didn't ask for my phone number."

"Girl, do you know who that is?" she asked with excitement.

"Nah, not really, he told me his name was Jarron." I walked out the stall and washed my hands.

"Jarron?" she responded, shocked by my reply. She shook her head. "Nah, boo, homeboy's name is Texas... Texas...um...um... hold up, lemme think." She paused. "Texas Reynolds," she replied confidently.

I rolled my eyes in the back of my head because it was apparent that Sasha was drunk and didn't know what the hell she was talking about.

"The dude you was talking to is one of the highest paid wide receivers in the league."

"Nah." I shook my head unconvinced. "That dude said his name is Jarron and he a janitor at an elementary school. You got him mixed up with somebody else. Plus, I can't tell he no major playa, cause he had on a li'l cheap ass watch and his homeboy was buying the drinks."

"Rae... that nigga lying. That's Texas Reynolds," Sasha slurred. "Hold up, let me Google him right fast." She pulled out her IPhone and Googled Texas Reynolds.

I dabbed the sweat off my face as Sasha waited patiently for the image to upload. Sasha enlarged the image and held the phone to my face; sure enough, it was him, Jarron Texas Reynolds.

"Damn, that shole is him." I grabbed the phone and stared at the picture, scrolling through her phone looking at different images and articles about him.

"He used to play for San Francisco, and this year he got traded to the Tyrants. Girl, I told yo' ass! That nigga is all that and some." I saw her excitement through the reflection in the mirror as she smeared her lip-gloss on.

"Damn, he told me he lives in Nashville and he's a janitor at an elementary school, but something told me he was lyin' cause he kinda hesitated when I asked him why he moved to Nashville." I handed her back her phone. "I wonder why he lied and said he was a janitor." I shot her a fleeting glance while dabbing sweat from my face with a paper towel.

"I don't know, I guess he didn't want you to know his profession. I'm sure chicks be at him 'cause they know he paid." She massaged her lips together to smear her gloss over her lips. "And I know his paper is stupid long because he's been in the league for a minute. That janitor front must be his li'l cover up."

I briefly glanced at her in the mirror as I was powdering my nose. I turned to her. "I'ma ask him why he lied."

"Girl, don't ask him nothin; just play along with his game."

We walked out the bathroom. There was a chick in front of us that had toilet paper stuck to her shoe. I tried to step on it to get it off, but she was walking too fast. Sasha and I fell out laughing. I don't know why that is always so funny to me. I guess because folks are in the club thinking they got it going on with tissue stuck to their shoe.

We walked back to the VIP section. Texas was standing right by the entrance waiting on us. He told the bouncer we were with him, and we followed him to a table. I introduced him to Sasha.

"Are y'all okay on drinks?" he asked.

"I would like a glass of champagne," Sasha replied. He signaled the waitress and told her to bring two more bottles of Ace's and some bottled waters.

The waitress came back and sat the champagne buckets on the table; she poured us each a glass. I knew I wasn't about to drink my glass. I just picked up the glass so I wouldn't fidget with my hands.

"Rae, I'ma go get Pace. I'll be back in a few minutes." Before she strutted off, she whispered in my ear. "Broad, you need to snatch that nigga up."

After she walked off, I felt him looking at me, but I was too shy to turn around and face him. I took a few more sips of my champagne to calm me down. Now that I knew this man was not only fine as hell, but he was paid, it made me a little nervous.

"So, Rae, where ya' man at?"

I turned and our eyes connected. I smiled. "I don't have one."

"What?" he replied unconvinced. "Aww, c'mon. Don't give me that. I know you got somebody. You too pretty not to have a man."

I blushed. "Well, I have a few friends, but nothing serious." Knowing all the time, I was single as a man on death row. "I really don't have time right now for a relationship, with school and work."

"Ahhh, where do you work?"

"I wait tables at Andrew's Crab House and I work in the biology lab on campus."

"Andrew's Crab, y'all have them cinnamon biscuits; every time I'm in there I eat like twenty of them joints."

"Yeah, that's our signature item." I smirked. "So, what about you."

He paused. "What about me?"

Dude don't play. I swallowed. "Where yo' girl at?" I asked.

He sighed gently. "I ain't found her yet; I'm still looking."

"Mmmm-hum," I gently nodded my head.

By this time, the VIP section had started getting crowded. There were some people who came and sat on the sofa beside us, so Texas scooted closer to me. We were sitting so close together I could feel his body heat. He shifted a little so I could lean back on the seat, but it was so crowded I had to lean most of my body on him. His sweet breath fluttering on my neck gave me goose bumps so I sat back up.

"Are you okay?" he whispered.

"Yeah...why?"

"Well, you look a little tense." He smiled.

I relaxed and eased back on the couch and nestled on his upper body. The rhythm of his heartbeat surged through me as my body rested on his. I turned to him and immediately felt his eyes on me. I kept my gaze low; I was too intimidated to look him in his eyes. I nervously hammered my leg up and down and bit down on the corner of my bottom lip. When I finally got enough courage to look him in the eyes, a fire ignited in my soul and turned me on.

"Man...you are so beautiful," he whispered. His intoxicating voice warmed me, making me lightheaded. He rubbed his fingers across my shoulders, sending a fiery shiver through my body. I finished the rest of the champagne.

"Thank you." A timid smirk parted my lips.

He leaned close to me and whispered in my ear, "Relax." His velvety lips brushed my ear lobe. My throat tightened as he moved closer to me. "I'ma marry you." His raspy voice whispered.

Huh? His soft lips nestled on the nape of my neck; a light sigh escaped me. I closed my eyes and let go as he placed soft gentle kisses on my neck. "Mmmm." His teeth grazed my skin as he gently suctioned my warm flesh into his mouth. *Ooohhh.* My body shuddered with pleasure. My nipples hardened and my pussy tightened and dribbled with hot juices. I was light-headed. This man was making me high. "St--op," I whispered, but he didn't acknowledge my pleas. He turned my face to him and his succulent lips met mine. His tongue slid deep into my mouth, and we eagerly sucked each other's tongues like a melting popsicle on a hot summer day. I wanted to pull away so bad but I couldn't; I was under his spell. He grazed his hands across my swollen nipples and then massaged my thighs. His hand slipped underneath my skirt. "Oohh," I sighed. I uncrossed my legs and he slid two fingers into my aching wetness.

"Mmmm, damn, baby, I want this pussy," he groaned. He slowly slithered his fingers in and out of my buttery wetness. I couldn't get enough. He dug deeper, and I slowly rotated my hips while gripping my tight pussy around his fingers like they were a fat, juicy dick. He was like a dangerous drug and I was addicted. I couldn't get enough of this man. He was makin' me feel like I never felt before. My womanhood began to salivate; pounding like a baby drum. I was about to cum. He buried his fingers inside me one last time and tickled my g-spot. At that moment a silent burst of ecstasy ruptured over me.

"Ummmmm." I cringed, as hot cum seeped from inside me; my body trembled and embarrassment struck me like a thief in the night. Cum juices slobbered over his hands and soaked my creamy thighs. We had kissed for about two minutes but it seemed like an eternity.

The lights in the club came on and reality set in. I sat up right in my seat and pulled my skirt down. We were both squinting our eyes from the brightness of the lights. He rubbed my hair and moved forward in an attempt to kiss me again but I moved back.

"I'm sorry," he said

"Oh… no… that's okay," I stumbled and shifted my gaze; it was hard for me to look him in the eyes. I believed if he looked in my eyes, it would reveal how weak I was for him.

"Come on, baby, let's get outta here."

Excuse Me. My mind was still on what had just happened. I licked my dry lips, and looked around to see if anyone had seen what had just taken place. I guess not because everybody was getting up headed for the exits.

"Aye, what's up?" he spoke in a low, raspy voice.

"Nothing," I whispered still avoiding eye contact.

"C'mon, let's take this to the room."

"Huh?"

"Let's go to my room. I'm staying at The Marriot. Let's finish this up there."

Then it dawned on me what had just happened. *I can't believe what I have just done. Oh, my God, I let this guy finger fuck me, and I barely know him, and he thinkin' we about to fuck.* I was so embarrassed. I had never done anything like that before. Then the words of my brother came to mind clear as day. *Rae, them NFL niggas just tryin' to fuck.*

"Raechel–"

The sound of his voice interrupted my thoughts. "Uhhh, I'm sorry, I have to go."

"Huh, what?" He looked puzzled by my response.

"It was nice meeting you," I replied coldly. I grabbed my clutch and stood up.

He gazed up at me with a shocked expression on his face. "Damn, it's like that… You can't come to my room and chill?"

"Hell, 'nah, I ain't coming to yo' room! Who do you think I am?" I snapped and walked off.

He came after me. "Hey," he grabbed my hand and pulled me close to him. "Relax, Ma, it ain't even like that. I just wanna talk and get to know you. Look, if it's anything I've done, I apologize; let me make it up to you."

I shot him a firm smile. *No, thanks.* I yanked my hand from him and quickly walked towards the exits.

"Raechel," he yelled. I ignored his call and kept pushing toward the crowd.

"Raechel!" He came after me but I was able to get lost in the crowd. Everyone was leaving out the club and there were swarms of people trying to get out the door. I pushed my way into the crowd hoping he wasn't behind me. I didn't turn around until I was outside. I sat in my truck, and laid my head on the headrest, and took a few deep breaths. After I regained my composure, I called Sasha but she didn't answer her phone.

I sat in my truck and replayed the events over in my head. It was something about that man I just couldn't place. Ever since the first moment I laid eyes on him, I knew he was special. I kept thinking about the way his eyes sparkled when he looked at me. It felt as if he was looking deep in my soul. I couldn't believe I kissed him, and let him finger fuck him in the club. I can't even explain how that shit happened; I don't even get down like that. It was something magnetic about him that was almost impossible for me to resist. I don't know why I couldn't pull away from this man. It was like I had no control over my mind, my body, or my emotions. One thing about me, I have to be in control of myself at all times. It was a good thing I didn't give him my number, and a part of me hoped I never saw him again. Texas Reynolds was one man that I could not trust myself to be around.

My phone rang. I looked at the screen; it was Sasha. When I reached to answer the phone, I noticed I still had on Texas' bracelet.

Chapter 3

I was on my way back to Nashville to start summer school. I had a ball the two weeks I was in Memphis. Sasha and I had gone out every night. Plus, I enjoyed the time I spent at home with my mom and brother. While driving back to Nashville, I thought about the night I met Texas. I had somehow pushed the encounter to the back of my mind. I kept reminding myself that I had to stay on my grind. I had to stay consistent with my workouts because in July, me and the girls were going to the Essence Festival and I wanted my body to be looking super tight. Prince was the headliner and was going to do his last concert tour ever and we were going to kick it in New Orleans or Nawleans as the natives would say. Also, I had to stay on track with my summer school classes as well as pick up extra shifts at Andrew's Crab so I could stack my paper for the Essence Festival. I had to be about it!

Monday morning Sasha and I got up and went running on West End near Vanderbilt's campus. It gets awfully hot in Nashville during the summer so Sasha and I would run in the early morning before temperatures hit the ninety-degree mark. After we ran, we would do what we called fellowship. When we fellowshipped, we talked about everything from careers to love, life, relationships, any kind of typical girl conversation.

"Girl, we need to step up our workout this month; maybe do an evening and a morning workout so we can be right for the Essence Festival."

"Yeah, that's cool. You know I'm game as long as we're finished by three o'clock so I can make it to work on time." I stretched my calves. "I heard the Essence be off the chain."

"I want to work on getting my thighs a little more toned, so when I put on my shorter than short hot pants, ain't nothing scrubbing or jiggling," Sasha commented and studied her thighs.

"Aiight, that what's up, let's do two-a-days. Let's meet in the morning and the evening. We can start today if you want to."

"Cool, let's meet this evening at two o'clock."

"Okay, I'll bring my work clothes and change at the Sports Complex," I said.

"Alright, I'll see you later."

I went home, showered, and went to class. My classes were cool. I love summer school because the teachers are so laid back. The classes I was taking were prerequisites I hadn't taken my freshman year so they were easy. After class, I ate a huge salad before going home and taking a nap. I was sleeping good when Sau called me.

"What's up, girl, are you getting ready to meet me?"

"Ah, dang, I forgot, girl. I was sleep. Yeah, I'll be there." I sheepishly crawled out the bed.

I got dressed, packed my work clothes and hygiene items. Checking to make sure I didn't forget anything, I looked through my bag. I had soap, toothbrush, my comb and brush, towels and deodorant. I walked out of the apartment.

Damn, it's blazing out here. We gon' pass out. I got to the park on time. Sasha and I jogged around twice. Although it was hot, it was still breezy because the park is full of trees and provides a lot of shade, but we were still sweating bullets and my hair was drenched.

"Woo, girl, that was a good workout," I huffed trying to catch my breath.

"Yeah, it was."

"Well, I'm about to leave. I'll call you tonight when I get off."

"Okay," Sasha responded, still breathing heavy from our workout.

I had to rush to get ready because I wanted to beat the evening traffic. I showered and put on my work clothes and changed at the Sports Complex across the street from the park. But my hair was so nappy that I couldn't do nothing with it. It was time for my retouch and my new growth was thick as Heinz. I tried to put some gel on it to slick it back in a ponytail. It helped a little but my shit was still through bookin'. *Oh, well, I'm going to the beauty shop in the morning. I'll just make my face up real good.*

After fooling with my hair for twenty minutes, I looked in my purse for my make-up bag and it wasn't there. *Damn, I know I didn't forget my make-up bag.* I poured all the contents out my purse but my make-up was nowhere to be found. There was nothing I could do about it because I didn't have time to go back home and get it. I looked in the mirror. I was busted. *I ain't gon' worry about it. I need to go and make me some money.*

♣

When I got to work, I could hardly get through the door because there were so many people waiting to be seated.

My manager came to me breathing hard and sweating. "Raechel, I'm getting ready to fill your section up."

"Okay, cool; I need the money." All at once, they sat me a five-top of Chinese people that couldn't speak English, a table of three hood rats with blue and green hair, and two old people that had the menus so close to their faces, they couldn't read it.

Then my manager came to me and said, "Rae, can you take a ten-top?"

"Yeah, just give me a minute to get the drinks and salads out to my other tables."

"Okay," she said.

I guess she must have disregarded what I said because when I came out of the kitchen with the tray full of drinks and salads, the table of ten was already seated. I noticed it was a table full of men. I really couldn't get a good look at them because I was so busy trying to do refills at my other tables, pass out salads, and take the order of the two old people that kept asking me a million questions.

Finally, I turned to greet the table, and it was ten of the finest men that I had ever seen. *Oh, my God, these are some of the Tyrant players.* I immediately ran to the back and tried to fix my uniform and hair but it was useless because I still looked like boo-boo the fool. *They would come in here when I'm lookin' a hot mess. Well, ain't nothing I can do about it right now.* I went back out to greet the table.

"Hello, I'm Raechel. Are you all doing okay?" Everyone was still talking amongst themselves; some of them had their heads down buried in the menu. No one was paying me any attention. I lightly cleared my throat and spoke louder.

"Ahem...Ahhemm...excuse me, can I get you all something to drink?" Suddenly, everyone turned their attention toward me and the first face that caught my eye was Texas Reynolds. *Fuck!* I damn near fainted. My heart started racing and a wave of anxiety struck me.

"We ready to order. U'm hungry," one smart ass commented. I started walking around the table to take everyone's order. I could feel the weight of Texas' glare upon me as I was taking each order. I purposely hesitated getting around to him.

When I finally got to him, he looked at me and then looked at my nametag as if he didn't know my name.

"Hello, Raaachel."

"Hi, may I take your order?" I asked. I wouldn't give him any eye contact. I had my pen in hand ready to jot down his order.

He looked back at the menu. "Why did you leave that night?" he asked in a low voice.

"I don't know," I sighed impatiently. "Can I please take your order?" No one at the table was looking at us; they were all engaged in small talk.

"Hey, why did you leave?" he asked again.

"Why did you lie?" I asked with my teeth clinched together.

"If you tell me why you left, I'll tell you why I lied," he said while his eyes were still glued to the menu, as if we were discussing entrée options.

"I think I had too much to drink, I started feeling sick," I told him. This was a total lie. I couldn't tell him the real reason I left was because when we kissed I felt something magical. And if I hadda gone with him back to his hotel, I would've became just another notch under his belt.

"Why did you lie?" I asked and eagerly awaited his reply.

"I'm not going to tell you," he said, while looking intensely in my eyes.

"Why?" I asked.

"Because you're lying right now," he said with a parted smile.

"Look! What do you want to order?" I snapped, trying to contain my smile.

"I don't know, get me whatever you think I should have."

I started smiling. "Come on," I insisted.

"No, seriously, get me whatever. Put it all on one check and give it to me."

"Kay," I replied. I had everyone's order. By the time I got back to the kitchen, I had food up everywhere. I had to get my other customers' food out and get drinks out to my new table. I was so far in the weeds I couldn't see straight. I walked out with the hood rats' food. Those chicken heads kept kee-keein and cackling. They were high, because every time I went to their table to refill their drinks a stench of weed tickled my nose. They kept asking for stuff. First, it was ketchup then tartar sauce. After I brought that, they would ask for something else.

Finally, I said. "Look at your plates and see if it's anything else you need." They started laughing. Even if they needed anything else I was not going back to their table until it was time for them to pay. *These hoes ain't about to run me for no two dollars.* Then the Chinese people, I got their order all wrong because I couldn't understand what they were saying. The older couple was sitting just looking dumbfounded. Every time I went to the table, they kept asking me what were the side items after I had already told them what they were five times. I was so blown away I just shook my head.

Thirty minutes had gone by and I didn't see my ten-tops food in the window. I went to check the computer to see if I had rung in their order. I went through every screen and didn't see their order.

"Oh, shit! I forgot to ring in their order." I quickly rang in the order and then ran to the kitchen. My heart was pumping like a freight train.

"Anthony, I fucked up. I need this order like yesterday; it should have been out at least thirty minutes ago."

"Alright, Rae, relax; I got you." Anthony was a cool brother that came in high every day. I don't know how he could function in a fast paced kitchen on the purp, but he did, and he was fast. My food always came out on time. He had always liked me but he was a little too hood for my taste, but he always had my back. When I fucked up somebody's order he'd get that shit out on the fly.

I went back to Texas' table; I cleared my throat to get their attention. "Umm, guys the computer lost your check so it may take a few more minutes on your food but it will be out shortly."

"Whatever, you probably forgot to ring in our order," one of the guys remarked.

"Ahhhh," all the them started laughing. I ignored the comment and went and checked on my other tables. By the time I made it back to the kitchen, their order was ready to be served. It took an hour but at least it was ready. My manager and I walked the food out. My manager apologized for the delay. We passed out the food and they began to throw down. They acted like that was the last meal on earth. I handed Texas his entrée, which consisted of lobster, crab, and shrimp.

"Mmmm, good choice." He smiled.

I finally cashed out my other tables and recollected myself. Every time I went to Texas' table to ask if they needed anything, I couldn't help but smile. I tried to keep a serious look on my face but I couldn't; I kept on blushing. I was trying to avoid Texas' constant stare. I refilled everyone's drink but his. For some reason, he made me so nervous that I felt like I was back in junior high.

When everyone appeared to be done, I brought the check to the table and laid it next to Texas. I collected the tab, ran his American Express black card, and gave him back the bill. As I set the credit card down, he grabbed my hand and held it for a few seconds. The guys at the table began taunting him.

"Ahhhh, Tex, uh oh," one of them shouted.

I was so embarrassed. "Thank you all and come again," I said and quickly left the table. I went to the kitchen. *I can't believe what just happened. I'm not going back out there until every single one of them has left.*

Making sure they were gone, I went to clean off the table, and picked up the credit card slip. There was no tip on it. I started looking on the table for a tip. "Wait a minute, I know these niggas didn't come in here and not leave me a tip on a six-hundred dollar check. Ah, hell, 'nah!" I couldn't believe it.

Then my manager came up to me and said, "Rae, one of those guys must've had the hots for you."

"I can't tell, they didn't leave a tip," I snapped, as I was helping the busboy clean off the table.

"Oh, yes they did; they left you a fat tip." That is when she handed me five, crisp one hundred dollar bills.

"Oh, my God; is this what they left?"

"Yes, and one guy asked me to give this to you." It was a little sheet of paper.

Rae, thank you for the service. I need to talk to you. You have something of mine. Will you meet me at Café Java on West End at 11 o'clock? I'll be waiting. Tex

Dang, what should I do? I didn't have time to go home and freshen up. I knew I wasn't going to leave work until eleven and that wouldn't be enough time to run home and change. Plus, I didn't have his bracelet with me, and he didn't leave a phone number. *I can at least meet him to tell him thank you and make arrangements to give him back his bracelet. Besides, I don't like him anyway.* At least that's what I kept telling myself. *I'ma go by there and holla at him for a minute and then leave.*

As I approached the coffee shop, I began to get a little anxious but I still managed to remain calm. I pulled up at the coffee shop at about eleven fifteen. I took off my work shirt and threw my Ralph Lauren cardigan on over the tank top I had on underneath, and put some chap stick on my lips.

Café Java is a coffee house and a bookstore that stays open until three a.m. It also has a neat little bakery that is world renowned for its homemade muffins. I walked inside. *I hope he's still here.* When I didn't see him, I purchased a cup of coffee and the latest, *It Girl* magazine and had a seat at one of the tables. *Okay, if he ain't here in five minutes I'm leaving.* I was flipping through the magazine and turned to an article entitled, *Fun Sex Positions* that showed pictures of various sex acts and poses. I was looking at the doggy style position when I heard a voice from behind me.

"Humm, looks like you're reading an interesting article."

It startled me. I turned around and spilled my coffee all over the table and magazine. "Gat dang it," I countered, trying to keep from cursing. He immediately went and grabbed some napkins and the waitress rushed over to clean up the mess I had made.

"Ma'am, I'm so sorry," I said while trying to help clean up the mess and dabbing coffee off the magazine.

"It's okay," she replied and began helping me and Texas clean up the mess I'd made.

"Would you like another coffee?" she asked.

"No, I'll just have a hot tea," I replied, still flustered from spilling my coffee.

The waitress turned to Texas. "What would you like, sir?"

"Just water for now, but I would like to see the menu." She handed him a menu. "Are you getting anything to eat?" he asked me.

"Yeah, I would like the pumpkin spiced muffin."

He quickly glanced at the menu. "I would like the turkey sandwich on the sesame croissant and an order of fries, please."

"Sure, your order will be right up," the waitress replied politely and turned to leave. I watched the way Texas ordered and interacted with the server; he seemed so classy. Plus, he was so sexy with a nice pair of L.L. Cool J lips.

"Soooo, Miss Rae-Rae." We both started laughing. "Can I call you Rae-Rae?"

"No, sir, you can't." We laughed again. "Rae-Rae is a li'l too hood."

"Yea, but I like it though." He smiled; our eyes locked briefly "So, Rae, how have you been?"

"I've been great. What about you?" I replied and offered him a soft smile.

"U'm good. I've been really busy lately with mini-camps"

"Yeah, I forgot, Mr. Janitor." We started laughing again, "Why did you tell me you were a janitor?"

"I don't know." He sighed. "I apologize, but you gotta understand; I meet so many people and I get tired of the way they react to me when they find out I play ball. I use the janitor front as much as possible. But it doesn't work because most people recognize me or either don't believe that I'm a janitor."

"Yeah, I understand."

"Are you in summer school?" he asked, changing the subject.

"Yeah, I'm taking two classes; both of my professors seem cool." The waitress returned and sat our orders down. I poured myself a cup of hot tea and let it cool before taking a long sip. The chamomiles began to unwind and relax me, and I started loosening up.

"Didn't you tell me that you were single?"

"Yeah, I'm single," I answered as I opened a package of sugar and added it to my tea.

"Why?"

"Well, like I said before, I don't have time for a relationship right now. My main focus is getting into Med school."

"When was the last time you were in a relationship?" he asked.

"The last serious relationship was about two years ago."

"What happened?"

"I really don't want to talk about it."

He took a bite of his sandwich and then looked at me. "Come on, it can't be that bad. If you tell me your story, I promise to tell you mine."

"Okay," I agreed with reservations. I took a deep breath. I hated talking about my ex, even though I was well over him. I was still pissed on the inside and I tried to think about him as less as possible.

"Well, I had been dating this guy, David, for two years. We were the perfect couple because both of us have similar personalities and we both are going to be doctors. As a matter of fact, he is in his fourth year of medical school. One night we was out having margaritas at this Mexican restaurant, and my girl Jada called. She had just broken up with her boyfriend and was kinda goin thru, so I invited her to meet us out. We all sat and had dinner and drinks. David and Jada seemed to hit it off, but I really didn't think nothing of it because my friend was an outgoing person and my ex was an outgoing person as well." I cut into my muffin. "It wasn't even a week later and David started acting funny. I couldn't reach him and he never returned my calls. I could never get in touch with him and when we did get together, he would try to pick a fight over little stuff. I just chalked it up that he was stressed with school and all. So a month or two went by and my friend, Jada, stopped calling me as much. I would call and leave her messages to meet me for lunch but she wouldn't return any of my calls. I would see her on campus and she would walk in the opposite direction to avoid speaking to me. Finally, one afternoon David told me he needed space. Of course, I was hurt but I thought we would get back together, because we had broken up so many times but we would always get back together. Like a week after he told me he needed space, I was in the mall when my best friend, Sasha, called me. I began to think back to that dreadful day.

"Girl, guess what?"

"What?" I said.

Sasha paused. "Rae, where are you?"

"At the mall."

"Do you have a minute?"

"Yeah, what's up?" I knew by the sound of her voice something was up.

"You probably want to sit down."

"What is it?" I asked concerned.

"Girl, David and Jada got married."

"David who?" I just knew she wasn't talking about my David.

"David, as in your ex, David. I saw their picture in the newspaper."

"Sasha, you're lyin'." Tears welled in my eyes. "Please, tell me you're lying."

"I'm sorry, Rae, it's true."

I was devastated. I left out the mall and sat in my car and cried for what seemed like hours. I was so shocked because he had just met her." I almost teared up just thinking about it.

"Maybe he already knew her," Tex said and took a bite of his sandwich.

"Nah, they had just met the night I introduced them. They had only known each other two months, then he married her. I felt like what does she have that I don't. Then the way he and Jada went about doing it; sneaking around behind my back. I don't blame one person more than the next because Jada was my girl and David was supposed to be my man. He owed me just as much respect as she did, if not more. That little incident kinda messed me up. My grades dropped and I became deeply depressed. I didn't want to deal with anyone. I just stayed in my room all the time."

"Have you seen that guy since?"

"Nope, and I don't want to." I sipped my tea. "The thing that destroyed me about that relationship was that at the time Sasha told me the news I was seven weeks pregnant. I had an abortion."

"Daaamn." He listened.

"After it happened I prayed and asked God not to ever let me see either of them because I didn't think I could handle it. But that was two years ago and I'm so over that now, but it took time. The abortion, the break up, took so much from me." I looked up at Texas and he was just staring at me. I couldn't tell if I had bored him to death or if he couldn't believe my story. "Dang, my bad, I didn't mean to bore you with talking about my past relationship."

"Nah, it's cool. I've been in a similar situations."

"Really?"

"Yeah," he said as he wiped his mouth with a napkin.

"Well, okay now it's your turn."

"Rae, I have a little girl."

"Oh, really?" I remarked with a smile on my face. *Damn!*

"Yea, really."

"How old is she?"

"Four years old."

"Are you and your child's mother together?"

"Heeeell, nah!" We laughed.

"What happened?" I inquired.

"Well, the college I went to, if you were an athlete you were treated like royalty. My freshman year I had all types of females throwing themselves at me--black, white, Asian, you name it. I really wasn't on no relationship tip because I was so focused on football. But this one chick was real persistent." He sighed and shook his head. "I'm talkin' 'bout she was damn near stalking me. Anything I needed her to do, she did it:-my papers, my laundry, whateva. So I started kinda diggin' her and we started dating."

"Okay...so basically you started dating her because of what she was doing for you?"

"Nah, nah, it wasn't even like that. I was really feelin' her. I mean I had met her parents; she met mine; we were a couple." He took a bite of his sandwich. "But my junior year, during the first game of the season, I broke my leg."

"Forreal," I said as I poured myself some more hot tea.

"Yeah, it fucked me up." Suddenly my world turned upside down. Everything changed. People started responding to me differently. The star treatment I was receiving went away. People was saying my football career was over; I was done. And ole girl she just started trippin'. She didn't wanna hang out no more. She stopped calling. Every time I looked up, she was rippin' and runnin' with different dudes. When I would ask her about it, she would always say they was her friends. He took a sip of water.

"Spring came and the new football recruits were visiting the college. When the new recruits would come in, my college tried to wow them so that the best recruits would sign with our school. So we threw a party for the recruits. They were all sitting at a booth in the club kickin' it, drinking, and having a good time. I went over to dap them up and welcome them to the school. While I was sitting there, one of the dudes was acting all funny…moaning and shit. I looked under the table. It was a chick under there giving him head. Guess who it was?"

"Who?"

"My child's mother."

"Huh," I gasped. "Damn, Texas, you're lying."

"I wish I was."

"I was so hurt. I left and what was really messed up was she didn't even know I saw her. Of course, I quit fucking with her. I realized at the point she was star stuck. She would do whatever to be with the best athlete. Instead of that situation defeating me, it motivated me. I went home for the summer, rehabbed my leg, worked hard, and when I came back I was starting, and was better than ever. But when I came back, she was pregnant and kept saying it was my baby. I didn't believe her. Soon as the baby came, we got a blood test and the test results confirmed ninety-nine point nine percent the child was mine. I love my daughter and would do anything for her, but her mother, I don't have nothing to do with."

"What's your daughter's name?"

"Charlie Renee Reynolds." His eyes lit up when he said her name.

"Ah, that's cute…Charlie."

Texas and I talked for hours about everything from relationships to childhood. It was like me and this man were old friends because he was so easy to talk to. After getting to know him, I felt really comfortable with him. When I glanced at my watch, it was after two-thirty. The coffee shop was about to close, and all the tables were empty. The waitress was sitting in the corner with an irritated expression plastered on her face; she was waiting for us to leave.

I glanced down at my watch. "Dang, I better get going because I have a very busy day tomorrow."

"Really?" he said as if he didn't want the night to end.

"Yeah, I have a hair appointment in the morning and I have to be in class at ten. So I better go home and get some sleep."

He grabbed my hand and stared directly into my eyes. "Damn, I ain't ready for you to go, but I know you got a big day tomorrow. Next time I'ma kidnap you." We both giggled.

The way this man looked at me I knew he was feeling me because I sho' was feeling him. The way he gazed into my eyes made my panties wet, and I knew I wasn't trying to fuck em' but he was so damn sexy. I could get lost in his eyes. They were so pleasant and hypnotizing, and the way he looked at me made me feel like he was looking into my soul.

He paid the bill. We both got up and walked toward the door. I was hoping he would ask me for my phone number; I was definitely not about to ask him for his. I believe if a man wants my number he knows how to ask and I was not about to step outside my role as a lady.

"Hey, what's your phone number?" He pulled out his cell phone.

"Five-five-six-thirty-three-forty-two." He programmed my number in his phone.

"Oh, yeah, thank you for the generous tip. I appreciated it."

"Aw, you good. You worked for it. You were getting your ass kicked, but you still got our food out even though it took nearly two hours."

We laughed. "Well, I guess I'll talk to you later." I started to walk away.

"Aye…you just gon' walk away?"

"What?" I asked, confused by his remark

"You ain't gon' give me a hug?" He looked at me with pleading eyes.

"Ah, you didn't ask for a hug." I blushed and walked towards him. He wrapped his huge body around mine. I felt like I was laying underneath a goose down comforter; that's how warm and cozy I felt in his arms. He held me for almost a minute. I snuggled my head against his chest, closed my eyes, and became lost in the moment. *I wish I could feel this feeling for the rest of my life.* Then I pulled away and felt the cool summer breeze regenerate. "Thanks again," I told him. "Oh, I didn't have time to go and get your bracelet."

He rubbed my face. "That's okay. I'll get it the next time I see you."

We both got in our cars. I started my car smiling on the inside. I waved bye as I drove off the lot. Driving home, I couldn't stop thinking about Texas. Just the thought of him gave me goose bumps. I kept on visioning his warm embrace, the way he touched me, the way he held my hand, I just couldn't get it off my mind. That's when my phone rung.

"Hello."

"What's up?"

It was him. "Aww, hey," I squealed, surprised that he called me so soon.

"Yo', you know I'm feelin' you, right?" His smooth voice caused me to shiver.

"Ahhh, forreal," I replied blushing. I was digging him too, but I wasn't about to let him know.

"When can I see you again?" he asked.

"I don't know, when do you wanna see me?"

"Tomorrow."

I paused for a minute. "Okay."

"That's what's up. Well meet me at Java again."

"Well, I gotta work so it's going to be late."

"That's cool with me, if that's okay with you," he added.

"Nah, it's cool," I replied in my soft, sexy voice. "I'll meet you there after work, around eleven o'clock."

"Aiight, then its official; it's a date," he said with eagerness in his voice.

"I'll see you tomorrow," I assured and hung up the phone.

I was so excited that after I went home and went through my nightly rituals, I climbed in the bed and fell asleep with Texas on my mind.

The next morning, I woke up and thought that last night had been a dream, and then I realized it wasn't. I had actually been on a date with Texas Reynolds, and we had a good time. *Oh, dang.* I suddenly remembered that I had to meet Sasha at the park to run then head to the beauty shop. I picked up the phone to call her

"What's up, girl? Where you at?"

"On my way to the park," Sasha said.

"Okay, I'll see you there." I hung up.

When I arrived, Sasha was ready to roll. "What's up with you, girl?" Sasha asked.

I took a deep breath, still sleepy from my late evening. "Girl, I went out last night."

"With who?" Sasha paused, anticipating my reply.

"Texas."

"What… chick how did that come about?"

"Girl, he came to my job and left me a note asking me to meet him at Café Java. So I met him there. We had a nice li'l time." I smiled reminiscing about my night. "Girl, dude got it going on. I like everything about him. Plus, he fine and sexy as hell. I'm supposed to meet him there again tonight. Broad, I can't wait!"

"Dang, Rae, calm down and tell me what happened." Sasha sounded eager to hear what I had to tell her about me and Texas. The two of us stood on the side of the walkway while I carefully went over the details of my night.

"He sound like he's straight, but remember you have to play them NFL types a little different. This ain't no average Joe you dealing with. You can't get too hype. You know how them cats are. They come off strong like they're really into you, the next thing you know they're into someone else."

"But he ain't like that tho...he different."

"Broad, you don't know what he's like. You don't know him. You've only talked to him a couple times. You have to play a little hard to get. If I was you, I woulda told him I had plans tonight and I would see him some other time. You stayed out late last night and you have to work today. Girl, with these men you can't act too giddy."

"Giddy?" I replied

"Yea, chick, giddy, too anxious; too ready and willing to drop what you doing in order to make accommodations for some man. Broad, you gotta let these niggas chase you. You see he came to your job to see you because you played his ass when you first met him. If a man wants you, he gon' do whatever it takes to have you, even if it means waiting to see you."

"Yea, you're right," I agreed after listening to her explain. "I probably should call and tell him to wait until tomorrow."

"Naw, girl. Go on and see him tonight since you done told him you would meet him. Just remember you have to remain a challenge. Don't call him, let him call you, and definitely don't fuck 'em."

"Aw, I know that." Sex is the farthest thing from my mind right now.

"Chick, I hope you don't think I'm hating," Sasha commented.

"Girl, I know you ain't hating. I know you just looking out."

"I am. So, broad, relax and be easy."

"Yeah, you're right." I didn't wanna hear what Sasha said but I knew she was right. Since last night, I know I had thought about Texas at least twenty times. I had to slow my role because in my mind, I had already pictured us together and we was walking down the aisle.

We ran our route and came back to our cars. "Well, chick, I'll holla at you later. I'm not going to run this afternoon because I need to get some rest."

"Aiight, girl, just call me when you get off," Sasha said and climbed into her truck. I did the same and we both drove off. I understood Sasha's concern and I agreed with everything she told me. I chilled but I just couldn't get Texas Reynolds off my mind.

Later that afternoon, on my way to work, my phone rang; it was Texas.

"Hello," I answered in a soft tone.

"Hey, beautiful." I immediately started smiling and butterflies fluttered in my stomach. "Have you had a good day?" he asked.

"Yes, I have. What about you?"

"It was cool; I can't complain. I was calling to see if we were still on for tonight."

"Sure. I guess I'll see you around eleven…. at Java, right?"

"Yea, Java," he paused. "Aiight, pretty girl, I'll holla at you later."

"Okay, bye."

"Bye, baby." *Umm* I smiled to myself. *He called me baby.* I went to work with a smile on my face and joy in my heart. The closer it came time for me to get off, the more anxious I became. I had brought a change of clothes. When I got off, I went in the bathroom, washed up a little and threw on my shorts and a tank top. I reapplied my make-up and sprayed on my *Body* by Victoria Secret perfume and ran my chi flat iron through my hair to straighten my hair out from being in that ponytail. I arrived at Café Java at ten-fifty-five. Since I was early, I went inside, sat down and continued my latest read, "Thong On Fire" by Noire. The author is so addictive. I was so entranced by the story that I lost track of time. I looked at my watch and saw that it was eleven-twenty. Texas hadn't arrived nor had he called. I called him twice and his voicemail picked up on the first ring. I hung up and called Sasha.

"Hey, girl."

"Hey, what's up?" she answered.

"Girl, I'm at Cafe Java waiting for Texas. He was supposed to meet me here at eleven o'clock and it's eleven twenty-five, and he ain't here. Do you think I need to leave?"

"Did you call him?"

"Yea, I called him but his voicemail picked up."

"Did you leave a message?"

"No."

Sasha paused for a minute. "Well, you wanna give him the benefit of the doubt. Maybe something came up. Give him another ten minutes. If he hasn't made it by then, call him again. If he doesn't answer, then send him a text, and tell em' that you're at Café Java waiting on him. Let him know you had intentions of returning his bracelet but since he didn't bother to show up or call, you're leaving, and he'll just have to get it when he gets it."

"Mmm-hum, alright." I got off the phone with Sasha, and waited on him ten more minutes and then I called him back. He didn't answer the phone so I left a message.

"Hi, Tex, this is Rae. It's eleven-thirty, and I'm here waiting for you at Java. I'll be here a few more minutes, then I'm leaving."

I didn't leave the coffee shop until an hour later. I ordered a Caesar salad. I kept looking at my phone but it didn't ring; I checked to make sure I hadn't missed a call. I even checked my voicemail - nothing. I paid my bill, left, and went home. That shit pissed me off so bad; I had been stood up. There is no excuse for standing a person up in the age of cell phones. I know things happen and plans change but at least he could've picked up the phone and called. *I guess that's why Sasha said don't get too excited. Well, he's not going to hear from me. If he wants that funky bracelet, he'll have to wait until I'm ready to give it to him.* When I got home, I turned my cell phone off and went to sleep.

Chapter 4

Sasha and I worked out hard the whole month of June. We were ready for the Essence Festival. We looked damn good and we knew it. The other members of our crew, Mimi and Cece, had it going on too. Those two chicks were born with the bomb bodies.

Cecily is the youngest member of our click. We call her Slick 'cause she a sneaky li'l bitch that's about her paper. I met her my junior year. She and I took a class together. She couldn't afford to get her book for class so I let her share mine. This was one of them crazy classes where you can't go strictly on lecture you had to have the book to pass. We just hit it off. I think what I love about my li'l sis is our birthdays are the same day. In a lot of ways we're the same person but from different backgrounds, and she's much more assertive and out spoken than me. At any rate, she told me she didn't have the money to get her book but if I helped her until she was able to, she would pay me back, so we became real close.

She was raised by a straight hoodlum…her momma. Her momma was a queen pin. She kept them living the life of Riley until she got popped and now she's serving two consecutive life sentences. After her momma got popped, her brothers and her dad were homeless. They had to live at the mission. The Feds took everything, and Cece's dad is paralyzed from the waist down. So her and her daddy put together a team and they went straight gangsta' on all the cats that snitched and had her mom locked up. All this happened her senior year of high school. She thought her plans of getting out of Memphis and coming to college was ruined.

She was determined to get up outta Memphis. She told me after her dad robbed the cats that set up her momma then they dealt with the niggas. I don't know what she meant by that, but I believe they killed the cats that set up her momma. She told me she took the money and got her dad and brothers a duplex in North Memphis, and she took the rest of the money and came to State. She all about her family. She told me she was going to make a better way for her and her family but she was gon' do it the right way, at least that's what she said. But to me she still living the same type of lifestyle because the dude she's dating right now is a big time hustler, Daddy Rich. He got plenty money and plenty hoes. Cece stay into it with one of his baby mommas. I mean he put her up in a nice li'l condo on West End and bought her a brand new Audi. The only thing is Cece don't look like she would be with someone like him. He's like sixty years old with some dreads. I mean some threads, his dreads so thin each braid like a mile apart. Cece only nineteen and she hot to trot. She has a vanilla oatmeal complexion and she petite but she got a nice, round ass. Her ass sit up so high you can play a game of chess on it. She acts like she just so in love with Daddy Rich. I just can't see it. Me, I'd rather wait on a few tables than to lay down with an old, shriveled up, cat like Daddy Rich. Gucci, Fendi, Louboutin's just ain't that serious to me, but to each its own.

The four of us were about to kick it and ball out at the Essence Festival. I wasn't looking to meet anyone. I was just out to have fun. Ever since that Texas incident, I was focused on nothing but me. He had called and text me several times and left messages for me to call. I placed the word *Never* by his number in my cell phone. So if he called I wouldn't know it because *Never* was placed by about five numbers in my phone and if *Never* comes up in my phone I won't answer it. One thing about me, when people show me how they are the first time, I believe them.

The crew and I arrived in New Orleans Thursday night. The city was already getting crowded. Walking into our hotel, we saw celebrities like Jamie Foxx and Monique. We even saw Reverend Al Sharpton. I don't know what he was doing here. I guess he was about to kick it too, and he was flexing in a Bentley. The five-star hotel we stayed in is called the Windsor Court. It's right across the street from Harrah's Casino. It's the same hotel the President stays in when he comes to New Orleans. Of course, we all stayed in the same room. We got a penthouse suite and divided the cost. The suite is huge. It's more than enough room for the four of us. It's like a mini loft with two bathrooms, two king size beds, a kitchen area and a let out couch, and it offers a spectacular view of the city. We walked in the room and everybody grabbed their luggage and went to various places in the room.

Cece yelled, "I got the couch," and plopped down on the couch.

"Well, chicks, this my bed," Sasha announced and placed her Louie canvas bag on the bed. She dared any of us to protest because she originally charged the room on her platinum American Express card. My cousin, Mimi, and I shared a bed. We weren't in the room ten minutes before Sasha announced, "Alright chicks, come on and let's get ready. Didn't y'all see all the celebs in the lobby? Let's shit, shower, and shave." She batted her eyes and got to moving around like it was time to make some moves and get out on the scene.

I was tired because I had worked the night before and we had driven eight hours. But her little speech gave me a second wind. It was all-good because I was on vacation and was about to get it in.

I slipped on a pair of khaki hot pants, a white tank top, and some flip-flops. I didn't want to get too dressed up because I knew we were about to do some walking.

"Let's go on Bourbon Street," Mimi mentioned when we finished getting dressed. Everyone agreed and we walked down to the lobby. We stopped at the front desk to get an extra room key. While Sasha and Mimi stood in line, I looked around the lobby. It was packed. There were black people from all over doin' it. There was a long line of people checking in and hanging out in the lobby absorbing the five-star elegance. A gray-haired white man played classical music on the piano among all these hood rich niggas, ball players and celebrities. I chuckled to myself. They finally got the other key and we headed for Bourbon Street.

Bourbon Street was so live. Everybody was drinking and having fun. I love the Essence Festival. It's an event that caters to black people from all walks of life. I mean you got yo' hood folks and you have your educated folks combined with athletes and entertainers. Everybody that attends the event is about progression. I mean you might have hood rich niggas kicking it right next to a doctor or CEO. That's what I appreciate about it because the common goal amongst the people is progression; how can I get more, how can I help my people, and everyone around me. The Essence Festival is one of the livest events of the year, and the parties at night are ridiculous.

As we were strolling down Bourbon, I noticed Ballistic, the hottest DC rapper, and his entourage coming out of Fat Tuesdays.

"Ohmigod," Mimi screamed. "That's Ballistic. Rae, look; that's Ballistic!" She nudged me.

"I see 'em, Mimi, chill."

"I can't believe it. I'm fixin' to go get his autograph."

Before I could protest she was running to get his autograph. I was floored. I just shook my head. *This girl out here acting like a groupie, like she ain't never seen no celebrity.* She stood over there and talked with Ballistic for a minute. Next thing I know, their entire crew was walking toward us.

Mimi introduced us. "These my homegirls, Sasha and Cece, and this is my cousin, Rae," she chimed in her sweetest, girlie voice.

Ballistic looked at Sasha. "What's up?" he asked. "Where y'all from?"

"Memphis," Sasha answered.

"Meen-fis," one of his homies repeated with a southern drawl, and they all started laughing.

"What's so funny?" Sasha shot back.

"Nothing, it's the way y'all talk. It's so country." Sasha loves when guys say that to her; she really starts to talk country then. I don't know what it is about northern men and country accents.

One of the guys walked over to me and introduced himself. "Whatup, ma...I'm Lucius...they call me J-love.

"Hey," I rolled my eyes indifferently.

"You sexy than a muthafucka'. I want you." He was cute, but he turned me off with his approach, plus his breath was funky as hell. It smelled like that man had eaten ten dookey sandwiches.

"His breath stank," I whispered in Sasha's ear

"Rae, his friend kinda cute. Plus, they're getting ready to take us to dinner." I knew that meant to just chill.

We walked down the street to Lalarue, this famous creole restaurant. Mimi and Cece were talking to the guys' friends. Everybody seemed to be hitting it off except for me. I started drinking. I had to do something to deal with this nigga. This cat would not shut up. He ran his mouth like forty going north, bragging about his cars and about how him and his crew was about to go on tour. I didn't give a fuck, because the nigga was gon' suffocate me with his hot ass breath. At one point I pulled out my gum. "Do you want some gum?"

"Thanks, Shawty." He put it in his mouth. That helped a little. After dinner we walked down Bourbon. I couldn't really get any action from anyone else because they were walking with us. At that point, it didn't matter because I was tipsy and we were all kicking it and having fun.

They walked us back to the hotel because it was time to get ready for the club. Sau, Mimi, and Cece all exchanged numbers with the crew. I knew Lucius was about to ask me for my number. He licked his lips and stood directly in front of me. *Ugh.*

"Aye, li'l mama, lemme get them digits."

"Let me get your number and I'll call you." He agreed and I programmed his number into my phone.

"You gon' be my boo-thang. I really wanna get to know you better," he whispered in my ear.

"That's what up," I smirked. I'd say anything to get him out my face. We all went to the room and started getting ready for the club.

After I got out the shower, Mimi told me, "Dang, Rae. You already got dudes calling you."

"What?" I replied as I was drying off.

"Some dude just called the room and asked for you, and when Cece asked who he was, he hung up."

"Girl, it was probably that J-Love nigga, but I didn't give him our room number."

"Well, how did he get it?" Cece asked.

"I don't know. He probably got it from Ballistic or one of them other niggas. I know y'all gave the room number to one of his homies.

"I didn't give him nothing," Cece declared while trying on her outfit that she was wearing for the night.

Then Mimi and Sau both agreed they didn't give out the room number either.

Cece smirked, "Rae, know she gave dude the room number. I mean, bitch, just because that nigga breath was funky that don't mean you can't get with him; that nigga paid." She sniggled. "Just hold yo' breath when you talk to 'em." They all started cracking up laughing.

We all got ready to go out for the night. Everybody was looking fly.

"Chicks, what party are we going to?" I asked.

"I don't know? Chick, call one of them Ballistic cats and see which party gon' be the livest.

Mimi called Ballistic. "Hey, what up? This Mimi. What party y'all going to?" She turned toward us and whispered. "They're going to Li'l Wayne's party at the Sheraton." We shook our heads in approval.

Sasha mouthed, "Ask them niggas if we can roll with them."

"Mmm-hum…uh-hu… ok that's what's up." She hung up. "They said we can roll with them, but they ain't getting out for another couple of hours."

"Ahhh, nah, fuck that. I ain't trying to wait around all night on them niggas. Chicks, we fixin' to go." We all agreed.

We walked on Canal to the Sheraton. It was a good thing the party wasn't far from our hotel because my feet were already starting to hurt in the heels I'd chosen. When we strolled up to the party, the line was already wrapped around the building. We stood in line for about ten minutes when Pace and his homeboy walked past.

"Hey, Sasha." Pace said and gave her a warm hug. "I've been trying to get in touch with you," he told her.

"Really?" Sasha's smile widened.

"Yea, I need to get your number again," he said.

"Okay." They exchanged numbers.

"Y'all going in here?" he asked.

"Yeah," Sasha answered.

"Okay, well come with me."

"Pace, we don't want to lose our place in line," Sasha countered.

"Don't worry, y'all with me." *That's what I'm talking about*. Sau turned around and motioned for us to all follow Pace. We walked straight to the door. He approached the bouncer and whispered in his ear.

"How many you got?" The bouncer asked. Pace counted us with his eyes.

"I got seven, Big Dawg." He pulled out a bankroll and peeled off about two G's and we all walked straight in. We all turned and thanked him. When we walked into the party it was a star-studded event. Everybody from T.I to Diddy was in there. Every NFL and NBA player you could think of. I thought I was in heaven. I had danced for about an hour when I decided to go and get me a drink.

While I was at the bar, J-Love snuck up behind me and kissed me on the lips. I pushed him off me so hard he almost fell down.

"Dude, what's yo' problem? Don't be puttin' yo' lips on me," I replied irritably and wiped the spit off my mouth with my hand.

"Aw, my bad. I'm sorry. It's…it's just that you look so good, ma," he stammered with remorse. He was sloppy drunk.

"Nah, you straight. I relaxed the frown on my face. "It's just I don't really know you like that." I was trying to be nice but I had to ditch dude as soon as possible. He was not about to ruin my action for the night.

"I'm sorry, baby. I'll make it up to you," he slurred. I walked off from that nigga. I didn't even get my drink I had paid for. We danced all night. Sau was kicking it with Pace, Cece was dancing with his friend, and Mimi had left early and went back to the hotel with Ballistic. The music was so loud in the club that we had to scream just to hear each other talk. After the party, Pace and his boys walked us back to the hotel.

"Damn, we kicked it in that joint," Sasha remarked.

"Yeah," I squeaked. I had been talking so loud over the music that my throat was feeling scratchy and I was getting hoarse.

When we arrived at the hotel, the girls sat in the lobby and chilled with Pace and his boys. I was beat, after Bourbon Street and partying all night. I told everybody goodnight and thanked Pace and his friends for sponsoring us, because they didn't have to. *I really didn't spend any money today*, which was a blessing. You know what they say, "If ya' looking like something you rarely have to open your purse."

I walked to the elevator. *Dang, all my girls met somebody they liked but me.* Then I told myself, "Rae, don't go there. Don't even focus on meeting someone; you came down here to have fun, not to meet a man." The elevator finally arrived. I stepped on and took off my shoes. My feet were aching so bad, I couldn't wait to get to the room. Drinking and kicking it all day had finally caught up with me. I walked in the room, put my purse, and key down. I didn't even turn on the lights. I laid down on the couch and passed out in my clothes.

The girls walked in the room about five in the morning, laughing and talking loud as hell. I sat up when I heard all the noise. They turned on the lights and woke me up.

"Daaang," Cece slurred still drunk. "Where all deez roses come from?"

I was still a little disoriented from my sleep. I opened my eyes and looked around the room in awe. We all paused for about five seconds. The room was filled with ten dozen red roses.

Cece plopped down on the couch beside me, reeking of alcohol. "Rae... Rae..." She tapped me on my leg, "Who sent deez flowers?"

"I don't know. I didn't even know they were here."

"Didn't you see them when you walked in?"

"Nah, I came in here and passed out." We all started to contemplate who could have sent the roses. "Maybe it was Pace," I said.

"Nah, it couldn't have been him. He didn't even know I was coming here," Sasha said, while looking through the roses for a card.

"Maybe it was one of them Ballistic cats," Mimi commented suspiciously.

"Girl, I doubt it. Them cats ain't no I'ma-buy-a- bitch flowers type of dudes. But I don't know, it may be a mistake." Sasha shrugged. "I'ma call the front desk and see. They may have been sent to the wrong room. She picked up the phone and dialed the front desk. "Hi, this is Sasha Houston in 1343 and there are ten dozen roses in our room." She paused. "Can you tell me if they were delivered to the correct room? Mmm-hum, did the sender leave a name or phone number?" We all looked at her while she was talking on the phone.

"Mmm-hum...Uh-huh...okay. Thank you."

"What did they say?" Mimi asked anxiously.

"He said they were delivered to the right room, but the sender wanted to remain anonymous; and he said there's a package at the front desk for Rae."

"What?" I pondered. *What type of package could be at the front desk for me?* I put on my flip-flops and went downstairs to the front desk.

"Hi, I'm Raechel Jones. I was told that I have a package waiting for me."

"Ms. Jones, may I see your identification?"

"I'll have to go back to my room and get it." I rushed to the room to get it and hurried back to the lobby.

"Okay, here's my ID."

"Ma'am, I need you to sign right here showing that this package was released to you." I signed the paper, and in return he handed me a card and a small box. I walked to the elevator, totally confused.

When I walked back in the room, "Girl what is it?" Sasha asked

"I don't know." I opened the card. There was a note that read, *Raechel Jones, meet me at Mike Anderson's Restaurant on 18th and Canal at 4 o'clock on July 3rd, From, your Secret Admirer.*

"Girl, open the box," Sasha urged.

I opened the box. Inside was a David Yurman platinum tennis bracelet with baguettes all around it.

"Damn, bitch. What nigga did you fuck while we were out?" Cece drunk ass screamed.

"Chick, please. I haven't had sex in forever. And I definitely haven't met anyone in the past twenty-four hours that I would even consider giving some. Besides, why in the world would I bring somebody up to this room and try to have sex with them before you nosy bitches came back in here." We all started laughing. "I don't know who could have sent this."

We all pondered then Cece said, "I know who it was, it was; Lucius...J-Love."

"How do you know?" I asked.

"Because I saw him in the party, and he kept on asking me where you was at." A light bulb went off in her head. "And...and he told me he had a surprise for you," she confirmed.

"Are you talking about the dude with the funky breath?" Sasha asked.

"Ahhhhh." They all fell out laughing. I was mad but I even started laughing with them broads.

"Well, I'ma go tomorrow and give him back his bracelet and tell him, thanks but no thanks."

"Girl, you a damn fool," Mimi protested, "Ain't no way I would give him that bracelet back. I'd keep it if I was you."

"Mimi, you know I'm not like that. I'm not going to keep this bracelet. There is absolutely nothing about that dude I liked, and I am not going to lead him on, so I'ma give it back to him."

"What you decide to do about the bracelet is on you, but keep the roses; they brighten up our room," Sasha commented.

"Well, ladies. I'm not going by myself. Y'all gotta go with me. He might be crazy. He's done all of this and he don't even know me," I added.

"Girl, please," Mimi scoffed.

We all put on our nightclothes and laid down and went to sleep.

A few hours later we woke up to a loud ass fart.

"Gat dayum, who did that?"

Cece yelled with a frown on her face. Sasha was giggling. I knew it was her trifling ass.

"You, funky bitch," Cece shouted while pulling the curtains back and opening the patio door.

"Girl, my bad. I musta had too much to drink last night." We all started laughing. We all got up and started to move around. "So what is on the agenda for the day, ladies?" Sasha asked.

Cece grabbed the Essence Festival itinerary off the nightstand and read the contents aloud. "There's a seminar on women fighting cervical cancer. The seminar is supposed to be about the importance of getting regular checkups and making sure you go for your annual pap smears. Then the annual bikini contest is supposed to start at five o'clock. It's not part of the itinerary, but it's where all the ballers come out to play."

"Where is it going to be?" Mimi interrupted.

"I don't know, but we'll find out today. They say that joint is always off the chain," Sasha countered.

"Okay, cool. We need to go to the different seminars, and then we can hit up the wild stuff this evening," Cecily added.

That's when I opened my mouth but nothing would come out. Then I squealed in the ugliest voice, "Y'all know." I swallowed. "I have to meet Lucius to give him back his bracelet." Everyone turned and looked at me.

"Damn, girl, what happened to your voice?" Sasha asked. "You sound like a dude."

I couldn't believe it; I was so hoarse I could hardly talk and my throat was kinda sore. I guess it was the New Orleans humidity, combined with my extensive sinus problems that caused me to lose my voice.

"Oooooh, girl. I don't know what happened to my voice," I whispered while holding my throat and trying to swallow. *Oh well, at least I won't have to talk to him.*

"I got the shower first," Mimi announced.

"Then I'm next," Cece stated.

"I'll go after y'all," I said, in a scratchy, hoarse, baritone voice.

"Girl, just be quiet. Your voice so ugly, just do sign language," Sasha mocked. "Lucius is going to think you're a tranny with that ugly ass voice." We all started cracking up laughing.

We were finally ready. Sasha is always the last to get ready, but when we step out all of us always look so cute. Each of us has different styles. Sasha and Mimi always keep their weave long and it always looks good on them. Cece loves wearing her hair short. Right now she was rockin' a sexy li'l Mohawk. She was always in some type of Bohemian wear, maybe some cargo pants and a fitted jacket, or just a T-shirt and some hot pants; she was always simple and cute. I had my everlasting layers. I keep my hair cut in long layers with a nice swoop bang. I might have Mrs. Sylvia, my hairdresser, to throw a few tracks in for length but I pretty much wear the same hairstyle because that's what works for me. I was dressed in a cute little Calvin Klein mini-dress, and a pair of wedge heel flip-flops.

We arrived at the convention center. We met Susan Taylor, editor-in-chief of Essence Magazine. I was in awe by her presence. She was such a spiritual black woman. When she spoke to us, it was amazing. It was like she was just full of peace. There was something different about her that made me think that I want to one day be just like her, helping women to move forward, and giving back to women, and empowering, and motivating women to be the best they can be.

We all sat down to listen to the seminar on cancer. I looked around the room. There were hundreds of beautiful black women in the crowd. Young, old, rich, poor but we were all together.

This guy stood up and walked towards the podium. "Hi, I'm Doctor Marcus Linder. Ladies, I'd like to ask a question. How many of you have a pap smear done annually, raise your hand?"

It looked like almost ninety percent of the audience raised their hands. He looked around the audience.

"Don't be trying to show out in front of your girlfriends. Some of y'all are lying." The crowd laughed. "Statistics say only forty percent of African-American women get annual check-ups, which is sad. The other sixty percent only get checkups when they're either pregnant or when they believe something is wrong with them. The expression on the doctor's face changed to a rather serious look as he continued talking.

"I met a woman four years ago that I fell in love with the first night we met. We got married a year later. We had such a perfect marriage that I used to ask God what had I done to deserve such happiness. She had two children from a previous relationship but I loved her so much that I was willing to raise them like they were mine. My medical practice was doing well and my wife and sons were everything I had ever dreamed of.

A year after we were married, we went to the Pacio-Mayweather fight in Las Vegas. We were at the fight having a great time when she started complaining that her stomach was hurting and she wasn't feeling well. We left the fight and went to the emergency room after the pain increased. She was admitted to the hospital and tests were ran on her most of the night. The next day we found out she had cervical cancer, and an emergency hysterectomy was performed."

The crowd gasped. "We were devastated. The hysterectomy did little to help her because the cancer had already spread throughout her body. The doctor told us she had six months to live. I couldn't believe it, she was going to die." He paused and held his head low for a moment. "I had gone to medical school, spent my life studying medicine only to learn that the woman of my dreams was dying. I had just met her two years before and now I was going to lose her. I stayed by her bed day and night, until she was released from the hospital. When we got home, we never talked about death. Instead, we acted as if she would live forever. We went to the park every day that she felt up to it, and I would read to her every night. Those were the best days of my life." He paused and looked into the sky. "My wife, Regina, died exactly six months later. She was my life, my world… my everything." Tears streamed down his face.

It was so quiet in the auditorium, except for the sniffles from the crowd. "After she died," he explained, "I mourned her death and became very angry. I was angry at God, angry at Regina. I was so mad."

He slammed his hand on the podium. He paused for a minute to regain his composure. A lady out the crowd handed him a tissue. "I was mad because she would still be here with me and our sons if she had only gone to the doctor regularly. Ladies, that is why I am here talking to you. Please, get an annual pap smear. Please, there are services that offer pap smears for free if you don't have insurance, but please take care of yourself." We were all crying when the doctor was done speaking. We had to go to the bathroom and touch up our make-up.

"Okay, chicks, what's next?" Sasha asked after we recollected ourselves.

"It's almost three o'clock; let's make our way over to Canal Street so I can meet Lucius," I screeched.

Mimi cringed. "Okay, cool, but will you please shut up with that annoying voice."

We walked over to Canal Street and arrived at Mike Anderson's at about three-thirty. The place was already crowded. We waited for about fifteen minutes before we were seated.

"I'm starving," Mimi whined. When the server came Sasha and I decided to split a bottle of wine. Cece and Mimi each ordered a cocktail. We each ordered an appetizer and an entrée. I knew we wouldn't eat all that food but you know how it is when you're on vacay, you splurge a little and that's what we did. It was about four-thirty when our entrees arrived. The food looked and smelled delicious.

Sasha spoke up after taking a bite of her food. "Raechel, do you see Lucius anywhere?"

I glanced around the restaurant and shook my head, no.

"Dang, it's four-thirty. I thought he said he would be here at four," Mimi stated avidly.

"Well, if he ain't here by five o'clock, you gon' have to apologize and give him that bracelet later on, because we need to get going so we can make it to the pool party on time."

I shook my head in agreement. I didn't feel like a conflict about it because it was too difficult for me to talk. We finished our meal. Sasha asked the server to bring the check.

Mimi got up from the table. "I'm fixin' to go to the bathroom."

"C'mon, Rae, we'll walk around to see if we spot Lucius on the way to the bathroom." We walked around but we didn't see anyone that even resembled Lucius, or his boys. We went to the bathroom, freshened up, and walked back to the table.

"How much do we owe on our portion of the check?" Mimi asked.

"The server hasn't brought our check yet," Sasha said

"Damn. He needs to come on. We gotta go," Mimi snapped. She got up to go look for the server. When she came back, she had a puzzled expression on her face.

"Where is it?" Cecily asked.

"He said our check has already been taken care of."

"By who?" Sasha asked and stood up and looked around the restaurant.

"I don't know."

"Maybe it was Lucius." Cece assumed. We all began to look around. We still didn't see Lucius. Our server finally made it back to our table.

"Thank you, ladies. It was a pleasure to wait on you." He smacked his glossed up lips.

"Sir, we would like to know who paid our bill," Mimi asked

"Oh, it was the gentleman over there in the booth by the window...and girl, owww, he is one beat for the gawwwds. If neither of you ladies want him, I'll take 'em." The flaming server remarked, we all started laughing. "Girl, that brotha so fine he gets three snaps in a Z-formation, twirl, bump, and a dip. Bottems Up," he stated and did a little prance. We couldn't see the guy in the booth because it was on the other side of the restaurant. We thanked the server and began to walk toward the booth where the server told us the gentleman was.

"Rae, make this short and sweet. I'll do the talking since your voice is gone. Just give dude the bracelet so we can bounce."

When we made it to the other side of the restaurant, the back of the guy's head didn't resemble Lucius. We kept walking and my stomach began to flutter because the closer we got to the booth, I realized that it wasn't Lucius. When we approached the booth, I was shocked to see it wasn't Lucius at all; it was Texas.

"Hey, pretty girl." I was totally in awe. He stood up and embraced me like I was a newborn baby. He looked at everyone else. "What's up, ladies?" They all introduced themselves. He immediately put his eyes back on me.

"I missed you, mama."

I smiled.

"Texas, Rae has a mild form of laryngitis so she can barely talk," Sasha explained.

"Do you feel okay?" he inquired.

I nodded.

"Did you pay our check?" Sasha asked.

He smiled. "Yes."

"Did you send the roses?" she asked.

"Yes."

"How did you know where we were staying?" she inquired.

"I was walking pass the Windsor Court when I saw y'all come in yesterday. I'm staying next door at the W."

"Oh, really," Sasha replied and glanced at me with a half-smile on her face.

"Ladies, I'm going to the bathroom to freshen up," Cece interrupted.

"Hold up...I gotta go too," Sasha said.

"Rae, we'll be back."

Mimi was the only one that didn't get up to go to the bathroom. I knew Sasha and Cece were going to the bathroom to give me some alone time with Texas. Mimi sat there and pretended to be texting on her phone, but I knew she was just being nosey.

"Raechel, I'm so sorry about the night I didn't meet you at the coffee shop. Something really important came up. I called you several times after that but you wouldn't return my calls."

My expression indicated that I forgave him. He smiled, and so did I. I remembered the tennis bracelet. I pulled it out of my purse. It was still in the box. I handed it to him and shook my head.

"Nah, ma, I bought that for you. Please, keep it, but I want my other bracelet back.

Oh yeah. I forgot I still have his grandmother's bracelet.

"Did you like the roses?"

I nodded and smiled.

Texas looked at me as if he could read my thoughts. He gently reached over and rubbed his hand across my chin. "Raechel, do you believe in love?"

I looked at him curiously. I was shocked that he had asked me that question. Then I noticed the girls were on their way back from the bathroom. I knew they were ready to go.

He grabbed my hand and our gaze connected. "Can I call you later?"

I nodded.

"I know you can't talk. I'll be satisfied just to hear you breathe.

Ooooh, how romantic. We all looked at him. Texas and I stood up. Sasha, Mimi, and Cece thanked him again. He grabbed my hand. I gently squeezed his in return to indicate I was thankful for what he had done. He walked us to the door. While walking through the crowded restaurant, he held my hand so tight that I could feel his heart thumping. The girls walked ahead and waited for me outside the restaurant. When we got to the door, he gave me a peck on my forehead; he acted like he didn't want to let my hand go. I gently pulled away. I waved bye and so did he.

Chapter 5

After the pool party, I went back to the hotel and fell into a deep sleep. I was awakened by my cell phone. I looked at the clock; it was nine-thirty at night. Sasha and Cece were still asleep. Mimi had gone to dinner with this guy she had met at the pool party. I picked up the phone but forgot I couldn't talk, so I hung up and laid back down and dozed off. My phone rang again. I picked it back up, "Hello" I whispered.

"Hello, is this Raechel?" I nodded my head as if he could see me through the phone. He called my name. "Raechel, is that you?" I didn't know what to do so I just pushed the buttons on the phone to indicate it was me.

"Hey, Princess. I told you I just wanted to hear you breathe." I smiled. "I wanna see you tonight if you are up to it. I've been thinking about you all day. I wanna see you, even if it's only ten minutes. If you are up to it, push three buttons." I paused for a moment then I pushed three buttons like he asked me to do. "Can you meet me at the bar in the lobby in about twenty minutes? If twenty minutes is okay then push one button. If you need longer, push two buttons." I pushed two buttons. I knew it would take me longer than twenty minutes. "Okay what about forty minutes? Push one button if forty minutes is okay." I pushed one button. "Cool, I'll see you downstairs in the lobby in forty minutes."

I hung up the phone. *Dang that felt like I was on the phone with my bank, checking on my checking account.* I jumped in the shower. After my shower, I flat ironed my hair into a soft windblown look and put on a little make-up because I didn't want to look like I had tried to get all dazzled up. I threw on some shorts, a tank and some flip-flops. All the noise I was making woke up Cece and Sasha.

"Chick, where you going?" Cece asked

"To meet Texas," I whispered, and smiled.

"Oooh, gon', diva." We all giggled.

"How do I look?" I whispered

"You look cute," replied Sau. "What time are you coming back?"

"In a couple of hours."

"Aiight. We'll call you if we decide to go out. Have fun."

One thing I like about the crew of girls I roll with was that we all respected the fact that each one of us was grown and everything we did didn't have to consist of a group. If one of my girls met someone they wanted to go out with for the weekend, none of us had a problem with it and no one judged the person for the choices they made. Our motto is when out of town you can be whoever you wanna be.

My girls always got their money when it was time to roll out and none of my friends are cheap. When we do roll out we do it in class and style always staying in the finest hotels and resorts. I can't stand friends that are always hollering about they want to go and kick it but when it's time to make travel arrangements they always back out. Hell, if you know you don't have the money, don't say you're going in the first place.

I glanced at myself in the mirror one last time before going downstairs to meet Texas. I walked to the elevator; I felt a little tense. I waited patiently for the elevator and then I noticed my dumb ass hadn't even pressed the button yet. I pressed the button and the elevator door opened, as if it was waiting just for me. *Ok, Rae, stay cool, calm, and confident.*

The elevator arrived at the lobby floor. I stepped off and walked around to try and find the hotel bar but it was nowhere in sight. Then I noticed as I was walking around the hotel my panties kept giving me a wedgie, which was making my hot shorts ride up my butt. They were not tight. They were a loose fitting pair of shorts. But I had worn the wrong type of panties with them. I became even more nervous. My shorts were riding up my ass, I couldn't find the bar, and sweat beads started to form on my nose. I walked around the lobby one last time. I finally decided to ask the hotel attendant where the bar was. He was an older white man who looked to be in his mid-sixties.

"Sir, where is the hotel bar?" I whispered.

"Excuse me, ma'am. I can't hear you," he screamed.

I pointed to my throat. "Laryngitis." Then I mouthed, "Where is the bar?"

"Oh, the bar." He pointed his finger. "It's right over there."

I looked in the direction he was pointing in. I can't believe I've passed that bar at least five times and didn't even see it. When I stepped inside the bar, I became a little more nervous. I immediately went to the bathroom and took off those panties and stuffed them in my purse, straightened up my tank, powdered my nose, and put on a little lipgloss, and went to the bar. I didn't see Texas.

"Excuse me, may I have a shot of Patron?" I whispered. I knew the alcohol wouldn't help my throat but I needed something to calm me down. I'm always kind of goofy around a guy I like. Either I say or do something stupid. I was not about to do that tonight.

"Would you like the shot chilled?" I shook my head, no. "What about salt and lime?"

"Yes."

I didn't have time for him to chill that shot because I didn't want Texas to catch me throwing back shots of Patron. The bartender handed me the shot and I immediately licked the salt, swallowed the tequila, and sucked the lime.

"Would you like another one?" I shook my head, no, and asked for the check. I quickly paid and moved from the bar to a quiet little table in the corner. Just as I started to sit down I looked up and saw Texas walking straight toward me. He walked toward me and gave me a big bear hug.

"Hey, pretty girl." I smiled. It was something about the way he said, 'Hey, pretty girl' that made my stomach twirl upside down.

I sat down and leaned back into the chair. The balmy effects from the tequila calmed my entire body right away

"Have you been here long?" he asked. I shook my head, no. Our eyes connected for a brief moment and I felt as if Texas had completed me. I instantly darted my gaze in another direction.

"You want something to drink?" he asked.

I whispered, "A red wine." We both looked in the direction of the bar to get the attention of the bartender. As the bartender walked pass the bar to our table, I noticed something red on the floor near the barstool I was sitting at. I looked in my purse. *Ohmigod! Those are my panties on the floor; they must've fell out when I paid for my tequila.* I giggled to myself.

"What's funny?"

I shook my head. "Nothing," I whispered.

"Hi, what can I get you to drink?" the bartender asked.

"I'd like a shot of Remy VSOP and the lady would like a glass of your best Cabernet."

"Okay, I'll be right back." He looked at me again. I smiled and shifted my gaze in another direction.

"You look great." I tried to say thank you and the squeakiest voice came out."

"Sweetie, don't." He grabbed my hands. "I told you I just wanted to look at you. I'll do all the talking."

The waiter returned with our drinks "Are you all ordering tonight?"

"Yes, give us a minute to look at the menu. Baby, what do you want to eat?" Texas asked. I looked at the menu and pointed to the Mediterranean Rolls.

He looked over the menu. "Yeah, I'll have an order of those. As a matter of fact, give me two orders," he told the server. I took a sip of wine. I was feeling warm and sensuous.

"Rae, I'm so happy you came out tonight. I was going out with my homeboys but these niggas down here off the chain. One of 'em got arrested last night."

"For what?" I whispered.

"Indecent exposure." Texas shook his head. "He pulled out his dick last night on Bourbon in front of these li'l females and the cops saw 'em. I had to get up early this morning and go get that nigga outta jail. Then these females down here goin' ham. I ain't never been around chicks so persistent. Everywhere we go chicks are jocking us, offering to buy us drinks, or they're trying to come back to the hotel with us. I don't understand. Women aren't like they used to be. They're too busy trying to make it happen on their own. It just gets old. But my niggas, they love it. They getting it in. They tryin' to freak as many chicks as possible."

I shook my head and agreed.

"What about y'all, are you and your girls having a good time?"

I nodded, yes.

The waiter stopped by and asked, "Would you like another drink?" I shook my head, no, and Texas ordered another Remy VSOP. I touched the waiter and gestured a writing motion.

"Do I have a pen, sure?"

He handed me the pen and I grabbed one of my beverage napkins and wrote on the napkin. "Do you have any siblings?" I wrote.

"Nope, it's just me." He paused for a moment. "Well…actually, I had a sister." I smiled; I noticed he had an expressionless look on his face. "But she died."

I wrote, *I'm sorry.*

"Nah, it's okay. It happened a long time ago." He took a sip of VSOP. "When I was seven years old our house caught on fire. Me and my sister always slept in the same room. Even though she had her own room she still wanted to sleep in the room with me. When our house caught on fire, I jumped up and grabbed my sister's hand and ran out of the house. When I turned around I thought I was holding my sister's hand but it was the doll she always carried."

I looked down because I hated I brought the subject up.

"It happened so long ago that I really don't remember that much about her. I do know we loved the same things and we were inseparable. My mother never got over it and please don't bring it up. My father was devastated but it nearly destroyed my mother." He took a sip of his drink and grimaced. "My mother is very over protective of me. She is quite a character. If you ever meet her, you'll see what I'm talking about." He raised his eyebrows and gave me an apprehensive look. "But my dad, that's my ace…he's a doctor."

"Forreal… What kind?" I wrote.

"Neurosurgeon. My father is one of three black neurosurgeons in the country

My mother went to nursing school but she's never worked. She's become a shopaholic."

I wrote on the napkin. "Where do they live?"

"Houston, but we're originally from Philadelphia."

Our waiter brought our food. I picked up one of my Mediterranean rolls and took a small bite. There were six rolls on my plate but I only ate three. I was not about to dog that food even though I was hungry as hell. I just don't believe in cleaning your plate on the first couple of dates.

He looked at my plate. "Baby, are you done?"

I nodded my head, yes, and sighed as if I was full.

"Are you sure?"

I whispered, "Yeah." Then he grabbed my plate and ate my Mediterranean rolls as well.

The waiter came and asked if we would like dessert. We shook our heads, no.

"Well, here's your check." The waiter placed the check on the table. I didn't want the night to end. I was hoping he would ask me to go for a walk.

"Rae, do you gamble?" I wrote on the napkin, *not really*.

"I'll teach you. C'mon, let's go to the casino."

I wrote, *k*.

Texas paid the bill; we got up and walked across the street to Harrah's. It was packed. During the Essence Festival, after everyone is done going to the many concerts and after parties and hanging out on Bourbon, almost everybody goes to the casino to gamble, eat, and mingle.

"Do you know how to shoot craps?"

I shook my head, no.

"C'mon, I'll teach you." We walked to the craps table. "Okay, the object of the game is to get the dice and roll them to the edge of the table and not to roll a twelve. If you roll a twelve, you shot a craps and you're out and you lost your money. Understand?

I shook my head, yes, although I really didn't fully understand, but I knew if I watched a couple of people, I would catch on quickly.

Texas pulled out five hundred dollars and gave it to the dealer. The dealer handed him a stack of chips. The dice revolved around the table to Texas; it was his turn. He took the dice and rolled a twelve on the first roll. I started laughing.

"Damn," he scoffed. The people at the table were trippin'.

"Y'all need to gon' back to where y'all came from, coming over here rolling a damn craps," this older black woman mocked. Everybody started laughing. Then it was my turn on the first roll. I rolled the dice too hard and they went over the table.

"And be sure you take her too. She don't even know how to roll the dice," the woman yelled.

The dealer gave me another shot. This time I rolled a seven. Everybody got excited.

"Yea, now that's what I'm talkin' bout," the woman remarked.

70

I rolled the dice again. I rolled another five. The dice kept revolving around the table. Texas decided to just let me play.

"Baby, you got beginner's luck," he commented. Every time the dice got in my hand, I rolled a two, four, five, or nine. Our table was crunk. People started coming over standing around watching. Texas was standing behind me. My butt kept rubbing against him. I felt something hard. I thought maybe it was his belt then I realized that it was too far up to be his belt. *Damn, that's his dick.* Instead of moving, I leaned back into the grove of his crotch and propped my ass up a little, feeling his hard dick grinding on my ass had me dripping wet. I was having a good time until I looked up and noticed this chick glaring at us. First, I looked off to see if she would stop looking. When I looked back in her direction she was still staring at us. *Damn, what is this bitch looking at?* I ignored her. *If she wants to stand there and stare at us like a fool, that is on her.*

"Baby, let's get out of here," Texas whispered in my ear.

"Okay, I need to go to the bathroom."

"Aiight, I'ma go cash in our winnings and meet you at the exit," he whispered in my ear.

I went and freshened up. He was making me so wet I had to go regroup and get my mind right. As I walked out the bathroom it occurred to me that the bathroom had an exit on each side. I went out the wrong exit. I was lost for a moment. I walked around looking for Texas, and then I spotted him talking to the girl that had been staring at us. It appeared as if they were arguing. She was pointing her finger and shaking her head. Then suddenly I saw her slap the shit out of him. A security guard came over and must have asked them what the problem was. Texas and her were exchanging words and she attempted to slap him again. At that point the security guard escorted her out the casino.

She had caused a major scene. People were stopping and staring at the altercation. I'm sure he was embarrassed. I immediately turned and walked out of the casino. I walked across the street and back to my hotel. He started blowing my phone up. I turned it off. When I walked in the room, Cece and Sasha were asleep. I didn't want to wake them. I put my nightgown on and wondered what in the hell had just happened. Maybe that was his girlfriend or someone he hooked up with for the weekend. Maybe it was just someone from his past. Whoever she was, she was furious. I laid there for a moment and finally dozed off and went to sleep.

It's the Fourth of July and the Prince concert is tonight. The girls and I are excited. We had purchased our tickets when we first found out he was performing at the Essence Festival. Sasha woke up first. "Damn, chicks, what time did y'all get in last night?"

"I just got in at about six," Mimi yawned. "And, bitches, I shook it last night."

"Girl, tell us all about it," Sasha urged.

"Girl, first I'ma go back to sleep. I'll tell y'all when I wake up," Mimi murmured and curled up in the bed.

"Rae, what about you? I heard you stroll in early this morning too," Cece said.

"Nah, chick that was Mimi. I got in around midnight. My li'l date got cut short."

"What? What happened?" Sasha inquired.

I got out the bed to go wash my face and brush my teeth. They were all sitting there waiting for me to tell all when I walked back in the room. Even Mimi was anxious to hear about my escapade. Sau had ordered room service and we were all nibbling off her plate.

"Okay, first we went to the bar in the lobby and had some drinks; we chilled and had a good time. Then we went over to the casino and shot craps. We were kickin' it and having fun when all of a sudden, I saw this chick staring at us. At first I didn't pay her no attention. I thought maybe she was a groupie or something, and Texas obviously didn't care about her because he was all over me." I took a bite of Sau's pancakes. "So things started getting a little heated between me and Texas and he was like, 'Baby, let's go.' I told him I needed to go to the bathroom first so he told me he would meet me at the exit."

"Ooooh… heated like what? Y'all must've been ready to fuck," Cece interrupted.

"Nah, hell nah." They all started taunting me. "No, bitches, we were not about to fuck. We just wanted to get out of there to get some fresh air."

"Fresh air, my ass," Sasha chimed in.

"Anyway, before I was rudely interrupted," I rolled my eyes at Sasha. "When I came out the bathroom, I saw him arguing with the same girl that had been staring at us."

"Girl, forreal?" Sasha commented.

"Then she just hauled off and slapped him."

"What?" Sasha exclaimed.

"That bitch smacked fire from that nigga mouth." We all laughed. "Then the security guard came and put her out."

"What did you do?" asked Cece.

"I left; I didn't even want him to know I saw it."

"Why didn't you stay too so you could find out who it was?"

I shrugged my shoulders. "I don't know. I should have, but it really ain't that serious to me, because I know this dude got plenty bitches he fucking with, and I definitely wasn't gonna be in the casino arguing with one of his hoes."

"It probably was his woman," Mimi said skeptically.

"Or it could have been someone he met for the weekend," Cece added. "But it ain't no sense in her getting mad if she hooked up with him for the weekend. She ought to know what time it is. Guys down here just want to hit it and quit it."

"I hope it wasn't his woman. That's fucked up if he all out at the casino *booed* up with Rae and knows his woman down here too," Sasha said.

"Whoever it was, she was wrong for slapping the man," I added, as I ate the last of Sasha's pancakes.

"Hell, it might have been his wife. Y'all know them ball players scandalous like that. They be cheating on their wives out in the open, and the wives just stick around for the money," Sasha commented, while sucking on a strawberry and smacking her lips.

"Well, they stupid as hell. It ain't enough money to make me stay in a marriage where my husband is openly cheating in my face," I said.

"Shit, I'll stay in the marriage if he has enough money to take care of me and his mistress, but that nigga better believe I'ma be out cheating on his ass too, and then I'll divorce him and take half," Mimi said and gave Cece a high-five.

"Rae, are you sure he ain't married?" asked Sau. "Girl, look it up on the internet; you know niggas be lying."

"Yes, I'm sure he's not married," I replied sarcastically. I knew Texas wasn't married and I don't think he has a girlfriend. I didn't believe he would lie about something like that. But I did want to know who that mysterious woman was at the casino. I laid back down. I knew I wouldn't ask Texas about that woman, it's just not my style.

We kicked it at the Prince concert; he put on a bomb ass show. But me and my girls was trippin' at how short he was. He doesn't look that short on TV, but he was still sexy, and kept the crowd hyped from beginning to the end of the concert.

Chapter 6

I was back in Nashville and had just finished up my work-study. When I walked outside it was blazing. I'm talking about that the type of heat that makes you feel like you're suffocating. I was starving and was about to go and grab a bite to eat when I looked at my phone, and noticed I had a missed call. It was a number I didn't recognize. I called the number back

"Hello, beautiful," the voice on the other end said.

"Hi." I smiled, it was Texas.

"What are you doing?"

"Nothing, just leaving class."

"Are you hungry?"

"Yes."

"Meet me at Café Java."

"When?"

"Right now."

I hesitated for a moment because I still was a little unsure about Texas. I didn't know if I could really trust him and I was still tripping off the fact that I seen him cussing and fighting with that chick at the casino. But I knew if I went back to my apartment I wasn't going to do shit for the rest of the day but watch reality shows.

"Okay, bye."

"Wait…hello. Are you hanging up?" he asked.

"Oh, I thought you were done."

"I wanna talk to you." I got in my truck and immediately jumped out; the leather seat burned the hell out of my legs. I stood outside and let the truck cool off before getting back in.

"Okay." We talked on the phone as I drove to West End. I was smiling the whole time I was talking to him. I was acting like a little giddy schoolgirl. Before I got out the truck I sprayed on a little Victoria Secret *Heavenly* and shined up my lips. When I arrived, he was already waiting inside. He stood up and hugged me so tight my feet slightly lifted off the floor.

"Mmmm, you smell good."

"Thank you." I smiled. This time I felt a little more relaxed.

We ate, drank, laughed, and had the best time. He was so easy to talk to. We had been at the restaurant for about three hours, when I noticed the time. "Dang, I didn't realize what time it was. We've been talking for hours. I'ma about to get ready to go." I really didn't want the night to end, but I didn't want to seem desperate and have him end the date first. He paid for the bill. As we were walking out the restaurant he grabbed my hand. I think it is so romantic to hold hands. That made me feel special. I loved the fact that he would always grab my hand when we were together.

He walked me to my car. We stood silent for a moment. I started looking for my keys.

"I really had a good time tonight," I told him and hit my alarm. When I grabbed the door handle he gently turned me around. His touch sent a warm chill through me. He looked at me for a moment then pulled me close to him.

"Hey, come with me."

"Where?"

"To my crib, please, I just wanna talk to you some more."

"Umm...I don't know." I pondered for a moment, knowing I wanted to go bad as hell but I didn't want to put myself in a situation where I would have sex with him too early and complicate things between us. I was feeling Texas Reynolds, and I didn't know how long I could resist the mad sex appeal he was throwing at me.

I hesitated for a moment. "Okay, cool, but I can't stay too late."

"Alright, just follow me," he said. I got in my Isuzu; he got in his Range Rover and we headed towards his house.

I called Sasha. "Hey, girl, what's up?"

"Nothing, what's up, diva?"

"Chick, Texas invited me to his house," I said anxiously.

"Aw, hell." We both laughed. Because we both had been in similar situations. Situations where I would be kickin' it with a guy and everything was going good; the guy would be into me, calling me all the time leaving sweet messages. I'm talking about the whole nine. But the minute we had sex things would change. He would start acting funny, not calling as much, not being as attentive as before. Just put it this way,

I was smart enough to know that you better make sure a man is in love after the chase is over.

"Chick, that's cool. But, Rae, please try to control your raging hormones."

"Girl, I know, but, Sasha, this man got me so gone. I'm so attracted to him. The way he touches me just does something to me on the inside."

"Well, I feel ya'; he is all that. But if you do have sex with him, you got to be able to except the consequences. It may bring y'all closer together or it may make him lose interest." She paused. "We've had this discussion a million times. If you have sex with a man too early, nine times out of ten you are gonna fall off. Right now, it's obvious that he likes you and you're keeping his attention. But the minute you have sex with him things are going to become a little complicated. Wait a while; let him get to know you, find out about you, your likes and dislikes. Don't even think about a relationship right now. Just kick it and take it for what it is. Right now it is about developing a solid foundation and then maybe in the near future you can build something more."

"Girl, we pulling up at his house. I'll call you back." I pulled down the mirror and checked my lip-gloss.

"Wait a minute, broad. What his house look like."

"Phat...a fucking mansion."

"Damn, chick, I'm jealous...girl, have fun." We both giggled.

"Alright, bye."

I got out my truck and walked up the driveway. This man's house was huge. I mean enormous. He had a roundabout drive way. I'm talking about one of them joints where you just drive around and park your whip right there in the front. There was a water fountain that sat in the middle of his manicured lawn that looked like it was straight from the MGM Grand. I dared not act like I had never seen anything like it before, even though I hadn't. We walked inside. There were vaulted ceilings with an immaculate stairwell, and ceiling-to-floor windows throughout the house. The windows didn't have any curtains or blinds. That was the first time I had been to a black person's house without any window treatments. White people are the ones who don't like curtains. Black folks have curtains, blinds, drapes and some more stuff on their windows; they'll even throw some bed sheets up to the windows.

"You have a very lovely home." The interior of his living room was cocaine white. He even had white carpet. "Oh, you have white carpet; let me take off my shoes."

"Baby, you don't have to worry about getting the carpet dirty. That's what carpet cleaners are for." *That's what I'm talking about. Why buy white carpet if you can't afford to walk on it.* "Come on, let me show you around." We walked around the house. "Do you want something to drink?"

"No, thank you." We walked upstairs to the theater room where there was a built-in aquarium with an assortment of exotic fish, sharks, and eels. There was a 100-inch screen on the wall. It was just like I was at the movies.

"Do you wanna watch a movie?"

"Yea, that's cool," I said as I sat down on the couch.

"What chu' wanna watch? I got that new Will Smith joint."

"Ah yeah, I heard that was good. That's cool, we can watch that." I really didn't know what movie he was talking about it. Seems like Will Smith got a new movie coming out every other month. I just wanted to hurry up and pick something so I could go to the bathroom and freshen up.

"Hey, where's the bathroom?"

"It's down the hall on the right."

I went to the bathroom and freshened up. I looked at myself in the mirror and exhaled a deep breath. "Raechel, be cool." I quietly told myself. I came back out and sat down on the couch. Texas put the movie in as I walked into the room.

"Hey, I'ma go change. Do you need anything?"

"Oh, no, I'm fine."

He was gone about ten minutes. When he came back in the room he handed me a blanket.

"Thank you." I unfolded the blanket.

"I figured you might need it. Y'all women are always cold."

"You're right, because it seems like I'm always freezing."

"I'm just the opposite; I'm always hot," he smirked.

I took off my shoes and folded my legs Indian style on the couch. Texas had put on a white T-shirt and some gym shorts. That negro looked so sexy standing there in that T-shirt. His biceps bulged through his T-shirt. I grabbed the blanket and laid it on top of me. He walked to get the remote from the bookcase, and then started walking towards me. *I know he is not about to come and sit on this couch. I had the blanket on top of me for a reason; to show him I am comfortable, so please don't come over here and wreck my flow.*

"Uhhhh, can I sit down?" he asked.

"Oh, yeah." I started to put my feet back on the floor.

"Rae, you don't have to move. I'ma sit right here if you don't mind." He took a seat directly beside me on the couch.

He pushed Play and the movie came on. I made myself comfortable. I turned my back and leaned it against the armrest of the couch and stretched out my legs. Next thing I know he had scooted between my legs and leaned his back and head on my lower torso.

"Am I too heavy?" he asked.

"Nah, you're fine."

He looked up at me. "Are you sure?"

"Yeah." I opened my legs wider so I could get more comfortable. We turned towards the screen and continued to watch the movie. I was trying to act cool; like I wasn't nervous but inside I was a nervous wreck.

After a minute or so I was comfortable. The movie was so good that I had forgotten he was there. Toward the middle of the movie, his breathing had changed. I looked down and he was knocked out. My eyes roamed over his body. The rise and fall of his chest made me appreciate his mere essence. He was sleeping so soundly I didn't want to wake him, even if it meant me being a little uncomfortable. So I scooted down a little and got more comfortable and went straight to sleep.

I woke up the next morning to the warm sun shining in my face. I was a bit disoriented, and didn't quite remember where I was. *Ahh, I'm at Texas'.* As soon as the thought popped in my head, he walked into the bedroom.

"Good morning, Sunshine."

I hesitated. "Good morning," I said in a raspy voice. I sat up in the bed and glanced in the mirror that was attached to the dresser in front of the bed. I didn't look too bad. My hair was a little fluffed but it had more of a windblown look. My skin always looks good in the morning unless I had been partying the night before.

"What time is it?" I asked.

"About six."

"How did I end up in here?"

"I carried you in here last night. Remember, you fell asleep on the couch."

"Ahh," I pondered for a second to recall the events from the previous night. "Did you sleep in here?"

He smirked. "No, baby, this is my guest room. I slept in my room."

"Oh…you're up awfully early."

"Well, I'm on my way to work." He called football practice, work, but when I think about it, it is his job and that's what he's getting paid to do.

"I'm getting up." I started to get out the bed and noticed I was only in a thong. "Where my shorts! Did you take them off me?" I snapped.

He started laughing. "Hell, nah. I wouldn't take your shorts off."

Then I remembered taking them off after he brought me in the room. "Well, I didn't mean to stay the night; I was going to get—"

He interrupted. "Rae, please. If I had wanted you to leave, I wouldn't have carried your ass in here last night." He sat on the edge of the bed. "Look, you don't have to get up, you can stay here if you want to. Please, go back to sleep."

"Nah, really, I'm about to get up; I have a twelve o'clock class."

"Aye, you good. Lay back down and get some rest," he insisted. "I'll leave my spare key and you can give it back to me tonight."

"Okay," I agreed. He left out and I laid back down and went to sleep. I woke up at about eleven-thirty. *Oh shit! I gotta be in class in thirty minutes.* I immediately threw on my clothes, grabbed my purse and keys and bounced. I was at the end of his street when I started looking around for my cell phone. I was steering with one hand and searching for my phone at the same time.

"Damn, I'ma be late for class," I screamed and pulled to the side of the road and dumped everything out my purse onto the seat. I unbuckled my seat belt and thoroughly searched my car seats, the floor, and console looking for my phone. I wasn't going anywhere until I found my phone and I was praying that I hadn't left it in Texas' house. *Here it is! Thank God.* It had fell on the side of my car seat. *How did that happen?* When I lifted my head I looked in the rearview mirror and saw a car had pulled into Texas' driveway. A Latina looking chick stepped out of the SUV. She went around to the back of the passenger side of the vehicle and fumbled around. Then I saw her walk into the front of the house with a little curly-haired girl in tow with what appeared to be a diaper bag. She grabbed her key and walked straight into the house. *What the fuck! That must be his baby momma and there li'l girl. I can't believe that nigga had me laying up in his crib and his baby momma live there.* I pulled off trying to wrap my brain around the fact that Texas' baby momma lives with him.

My heart was thumping. I was totally astounded for a minute. *I knew I couldn't trust this nigga.* He's obviously still messing with his baby momma. I began to tell myself, "Rae, calm down. This is not your man first of all, so he can basically do whatever he wants." I turned around and looked back at his house. That chick didn't emerge again. She was comfortably dwelling inside of his two-million dollar home. Hell, nah! I don't have time for no baby momma drama. Really, I didn't even tripp, because niggas are what they are and don't too much shit surprise me. But what pissed me off was that this chick got a key to his house and so do I. What if she had of strolled in there while I was sleeping. Or what if she had of seen me leaving this man's house? Anything could have happened. That's some bullshit and forreal. Then I ain't gon' even get in the baby momma drama shit. *That's a whole nother level.* Every time I've tried to date a brother with a child it has been straight turmoil, from the beginning to the end. I don't know what it is about them baby mommas, but dudes be having mad respect for them. I guess they should because them chicks believe in these men and have their child, so the man should respect them to the utmost. My thing is, don't be still trying to make it happen with your child's mother but trying to kick it with me on the side. Because the minute that baby momma finds out the father is dating someone else, there they go; all of a sudden they want the man back. Then there I am, caught up in the middle of some baby momma bullshit. That's some stress that I definitely don't need, but it's cool though cause I'm cutting his ass off. No phone calls, no explanation, no nothing.

Chapter 7

Ugh! I was pissed. Dude must be out of his mind if he thinks I'm about to be the other woman. I don't play that. I don't fuck with married men or men in relationships. I don't have to. There are too many men out here for that. That shit had me heated. I kept replaying the scenario over in my head.

I put in my Nicki Menaj "Pink Friday" CD. I was deep in thought when I looked in my rearview mirror and noticed a car riding on my tail. I sped up and the car sped up right behind me. I tried slowing down to see if the person behind me would slow down but they didn't. I was coming up on a sharp curve, when suddenly the car drove up beside me and pulled over on me, causing me to slightly swerve off the road. I steadied my truck and got back on the road. Then the person pulled over on me again, this time causing me to lose control of the wheel. My truck started tilting. The passenger side of my truck came off the pavement and I was riding on two wheels. I immediately jerked the wheel to try and make the car level back out on the road, but I lost control of the wheel and my truck started flipping over.

My world stopped. It was like a movie. I was going in slow motion as the truck just kept flipping over and over. I closed my eyes. "Heavenly father, please protect me."

My truck ended up in the median, upside down, and facing the opposite direction. I was knocked unconscious. I waited for the bright light they say you see when you die, but I didn't see one. My consciousness slowly set in.

"Uhhhh," I weakly moaned. It felt like a ton of bricks had landed on my head. It took me a minute to realize that I was still alive. That is when this man pulled me out the truck. I tried to open my eyes, but I could only see out of one eye. I was totally delirious. As the man was pulling me out of the truck, I was praying, "God, please don't let me die." My entire head was throbbing. It felt like Mike Tyson had hit me in the eye twenty times and bit off my ear lobe. I kept trying to focus my right eye but all I could see was a blur. I slowly opened my left eye. When I looked up at the man who had pulled me out of the truck, he had a white face, white hair, and white eyebrows. A peaceful sensation came over me. He comforted me.

"Everything is okay. Jesus is here with you right now," he told me.

I laid back on the ground and closed my eyes. My serene moment was interrupted by ambulance sirens. When I opened my eyes back up the man was gone. The paramedics had arrived. They checked my vital signs and then put me onto the gurney and strapped me down.

I lifted my torso off the gurney. "Where is the angel?" I asked.

They strapped me down tighter. "Ma'am, you have just taken a pretty bad bump to the head and we're going to get you to the hospital as soon as possible," one of the paramedics said.

I laid my head back down. I must've passed out because I woke up in a hospital room strapped down and I couldn't see out of my right eye. I laid there trying to remember exactly how I ended up there. Then my thoughts were interrupted by someone walking in the room. The person was standing in my room but I couldn't see anything I couldn't move my head because of the neck brace I had on. All I saw was a figure and I heard the person breathing.

"Is...sssomebody there?" I asked woozily.

I heard footsteps coming closer to the bed, but the person just stood there.

"Are you the doctor?" An eerie feeling came over me. I already hate hospitals.

There was no response. I tried again to lift my head but I couldn't. They had me strapped down like I was headed straight to the loony bin. I moved my hand around the side of the bed in search of the call button, and then suddenly I heard the person leave. I wiggled my hands up and unloosened the straps on my arm. I had unloosened the straps around my neck. I was maneuvering my body upward in the bed when the nurse and doctor walked in.

"Oh, dear, what are you doing?"

"Why y'all got me strapped in this bed?" I snapped.

"Oh, sweetheart, it's so if you have any broken bones or other injuries you won't hurt yourself more."

"Ahhh, what happened?"

"You were in a car accident. It looks like the airbag ruptured in your face." She pulled off all the Velcro straps and helped me to sit up. As she helped me sit up, my head was swimming. I was so dizzy. I slowly opened my right eye but I couldn't see anything but shades of white and gray. "Now is that better?" the nurse asked.

"Yes, ma'am, thank you," I murmured while trying to catch a glimpse of my surroundings. She was an older white woman with a round face and she smelled like peppermints and carmax. She was nice and very gentle.

I finally positioned my body so that I was comfortable. That's when the doctor rolled over to me on his stool.

"Hello, I'm Dr. Larry." He was a young, white doctor. With limited vision, I was still able to see that he was sporting a pair of red Converse.

"I'm Raechel," I replied weakly.

He checked my heart and pulse and then took a bright light and shined it directly in my eye.

I flinched, as he pointed the light in my eye.

"Close your left eye and try to focus. Can you see this object?"

"Not really; what is it?"

"It's an ink pen. What do you see, Raechel?"

"It's blurry... it's hard to tell," I said while still trying to focus my eye, but all I kept seeing was white.

"Hmmm, looks like you got socked in the eye with the air bag."

No shit. He continued to examine my eye but wasn't saying anything, just constantly looking at it and going, "Humm."

I became aggravated. "Is my eye going to be okay?" I impatiently snapped.

"Yes, the nurse is going to take you to the examination room to run a few tests just to make sure there isn't any serious damage."

"Test," I shouted. "What kinda test?"

"They're just standard tests for patients that have had trauma to their eyes. Don't worry, you'll be fine."

My head was banging. I couldn't see out of my right eye, then it dawned on me my car was fucked and I didn't have a lick of insurance.

"Ms. Jones, do you have any relatives we can call?"

I gave the nurse Mimi's and Sasha's phone numbers. I was not about to give him my mother's phone number because she would have been on the first bird up out of Memphis. Plus, I wanted to be the one to tell her what happened.

They wheeled me to the examination room, and ran a series of tests then escorted me back to my room. As I sat in the room waiting on the test results, my mind lingered back to the individual that was in my room, and why were they standing so close to my bed. My thoughts were interrupted by Dr. Larry. I could tell by the expression on his face that everything was okay.

He glanced at his chart. "Ms. Jones, you're going to be fine. Your cornea is slightly bruised, but it will heal in a few days. I'm going to prescribe you some eye drops to apply twice a day. You should have your full vision restored in your eye in a few days. But you are going to be pretty banged up for a while, and the blackness around the eye will probably last about a week or so. I'll give you something for the pain as well. Ms. Jones, when was the last time you had a tetanus shot?"

"Um, I don't know. I can't remember." *I don't think I've ever had a tetanus shot.*

Out of nowhere, he pulled out a long needle. "Okay, turn over."

"Oh, no, I hate needles," I cried but I turned over like he told me to do. He rammed the needle directly in my ass.

"That wasn't so bad now, was it?" he said in a mild tone.

Hell, yeah, it was bad. It hurt like a muthafucka! I cringed and rubbed my ass and gently shifted my weight to the other side.

Sasha and Mimi walked in the room at the same time. They both looked at me.

"Daayum!" they shouted almost simultaneously. They both rushed toward me and gave me a hug.

"Are you okay?" Sasha asked, glaring at my eye.

"Yeah, I'm straight," I replied in a hazy moan.

"What happened?" Mimi asked, as she moved my hair from in front of my eye."

I leaned back on the pillows in the bed. "I don't know." I sat there for a few seconds trying to recall the events from my wreck. "All I remember is I was driving and this car pulled up behind me, driving on my tail, so I slowed down hoping they would pass. Then all of a sudden, they pulled up beside me and swerved over on me causing me to lose control of the truck."

"Did you see what the person looked like?"

"No, the car had tinted windows. It looked like one of them Dodge Chargers." I paused. "But I'm not sure; everything happened so fast."

Sasha looked at me with a worried expression. "Rae, you need to go file a police report. Do you think that somebody may have been following you?"

"No, I don't think so." I paused, trying to recall the events from the wreck. "I didn't notice the car until it was riding on my bumper."

"Sounds like to me somebody was trying to run you off the road," Mimi said.

"But who? I don't have any enemies that I know of."

"Girl, please; it's people that will be right in your face skinnin' and grinnin' but all the time hatin' on you," Sasha said as she helped me up out the bed.

"True, but I don't feel like that's the case. I think it was a person in a hurry and I panicked and lost control of the car."

"Alright, Rae, whatever you say. But I would at least go file a report."

"Nah, I'm ready to go home," I insisted. I was tired and my head was throbbing. The doctor placed a white bandage over my eye and gave me my prescriptions and then he released me.

"Where is your truck?" asked Sasha.

"I don't know, but I got a glance at it before I left the scene. I know it's totaled."

We all walked out the hospital. They both helped me into Sasha's Land Rover. Sasha handed me a pair of shades to put on. I don't know where she got them from but they were dark as hell. I put them on because the sun was blinding me. I could have sworn she gave me a pair of them Blue Blockers that old people be wearing. I was so glad to be out of that cold hospital and was glad I wasn't seriously hurt. I was messed up about my ride, but I was thankful to be alive.

"Rae, I think you should come over to my house tonight."

"Nah, girl. I just wanna go home. Take me to my apartment," I mumbled as I closed my eyes and reclined in the seat.

"Girl, shut-up. I'm not about to take your blind ass-home. You can't even see. You going to my house tonight. I'll take you home in the morning. The end, period."

I hated when she said 'the end period' because that meant conversation over. I was not about to argue with her. I could barely hold my head up. I'm blessed to have a friend like Sasha because good friends are hard to find. We went to Walgreen's to fill my prescriptions and headed to Sasha's house. My head started killing me and my medicine was wearing off. I needed to lay down. Sasha helped me up the stairs and helped me get undressed. I took two Lortabs, laid down, and went to sleep. I didn't wake up until eleven-thirty that night. I had several missed calls on my phone. Five calls were from Texas. Of course, my Mom had called a million times. While I was checking my calls and text messages, my phone beeped; it was Texas calling again. I pressed the Ignore button and laid back down. I was not about to be involved in any baby momma drama. I turned on the T.V. I watched Law and Order with one eye, until I fell back to sleep.

♣

A week had passed since the accident. The vision in my eye had come back, and the swelling had gone down, but there was still a little dark circle around my eye. I had been going to class all week and had worn shades every day. People in my class probably thought I had been in a fight and someone had beaten me up. I didn't even bother to explain what had happened to anyone. It wouldn't have mattered. People are going to lie and make up rumors anyway, especially on college campuses. I didn't care; let them think what they want to think. I had enough stuff to worry about. I had missed a week of work, I didn't have any transportation, and in Nashville you're basically fucked if you don't have a car.

It was Friday and I didn't have anything to do. I was stuck on campus until someone came and got me. I wasn't about to bug anyone because I hate asking folks to do stuff for me. Plus, I wanted to save them until I really needed them.

Sasha called about noon. "Hello."

"What's up, girl?"

"Nothin'," I replied in a dreary tone.

"You wanna go to lunch?"

"I guess, what time?"

"About twelve-thirty."

"That's cool."

She arrived exactly at twelve-thirty; I was shocked because she's never on time. When I got in the truck the first thing she did was look at my eye.

"What do you think?"

"It looks a lot better," she remarked.

"You think so?"

"Yeah."

I pulled down the passenger side mirror and examined my eye up close. "Yeah, it does look better," I agreed.

"Where do you wanna eat?" she asked.

"South Street."

"Okay, cool."

Sasha and I arrived at South Street. It was a beautiful summer day. I was glad to be off campus. I had been stuck on that damn campus most of the week, which had put me in a foul mood. South Street is this cool, hip, hang out, that has a patio and balcony with a humongous oak tree that goes straight through the building. Sasha and I love it. We dine there at least once a week. We caught up on the latest gossip and had a delicious lunch.

"So, what are you doing for the rest of the day?" she asked.

"I gotta be at work at five." I took a sip of my fruit tea.

"Aw, you goin' back to work?"

"Yeah, I have to. I'm broke as hell. That wreck fucked me up."

"Girl, you know I got you if you need a loan."

"Nah, girl, I'm good. You've done more than enough, taking care of me after the accident. After this weekend, I'll be back on. Plus, my refund money from my scholarship is supposed to be on my student ID on Monday." I lied about that, but Sasha is the type of person that will keep insisting I take some money, and that is not my thing. I can't sleep if I owe somebody money. A couple of shifts at Andrew's Crab will hold me over until I get my shit together.

"How are you getting to work?" Sasha asked, and gathered the napkins that a light breeze had scattered across the table. "Do you need me to take you?"

"Nah. Wren supposed to let me use his car." Wren is my play brother. I met him through Mimi. He sells weed. And Mimi who is a weed connoisseur used to fuck him to get her weekly stash. He was always hanging out in our dorm room. Then I realized we were the same major, so we started studying together and all of a sudden, Mimi quit fuckin' him. I think she got jealous because he and I used to hang out so much. Our relationship is strictly platonic; he ain't never tried to holla at me. I guess she couldn't stand the fact that somebody she was fuckin' was paying me more attention.

"What? His Escalade?"

"Nah, that other li'l car he got." We both got quiet. I saw a slight smirk on Sasha's face and then we both started laughing because Wren's other car was a straight hooptie.

"Girl, you sure you don't need me to take you?" Sasha insisted, still trippin' off the fact that I was gon' be driving Wren's hoo-ride.

"No, girl, I'll be straight. I ain't too good to drive a bucket. I just need to get from point A to point B."

"That's what up," Sasha smirked, as she finished off her virgin strawberry daiquiri. "Well, do you wanna go out tonight?" she asked.

"Sau, look at me. Don't you see my eye is still jacked up?"

"Girl, please. Throw a little Mac on that eye, and you'll be straight." She swirled her straw in her glass and slurped the last of her daiquiri, which made the hairs stand up on the back of my neck. I hate when people do that. It's just a sign of no home training. She slurped again.

"Girl, stop. I know that shit ain't that damn good." I turned up my lip.

"Aw, girl, my bad." She giggled. "Come on, Rae. You know we haven't been out in forever." It hadn't really been a long time, but a long time to me and Sasha meant two weeks. "Tonight Cali is having his White Linen party, and it's gonna be plenty niggas there 'cause it's hosted by Angelina Applause."

"Who is Angelina Applause?" I asked confused.

"Wait a minute…you ain't never heard of Angie Applause?" I shook my head no. "She a porn star with a big booty… I'm talking about the biggest booty you ever seen in yo' life and niggas be going crazy over her."

"What? Well why they call her Angie Applause?"

"Because they say when she clap her ass cheeks together it sound like a round of applause."

"Girl, please, that's ridiculous," I rolled my eyes nonchalantly.

"Well, chick, I'm just telling you why they call her Angie Applause. So, chick, you going?"

I pondered. I hadn't been out in a minute, and I did have a badass white short set, that I got from BeBe, that I couldn't wait to rock.

"If I go, you gon' have to pick me up," I said indifferently.

"I got you; just bring some clothes so you can spend the night over my house."

"Okay."

Sau dropped me back off at my apartment and I got some rest before it was time to go to work. I was so depressed about not having any transportation. But my cousin, Diamond, heard I was in a wreck and called and told me she was sending me a little something. Diamond is Mimi's sister. She said she wouldn't be able to send it until Monday because she was out of the country. I just needed some money to hold me through the weekend. I had been off work for a week, but one thing about waiting tables; I can always go in and make some money. I didn't have to wait around for a check.

I got ready for work about three o'clock. Wren and his girlfriend bought me his, no air, busted, '94 Sedan Deville, with a ragtop, or maybe I should say, raggedy top car. But I couldn't complain, at least I had a way to work. I left extra early to avoid the five o'clock rush hour traffic.

While driving to work I thought I was going to suffocate. I was straight sweating bullets, plus my hot ass Andrew's Crab uniform was not making the situation any better. I tried to turn on the radio but it didn't work, and it felt like hot air was blowing into the car. *I'm about to die in this piece of shit car.* I was so pissed I didn't have my own car or the money to rent a car, tears welled up in my eyes. I pulled up to the traffic light and heard somebody honk their horn but I paid it no mind. Then out of my peripheral I noticed the person in the car beside me motioning, trying to get my attention, but I looked straight ahead. I was embarrassed of Wren's whip and I didn't want nobody to see me in that joint. The light changed. I took off and the black sports car pulled behind me. I couldn't see who it was because of the glare from the sun. Then my phone rang. It was a number I didn't recognize.

"Hello," I answered.

"Hey."

"Who is this?" I asked in an agitated tone.

"Ahhh, you done forgot about me already?"

"Ah, hey," I replied indifferently. It was Texas.

"Where you going, pretty girl?" *Dude whatever, don't try to sweet talk me. You ain't slick.*

"I'm on my way to work," I replied firmly.

"Yeah," he said.

"Mmm-hum," I shot back with an annoyed sigh.

He hesitated. "What time do you have to be there?"

"Five."

"Pull over and talk to me for a minute."

"We talking now."

"No, I wanna talk to you face to face."

"No, I can't. I have to get there early. I gotta talk to my manager about something," I lied. I was not about to pull over. It was sweltering outside and I had sweat rolling like a river down my face. My face was so shiny it looked like somebody had poured a bucket of Crisco on it.

There was silence on the phone and then Texas spoke up. "Where you been, ma? I've been blowing ya' phone up all week. I know you seen me calling. I left several messages, you ain't called me back. I've gone by your job but you haven't been there, so tell me, what's up?"

"I was in a wreck."

"Forreal, when?"

"Last week, right after I left your house."

"Are you okay? Did you get hurt?" he asked anxiously.

"Yeah, well the air bag hit me in the eye, but I'm alright now."

"Damn, baby. I'm so sorry, Rae. How am I gonna take care of you if you don't call me and let me know what's going on?"

"Whateva," I remarked dryly. *Yea, nigga whateva. If I hadn't been over your house I wouldn't even be in this situation, broke and driving this whack ass car. Then to top it all off you left me in your house asleep and yo' baby momma got full access to yo' crib.*

"Rae, forreal. You mean you couldn't pick up the phone and at least call me one time?" he asked in a disappointing tone.

"Nope. I sure couldn't," I remarked annunciating each word loud and clear.

"Damn, its' like that?"

"It mo' certainly is," I returned with much attitude in my voice.

He hesitated. "Aiight. Well, If you don't want me calling you no more, I won't."

"I would really appreciate that…bye," I remarked smartly and hung up the phone.

Fuck that nigga. Who does he think he is? He gon' try to play me. Like I'm some li'l dumb ass hood rat that supposed to be star struck 'cause he a NFL player. Dude, you can't treat me no any kinda way. I shoulda cussed his ass out!

Texas had me heated. I was already pissed off about my current situation and he didn't make it no better with his little bullshit ass. I pulled up in the parking lot at my job, and low and behold there he was sitting in the parking lot waiting on me. I got out the car and walked right pass his car. I put my mug on trying to conceal my smile, and proceeded to the front of the building as if I didn't see him.

"Raechel," he screamed. I turned around and looked into the car like I didn't know who was calling me.

"What?"

"Come here!"

"I'ma be late for work," I yelled and continued walking.

"Girl, come here," he demanded. I drew in a deep breath and walked to the car trying my best to contain my smile.

I climbed into the buttery seat of the black Lamborghini Murcielago. The air was on blast blowing straight snowballs. I shivered.

"You cold?" he asked. I nodded my head. He turned down the air. He leaned back in his seat and cut his eyes at me. "Aye, what the fuck is yo' problem?" he asked calmly and trying to read my behavior.

"Nothing," I replied nonchalantly avoiding eye contact with him.

"Well, what's this about you don't want me calling you?"

"Because you playing games and I don't have time for games. I got too much shit going on for me to be adding unnecessary drama in my life."

"Games? What games?" he asked like he was totally confused. "What are you talking about?"

"You know what I'm talking about!"

"No, I don't!" He spat, his frustration apparent in his voice.

"I'm talking about you still fuckin' with yo' baby momma and you putting me in that fucked up situation."

"What fucked up situation?" He sat up in his seat, trying to figure out what I was talking about.

"Look, the last time I was at your house, I saw yo' baby momma walk in with y'all li'l girl and I'm not trying to be caught up in no baby momma bullshit. And you had left me in your crib asleep what if—"

"Hooo..ld up," he interrupted me mid-sentence. "Is that the reason I ain't heard from you?" he asked taken aback.

"Well…yeah. What you think?" I rolled my eyes and looked out the window.

He leaned back in the seat calmly and stared at me, there was an awkward silence. "Let me get something cleared up 'cause I don't know what type of niggas you use to fuckin' with, but you need to realize I ain't them. I'ma grown ass man and I would never put you in no situation that would cause you harm or danger. First of all, the woman you saw was my housekeeper. She's the only person that has a key to my crib. Sometimes she bring her shorty to work with her when she can't find a baby sitter." He paused and stared at me, making me feel like I was two feet tall.

"Secondly, you ain't never got to worry about my baby momma." We have absolutely nothing in common but my daughter. I respect her because she is the mother of my child but that's it. I'm not in love with her, I'm not seeing her, nor do I have anything to do with her unless it concerns my daughter."

I was speechless. I felt like a damn fool. I was avoiding this man thinking he was trying to be a playa.

"Rae, listen. I told you the woman I wanna be with is you." My heart fluttered when he said that and a wide smile came on my face.

"Rae, I need you to do me a favor."

"What's that?"

"I need you to trust me. Give me a chance to explain myself before you go jumping to conclusions."

I hesitated. "Alright," I whispered embarrassed by my behavior.

"What are you doing tonight?" he asked.

"Me and my girls are going out."

"Where y'all going?"

"Um-mmm, I don't know."

"Well, hit me up when you get off."

"Okay, bye," I said and got out the car. I knew all along where I was going, but with men you can't give up too much information. I knew I was going to be at the White Linen Party along with all the local celebs, ballers, and shot callers.

Chapter 8

Sasha and I arrived at Blu Diamond. It was packed; everybody was decked out in their Miami white linen. The line was wrapped around the building. I definitely was not about to stand in that long line, especially in my all white linen short set. I looked up and saw Blu, the owner of the club, walking to the front door. Thank God we knew him.

"What' up, Blu?"

"Nothin, what's up, Ma?" he hugged me and Sasha.

"What's up, I know you gonna let us in."

He was a little hesitant. "Well, Cali them done rented out my spot. This they shit, and I ain't tryna step on no toes by letting people in free."

"Ahhh, you know we ain't trippin' about paying; we just don't wanna stand in this long ass line," Sasha admitted.

"Aiight, that's what's up." He walked away and whispered in the bouncer's ear at the front door. Next thing I know, the bouncer was waving for us to come on through. Sasha and I each paid thirty dollars to get in and proceeded into the party. The heat and humidity hit me as soon as I walked through the door. It felt like I was walking into a sauna.

"Damn, is the air on in this joint?" Sasha commented, while lifting her hair off her neck.

"I don't know, but it sho' don't feel like it," I replied while fanning my face. I glanced around the club. All I saw was a sea of white linen. Everybody had come dressed in their finest white get ups. One thing about black folks, we sure do look good in white.

Sasha and I went and found a table. I texted Mimi. *"Where are you?"*

She texted back, *"Near the patio."*

Me and Sasha went and sat at their table so we could at least feel a little of the summer breeze. We all ordered a round of drinks and started to kick it. Sau and I went to the bathroom. On our way to the bathroom we heard the D.J announce, 'The Tennessee Tyrants are in the house, Super Bowl Champions.' The crowd roared. In Nashville they treat our professional athletes like royalty. Everywhere them cats go they get mad respect and props throughout the city. We went and freshened up. When we got back to the table, Cece couldn't wait to tell us.

"Girls, you know the ballers in the house." She and Mimi always got so excited about the ball players being in the club–them and every other female that was there.

I sat down and absorbed the vibe in the club. I have to marinate when I first get to the club, have me a few drinks before I get to doing my thing. I looked down and noticed my phone vibrating on the table. I had a text message; it was from Texas. *"Lookin good, ma."*

"Thanx, where are you?" I scoped the crowd. I stopped when my eyes connected with his across the room. I smiled and waved. He texted me back, *"Come here."*

"K." I texted back.

"Sasha, come go to the bathroom with me." I had to play it off because I knew Cece and Mimi would have wanted to go in VIP. I wouldn't have minded but I was not about to look like a group of little girls flocking up to VIP in a single file line. As Sasha and I were leaving the bathroom, some dude pulled her hand and they began conversing. While I was standing there waiting on her to wrap up, the D.J came on the mic.

"Throw yo' hands in the air for Angie Applause." I glanced in the VIP section. Angie Applause was parading around the VIP in a white bikini top and this white mini skirt with two slits on the side, with her ass cheeks hanging out. Sasha wasn't lying when she said she had a big booty because her butt was so phat looked like she had ass implants. What was shocking to me was I couldn't understand how her ass was so big but her waistline and stomach were small. There were a slew of other bitches up there. I'm talking about white, black, Asian, I think I even saw one or two midget bitches. Chicks were doing any and everything to get noticed by one of the ballplayers, or just by one of the ballin' cats that was in VIP flossin' and flashing money. However, every guy in the club had their eyes glued on Angie Applause's humongous ass. Then this wild Tyrant player name, Duck, stood up. I guess he was trying to show out for the Angie Applause broad cause he started makin' it rain. It was a chain effect because the hood rich niggas wasn't gon' let him shine so they started making it thunder, tossing up straight hundred dollar bills and hoes went berserk. Mad bitches started diving for that dough. Other chicks was shaking and droppin' it like it's hot so they could be showered in bills.

Top Dolla, this fine ass rapper from Nashville, was standing on the couches with his crew dousing chicks with bottles of Rose' and them hoes gladly let them do it. I was mesmerized by the entire scene. Then the D.J made all the chickens move out the way so Angie could make her ass clap. They turned down the music and Angie went to town clapping and plopping her ass cheeks together like she was giving a standing ovation. Every dude on that stage started throwing money at her, including Texas. I shook my head. *Nah, um good... ain't no way I'm going to VIP and starve for this nigga's attention. If he wants me, he gotta come and get me.* Sasha finally stopped running her damn duppaloops.

"Okay, Rae, let's go."

"Girl, I changed my mind. Look at that Angie Applause bitch."

Sasha's eyes widened. "Gatdamn! That bitch's ass is huge...that's gotta be fake."

"Nah, broad, no it ain't. That chick wouldn't be able to shake her ass like that if it was fake." I said still taken aback by the scene.

"Girl, and look at them niggas, that's all they care about is a fat ass, and that bitch is a damn porn star and they acting like she the Queen of England." She rolled her eyes.

"Nah, we definitely can't be a part of that scene. We went back to the table. Mimi and Cece were chilling. Each of them had a glass of champagne, and two bottles of Rose' was on the table.

Sasha's eyes roamed the spread. "Damn, y'all poppin' bottles ain't it? Where this come from?"

"Girl, from my li'l' friend." Cece pursed her lips nonchalantly and took a sip from her glass.

"Who? Cali?" I asked

"Mmm-hum," she replied casually. Cali is this big time hustler that got major operations throughout the south east and owns a hip-hop clothing store here in Nashville. He in school at State. They say he smart as hell too and he just a cool nigga. He been trying to get with Cece for so long, but for some reason she won't get with him. She claim he a playa, but I don't think he is, because I ain't never heard his name ringing around campus and I don't ever see him with no chicks up at

State. The main reason she won't get with him is because of Daddy Rich. He got her on lock and I don't know why because Daddy Rich got kids all over Nashville. As a matter of fact, his oldest daughter is the same age as Cece. I declare I don't know what she likes about his old ass. She stupid. If I was her, I woulda got with Cali a long time ago.

One thing about the dope game in Nashville is it's very profitable. And the local D-Boys love girls in college. There are times when D-Boys would come on campus, pick him a Shorty he like, take her to the mall and just ball out. It often went down like that, and I'm talking about no sex involved. These dudes did it just to be trickin' off some dough.

Sasha and I each got a glass and sipped on some of the champagne. I felt myself getting tipsy. I knew it was time for me to do what I did best, and that is hit the dance floor. I love to dance. Once I get on some drinks and unwind, the dance floor is the best thing going. Sasha often follows right behind me. We don't care who we dance with, how we dance, we just get on the floor and move to the beat. My sorority gave me the line name Rhythmless Nation instead of "Rhythm Nation" because I can't dance one bit, and I don't have a lick of rhythm. But when I'm on some drinks, you can't tell me nothing.

I was in a zone, feeling the music with my eyes closed, swinging my hair from side to side having a good time. When I opened my eyes, I noticed two dudes arguing near the pool table. One of the guys broke a beer bottle across the other dude's head, and then the other guy slapped him across the face with a pool stick. At first no one seemed to notice them fighting.

I nudged Sasha. "Look, they fighting." I pointed in the direction of the fight.

"Aw, hell. Let's get the fuck outta here."

As soon as she said that, all hell broke loose. One of the dudes pulled out a gun and started shooting in the air. Bullets went flying everywhere. At that moment, it was straight pandemonium. Everybody was screaming and running towards the door. People were pushing and shoving. I lost Sasha in the crowd. As I was trying to make my way to the exit, I felt somebody directly on my heels. Suddenly, a hand squeezed my ass like it was a roll of Charmin. I turned around; it was this bald-headed dude with a dreaded beard. Before I had time to tear into his ass for touching me, he yelled something to me in a Jamaican accent, but I couldn't understand what he said.

He had a sneaky smirk on his face, then he pointed his index finger toward me and mouthed, "Bang." He laughed, and then faded into the crowd. I was looking back trying to get another glimpse of him when I ran directly into a pole. BAAM! *Motherfucker.* I stumbled back almost falling to the ground, but I caught my balance. *Ohmigod.* I was disoriented. Then mace started stinging my eyes and nose; I couldn't see anything. My heart started pounding so fast, there was so much commotion. I was getting lightheaded. My breaths became shallow and my knees turned to Jell-O. At that moment I felt myself about to pass out. Then out of the clear, blue sky this hand grabbed me from the crowd. He picked me up as if I was light as a feather and carried me through the kitchen and out the back exit. He had me across his shoulder with my ass up in the air.

"Put me down. Put me down," I shouted while trying to squirm my way outta his arms. When he put me down, I looked up. It was Texas. "Ahhu, ahhu, ahhu." I was coughing and wheezing. My nostrils were on fire from the mace Security had sprayed in the club.

"Raechel, Raechel…are you okay?" He shook my shoulders while trying to get a response from me.

"Y…ea." I sighed while still coughing; he smiled and wiped a strand of hair from out my face. I rubbed my head, "Ahhh, my head."

"Do you need to go to the emergency room?"

"Nah," I hesitated. "I'm straight." I was dizzy from me running into the pole. "What happened?" I asked.

"Some niggas got to fighting in the club. Shots were fired; everybody panicked and ran." He touched the bump that had formed on my head. "Are you sure you don't need a doctor?"

"Yea, I'm sure." I answered in a confused whisper.

"Come on; let's get out of here."

"Nah, hold up a minute. I gotta find my girls." We walked back to the front of the club. At first I didn't see them. I pulled out my cell phone to call. That's when I saw Mimi and Cece walking toward us.

Them hookers was tore up. Mimi's shirt was ripped and one of her titties was about to pop out. She had broken one of her heels off her Christian Louboutins and scarred her elbow. Cece's weave pony tail had fallen off her head and she only had a little twig sticking straight up on the top of her head.

"Damn, are y'all okay?"

"Hell, nah, we ain't okay," Mimi snapped an unbuckled one of her sandals. "Them ignorant ass niggas got to shooting up in the club and shit."

I held her purse while she took off her other shoe. "I'm asking are you hurt or do you need to go to the hospital?"

"Nah, I'm good," she seethed taking her frustrations out on me. "I'm about to get the fuck outta here."

"Girl, I'm just happy to be outta there," Cece added.

"Where Sasha?" I asked.

"I don't know." Cece shrugged. We began to scope the parking lot for her. Then I heard someone calling my name. We looked and Sasha was walking out of the club, flawless.

"Girl, these niggas so ignorant. I'm fixin' to stop coming out because they don't know how to act."

"Mmm-hum, they shole don't. Girl, where were you?"

"Chick, I jumped behind the bar with the bartenders and waited for the commotion to stop." She looked at Mimi and Cece. "Damn, what happened to y'all?" She paused for a minute, and then burst out laughing. She laughed so hard she was crying.

I tried to contain my laugh, but seeing Sasha bowled over in laugher I couldn't help but laugh too.

"Hoes, what's funny?" Mimi fumed. Sasha was laughing so hard she couldn't even answer. "Bitch, that shit ain't funny. We coulda got seriously hurt in there and you laughing. "C'mon, Cecily. Let's go."

They stormed off to their car. I was happy everybody was okay and no one was seriously hurt. They were so mad they left, because we were laughing.

Black folks were still riding around and dancing in the parking lot. Everybody was getting ready to head to the after-hours club BLU ICE.

"So what's up? What are you about to do?" Sasha asked.

"Texas is going to take me home."

"Ahhh…okay." Sau flashed a playful smile. Just then valet pulled up with Texas' Benz. The valet opened the door for us. Texas drove

Sasha to her truck so I could get my night bag. I gave Sasha a hug and we parted ways.

Texas looked at me. "Are you sure you're okay?" he asked again.

"Yeah, I'm straight." My headache had subsided but I did have a small knot on my forehead.

"You hungry?" he asked as he put the car in gear.

"Nah, not really."

"Do you wanna hang out a little longer?" he asked

I looked at the clock "That's cool." It was only a little after midnight. That fight had caused the party to end early.

"Are you cool with going to my place?" he asked as he got on the Interstate.

"Yea… okay."

"So, why didn't you come to VIP?"

"I was coming but I decided to dance first." *Dude, actually I didn't come because I didn't wanna look like a fool while you gawked at Angie Applause shake her ass.* But I definitely was not about to mention that. I didn't want to show any signs of insecurity. He glanced at me for a second then put his eyes back on the road.

"You coulda at least came and danced with me." I didn't respond to his comment. I smiled and looked out the passenger side window. "Did you have fun?" he asked.

"Yeah, I was having fun until them dudes got to fighting. What about you?"

"It was aiight. I don't really do spots when they packed out like that." He glanced over at me with one hand on the base of the steering wheel. "I mean it was so crowded you could hardly walk. Niggas was bumping into me, stepping on my shoes and shit."

"Yeah, I don't like crowds like that either I always get kinda of nervous." I told him.

"Mmm-hum," he sighed. You didn't seem too nervous when that dude was dancing all on you." He lifted an eyebrow and looked at me for a few heartbeats.

I glanced at him. "What dude?" I asked.

"I don't know. Some nigga was all on you on the dance floor." He turned on the radio.

I pretended as if I didn't know what the hell he was talking about. I played it off. *I know he ain't jealous.* There was a comfortable silence. I chilled and absorbed the moment.

"What type of music do you like?" he asked

"I like all types, of course Hip Hop and R&B. You know, the latest songs–the top forty."

"Okay." he nodded his head, "Who's your favorite artist?"

"Humm, let me think, Jay Z and of course Yo' Gotti 'cause he from Memphis, and as far as R&B I'ma say Maxwell, R. Kelly, and Prince. What about you; who do you like?"

He was silent for a few seconds while he was contemplating his top favorites. "I have several," he said.

"Okay, who are your top three?"

"Marvin Gaye, Jay Z, and Sade."

"Awe, yeah, Sade' is one of my favorites too." He turned the disc changer to the *Best of Sade* CD. As the music played, I sat back, turned my seat warmers on, and relaxed, as his Benz floated down the freeway. The plush, diamond white, CL600 coupe, with cognac leather interior was so luxurious. The seats massage you as you're riding. I felt like I was riding in a mobile day spa. As we glided down the road, I noticed that he'd passed the exit to his house.

"Where are we going?" I asked.

"You'll see." We drove another fifteen minutes outside of Brentwood. We turned onto a narrow private road that led to a beautiful log cabin situated next to a small lake on a large expanse of land. We got out of the car.

"Where are we?" I asked.

"This is one of my properties. Actually it's a farm."

We walked into the cabin. The interior was gorgeous. It was all wood with an upstairs loft. There were three bedrooms and two bathrooms, which were all huge. I looked out the patio window onto the deck.

"It's a little warm in here," I remarked as I took off my stilettos and wiggled my toes against the hardwood floor.

"My bad, I didn't leave the air on." He twisted the dial on the thermostat "It'll cool off in a minute."

"Where are the animals?" I asked.

"Actually, the only animals I have are horses."

"You have horses?"

"Yes." The sides of his mouth broadened.

"Where are they?"

"They're out back in the stables."

"No, they're not," I remarked apprehensively. I didn't see any place around the cabin that could've possibly housed a horse.

"Yes, they are. Come on; I'll show you."

I grabbed my flip-flops out of my overnight bag and put them on. We walked out the back door and onto the deck. It was pitch black except for the light on the deck and the light from the stars and moon. The land was so vast, I couldn't see past the lake. I followed Texas to the stables. There were four horses. I don't think I had ever been that close to a horse before.

"Can I touch it?"

"Yeah, go on," First, Texas rubbed the horse, then I followed suit and stroked the horse's beautiful, brown coat. The animal just stared at me.

"Ooooh, I wanna ride it," I said while admiring the texture of the animal's coat. He started laughing. "What are you laughing at?"

"Nothing, it's just the way you said it. Ooooh, I wanna ride it." He repeated what I said in a womanly voice. We both started laughing.

"No. That came out wrong. I meant that I want to go for a ride on the horse."

He nodded at me and smirked. "We'll go for a ride in the morning." *In the morning, he must plan on me staying the night.*

"Okay," I said smoothly as we walked back toward the cabin.

"What made you buy this house when you have another house just a few minutes away?"

"Well, I love horses. Also, this is a business." He opened the sliding door and we walked back into the cabin. He left the patio door open and closed the screen.

"A business?" I asked curiously.

"Yeah, I'm going to turn this into a stud farm, and a place where families can rent the land out to host family reunions, birthday parties, and things like that. They'll have the land to ride the horses on and also be able to fish and cookout. And that land that's on the other side of the lake I'm going to have some cabins built just like this one that the families can stay in. When I retire I'll be able to devote more time to it, but right now, I have a guy that sees after the property and takes care of my horses."

"Oh, that sounds interesting." *That's what I'm talking about, he thinking about more ways to make money. Dude got it goin on.*

"Do you want something to drink?" he asked.

"Sure."

"What chu' want?"

"I don't know. Surprise me."

We went into the kitchen and I sat behind the bar. I looked outside the window and noticed it had started sprinkling. Suddenly there was a loud thunder and then it began to pour down raining. I knew that was it for me going home. As the storm increased, a fresh rain scent consumed the air. It was still a little stuffy inside the cabin. I noticed little sweat beads had formed on Texas' head. He took off his linen shirt and left on a wife beater underneath. I took a moment to study him, but I didn't want him to catch me admiring his fine ass body so when he looked up at me I cut my eyes in the opposite direction and pretended as if I was looking at the rain. All the time, I was secretly lusting after his body, his broad shoulders and tight abs. Each time he moved, the thick muscles in his back contracted like he was lifting one hundred pound barbells.

The white linen pants he wore slightly hung on his waist like pajamas, displaying that V shape above his waistline. Right below that was his dick and when he turned around I could see the fat bulge through his pants.

"So much for horseback riding in the morning."

"Huh?" I blinked, startled by the sound of his voice. I was daydreaming about me on top of him riding his dick in the morning.

My response pulled his attention from the drinks. "Horseback riding...it'll be too muddy." He smiled.

"O---oh, yeah," I agreed caught off guard.

"You okay?"

"Yea, I'm just tired." I yawned and pretended like I was sleepy, knowing all the time I was wide awake and my eyes was glued on that man's ding-a-ling like a dog waiting to be fetched a bone.

"Guess what?" I said. He looked up.

"What?"

"Tonight in the club when all the commotion was going on, some dude grabbed my ass."

"Did you know him?" he asked confused by my statement.

"Nah, I couldn't really get a good look at his face because of the mace that was sprayed."

"Damn, what was up with that?"

"I don't know and he did it when everybody was running towards the front." I got up to demonstrate. "He just grabbed a big hunk of my ass just like this." I grabbed his ass like I was palming a basketball, he jumped and started laughing.

"Damn, forreal? That's crazy as hell."

"Tell me about it, his perverted ass." I pursed my lips. "Instead of him worrying about tryin' to get out the club he was trying to fill on somebody's booty." We laughed. "I woulda told Security but there was so much commotion going on I couldn't get to them."

"Damn niggas are a trip." He smirked and poured my drink in a martini glass and handed it to me.

I took a sip of the fruity concoction. "Mmmm. What is this?" It tasted like a Mai Tai.

"It's a Texas Sunset." He smiled.

"It's delicious." He stared at me through the open space. I looked away and started blushing.

"Baby, I'ma go change clothes. I'll be right back," he told me.

"Okay."

I went into the upstairs loft and sat down on the couch. The house had cooled off considerably. I was freezing as I searched for the remote to the T.V. After I found the remote, I couldn't figure out how to turn the damn thing on. I was fooling with the remote when I noticed the light in the kitchen and hallway go off. The entire house was dark; except for the moonlight that danced through the window blinds. Texas walked in the room and pushed a button that ignited the fireplace. I took a few more sips of my drink. *If this man comes on to me, it's fixin' to be on 'cause I know I can't resist him.*

He grabbed the remote from my hand and turned the surround sound on. He glared at me from where he was standing near the fire place. "Raechel, I want you to do something for me."

"What?"

"I want you to dance for me." Shocked by his request, a coy smile escaped my lips. I knew by the expression on his face he was serious.

"Kay." I got up and slowly swayed to the smooth melody of R. Kelly's "Imagine That." His gaze lingered over my body.

"Rae, take off your clothes."

"Huh?"

"Take off your clothes." He spoke in a low tone. I undressed slowly while seductively moving to the rhythm of the song. His eyes were glued to me as I slowly removed each article of clothing.

I closed my eyes and moved to the rhythm. I was lost in another world. I imagined what it would be like when he finally touched my body. When I opened my eyes, his gaze pierced my soul, sending chills up my spine.

He got up from the couch and stood behind me slowly gliding his hands over my entire body. I relaxed and lived in the moment, then he slid his hands into my wetness and gently massaged my tight, wet pussy. "Mmmm," I moaned. He placed soft kisses on my neck. A deep chill flowed through my body; he cupped my breasts and lightly caressed each nipple with his fingertips. "Oooooh," I moaned and arched my back and slowly gyrated on his fingers.

"Damn, baby, you're so wet." He entered his finger in again, pulled it out and licked it. "Mmmm, and you taste so good. Get on your knees and bend over the couch."

I got on my knees facing the back of the couch with my butt sticking out. He got behind and placed soft kisses on my back, then he made a trail with his tongue from the top of my back to my ass crack. He spread my legs wide and licked my pearl tongue, then he spread my ass cheeks open as he went in deep with his tongue. He started feasting and sucking like he hadn't eaten in ten days.

"Ooooooooh, Teeexxas," I screamed in ecstasy. "You 'bout to make me cum."

"Baby, that is the objective."

"I don't wanna cum yet." He laid out on the floor and I sat on his face in the sixty-nine position, riding his tongue while he caressed my nipples.

His mouth-watering dick saluted me like the National Guard. It looked so juicy and scrumptious I couldn't resist. I laid on top of him while gyrating my pussy in his face. I stroked his fat pole with my hand while sucking on the head like a sweet chocolate ice-cream cone.

"Mmmmmm." I slurped and licked on his shaft making it slick and wet. At first I was gentle and soft but he started licking my pussy and *ooooh*, it was feeling so good. I wrapped my lips around his dick, trying to stuff all of his thick, fat, dick in my mouth but it was so big I could only fit half of it in my mouth. I cupped his balls and massaged them while sucking his dick like my life depended on it. I was in pure ecstasy. I arched my back and rotated my hips as he fucked me with his tongue. He must've known I was about to cum because he wrapped his arms around my slim waist and held me tight, sucking on my throbbing clit until it burst. "Ooooooh...... I'm cummin'." I clinched my ass together and grinded his face, as a wave of pleasure rushed over me.

He sucked on my pearl tongue, drinking every drop of my sweet juices. I bobbed my head up and down his dick sucking it like no tomorrow. I felt it throbbing and suddenly a salty eruption filled my mouth.

He picked me up and carried me into the bedroom. I knew we weren't finished. "Kiss it for me, baby." He sat on the edge of the bed. I got on my knees and started licking his balls and stroking his dick to get it back hard. It wasn't long before I felt his hardness growing in my mouth. I sucked even harder as he grabbed my head and thrusted his dick in and out my mouth. "Yeah, baby...that's what 'um talkin' 'bout." He massaged my nipples as I massaged my clit. I felt my juices flowing down my leg. "Get up and turn over so I can see that ass." I climbed on the bed, and got on all fours. He got behind me and plunged his dick deep inside me

"Ooooooh," I screamed, "Texas, it's too big."

"My bad." He took it out and rubbed the head on my clit getting me dripping wet then he eased the head in and slowly took it out. Then he slid it in deeper than before. "You gon' take this dick for daddy?" he asked while playing with my nipples.

"Yes," I moaned and grinded my tight pussy trying to take in all his dick.

"Yeaaaaa....there you go, baby. Take that dick."

"Mmmmm," I moaned as my pussy became soaking wet. He eagerly rammed his dick in and out of my pussy. "Oh, baby… it…. feeeel… soooo good," I cooed. With each stroke it was pure delight. He put one hand on the small of my back and slapped my ass with the other.

Smack, Smack. "Take that dick, baby," *Smack smack!* "You like this dick?"

"Yeeeess," I moaned

"I like this pussy too." *Smack, smack,* "Shake that ass for daddy." I bounced my pussy on his dick wiggling and bucking my ass. "Ohhhhh, shit, baby, this some good ass pussy. Gat-damn you gon' make a nigga marry yo' ass." Every time he entered, my tight pussy slurped every inch of his long, thick, dick like a triple-thick strawberry milkshake. "Damn, baby," he moaned, "Slow down; you gon' make me cum." I stopped for the briefest second. I couldn't hold it any longer, I squeezed my pussy walls on his dick.

"Teeeeexas, I'ma bout' to cum."

"Hold on, baby, 'um about to cum too." His breathing intensified and he started thrusting faster and harder, He rubbed my clit and that was it. I couldn't hold it any longer.

"Ooooooooohhh, Texas…..oh, baby!" I screamed as shock waves surged throughout my body.

He grabbed my hair and started pumping in and out of my pussy. I felt his dick throbbing. "Here it come, baby. Oh, shit!" he screamed as he pulled his fat dick out and shot hot cum all over my ass. "Fuuuuuuuuck…uggghhhhh," he growled stroking his dick, trying to get every drop of cum out. "Damn, baby…. you got some good pussy," he whispered, still breathing heavily. He collapsed on top of me and within minutes we were both fast asleep.

Chapter 9

I awoke the next morning to the sound of raindrops and a smiling Texas looking intently in my face.

"Hey," I whispered and returned his smile. "What are you doing?"

"Watching you sleep." He smiled and stared into my eyes. "Did you sleep well?"

"Yes, I did," I assured him with a smile. "Man, you wore me out last night," I continued. At that moment, as I gazed into his brown eyes, I became instantly aroused. He looked so sexy. But no matter how wet I was getting at the sight of him, I still had to turn my head when he attempted to kiss me. I had no intention of giving him a taste of my early morning dragon breath.

"Come on, Rae, give me a kiss," he said playfully.

"No," I declared. "I haven't brushed my teeth yet."

"I don't care. I haven't either. So give me a kiss."

"No, Texas," I said as I shook my head from side to side while covering my mouth with my hands.

"Yes," he countered cheerfully. He then started kissing me all over. Wherever there was exposed skin, he planted a swift but delicate kiss. At the same time, however, he began to tickle me in my most sensitive places. My hands dropped from my mouth, and I burst into a peal of laughter. I'm very ticklish, so I couldn't help it. Of course, as soon as I presented him with an opening, he moved in and stole a peck. That peck turned into a long and passionate kiss.

"Mmmm, baby you taste good," he moaned. "I want some more."

As we kissed again, I went from moist to dripping wet. He gradually slid under the covers and began to suck my sweet nectar, while simultaneously massaging my g-spot as he moved both his index fingers back and forth while licking my pussy. I came twice, which is not the norm for me. I have always been the type of person that could only have one orgasm at a time. But with Texas, I had cum at least seven times in the past twenty-four hours.

We made love again that morning and then went back to sleep. I didn't wake up until late that afternoon around two o'clock, and I still didn't want to get out of bed. The air conditioner combined with the rain had cooled the house off dramatically to the point it was freezing. It felt so good beneath the thick down comforter, as I laid in his arms with my head resting on his warm chest. I tried my best to capture the moment in my mind because it was almost too good to be true. I'm in bed with one of the finest men I have ever seen; and I've seen some fine ass men. He also has an amazing personality to go along with the looks. Plus, he has it going on in the bedroom. He is sensitive to my needs, but also has just enough aggression and freakiness to keep things interesting. Finally, and most importantly, is the fact that he's into me. I don't know how to take it all. Is this forreal? If it is, then how long can it last? Well, at this moment in time, it feels real and right. So, all I can do is live in the present and take it for what it's worth.

Texas was still asleep. I got up to go to the bathroom. When I came back, he was propped up in the bed. *Ohmigod, I can't believe I put all those hickies on him.* I didn't comment on them. I definitely didn't try to do it but in the heat of passion, I didn't realize what I was doing. I climbed back in the bed.

He smiled at me. "So, baby, what you wanna do today?"

"I have to be at work at five," I told him.

"Work?" he exclaimed.

"Yes, work." I got back out the bed and started looking for my clothes from the previous night. Then it occurred to me they were still on the floor in the bonus room where I left them the night before.

"Baby, you can't go to work today."

"I have too, Texas. I was off all last week except for last night, and my bills are starting to roll around. I can't afford to miss any more days."

"I have a proposition."

"What?" I asked suspiciously, and sniffed and sprayed the variations of colognes he had on his dresser.

"How about if I pay you to spend the day wit' me?"

I sighed, while shaking my head, no. "No, Texas I can't accept any money from you."

"Rae, how much do you make?"

My eyes wandered as he asked me. I sprayed a dab of his Lacoste cologne on my wrist and smelled it. "Texas, don't act like that. You know I have to go to work."

"So you have to go to work?" He got out the bed and left out the room.

"Yes," I stated avidly.

He came back with two rubber band stacks. He removed the rubber band and all I saw was hundred dollar bills. He peeled off three hundred dollars and laid them on the dresser. "So, you're going to work." My eyes lightly bulged at the sight of the money.

"Yes," I said convincingly. He placed another one hundred dollar bill on the dresser. I took a fleeting glimpse at the money. He asked the question again.

"Yes, Texas, I'm going to work." This time I said it firmly. He put another one hundred dollars down.

"Yes, Texas I'm going to work."

At that point there was seven hundred dollars lying on the dresser. Now I ain't no gold digger but I ain't no dumb bitch either. I looked at him then I looked at the money and smiled.

"Hell, nah, I ain't going to work. I would have to work at least five shifts at Andrew's Crab in order to make seven hundred dollars." Then he gave me the other stack of bills.

"Here, this should take care of your bills." I was so shocked I stood there with my mouth hanging open; it was at least three thousand dollars.

"Texas, I can't accept–"

He interrupted me in mid-sentence. "Raechel, this is pocket change to me. Take the money, and do something nice for yourself. Besides, you deserve it. You've had a rough time lately."

I thought about it. I had been having a difficult time. With the car accident and almost getting stampeded in the club, I did deserve to do something nice for myself.

"Texas, I don't want you to think I'm here for money or your fame." I looked in his eyes, which was still difficult for me to do.

"Baby, you don't have to tell me that. Believe me, if I thought you was like that you wouldn't be here right now. I know what type of woman you are. I know you are hardworking and independent, and that's cool. That's what I like about you, but, baby, stop being so independent for once and let a man take care of you." He rubbed me across my cheek and then gave me a sweet peck on the lips. "Now, come on so we can get the day started." Then he slapped me on the butt.

"Ouch," I shouted. "Aiight, boy, quit playing."

"Who you calling a boy?"

"You," I said while trying to suppress my smile. I started trying to slap him on the ass but he was too big. He kept dodging me; we started running through the house trying to slap each other's butts. I was having so much fun. Texas caught me and bent me over his knee and pretended to spank me like a bad, little child.

"Uhhh, and this is for putting all then damn hickies on my neck." He slapped me on my butt even harder.

"No, no, I'm sorry." I yelled as he kept slapping my ass. I was laughing so hard my stomach was hurting. At first we were playing, but then it started to kind of turn me on and we ended up having sex again.

I called my co-worker, Tangerine, to pick up my shift and she agreed right away to work in my place. She was always trying to pick up extra shifts whenever possible. She had six kids with three trifling baby daddies, but she was holding it down. She worked at Andrew's Crab and stripped on the side and every time you saw her kids they was neat and clean. I knew she could use the extra money.

Texas and I pulled up and walked toward the entrance of the Green Hills Mall. I stopped in front of the door while he held the door open for me. I never touch a door while a man is present, and there is never a time that I remember having to. It seems that most men know that it's the gentlemanly thing to do. I learned from my cousin, Diamond, who told me, 'Stay in your place as a lady and you can get almost anything from a man. Most of the times you won't even have to open your legs.'

My cousin, Diamond, starting hooking when she was sixteen, then she met a lady that ran an escort service with her husband. Diamond became a high price call girl. She worked for the escort service for a few years. Then she fell in love and married a rich oil tycoon. I'm talking about her life is like the movie *Pretty Woman*. I've always admired my cousin and her friends because they have always demanded respect from men. She is always dressed in the finest gear from head to toe and wears some of the most expensive jewels. The bitch got it going on. Her motto is: Always make a man jump through hoops because they love a challenge. And if he won't jump through hoops, fuck'em because there is always another brotha' who will."

I often times used Diamond's advice because I recognized at a young age that I could learn a lot from people who were older, wiser, and more experienced than me. I need all the advice I can get because I stay falling off and doing some dumb shit that could have been avoided if I had just listened. My cousin started her life off rough and in the streets, but now she's living a life of bliss and luxury. She is always trying to educate me and Mimi about men and how we should demand to be treated.

Texas and I walked in the mall. I was full of excitement. I was wondering what Texas had planned for us when to my surprise, we stopped at a day spa. As soon we walked in, a Middle Eastern woman, who looked to be in her mid-fifties, greeted us, and kissed Texas on the cheek.

"Greetings, Texas," she said in a thick Arabic accent.

"Greetings, Bella."

Her eyes shifted to me. "Who is this beautiful woman you have?" She asked with a smile still on her face.

Texas turned and looked in my eyes. "This is my wife."

"Oh, you got married?" she replied.

"No, not yet, but soon."

She winked at me. "Well, you're a very lucky girl."

"Yes, I know." To hear him call me his wife made me feel like a million dollars, I was cheesing from ear to ear.

"Come, follow me," she instructed us. She escorted us into a secluded room with candles burning. The aroma and the ambiance was so exotic. Inside the room there was a huge tub that resembled a Jacuzzi. *What are we were about to do?* "This is the first part of your spa package, a coconut milk bath with imported oils to help you relax and let everything go." She smiled at us, "Enjoy," and exited the room.

After the milk bath, we both were wrapped in seaweed to exfoliate our skin, and then we got hour-long massages and manicures and pedicures. After we left the day spa, we were famished.

"Rae-Rae, what do you want to eat?"

"Cheesecake Factory?" I suggested since it is my favorite restaurant.

"The Cheesecake Factory it is," Texas replied and kissed me on the cheek.

We sat outside on the patio at the Cheesecake Factory and there we talked for hours. I ordered my jambalaya pasta without the shrimp. We shared a bottle of wine and had the most fabulous evening. Even though I didn't want to admit it, I knew I was in love with Texas Reynolds.

Chapter 10

Texas and I became inseparable. We were together almost every night of the week; we were definitely in love with each other. I would do almost anything for him, and he would do the same for me. In fact, he told me to save up my money so that I could get the car I really wanted, and he would match whatever I had when I went to the dealership. In the meantime, however, he had given me the keys to his Range Rover, and told me to drive it until I was ready to purchase a car of my own.

School had started back and campus was crunk. I was on cloud nine and was loving life. I had one more year to go, and I would be entering medical school. I applied to several medical schools, but the one I wanted the most was Meharry Medical School. I'm interested in it because it's here in Nashville and if I'm accepted I wouldn't have to relocate. Also, if I wanted to ride home for the weekend to visit my family, Memphis is only a couple of hours away.

Sasha and I still ran a few laps every day. I really had to stay on top of that. I gained about ten pounds when Texas and I first started dating. We were going out to eat every night and fucking like rabbits, which was as close as I got to a workout. I noticed the couple of extra pounds, but I ignored them. Of course, Sau was not about to let me slide.

"Alright, Rae, your ass is spreading. Laying up eating and fucking every night. Don't get fat. You know what type of man you have. You gotta stay ahead of the game. Stop all that eating. I know the dick is good, but, hell, when y'all finish, chick, you better eat some air," Sasha told me.

I didn't want to hear it, but she was right. I love Sasha. We always keep each other in check, and she isn't a hater. Some friends will be jealous because they aren't with anyone, and try to fill your head with negative thoughts about your relationship. Sasha is just the opposite, because even though she wasn't with anyone at the time, she was happy for me and wished me the best with Texas.

♣

It was Sunday morning. I got up and went to nine o'clock church service at Born Again Church. I had to go and get my praise on. I left right after the sermon because I had to meet Sasha at her house so that we could get ready to go to the first Tyrant's football game of the season.

Texas was so excited about the game. The only thing he could talk about all week was how he was ready to kick some ass on the field. I loved football before I met him, but our relationship intensified my love of the game. I hadn't seen him all week because the team was on curfew. They didn't want the players getting distracted and having sex because it decreased their testosterone levels. The coaches wanted the players' minds strictly on football.

I couldn't wait to see my baby get on the field and do his thang. When Sasha and I arrived at the stadium, it was packed. Everyone seemed just as excited as me. Sasha and I walked around and tailgated. I had never been to a professional football game before. I thought we had kicked it at the games at State, but these people were having a party at ten o'clock in the morning. Sasha and I were pleasantly surprised at how much fun we were having celebrating the start of the season. The biggest surprise for me was that white folks were kicking it harder than most of the black folks. In my experience, it's usually the other way around.

When we noticed a mass of people walking toward the stadium, Sasha and I hurried to pick up our tickets that Texas left for us at Will Call. It was early September, and it was sizzling hot. In an attempt to beat the heat, I'd worn shorts and a Tyrants tank and matching hat. Sasha was dressed similarly. We both wore comfortable flip-flops, because we had a lot of walking to do. When we located our seats, we discovered that we were on the fifty-yard line, directly behind the cheerleaders. We could see everything. As soon as I sat down I looked for Texas. It seemed like our eyes met at the same time. I smiled and waved. He smiled and waved back.

With a spectacular kick return for a touchdown, on the game's opening play, the Tyrants took an early lead. After joining the crowd in hollering and cheering for the home team, I was then able to sit and take notice of my surroundings. Sasha and I were seated with many of the wives, girlfriends, and baby mommas of the Tyrants' players. As we were absorbing our surroundings, this blonde chick sashayed down the aisle. Sasha and I stood up to let her by and she still managed to step on my toe. *Damn, that bitch could've at least said excuse me.*

The Tyrants scored first, but most of the first half was a defensive struggle. Both teams moved the ball, but aside from the initial Tyrants touchdown, neither could put any points on the board. My baby was on the field cutting up, though. The position he plays is wide receiver, and he had a couple nice catches. What was even more impressive was his blocking abilities. He put some dudes on their asses. I wouldn't have been surprised to see one of them hits on the top ten plays of the day on ESPN. He hadn't scored a touchdown, though, but I was praying that he would. Then, near the end of the second quarter, Texas got his chance. The Tyrants had the ball on Miami's twenty-yard line. On first down, the quarterback threw the ball to Texas in the end zone. Sasha and I jumped up thinking he was about to make the catch, but the ball was over thrown.

When I sat back down, the blonde chick was still standing up and screaming for a pass interference call. This time she nudged me. I ignored her first couple of bumps because we were at a football game and people do tend to get rowdy, but she was doing a little too much. Then, after a seven-yard run on second down, with the ball on Miami's thirteen-yard line, everyone stood to cheer on the home team right before half time. There was thirty-eight seconds left on the game clock. We definitely needed to score. Then, at the snap of the ball, this bitch bumped into me again causing me to bump into Sasha. Both of us glared at her and waited on her to apologize or say something but she didn't say a word or even acknowledge that she had literally shoved me into Sasha. She had an unconcerned look on her face as if she didn't do anything.

"Now, I hate to get ignorant, but if this bitch bump into me one more time, then I'm going to smack the shit outta her," I told Sasha.

When we turned our attention back to the field, the ball was in the air. The crowd grew quiet with anticipation. Texas stretched out and made a fingertip catch at the back of the end zone.

"Yeessss," I squealed as Sasha and I jumped up and down, screaming and high-fiving each other. Of course, when the lady beside me started celebrating, she shoved me again. This time she made me knock over my drink and popcorn. That was it. I glared at her, and then my mouth took over.

"Look, li'l momma, this is your second time bumping into me. You made me spill my drink and popcorn. You need to watch it," I snapped.

"I didn't make you do anything," she returned.

"Yes, you did."

"Well if–"

I interrupted her mid-sentence. "Look, I'm not trying to hear what you got to say. Bump into me one more time and we gon' have a problem." *Clumsy ass bitch.*

"Whateva." She rolled her eyes and flung her hair in my face. It took every ounce of will power within me not to reach over and rip that shit out by the roots. It was half-time, so Sasha and I went to freshen up.

"Girl, what's up with that chick beside you?" Sasha asked, while lifting up her hair and wiping the sweat off her neck.

"I don't know, but she got me fucked up."

"Raechel, you gave that bitch one too many chances. It couldn't have been me. I woulda had to check that bitch the first time she bumped me, and didn't immediately say 'excuse me'."

"Girl, I was tryin' to hold my composure. I don't wanna be at Texas' game fighting and arguing."

"Yeah, but that bitch kept trying you. After you let her slide the first time, she just kept bumping you. One time she almost knocked both of us down. And did you see she got on Texas' jersey."

"She does? I didn't even notice," I said while dabbing the sweat off my nose.

"I hope that ain't one of his hoes."

"It better not be 'cause I'll cut that nigga off and never in life speak to his ass again." Just the thought of Texas having me at his game with another chick he was dating was making me heated.

"Girl, calm down, I'm just saying, that chick probably acting silly because she wondering who we're here to see, and how we got those seats. Girl, who knows? The bitch might be mad just because the sun is shining." We giggled.

"I do know one thing. She has one more time to bump me," I remarked sternly. We went to the concession stand and ordered some nachos. Sasha got a Bud Light, and I got an extra-large strawberry slushy. The heat was unbearable, and I needed something to help me cool off.

We walked back into the stadium. Mostly everyone was back in their seats, but when we got to our seats they were taken. The same blonde bitch who was bumping me was sitting in my seat.

"Ma'am, you're sitting in my seat," I snapped as I stood over her. When I looked at her, she looked familiar but I couldn't place where I had seen her. She kinda resembled Coco, Ice T's wife, because she had some humongous fake titties.

"No, this is my seat," she sneered with much attitude, and then turned her attention back to the game.

"Excuse me, ma'am, I was sitting in A-27," I said.

"Let me see your ticket," she demanded.

"Sweetheart, I'm not letting you see shit." I was not about to argue over a seat that I knew was mine. Sasha and I turned around and walked all the way back down the aisle, stepping on peoples' toes. We then had to go up several flights of stairs to get the attendant. It was hot as hell. When we finally found the attendant, an older white man who was obviously drinking on the job because his breath reeked of alcohol, I explained the problem to him. We walked back down to our seats with the attendant and my, seat was vacant. The blonde bitch had moved. The attendant looked down the aisle.

"Der ain't nobody in dat seat," he slurred.

"Sir, they were taken but the woman that was sitting there moved," I explained. He looked at me like I was lying.

"Maayum," he sighed. "Puhlese, don't bother me unless this stadium is about to blow up." Each word was like a blow to the face as the stench of alcohol and poor dental hygiene permeated the air between us and assaulted my nostrils. Shaking his head and muttering to himself, he turned and walked away.

"Sorry we're asking you to do your job, you dusty hillbilly," Sasha yelled after him. We sat down in our seats. I rolled my eyes and gave the blonde a nasty look. A devious little smirk was plastered on her face. By the time fourth quarter rolled around, I wanted to leave. Texas had scored again and Tennessee seemed to be in control of the game, but I hadn't been able to enjoy it because of this stupid ass bitch.

"I'm ready to go," I whispered to Sasha.

"Rae, are you sure?" By the tone of her voice and the look on her face, I knew she wasn't ready to leave. I nodded my head.

"Yeah, but let's wait a few minutes. I have to do one last thing before we leave," I told her. There was four minutes and forty seconds left in the game. Tennessee held a ten-point lead, but Miami had the momentum and the ball on the Tyrants twenty-two yard line after starting on their own one-yard line. "If Miami scores a touchdown here and get an onside kick, then they may be able to tie the game or retake the lead," I nervously told Sasha. The crowd was standing.

Sasha and I joined in. "Defense, defense, defense," we chanted. It was third and three. Miami needed to score or get a first down. If they didn't, then they would have to decide whether to kick a field goal or go for it on fourth down. The quarterback took the snap and dropped back to pass.

"Get that bastard," I heard someone scream. The Tyrants' defense was in an all-out blitz. Just as the quarterback was surrounded by three defenders, I decided the time was right to do what I'd planned. I removed the lid from my still ice-cold strawberry slushy in its insulated cup. All eyes were on the field as the play unfolded. I had to time it just right. I steadied myself and smiled. The instant that Miami's quarterback was flung to the ground the crowd went wild, and so did I. I turned and doused that rude bitch with my slushy. Her Tyrants jersey was soaked with sweet, sticky strawberry slushy.

"Uggh," she gasped and gritted her teeth at me. I also accidentally splashed a little slushy on this older black lady that was sitting beside her. It got in her hair as well. I just played it off like I didn't see it.

"Oh, I'm sooo sorry," I chimed with mock sincerity. I handed her some napkins. "You may need these."

She snatched the napkins from me and glared at me with pure rage.

"Sorry," I smirked. Sasha and I walked away laughing our asses off.

Chapter 11

After the game, Texas had invited Sasha and me to the Stadium Club where the Tyrants team hung out after the game with their families, friends and permanent ticket holders. We walked inside the stadium club and it was decked out. They had a DJ and a buffet table laid out for kings with everything from lobster to crab legs. They had a carver there to slice whatever meat you wanted. There was all types of fruit and dessert assortments. Everything looked so good, and I was starving. I didn't see Texas upon our arrival so I walked around until I spotted him.

I walked over to him, and smiled. He wrapped his arms around me and picked me up. My feet were dangling off the ground. I wrapped my legs around his waist as he gently swung me around. We kissed for almost a minute. Then he put me down.

"Hey, princess." He hit the rim of my Tyrants ball cap. "You look so cute."

I blushed. "Thank you."

He looked at Sasha. "What's up, Sau?"

"Hey, Tex. Y'all played a good game."

"Yeah, baby, you were cutting up," I added.

"Thanks, did you have any trouble with the tickets?" he asked.

"No, they were waiting on us at Will Call."

"Good, did you like the seats?"

"Uhhh…..yeah, they were perfect," I answered with hesitation." Sasha glanced at me.

"What? Baby, what happened?"

"Oh nothing, there was just a rude fan beside us but nothing serious." Sasha, cut her eyes at me with a smirk on her face.

"Yeah, you run into people like that at football games."

"Tell me about it," I agreed and inconspicuously cut my eyes at Sasha.

The coach walked up and Texas introduced me and Sasha.

"Baby, let me holla at my coach for a minute, then I'll be right with you. Don't go too far because I got somebody I want you to meet."

"Okay," I responded. He leaned down and gave me a peck on the lips. Sasha and I went to the bar and ordered two Cosmopolitans. While we were sitting at the bar talking, I noticed this fine ass brother had come and stood beside Sasha and ordered a drink. Sasha didn't notice him because she was facing me.

"Girl, my feet are killing me," I said while sliding off one of my flip-flops.

"Yours, girl, my dogs are barking," said Sasha.

"I know they should be with all them hammer toes you got," I teased and took another sip of my Cosmo. The both of us laughed.

"Bitch, I know you don't want me to get on your Fred Flintstone toes, and that gnawed off pinky toe of yours that looks like a forehead," she shot back.

We started cracking up. Plus, I think that one drink had gotten to me because I hadn't eaten. The guy standing beside Sasha slightly chuckled at our conversation, which caught Sasha's attention, so she turned around to see who was behind her. When she turned around, their eyes connected. They both glared at each other for a couple of seconds. He was a chocolate brother with a shaved head and skin as smooth-as-silk. When Sasha turned back to me, she knocked over her drink, spilling most of it in her lap.

"Dang!" She grabbed some napkins and started cleaning up the spill. The guy grabbed some napkins and started helping her clean up the spill too. He even took a napkin and wiped her leg off, then he motioned for the bartender who quickly came over and finished cleaning up the spill.

"I'm so clumsy. Thank you so much," she said to the guy.

"You good," he said. "Aye, my man, can you get them another round," he told the bartender. He paid for the drinks and then left.

Sasha and I looked at each other. "Daaayum," we said simultaneously.

"Dude was sexy as hell," Sasha commented.

"He shole was," I agreed. Texas walked up on us talking.

"What y'all over here doing?" he asked suspiciously. Sasha and I was giggling like some school girls.

"Nothing," I said, trying to contain a smile.

"Mmm-hum, Rae, don't you be over here checkin' out no other niggas."

"Baby, I'm not."

"Mmm-hum." He leaned down and gave me a peck on the cheek.

"Tex, was that one of your teammates?"

"Who? The dude that was just standing over here?"

"Yeah."

"Yeah, that's my boy, Sean. I'll introduce you to him. "Yo, Sean," Texas yelled across the crowded room.

"Nooo...no," Sasha interjected, but it was too late; he was already walking back in our direction. Texas introduced Sasha to Sean and they seemed to immediately hit it off.

Texas grabbed my hand. "Come on, baby. I got some people I want you to meet."

"Who?" I asked.

"My parents." He smiled.

"What? You didn't tell me that your parents were coming to town." I felt an uneasiness sweep over me.

"I didn't know they were coming myself. They flew in this morning."

"Well, I wish I had known because I probably wouldn't have worn this outfit, Texas. I'm all hot and sweaty. I look a mess. What about I go home and change and meet them later."

"Rae...Rae... relax." He pulled me close and kissed me on my lips. "You're fine. My parents know you've been at the game. That's what people do at football games; they get hot and sweaty. You look great; don't worry."

"Okay." I sighed.

I looked back at Sasha and saw that she and Sean were engrossed in conversation.

"Before we go meet them I have to tell you something," Texas said and exhaled while displaying a disturbing look. "Eva is here."

"Who is Eva?"

"My daughter's mother."

"What is she doing here?" I was livid.

"She wasn't supposed to be here. I left a third ticket that was supposed to be for my daughter, but Eva took it upon herself to make use of it and left my daughter with her grandparents. Rae, believe me, I'm pissed about it, but I decided I wouldn't let it ruin my day. I've had a good day. We won our first game of the season, my parents are here, and I have the love of my life with me." He smiled at me. "Besides, Raechel, she needs to meet you because you are about to be in my life forever."

"Texas, I'm not about to meet your child's mother."

"Why not?" he asked.

"Because, first of all you sprung this on me. I'm not properly dressed, I'm sweaty and hot. I just don't think this is a good time," I said apprehensively.

"Rae, this is the perfect time. Come on, do it for me." He kissed me on the lips.

"Okay," I agreed. All it took was for him to look into my eyes and I gave in.

He gently tapped me on the ass, and grabbed my hand. "Now, come on."

Texas really threw me for a loop because I don't do mommas, baby mommas, my dude's momma—that just ain't my thing. And then two mommas in the same night was just too much for me. I've never been big on meeting my boyfriend's parents anyway. I mean, I know if I date someone long enough and there's a possibility that it's something more, then I more than likely have to. And I'm cool with that sometimes, but I will not kiss their asses just so they will accept me.

I remember Mimi was dating a dude whose momma was trifling as hell. She would call Mimi and expect her to take her places and even ask to borrow money without ever paying it back. All the time Mimi was ripping and running for that dude's momma, he was running to see some other girl. After seeing what Mimi went through, I learned then that I will respect his parents and be nice and cordial, however, I won't allow them to overstep their boundaries just because I'm dating their son. As for his child's mother, she needed to know about me and she needed to understand that I was the new sheriff in town. Also, if there was any inkling that she might want to get back with Tex, she needed to get those thoughts out of her head. Texas is my man now and as long as he's treating me right, and holding me down, I'm not about to give that up for nobody.

We arrived at the table and my heart stopped beating for a few seconds. Texas' parents looked intensely at me, along with his baby's momma. The smile on my face faded. *Oh shit*, it was the two ladies that I had spilled the slushy on.

Texas' attention turned to his parents. "Mom, Dad, I would like for you to meet my future wife, Raechel Jones."

His mother gave me a wicked frown. I'm sure it was because of the slushy incident between me and the apparent baby momma. She interjected, "We've already met."

Texas' smile widened. "I was hoping so, that's why I had the seats placed near each other. I wasn't sure you guys would show up but I'm glad you did."

I held out my hand.

"Hello, nice to meet you." His father gripped my hand with a firm handshake and we exchanged a pleasant smile.

"Hi, it's nice to meet you as well, Dr. Reynolds," I said. I extended an invitation to shake Texas' mother's hand but she ignored my gesture and began to study my outfit.

"Is this how you dress all the time?"

"Well, no this is what I decided to put on today, because it's ninety-degrees outside," I told her.

I didn't want to get smart with his mother, because I believe in respecting my elders, but girlfriend was not going to sit in my face and insult me, especially in front of Texas' baby's momma. Sorry, wrong one.

My eyes connected with his baby momma. She had changed into another Tyrants T-shirt; she probably bought it from one of the vendors. She had to do something because I had spilled that slushy all over her ass. Texas turned his view to her.

"Eva, I want you to meet Raechel Jones, my future wife." Then it dawned on me, this was the same chick Texas was arguing with at the casino that night. The only thing different about her was the color of her hair. I extended my hand and she grabbed it and gave me a flimsy grip. I glared directly into her eyes with a slight sneer on my face.

Texas and I sat down. I noticed his momma's lips were poked out giving me a real stank look. I wanted to apologize only because I realized that some of the slushy spilled on her too. But since she had such a 'tude, I decided not to.

Lightly clearing his throat, his dad asked, "So Raechel, where are you from?"

"Memphis."

"My wife is from Jackson, Tennessee, right outside of Memphis."

"Really?" My gaze turned to his mother with the corner of my lips slightly turned upward trying to get her to smile, but her lips didn't budge. She acted like she was more interested in engaging in small talk with Eva. I directed my attention to Dr. Reynolds.

"Raechel, what brought you to Nashville?"

"I attend State University"

"What are you studying?"

"Pre-Med with an enface in pediatrics."

"Oh really? Good choice." His eyes widened with obvious approval. "How much longer do you have?"

"This is my last year."

"What schools are you looking at?" he asked like he was genuinely concerned.

"I'd like to attend Meharry, but I've checked out other schools as well, like Emory and Howard. They all have great medical programs.

"Smart girl." I could tell Dr. Reynolds liked me. We talked for at least thirty minutes about school and medicine. Dr. Reynolds looked at me and then turned to Texas. "It seems like she has a good head on her shoulders."

"That's why I love her so much." Texas gave me a peck on the cheek. "And, Pop, she has a three-point eight GPA and works a part-time job."

"Really? That's great." Dr. Reynolds looked at me with pleasure. "Where do you work?" I really didn't want Texas to divulge that information but he seemed so proud to announce my GPA and my job.

"I'm a waitress at Andrew's Crab."

Mrs. Reynolds whispered to Eva, "I should have known another groupie after my son's money."

"That figures," Eva muffled under her breath.

I looked at Eva. "Excuse me, did you say something?"

She smirked and shrugged her shoulders, "Uhh, no."

Dr. Reynolds and I continued to talk while Eva and Mrs. Reynolds preceded having small talk amongst each other.

"Dr. Reynolds, Texas tells me you're from Philadelphia," I remarked inquisitively.

"Yes, I was born and raised in Philly. It's a wonderful city. Have you ever been there?"

"Actually, I have. I have an uncle who lives there. He's an engineer for Boeing." Dr. Reynolds nodded his head while intently listening. "My mother and I visited two summers ago and I really enjoyed it."

Texas' mother interjected. "Where is your father?" I turned toward her, still maintaining my composure, being that she hadn't said barely two words to me for at least an hour. *Now all over sudden she sees an opportunity to pry into my business.*

"My father passed away several years ago."

"Really," she said without emotion.

"Yes, ma'am…. really."

She asked with an attitude, "Was he a part of your life?"

"Yes, he played a significant part in my life. Our family was very close." Little did she know, or need to know, that I never knew my father, nor did he ever help my momma one bit. The one significant way he helped us was when he died and started receiving his Social Security checks, but that wasn't any of her business. I know I wasn't being totally honest but I tell people what I want them to know, because people don't play fair and sometimes they will use what they know about you as ammunition.

I immediately changed the subject and began asking them questions about how the two of them met. The mom still seemed like she had a little attitude but she had to warm up, because I was being so nice to her that she had no choice but to be nice back. I could tell she still had her reservations about me, but I wasn't going to try to change that in one meeting. She would just have to get to know me over time.

As for Eva, she didn't have much to say and that was perfectly fine with me. I didn't want to talk to her and I didn't want her talking to me. I wasn't the least bit threatened by her. She looked okay. It was clear she had breast implants and she had gotten them way too big and they looked fake. She didn't look better than me and I knew that for a fact.

That drink I drunk had run straight through me. Texas' father had talked a sore in my head. He had gotten on him some drinks and was running his mouth like forty going north. I didn't want to interrupt but I couldn't hold it any longer. I had to pee. I excused myself and walked toward the ladies' room. I was walking normal until I got out of their view. As soon as I turned the corner I made a mad dash for the ladies' room. I was about to pee on myself.

I ran in the bathroom. Good thing there was no line. I relieved myself. When I came out of the stall, Eva was standing by the sink primping but I ignored her. I washed my hands and took off my hat and began brushing my hair.

She glanced at me and said, "You have nice hair."

"Thank you," I answered.

"Is it yours?" she asked sarcastically.

I gave her a smile, "Why, of course." *Damn right it's mine, biatch.*

"Are those yours?" I pointed to her fake ass titties.

"They sure are. Courtesy of Texas Reynolds. Thank you. You might need him to invest in you a pair of 36C's.

"No, I'm straight. Texas likes these 34B's just the way they are."

"Yea, I forgot…why invest anything in a fuck buddy."

I chuckled, "Fuck buddy. I like that," I hesitated while still chuckling. "That's fine by me as long as I have the keys to the Range, the house in Brentwood, and as long as he keeps paying my bills. Oh, and my bad, I also have the keys to his heart, something that you don't."

This heifer was starting to piss me off but I wasn't about to give her the satisfaction. I'll play along in her little game. I rarely let a bitch know that she's getting under my skin. I usually hold my composure and just reply with sarcastic remarks.

"She smacked her lips. "Texaaas doesn't want you," she replied in her aggravating southern accent. "You're simply not his type." She smirked. "You're way too dark for him. He's gonna fuck you and leave you high and dry just like he does everybody else." She squeezed her fake titties together and tossed her hair off her shoulders. "You'll see. Next month he'll have another bitch sitting in the exact seat you were in today."

All the while she was talking, I was still applying my lip-gloss and ignoring her. I knew I was getting under her skin by ignoring her.

"After he gets done fucking on you, he'll be right back where he belongs, with me."

"Are you done?" I asked her and proceeded to the door.

"You'll see, ghetto, black bitch."

"Excuse me... what did you say?"

"I said, you ghetto, black bitch!" At that second, everything I knew about holding my composure and biting my tongue immediately flew out the window.

Wham! My fist landed directly on the rim of her nose. She tumbled over one of the sinks to catch her balance.

"Bitch! You got me fucked up. Don't ever call me out of my mutherfuckin' name again," I snapped.

"Bitch, I'ma get you," she screamed while grabbing her nose as blood dripped from the palm of her hand. Her entire face was red. I grabbed my purse and proceeded out the door as she began to rant and rave.

"Raechel, you are going to have hell to pay when I finish with you."

"Whatever, bitch!" I stormed out the bathroom. My heart was racing so fast I stood in a corner and calmed myself down. *That bitch made the North Memphis come up outta me.*

I scoped the crowd for Sasha because I had to get the hell out of there. I couldn't believe that bitch insulted me like that. It was the main reason I didn't want to meet her, because baby mommas are difficult to deal with. It takes a mature woman to realize when a relationship is over and it's time to move on. I was walking around but I didn't see Sasha anywhere. I noticed Eva at the table sobbing and talking to Texas' parents. I'm sure she was telling them all types of lies about me. I was surveying the crowd looking around for Sasha and bumped directly into Texas. The heat from his glare could burn a hole in me.

"Raechel, I need to talk to you."

"Texas, I'm looking for Sasha. I have to go."

He grabbed hold of my arm and led me outside on the terrace. "Nah, we fixin' to talk, now," he said with fury in this voice. As we walked outside, I saw Sasha on the bench with Sean drinking and having a good time. Our eyes connected and she waved.

Texas pulled me into a corner. "Raechel, what's wrong with you?" he snapped.

"What?" I acted as if I didn't know what he was talking about.

"Raechel," he gave me a stern glare with his arms folded across his chest. I bit the bottom of my lip as my eyes wandered. He grabbed my face and turned my gaze to him. "What happened?"

I hesitated. "Look, Texas. I was in the bathroom minding my business, when she came in there harassing me and talking shit about our relationship. Talking about I'm just your fuck buddy, and you're going to leave me in the ghetto."

"Raechel, are you my fuck buddy or are you my woman?" he asked.

"Your girlfriend," I mumbled softly.

"Then why were you arguing with her and why did you have to hit her?"

"Because that hoe disrespected me and called me a black bitch," I snapped.

"Aiight…well, maybe she deserved it. But, I still don't agree with you arguing with her in the first place."

"I told you, she started it."

He got in front of me so no one could hear our conversation. "I don't give a damn about who started it; I still don't want you are arguing with that silly ass bitch." He sighed. "Look, you are my woman. Whenever we're out together, you're representing me. We represent each other. I can't have you out here quarrelling and clowning like some project ass bitch."

"I ain't no project bitch," I snapped, rolling my neck and batting my eyes.

He grabbed my arm and pulled me close and clinched his teeth, "I didn't say you was a project bitch. I said, I don't want you acting like a project bitch."

I saw the anger in his eyes because of my behavior. I calmed down and thought about the situation.

"But, baby." I tried to touch him but he moved my hands from his face.

"But baby, my ass. Let me tell you something, Raechel. I'm a man first. I can handle my business and I don't need you arguing with Eva. I told you that she's childish and immature. She knows she can never have me. She's just fuckin' with you, trying to get you to come down to her level. If you have any discrepancies with her, you come get me. I don't want any woman of mine cussing, getting loud, and fighting in public. I'll straighten Eva's ass out. I'll never let her, or anyone else for that matter, disrespect you."

We were silent for a few seconds.

"Do you understand?"

I nodded gently as my eyes filled with tears. I held my head down because I had never had a serious argument with Texas. I tried to hold back my tears but they started to fall.

"Baby, please don't cry,"

"I'm sorry, Texas. I didn't mean to ruin this night for you. Eva has probably told your parents all type of lies about me."

"Baby, baby, don't cry. You know I can't take that, Rae. And you haven't ruined this night for me. I'm happy you're here with me. The next time Eva talks to you like that, let me handle her. Look, don't worry about my parents; they'll be fine." He wiped the tears from my face. "I'm going to go back in here and finish up. I'll meet you at the house in an hour."

"Okay." He kissed my forehead. "Bye, I love you."

"I love you too."

I went back to my apartment. I no longer felt bad about what had happened. I should have conducted myself in a more mature manner and never given in to that skank bitch's taunts. I usually handle myself a little bit better but this time I just couldn't. I guess it's because I really and truly am in love with Texas, and I believe he loves me too. I think when a person truly loves somebody, they'll fight for it. I didn't go to Texas' house. I took a little of Diamond's advice and let him jump through hoops. He was blowing my ass up. I wanted to answer, and I was missing him too, plus I was horny as hell. My body is funny like that. I can go for months without having sex and not even miss it or think about it, but the minute I start to have sex on a regular basis, the more I want it. I just can't get enough of it. I went under my bed and grabbed my silver bullet and dreamed about Texas devouring my pussy, until I passed out.

Chapter 12

Homecoming rolled around, and the city was live as hell. Homecomings at State are unbelievable. The whole week is one big celebration, but things really begin to jump off on about Thursday. That's when the alumnae usually start to arrive in the city. On Friday we have a pep rally where the band performs and the alumnae and entire student body congregate in the Student Union and socialize. It is always so exciting to see generations from the past mixing and mingling with the new generation. We all helped to build a historically black university that has educated some of the most famous people in the world. Following the pep rally, everyone goes to the annual Long Island Tea party hosted by either the Kappas or the Alphas.

The Alphas were hosting this year. This event is more for the younger State alumnae. It always starts at two o'clock but by one thirty, a line is wrapped around the door. If you're not in line by at least two you're not getting in. With free Long Islands until the liquor runs out, how can it not be off the chain?

Sau and I went, but I didn't follow my own advice. We got there after two and they weren't letting anybody else in. There was nothing that could be done about it, so we just drove around until it was time to meet Sasha's mother for dinner.

Sasha's mom is State alumnae and never missed a homecoming. I didn't mind spending time with her because Sasha's momma is always so much fun. Though very wealthy, she isn't stuck up at all. She drinks, smokes, and she'll cuss your ass out in a New York minute. Yet, she is the type of person who would give you the shirt off of her back. She even paid for my tuition once when my family was going through a financial crisis. She didn't do that for me because I was friends with her daughter. She's been known to do the same for other students who may have needed assistance. She is one of the most generous people I know. Sasha is the same way. The only difference is that Sasha's ass is spoiled rotten. It's either her way or the highway, but hell everybody has their little quirks.

Mimi and Cece met us at the restaurant for dinner. As soon as the waitress came, Sasha's mom ordered two Grey Goose martinis. I knew once Sasha's momma got on some drinks she was going to get started. Sasha had told her mother all about my new relationship. I knew why she'd done that, so I could be the butt of all the jokes. Sasha and her mother are very close, like best friends. Sasha feels like she has to tell Mrs. Houston everybody's business, but she won't dare divulge any of her own secrets.

"So, Rae-Rae, I hear you've been shacking up."

She always called me Rae-Rae. I looked at Sasha. She quickly held her head down while trying to suppress a smile on her face. I tightened my lips and gave her an evil look anyway.

"Uhhh, no, ma'am. I'm not shacking."

"Mmm-hum, now, Rae-Rae, let me give you a bit of advice," she said after taking a long sip of her drink. "Don't be shacking up until you get a ring on your finger. You'll never get married by shackin', suckin', and fuckin'. You make it too easy for a man when you shack up. If a man is good enough to sweat on you, then he is good enough to sweat after you."

"Uhhh, yes, ma'am." Sasha, Mimi, and Cece all started snickering. Then she got on Mimi.

"Now, Mimi, what's this I hear about you getting mugged?"

Mimi had the most astonished look on her face. A month ago Mimi was carjacked right behind the school. Mimi and this guy she had been dating were in a parked car in Hayfield Park. They were having sex when a gunman tapped on the window and told them to get out of the car, and leave all of their stuff inside. The gunman took the car and left them standing in the park butt ass naked. Mimi and the dude were running through the park naked trying to get back to campus when they were spotted by one of the campus security guards.

"Mmm-hum, you must've been working on a nut when you got caught with your britches down. What is it with you and parks anyway?"

"Ahhhh!" We fell out laughing.

Mimi looked at Sasha with a, bitch-I'ma-kill-you-look. Mimi was so embarrassed. She tried to play it off but she couldn't even lie.

Sasha's mom continued. "Come on, now. Why in the hell would you be in a parked car at midnight? There's only one reason. You two were getting your groove on."

We turned our attention to Cece after Mrs. Houston took a sip of her fourth martini.

"Cece, I heard you got fired," Mrs. Houston said.

Cece looked at Sasha and mouthed. "I know you didn't."

Cece and her professor had been dating. I know it's wrong to date your professor, but this man was too damn fine. His name was Professor Smith and Cece's boss on her job was named Mr. Smith. Cece and the Professor were always sneaking around making sure no one saw them from State and making sure Daddy Rich didn't catch her ass. They had to be very careful because if they were caught, the professor could lose his job. Cece told us that she and the professor often had phone sex, and they would *sext* each other. They would send each other explicit pictures of themselves. He would send her pictures of him jackin' off and she would text him pictures of her doing God knows what. One day, while they were participating in one of their phone sexcapades, Cece decided to send the professor nude pictures of her titties and of her spread-eagled on her bed fingering her va-jay-jay. She just got all into it.

When she got to work the next day, her boss called her into the office and immediately fired her for sexual harassment. He told her he didn't know why she had sent pictures of her fondling herself and behaving in such lewd acts. He was appalled. He told Cece his wife was the one who had discovered the pictures and suspected him of cheating.

Cece looked like she wanted to strangle Sasha. "Well, since Sasha is telling everybody's business, she forgot to tell everybody about when Cedric was eating her out and she let one loose and farted in his face."

We all looked at Sasha with the most astonished look on our faces. There was a stunned silence among us.

Uh-ooooh. "Cece, you're wrong for saying that in front of Mrs. Houston."

Mrs. Houston burst into laughter; and we all started laughing.

"Damn, I hope it wasn't funky." She turned up her lips and gave her a look of disgust. "Sasha, that's just nasty. Why in the hell did you do that?"

"Momma, I couldn't help it. I couldn't hold it in."

We laughed so hard that the waitress came over to ask us to quiet down. I was laughing so hard I couldn't even catch my breath. Cece and

Mimi both had tears in their eyes from laughing. Sasha was so mad but she couldn't help but laugh too.

Chapter 13

Homecoming Week was off the chain but they always are. I didn't go to as many activities as I used to. I guess because a lot of things I used to do as an underclassmen didn't really appeal to me as much anymore. I did go to the Greek Show. The red and white won like we always did. I wasn't in the step show because I'm one of those that can't catch on to simple steps because I don't have any rhythm. Good thing, I did have some in the bedroom while I was riding a dick. I guess because that was my favorite thing. I knew how to do it so well. I especially liked riding Texas because I loved gazing into his sexy eyes, while I slowly grinded on his dick, making sure he would hit every angle of my pussy. Sometimes I would tell him to hold still, then I would rotate my g-spot on his dick. I can cum so easy like that. Then he would flip me over on my back or stomach and thrust in and out until he exploded inside me. Sex with him was the bomb; the best I'd ever had.

♣

I had a pretty cool week but it was back to work. While school was in full session, I only worked the weekends. I had to focus all my attention on my grades because I didn't want anything keeping me from getting into medical school. There was one thing I had control over, and that was my destiny to become a doctor so I could make a better life for myself and help take care of my mom. I didn't mind working on weekends. I had done it for so long that I was used to it, plus I always got off early enough in case I wanted to go out.

Since football season had started, Texas was either gone on the weekends or he would be preparing for a game, which I definitely didn't want to interfere with. But sometimes when they had a home game I would sneak up to the hotel and spend the night. That was fun because they were on curfew and he had to sneak me into his room. One time I dressed up like a guy and played like I was delivering take out. It was so fun and sexy. I wore a fake mustache and dressed in men's clothes, but underneath my clothes I had on a sexy lingerie number from Victoria's Secret. Texas came down to the lobby to pick up the take out.

"Damn, I left my cash. Man, just come on up because I don't feel like walking back down here." The hotel attendant looked at us like, 'I don't care what you do.' We got on the elevator, and he couldn't keep his hands off me. He unbuttoned my shirt and began sucking on my nipples. All of a sudden, the elevator stopped. I quickly gathered myself and moved away from him. Texas' coaches got on the elevator and began looking at us strangely. My heart was pounding so fast. We were standing in the elevator as if we didn't know each other. I took a quick peek at Texas. He looked at me and started motioning for me to fix my mustache. I didn't realize part of it had come undone. No wonder the coaches gave me a strange look. As soon as we got to the room, we had the steamiest sex.

♣

The Tyrants had secured a spot in the playoffs, and they had an off weekend before playoffs began. Texas told me he had a surprise for me. I had been so busy studying and trying to pass Organic Chemistry. It is so hard. I had already failed it three times; well not really failed. But if by midterm I didn't at least have a C in that class I would withdraw from the course, because it would be too difficult to pass. The professor is a straight bitch. She's one of those angry black women that had it hard going to school in the sixties because of her color. So she feels like she should make life hard for us because in her opinion blacks got it too easy now days. She always has a frown on her face. And it seems like her main goal is to make the class ten times harder than what it is.

At any rate, we were out of school Thursday and Friday for winter break. I had taken off work because I was going to spend the entire weekend studying for this class. Thursday morning Texas called.

"Hey, mami, what you got up for the day?"

"Nothing, bae; what's up?" I asked curiously.

"Well, pack a bag," he said.

"What, Texas?"

"I said pack a bag. I'll be there to get you in an hour. Hurry up because I don't want us to miss our flight."

"What are you talking about, a flight?"

"Rae, I'll explain in the car, okay?"

I hung up the phone with him and started smiling. I put my face in the pillow and screamed. The phone rang again; it was him.

"Hello," I held my breath, trying to conceal the excitement in my voice.

"Oh, baby, by the way, pack light."

"Okay, bye." I got up and grabbed my suitcase from out the closet. I started pulling shit out the drawers and closet left and right. It looked like a tornado had been through my room.

I threw some of everything in my suitcase. I was running rampant through my apartment trying to get my stuff together. I had to go through my summer bags and find all my summer sandals, on top of jump in the shower and find something to wear on the plane.

I went to brush my teeth and looked at myself in the mirror.

"Oh, fuck!" My hair was a ridiculous mess. I was in desperate need of a perm and a rinse. "Oh, my God, what am I going to do about my hair?" I didn't have time to do anything to it. At least I may have time to wash it and put a black rinse on it. The rinse will help and give my hair a little shine. I can always straighten out my naps with my flat irons.

I jumped in the shower, washed my hair and applied the rinse. I got out the shower, blow dried my hair, and flat ironed it, put on this cute Prada sundress and my flip-flops. I was applying my make-up, when Texas knocked at the door.

He greeted me with a kiss. "Hey, baby."

"Hey," I cooed.

He stepped inside and grabbed my bags. He noticed my fingers and eyed them strangely.

"Damn, baby, why are your hands black?"

I looked at my hands and they were black from the rinse. "It came from my hair rinse," I answered.

"Where are the rest of your bags?"

"In the bedroom."

"Raechel, you have two minutes. Our flight leaves in an hour."

"Can we catch the next flight?" I yelled as I was stuffing all my sandals and clothes in my suitcase.

"No," he yelled. "I've already checked. The next flight doesn't leave until tomorrow evening."

While Texas was taking the bags down, I was in the bathroom trying to wash the rinse off my hands but it was barely coming off. *Well, forget it.* I quickly used the bathroom because I didn't want to have to use it on the plane. When I flushed the toilet, it over flowed and water poured out everywhere. *Oh fuck!, this shit would happen!* I hurriedly grabbed a gang of towels and threw them on the floor. As I was trying to soak up the water, I was sweating bullets and my hair started sticking to my face. Texas was outside blowing the horn almost constantly. If my suite mate comes in this bathroom she's going to kill me. Hopefully, she won't trip too much.

When I came to the door, Texas was leaning against the car with an irritated expression on his face. "Rae, come on," he shouted. "I told you, our flight leaves in an hour."

"Okay, here I come." We got in the car. I strapped on my seatbelt because his speed rapidly accelerated to about ninety miles per hour. Normally, I would be tripping off how fast he was going, but not today, because I was so excited. As soon as we arrived at the airport, Tex jumped out the car and grabbed my bags. He checked our bags with the curbside concierge. He kept his Louis Vuitton carry on.

The concierge gave us our boarding passes. "Your gate is B-12, the flight is boarding now. I hope you make it," he commented apprehensively.

"Are you ready?" Texas asked me.

"Ready for what?"

"To run." He took off running through the Nashville Airport. I followed suit right behind him. My flip-flops kept stubbing my toe. Texas had on sandals and kept slipping and sliding. We were balling through Nashville International Airport. My tittie popped out of my dress but I didn't even realize it. As I ran past a group of Chinese tourists they started clapping. I thought they were cheering us on because we were running so fast but I believe they were cheering because they saw my *Tig Ol Bity* pop out. I don't how long it was out but I didn't realize it was out until we arrived at our gate, B-12. Texas gave the stewardess our tickets and showed our identification. We walked through the tunnel. I said my prayer like I always do when I get on a plane.

"Lord, send your angels to protect this plane, and the pilot, and all of the passengers. In Jesus' name. Amen."

"Aloha." The stewardess greeted us as we walked on board.

"Aloha." Texas returned and put our bags in the overhead storage compartment. Our seats were for first class. We sat down and both sighed. I looked at him still trying to catch my breath and asked, "Baby, where are we going?"

As soon as I said that the stewardess came on the mic and said, "Sit back, fasten your seatbelts and enjoy the ride because in six hours you will be on the sandy, white, beaches enjoying the warm, sensual weather on the shores of one of the most exquisite islands in Hawaii…Maui!"

"We're going to Hawaii?" I beamed.

"Nah, we going to Russia." He shot me a dumbfounded expression. "Yeah girl, we're going to Hawaii. Didn't you hear the lady?"

"Oooh, baby, thank you so much. Texas, why are you so good to me?"

"Because I love to see you smile." He leaned over and gave me a warm, passionate kiss.

The plane wasn't even in the air good, and I was in dreamland. I don't know what it is about airplanes, but every time I fly I go to sleep.

I walked in the house exhausted from a long day at work. I showered and crawled under the warm, crisp sheets. As soon as I got into bed I moved my body close to Texas. His body heat immediately warmed me. He placed his arms around me and I fell asleep. When I woke up it seemed like I had been sleep for hours, but I had only been asleep ten minutes. The room was dark except for the moonlight peeking through the window. I turned and tried to move my body and noticed that my arms were tied to the bed post. My gaze rose to Texas. His sinister glare cut me like a razor blade. "Texas," I called his name, he didn't respond nor did his gaze budge. Then I looked again and his face became disoriented like he was being controlled by something else. He rose out of bed and grabbed a match and lit it. Flames immediately surrounded the bed. My skin began to melt like butter in a frying pan. I screamed for dear life.

I woke up and jumped.

"Baby, are you okay?" Texas asked.

"Yeah," I mumbled, still disoriented. "I just had a bad dream." I sat up in my seat.

"Baby, just go back to sleep and try to get some rest. We have a big weekend planned." He kissed my forehead. I laid my head on his shoulder and closed my eyes but I couldn't go back to sleep. I kept thinking what a strange dream I'd had.

We arrived on the island of Maui. When we stepped off the plane, the sunrays passionately kissed my face, which immediately made me forget all about Nashville. Texas and I went to retrieve our bags from baggage claim.

When we walked out the airport our driver was waiting on us in a silver Mercedes G-wagon.

"Aloha, Mr. and Mrs. Reynolds. I'm Javier, your driver for the weekend. I am at your service." We both shook the his hand. Javier loaded our luggage and we got in the truck.

"So you're staying at the Four Seasons Ocean Resort?" said Javier.

"That's correct." Texas agreed.

"It's paradise; you are going to love it," Javier assured us. "The hotel is amazing; and you are right on the beach." Javier took the scenic route to the hotel to give us a mini tour of the island. Texas and I were in awe. I looked.

"Baby, have you ever been here?"

"I've never been to Maui, but I have been to Honolulu."

"So, I'm not the first girl you bought over here?"

"No, you're the second. My mom comes every time I'm invited to play in the Pro-bowl."

"Oh." I felt stupid. He looked at me and smiled. His eyes were glistening from the sun. As we drove upon the ocean front, I inhaled a startling breath. "Oooh, the water is so amazing. Look at the color. It's aqua green; I've never seen anything so beautiful."

Javier pointed. "Over there to the right of the beach is a hospital for terminally-ill people. They say in that hospital every time someone checks in, they always get better because of the water. They look out into the water and it makes their sickness or illness go away. The name of the hospital is Return to Life."

"Wow." I was awestruck.

We drove by the ocean front. Texas and I were totally silent, absorbing the view and holding each other's hand. We arrived at the resort; two bell men greeted us and took our bags. We walked into the hotel, which was absolutely fabulous. I looked around while Texas checked us in. They gave us each a key to one of the penthouse suites. The room was breathtaking, with marble floors in the foyer. I immediately opened the balcony window. The view was magnificent and all I could here was the roaring of the ocean waves.

"Baby, can I leave the patio door open the entire time we're here?"

He walked up behind me as I was standing outside on the balcony. "Raechel, you can do whatever you want to do," he paused. "We're on vacation, how about that." Then he slapped me on my ass.

I ran and got on the bed. I started jumping in the bed like a little kid. I was so thrilled. Texas yanked my feet and I fell right on my butt on the soft comforter.

"Baby, what do you want to do first, eat or go to the beach?" he asked.

We both looked at each other and said simultaneously, "Eat."

When I went to the bathroom to freshen up I gasped at the huge Jacuzzi tub and a view that was directly facing the beach. I put this BCBG sundress on with my bikini underneath the dress. By the time we were finished getting dressed, the sun was setting. We went to a restaurant that was outside on the beach.

Texas ordered a bottle of wine, and we sat and listened to the ocean waves pounding against the shore. Texas dined on lobster, and I had steak marsala. The wine intensified the flavor of the food, and I ended up cleaning my plate.

Within a few feet of the restaurant there was a beach party going on. They had a live band, and the Hoola girls were dancing on elevated platforms. We went and joined in. Then the shot girl came around and was passing out Patron shots. We each tossed back a shot and continued to dance. He handed the girl a fifty and told her to keep the change. She returned minutes later and gave us another shot so we took that one and danced some more. Grooving to the beat, I started to fill the warm effects from the tequila.

We both knew we'd had too much to drink so we left the pool party and took a stroll down the beach. As we walked, I came out of my dress and ran and jumped in the water. I didn't swim because I can't. I was tipsy too. I laid on the beach, and let the cool waters just run up and down my body while Texas swam and floated in the water.

I was lying on the beach and he came up from behind me and slid my bikini bottom down, and placed soft kisses on my back, while rubbing his hands between my thighs. I immediately became wet. He unfastened my bikini top and started kissing me gently on my legs and thighs while softly caressing my ass. I moaned gently as he went further up my thighs. He sucked me so sweet and gently that I came instantly. Without stopping, I felt the thrust of his hardness inside me. He grabbed my hair and started pounding me hard. I screamed, "Fuck me harder." He thrusted his dick in and out forcedly. My pussy became even wetter. He was turning me on because he was being so forceful.

"Fuck me harder," I screamed again. Texas pounded my pussy until I screamed, "I'm... cuuummin!"

"Ugggghhh," he moaned. We both laid there as the intense sensation flowed through our bodies. The crisp ocean waves rushed over us like rain on a hot summer day. I was truly in paradise.

♣

We got up the next morning and headed straight to the mall. The shops were amazing with everything from Louis Vuitton to Yves St. Laurent. I bought some perfumes and a few summer dresses. We went to a jewelry store; Texas looked for a watch as I looked at the rings. I know why they say a diamond is a girl's best friend, because I fell in love with the diamonds I saw in that store. I must've tried on at least ten rings but the one that I liked the most was a canary diamond with white diamonds around the sides. The rock glistened on my finger.

I saw Texas cutting his eye at me but he wasn't trying to come nowhere near the rings. Anytime a man thinks you're trying to force marriage on them they get scared, but I didn't care. I still tried on the rings and had a fabulous time. He waved his hand for me to come on. We walked outside the building and my phone rang. It was my mom. I had forgotten to tell her I was in Hawaii. Texas told me to wait for him because he had forgotten his cell phone and had to rush back into the jewelry store.

My mom was fussing. "Even though you're grown you need to let somebody know where you are, Raechel. Anything can happen."

"Yeah, you're right; it's just that it was spur of the moment. Texas surprised me. I'm sorry, Mom."

I knew she was right. I just agreed with what she was saying and then told her I loved her and got off the phone. Texas came out the store, looking frustrated.

"I can't find my phone." We searched the bags and located his phone stuffed inside one of the shopping bags.

We went back to the room and put up our bags.

"Okay, baby. What chu' you wanna do next? Parasailing or the Jungle tour?" Texas asked me.

"Why not do both?"

"Okay." We put on our bathing suits and hit the beach again.

"Texas, remember that I don't know how to swim."

"Baby, you'll be okay. We're not getting in the water. Besides, you'll have on a life jacket." He kissed me on my lips. "I'm not gonna let anything happen to you."

I was a little apprehensive, but I trusted him and we decided to do the jungle tour first. We got into a small, two-seater boat and followed the tour guide far out into the ocean. At first I was doing fine but the farther we went into the ocean, the more intense the tide became. The waves from the current kept rocking the boat and causing it to bump up and down. My heart started racing. I could just see myself flipping out the boat and falling into the water. I looked around and all I could see was water. There was no land in sight.

"Texas, please let's go back. I'm scared."

"Rae, I can't sweetheart. We're in the middle of nowhere. We have to keep following the tour guide until we get back to the ocean front."

"Please, Texas," I begged as tears flowed from my eye. "I'm so scared." I cried and held onto the side of the boat for dear life. I put my head down and cried like a baby.

"Rae, calm down," Texas screamed. But I couldn't stop. I was too frightened. So he eventually waved his hand up for the tour guide to come. The tour guide asked me to climb over to his boat and he would take me back to shore while Texas stayed in the other boat and followed the other tour guide. I was so scared I wouldn't even stand up in the boat, Texas and the tour guide had to take me back to shore and then catch up with the other tourists. They dropped me off on shore. I was so happy to see land I got out the boat and forgot my flip-flops.

I caught a cab back to the room barefooted. *Hell, I know Texas is going to be mad at me, but I'm sorry, I hate the water.* I had almost drowned before and ever since then I have been afraid of the water. Mimi and I went to this water park, Adventure River, when I was in the eleventh grade. I was much bigger-fifty pounds heavier, and I had the nerve to have on a bikini I didn't realize how fat I was then, but when I look back on pictures, I was huge. I went to get on one of the tall slides where you sit your butt in the tire and go down the slide. When I got ready to sit my butt in the tire hole it wouldn't fit; my butt was too big. But it was too late to turn around. It was one way up and one way down, which was going down the slide. I sat down on the slide and as soon as I went around a curve on the slide, my ass came out the tire and it flipped me over, so I went down the slide face down on my stomach with my ass in the air. I went straight into the pool and of course I panicked. Though it was only like three feet of water, the life guard had to jump in to save me.

When I got out, Mimi was laughing so hard she had tears in her eyes. She said that while I was coming down the slide one side of my bikini was stuck in my ass. I was so pissed that I never went to that water park again.

I went back to the room and dozed off. When I woke up, Texas was back.

"Texas," I called.

"Yo', I'm in here." He was in the bathroom. I walked in and he was sitting in the Jacuzzi. It was filled with bubbles and he was laid back with his arms around the edges, smoking a Cuban cigar. He looked like Tony Montana from Scarface; the smoke from the cigar had clouded the air. There was also a bottle of Dom Perignon chilling beside the tub and two glasses. I smiled,

"Why didn't you wake me up when you came in?"

"I wanted to let my princess sleep, especially after today. Come on, baby, get in." I slipped out of my shorts and a chill came over me. When I sat down in the water the warm bubbles massaged my entire body. At first the water was too hot but then Texas poured me a cool glass of champagne and my temperature began to steady. The lights were dim and all I could hear were the waves from the ocean.

"Baby?" He puffed on the cigar. I knew he was going to mention what happened on the jungle tour. "What was up with that today?"

I was hoping he wouldn't bring it up; I shrugged my shoulders.

He released the smoke from the cigar. There was a long silence. He tapped the ashes in the ashtray. Then he burst out laughing.

"Rae." He was laughing so hard he couldn't speak.

I hit him in the arm as hard as I could but he just kept laughing then I started laughing too.

"If I had known you would act like that I woulda never suggested we go on the jungle tour. Baby, I gotta teach you how to swim. Because that stunt you pulled today was ridiculous."

I smiled, "Yeah I know."

We laid back and sipped champagne and just chilled. "I'm starving. What are we goin' to eat?"

"I ordered room service," he told me.

"What did you order?"

"It's a surprise?"

"I hope you didn't order me any seafood."

"Baby, I know you can't eat seafood; you're allergic."

Texas always remembered everything about me, which is one of things that I loved about him.

"Rae, you know I love you, right?"

"Ahhh, Texas, I love you too," I smiled.

"I fell in love with you the first night we met." He looked me directly in the eyes "Ever since the first moment I met you, I knew you were the one for me. I keep telling you I wanna spend the rest of my life with you."

I moved my body next to his and gave him a warm kiss on the lips. We were interrupted by a knock at the door.

"Damn, that's room service."

We both looked at each other because neither of us wanted to move."

"Baby, I ain't about to move. You gotta go get that," Texas told me.

"Ummph," I whimpered. "Okaaaay." I kissed him on the lips. I didn't want to get out of the hot tub either but I did. I climbed out of the

Jacuzzi and his eyes gazed leisurely over my nakedness. I put on my soft Teri cloth robe that was provided by the hotel.

I went and opened the door; the waiter rolled the serving table into the room.

"How do you want to pay for this?" Charge it to the room and add a thirty percent gratuity to the tab," I told him.

"Okay," he thanked me with a satisfied smile.

"Thank you, Mrs. Reynolds."

I smiled. "You're welcome." I liked the sound of Mrs. Reynolds.

He looked at me and winked his eye. "I hope you enjoy your dinner."

"Thank you." I closed the door. I was starving. I went straight to the serving dish to see what Texas had ordered. I removed the top from the platter. There wasn't a meal; there was a card and a black box. I picked up the card. It read: *There is no me without you.* I opened the box.

"Huh!" I gasped. It was the ring from the jewelry store. My eyes filled with tears, I turned around and Texas was standing right behind me. He kissed me and then got down on one knee.

"Raechel Jones, will you marry me?"

I didn't hesitate. "Yes, Yes, Yes!" I screamed and wrapped my arms around his neck. He picked me up and I straddled my legs around his waist and kissed him. He swung me around, and then carried me into the bedroom.

I couldn't control the tears. "Texas, I'm so happy." I said as I wiped the streaming tears away. He had gotten the ring I had tried on in the jewelry store. I couldn't believe it. It was a five-carat canary diamond with baguettes around the sides, absolutely gorgeous. Texas put the ring on my finger. It damn near blinded me.

"Texas, I'm so happy." I gave him a kiss. "Thank you so much, sweetheart. I love you so much."

"No, Raechel, thank you."

"Thank me for what?"

"Thank you for letting me love you, thank you for loving me." We kissed again. I interrupted the kiss. "Baby?"

"When did you want to do this?"

"We can do it tomorrow if you want."

"Huh?" I said with an astonished expression. He started laughing,

"I knew that would be your reaction." He paused. "Well, I want you to graduate first. and I'm sure you want a big wedding, so I was thinking next summer before you start medical school."

"Yes, that would be a perfect time." I gleamed.

"I'm getting ready to renew my contract with the Tyrants and hopefully you'll get accepted into Meharry. If everything works out, we will be happily married by next August."

"It sounds like a plan." We ordered room service forreal this time. After we ate, we made love, and I went to bed with thoughts of me walking down the aisle as Mrs. Raechel Reynolds.

For the next couple of days, Texas and I did some sightseeing and shopping but we mostly stayed in the room and fucked like rabbits. Good thing I was on the pill because I probably would have been knocked up; walking down the aisle with a swollen belly. And that's one thing I wasn't trying to do. I didn't want a baby right now. I wanted to finish Medical School first then we could have all the babies we wanted. Even though Texas has money, and I know we will be straight financially, I still want to accomplish my own goals. I don't want my life to revolve strictly around his.

♣

We both hated to leave Hawaii. Texas wanted to stay another day, but we couldn't because we both had obligations. Plus, I couldn't wait to get back to show off my ring to my girls. I had called them and told them about it and they were all excited for me. When we boarded the plane I was so high off of life. I had the man of my dreams. I was engaged and I was in love. I felt like nothing could go wrong. But, oh was I sadly mistaken. Not only did things go wrong—they went terribly wrong.

Chapter 14

When we got back from Hawaii, I was exhausted. I called my mom and told her the good news about me and Texas. She was happy for me, but she was also complaining because she had never met Texas in person. They'd only spoken on the phone. I told her that Texas said he would fly her to Nashville whenever she was ready, but she complained because she didn't like flying. She would just have to wait to meet him, because now Texas is in the playoffs and his schedule is very hectic.

Sasha and I met up after class and worked out. After we were done jogging, I told her all about my trip to Hawaii and about how Texas' proposed to me.

"I'm so happy for you, Raechel. I know you and Texas are going to have a wonderful life together," Sasha told me.

"Thanks, girl," I replied nonchalantly. "But that's enough about me. What's up with you and Sean?" I asked.

Sasha smiled. She had that kind of glow you have when you first meet somebody you like and y'all haven't had sex yet. You know when you check your phone every ten minutes to see if he's called or texted. And the moment he does you start smiling, your heart starts to race, and you get butterflies in your stomach. That's the glow she had on her face.

"Girl, he seems straight," she said while trying to act like she was not that into him. But by the tone in her voice, I knew she was definitely feeling him.

"Straight, huh? I know it is gotta be more than that."

"Well, of course we haven't had sex yet, but Rae, he's super cool. I just like everything about him." She started smiling. "He's kinda hood though, but you know that's the kind I like."

"Where's he from?"

"Miami. You know how them niggas from the MIA are. They just straight gangsta' and I love it." She screamed, we both just laughed.

"Girl, I'm just waiting for something to be wrong with him."

"Sasha, don't talk like that. You can't be negative. Give him a chance."

"Yeah, you're right, but it's always something. But I'll try not to focus on that right now." We stopped at our cars, drank our bottled waters and grabbed our cell phones. "So girl, when is the big day?" Sasha asked, while scrolling through her phone.

"What big day?"

"Duh... your wedding day," she mocked with a dumbfounded expression.

"Ah, girl. My mind was somewhere else. We haven't decided on a date yet, but it's more than likely going to be sometime next summer."

"Are you still going to medical school?"

I looked at her like she was crazy. "Damn right, I'm still going to medical school. Girl, you know I'm not trying to be totally dependent on Texas. Chick, I gotta have something to fall back on in case that nigga up and decides to leave me one day."

"Yeah, girl; I feel ya, but, Rae, Texas seems perfect. I know y'all gon' be together forever."

"Yeah, I pray so," I told her with uncertainty. My mind began to wander. I thought about the previous night when Texas and I were in bed asleep.

"Rae, are you okay?" Sasha inquired with an awkward expression. "What do you mean by you pray so?"

I exhaled a deep breath. "It's just that lately, Sasha, I've been having some crazy dreams."

"What kind of crazy dreams?"

"Dreams about Texas."

"What about Texas?" Sasha asked with her brows wrinkled like she was worried about me.

I sighed. "Dreams that he's..."

"He's what?"

I swallowed hard. "Dreams that he's trying to kill me,"

"What?" Sasha exhaled a deep breath and we both sat down on a bench in the park. "Are you serious?"

"Yeah, I'm serious Sasha, and last night some crazy shit happened."

"What happened?" I reflected on the previous night's events.

"Okay, I got outta class late last night and when I got over Texas' house he was already in the bed sleep. I took a shower and crawled into bed and snuggled under him like I always do. I was so tired. As soon as my head hit the pillow I was in lala land. I was sleeping hard.

Then all of a sudden I felt somebody's hands around my neck choking me. At first, I thought I was dreaming but then I opened my eyes and realized it wasn't a dream. I screamed, "Stop," as I gasped for air. That is when I realized the person that was choking me was Texas."

"Forreal, girl! What did you do?" Sasha's eyes revealed her nervousness.

"I managed to call his name and tell him to stop. It was crazy, Sasha because he quickly loosened his grip. I was so scared. I jumped outta of bed and turned the lights on. I held my throat and tried to catch my breath." Tears came to my eyes as I thought back on the dreadful moment.

"What are you doing? Trying to kill me?" I wheezed and watched him from the bedroom door. Sasha, I'm telling you, he looked like he didn't know what he'd just done to me. He looked more dazed and confused, like he was waking up from a nightmare or something."

"I can't believe that, Rae. Why did he say he was choking you?" Sasha inquired.

"He didn't say, he sat up in the bed and asked me what had happened so I told him. He looked at me with the saddest look on his face and told me he was sorry. He looked like he wanted to cry. He got out the bed and came and sat by me on the floor. He asked me if I was okay and I asked him the same. We sat on the floor embracing each other. That's when he told me that he had been having nightmares."

"What kind of nightmares?" Sasha asked

"Nightmares where somebody was trying to kill him. He said up until last night he could never see the face of the person that was trying to kill him."

"Well, who's face did he see?"

"The face he saw was his."

"What? That's crazy as hell," Sasha remarked with a worried expression.

"Then we laid back down, Texas went back to sleep. But I couldn't sleep. I was too scared. I kept thinking about Texas choking me, plus I've been having nightmares too. And for Texas to say he had been having strange dreams too it really has been bothering me. I don't know what's going on."

Sasha was silent. I'm sure she was trying to soak in everything I had just told her. She finally started talking.

"Maybe you should talk to Ma'Sadie. She's probably the only somebody who can tell you what's going on with you and Texas and these nightmares."

Sasha's godmother, Ma'Sadie, is a prophet who could predict things that were going to happen to people before they happened. Ma'Sadie said that her gift of prophecy had come from God. Sasha swore by Ma'Sadie, but Ma'Sadie couldn't predict future events in Sasha's life because Ma'Sadie couldn't see the future of people that was close to her like friends and relatives, only the future of strangers.

Sasha dialed Ma'Sadie and put her on speaker. "Hey, Ma'Sadie, How are you doing?"

"I'm doing well." She had a very pleasant but solemn voice.

"Ma'Sadie, I'm here with my friend, Raechel Jones. She's been having some disturbing dreams and she wants to see if you can maybe help her to understand them."

Sasha passed the phone to me, but I was kind of apprehensive so I wouldn't take it at first.

"Girl, take this phone," she mouthed to me in a forceful manner.

This time I grabbed the phone because I needed some answers.

"Hello, Ma'Sadie," I said uneasily.

"Hello, darling. Tell me about these dreams you're having, my child."

I took her off the speaker so that I could hear her more clearly. First, I explained to her the recurring dream I had on the plane and the most recent dream I had the night before.

"I stayed the night over to my fiancé's house. He left me in bed asleep. When I woke up, he was gone and I was running late for class. I rushed to get ready and opened the door. When I opened the door a huge snake fell from the hinge of the door and landed around my neck. I got the snake off me and noticed there was a colony of snakes swarming around the front door preventing me from leaving. When I ran back into the house there was a big rattle snake in the house hissing at me. I needed to get my phone to dial 911, but the snake was swarming just inches away from my phone that had fallen on the floor. I decided to be brave and make a dash for my phone. As soon as I picked it up the snake jumped up and bit me on my hand. I became weak as the poison flowed through my blood stream. I collapsed and all I remember thinking is I don't want to die, I don't want to die. Then I woke up."

Ma'Sadie was silent, and Sasha was staring at me with intensity.

"Hello…Ma'Sadie are you there?"

"Yes, my dear," she answered in a somber voice.

"So what does it mean?"

"The snakes in the dream represent evil. The fact that they were blocking the door means that the evil is trying to block you from goodness."

"What about the snakes in the house?"

"The snakes in the house mean that an evil presence will beseech that house."

"Is the evil presence Texas?"

"I don't know. I can't see clearly. I would have to speak with him. Do you know his date of birth?"

"Yes, it's seven-seventeen," I told her with fear resonating in my voice.

"I see an evil side and a good side. There will be a battle between the good forces and bad forces that will take place near water. The good forces will prevail if you follow your heart, but death will occur in threes. You must follow my advice from this day on. You are not to have intercourse until you are married. Now goodbye until later, my child."

"Huh? Wait, Ma'Sadie. No intercourse?" Her answer to me was a dial tone buzzing in my ear. "Hold up, wait just a minute. Nah!"

"What did she say?" Sasha asked.

"She told me what she saw in my dreams, and then said that I shouldn't have sex until I'm married. Then she says goodbye and hangs up the phone. I'm calling her back. I don't know why she said that. She must've made a mistake."

I was trying to press redial when Sasha yanked the phone out of my hand.

"Rae, calm the hell down. One thing about Mama Sadie is she doesn't make mistakes. If she told you not to have sex until you're married, you may want to follow her advice," Sasha said concerned. She glanced at her watch. "Look, I'm getting ready to leave."

"Where are you going?"

"I'm going over to Sean's house.

"Mmm-hum," I mumbled. Sasha gave me a sly look.

"Now, girl, Ma'Sadie told you not to have sex, not me," Sasha mocked.

"Whatever," I answered and waved her off. We got up from the bench and headed toward our cars. On my drive home, I kept replaying the conversation with Ma'Sadie over in my head. *What did she mean when she said the good forces will prevail if I follow my heart?*

Later during the day, I went to the library to study for a couple of hours then I went to see Texas. He was asleep when I got there. After I showered, I sat on the edge of his bed. As soon as I sat down, he woke up. I leaned down and gave him a kiss.

"Hey, baby, what's up?" he turned over on his back and looked at me.

"Nothing, baby. Go back to sleep."

"Princess, what's the matter?" he asked. He could tell there was something bothering me.

"Nothing."

He grabbed my hand. "Yes, there is." He sat up in the bed and turned on the night light.

"Tell me. What's up, baby?"

"Texas, what would you think if I told you I didn't want to have sex again until we're married?"

"Where did that come from?" he asked totally perplexed and confused.

I explained to him who Ma'Sadie was and the conversation I had with her.

"Raechel, I don't believe that psychic shit."

"She's not a psychic, Texas. She's a prophet; a prophet is different. A prophet gets messages from God."

"Whatever, Raechel."

"Baby, she wants to talk to you too." I got up and turned on the bedroom light.

"Talk to me about what?" he asked irritated.

"About the dreams we've been having."

"Raechel, those dreams are coincidental, and I told you the one last night was a nightmare. I told you them spicy tacos I ate caused that nightmare."

Texas got up from the bed and went to the bathroom, and I followed right behind him.

"Can we at least call her one time?" I went to retrieve her number from my purse and then walked over to the nightstand and picked up the cordless phone.

"Raechel, I said, no." He grabbed the phone out of my hand. "I don't want you talking to that lady again. All she's doing is scaring you. Nothing bad is going to happen to you. I promise." He kissed me on the top of my head, then he looked me in my eyes.

"As for sex, if you want to wait until we're married, then I'm fine with that. But it's not because of some premonition you got from a psychic. And I know one thing for certain."

"What?" I asked with some added reservation.

"Your ass can't be coming over here sleeping in them skimpy shorts and them li'l ass nightgowns." He smiled.

I smirked. "Okay," I agreed and we both laid down and went to sleep.

Chapter 15

Upon walking into work, I looked at my phone and saw that I had a text message: *"Blood is Red, Bruises are Blue. Bitch, if I see u with Tex again, u gon' die too!"* I kept trying to call the number back but no one answered the phone.

For the past week someone had repeatedly called my phone. When I answered, the caller would hold the phone and not say anything. Sometimes the number would come up Restricted. Other times it would be different phone numbers. I mean it was to the point I was thinking about getting my number changed. I thought about who could've possibly been harassing me and only one name kept coming to mind, Eva. I wasn't dating or seeing anyone but Texas Reynolds and she had a major problem with it. The constant calling and hanging up was getting out of hand. Now she was sending threatening text messages. I was going the next day to report it to the police and get my number changed.

I called Tex to tell him about the text message but he didn't answer the phone. I started my shift but I couldn't stop thinking about the intimidating text message. Several co-workers asked me if I was okay because I'm normally talking and joking, but today I mostly kept to myself.

"Rae, are you okay? You don't seem like yourself today," Tangerine asked.

I played it off and gave her a phony smile. "Yeah, girl. I'm straight."

Tangerine and I were in the same section. We each had five tables a piece and we rotated the tables. She came into the kitchen and told me there was a table in our section and it was my turn. I walked out to the section, checked with my other tables, and made sure they didn't need anything before I went to greet the next table. I approached the table and the customer held the menu, which shielded their face.

I greeted the table, "Hello, welcome to Andrew's Crab. What can I get you to drink?" The customer suddenly jumped up from the table and sprayed me in the face with pepper spray. "Ahhhh," I screamed and stumbled back trying to get away from her. I tripped and fell over a table and some chairs. It was a woman wearing a red wig and dark sunglasses. It was Eva. Before I could say anything, she bent down and kicked me in my stomach.

"Ummph!" I grunted as I grabbed my stomach.

"This is a warning bitch," she hissed before she stormed off.

Some guests in the restaurant came to offer their help. My eyes were burning and it felt like my skin was on fire. My manager and Tangerine came and helped me into the back office. I couldn't digest what had happened. Tangerine and my boss laid cold, wet towels on my face and eyes. Soon the burning sensation began to lessen.

My manager asked once she was sure I was all right, "Rae, what was that all about?" I was still trying to make sense of it myself.

"I don't know."

"Well, the police have been called. They should be here in a minute."

Two policemen arrived. One of them asked, "Do you know who the woman was?"

"Yes, it was my boyfriend's ex-girlfriend," I winced while still coughing and wheezing from the pepper spray. My eyes continued to burn and water.

"Can you give us a description, ma'am?" the other police asked.

"She was wearing dark clothes. She had on a red wig and dark shades."

"Ma'am, how was she recognizable if she had on sunglasses?"

"I know it was that bitch. When I came in to work, she sent me a text and threatened me." I showed him the text from my phone. Besides, she was the same height and build as my fiancé's ex."

"Are you sure?"

"Yes," I screamed.

"What's her name?"

"Her first name is Eva, but I'm not sure of her last name."

"What is your fiancé's name?"

"Why y'all need to know all that?"

"Well, ma'am, we just like to check all avenues, just to make sure your fiancé is not playing the field. You never know, he may have had something to do with this incident."

"My fiancé didn't have nothing to do with that crazy ass bitch. She came in here an assaulted me on her own. I know he ain't playing the field." I didn't want to drag Texas' name into it. All the media needed was something on one of the ball players and they would blow that shit way out of proportion so I gave them a fake name. They said they would investigate the incident.

"Do you want to press charges?" the first policeman asked me.

"Hell, yea, I wanna press charges." But I still needed Eva's last name." I called Texas repeatedly but I couldn't reach him. He didn't call me back until three hours later.

"Rae, what's the matter? Is everything okay?"

"Hell nah, everything is not okay. Your fuckin' baby momma showed up at my job today and sprayed me with mace."

"What," he shouted. "Eva ain't in Nashville."

"The hell she ain't. The bitch came to my job dressed in a wig and sunglasses. What's her last name?"

"Hunter," he stumbled nervously. "Why, what are you about to do?"

"I'm on my way to press charges on her. That's what I'm about to do," I screamed. "What type of psycho bitch is she? I can't believe that she came to my job and maced me. That bitch is bold 'cause she don't know who she fuckin' with. If I see that bitch I promise I'ma beat that shit out of her. Nah, I'ma get that bitch where it hurt. I'ma get that hoe locked up. She done messed up now. You said you would handle that bitch, Texas. But it's too late 'cause I'm about to handle it." I hung the phone up in his face, jumped in the car, and headed straight to the police station to file charges against her. Texas was blowing my phone up. I contemplated answering, but didn't.

Then he sent me a text. *"Raechel, please answer the phone."* He called again.

I picked up the phone. "What," I answered angrily.

"Look, Raechel. I don't know what the hell is going on, but I'm going to get to the bottom of it. I'm so sorry about what happened to you, baby. I can't believe that Eva would do some shit like that. That bitch done lost her damn mind. I've been calling her but she won't pick up. I've called her parents but they're in Spain for the next fourteen days. I don't know what's going on. And to top it all off, I need to know where my daughter is."

I could hear in his voice that he was upset. I hated to bother him on the day before game day, but fuck it; we have got to get this situation with this Eva bitch handled but I still felt bad. I hesitated and took a deep breath. "Texas, I'm sorry to slam this on you right before a game."

"Baby, please don't be sorry." He paused. "It's my fault for getting you involved in this cycle of bullshit."

Cycle of bullshit "Did you say cycle of bullshit?" He didn't immediately respond. "Texas, what's going on?"

"Rae, we'll talk about it later." I took a deep breath before losing it.

"Nigga, you better tell me what the fuck is going on right fuckin' now," I screamed.

"Rae, wait a minute. I didn't cuss you, so just chill a minute." There was a pregnant pause. "Eva is crazy."

"Crazy, like what, baby momma crazy, I want you back, crazy?"

"Nah, crazy like she needs to be admitted to a hospital crazy, psycho crazy. She had some major issues when we dated in college. She didn't cheat on me; I cheated on her."

"What?" I exclaimed. "You told me she left you."

"I'm sorry that I lied. It was the other way around. I cheated on Eva. Me and Eva was never really together. We was cool. She would help me with my papers and we would hook up every now and then–"

I interrupted. "Hook up like what?" He didn't respond. "Helloooo, hook up like what."

"Like we would fuck, we would fuck, Rae!" he screamed.

"If you wasn't with her then why was y'all still fuckin? And don't be getting no attitude with me," I snapped.

"Anyway, I started to get noticed at school for my athletics. I became more popular on campus, and with the popularity came the girls. Eva would literally lose it if I so much as looked at another girl, let alone speak to one. She became obsessive and started following me around, and going through my phone. She was even threatening the different chicks I was seeing. Then she scratched B-I-T-C-H in my truck, so I quit fuckin' with her all together because I was gon' mess around and kill that bitch about my whip."

"How do you know it was her?" I said irritably

"Didn't you just hear all the shit I said she was doing?" He breathed hard. "It was her. I know it was."

"Well, you said you was seeing some other chicks. It mighta been one of them."

"Anyway," he said ignoring my last statement. "There was this one chick that I had gone to high school with. She was real cool. Me and her just vibed together but our relationship was strictly platonic. I played football with her brother in high school, and practically grew up with them. Her name was Keisha. She was my homegirl. Keisha had a boyfriend that lived in another city. I would talk to her when I needed a woman's perspective on things. You remind me of her because y'all favor."

"Mmm-humm."

"So me and Keisha started spending a lot of time together and I started to like her as more than just a friend. I felt like it was time for me to settle down so I stop messing around and was devoted to her. She broke things off with her ex, and me and her made it official; we were a couple. One day we were in my room chilling and I looked at my phone. I had like twenty missed calls from Eva. Next thing I know she was banging on my door. When I opened the door Eva stormed in and started attacking me. At first I tried not to hit her, but then she started hitting me in my face. So I grabbed her by her neck and was about to choke her lights out before Keisha pulled me up off her. She was hitting me talking about I ruined her life; I was gonna burn in hell all types of crazy shit. I don't know why she was trippin' because from day one I had told her we wasn't nothing but friends. But she obviously got in her head we was a couple.

I told the campus police what had happened, and they escorted Eva away and told her not to come anywhere near me or Keisha. Before Eva walked off she looked at Keisha and said, 'Bitch, you're going to pay.' Keisha was from the hood so of course they had words; Keisha got in her face and mugged her, 'Bitch, pay me right now since you're so fuckin' bad.'"

"What did Eva do?" I asked Texas.

"Eva looked at Keisha and said, 'I'ma get you bitch. You're gon' pay for everything you done to me. You'll pay when the time is right.' Then she started laughing. The way she said it had me kinda of shook.

Because she had a li'l smile on her face when she said it. And the way she had been stalking me I didn't want her to do anything to Keisha."

I pulled up outside the police precinct and listened as he finished telling me the story.

"The next day, while I was in class the police came and arrested me. I was confused. I didn't know what the hell was going on. The cop told me I was a suspect in the murder of Keisha Greenlee. Murder? I was so taken back I didn't know what to do. On my way to jail I kept praying that they would realize that they had made a terrible mistake. I was pissed that I had been arrested, but I was hoping that there had been a mistaken identity for the death of Keisha. But when I went into the interrogation room and the investigators started showing the pictures of Keisha's badly battered body, I realized it was true and I just lost it. "Keisha had been found brutally murdered in her apartment."

"Oh, my God," I gasped. "Why were you a suspect?"

"Because she had been stabbed eighty-one times, and she was found wearing my college jersey, number eighty-one. I was the last one to be seen with her on the night of her murder. People had seen us arguing in the dorm lobby; she was upset because of the altercation that had occurred between her and Eva. I drove her home and I stayed with her until she fell asleep, then I left and went back to campus because I had curfew. I was devastated because Keisha was my best friend. And I was a suspect in her murder. My parents had to come to Alabama and hire an attorney as well as a private investigator. I spent twenty-one days in jail."

"Why so long?"

"Because the DNA analysis came back positive and the private investigator had to find evidence that would prove I wasn't the murderer. I was released, and the charges against me were dropped."

"Did they ever find the murderer?"

"No, but there is one person who I've always suspected."

"Who?"

He paused. "Eva."

"Why Eva?"

He exhaled a deep breath. "Beside Keisha's body there was a note that said: *Payback is a muthafucka.*"

I gasped. "Did you tell the police about the threat Eva had made?"

"Yes. I told them everything I knew. I told them about how Eva had been stalking me and the threats she had made, but they didn't believe me."

"Why?"

"Because Eva was pregnant." He paused. "And so was Keisha?"

"What?"

"Damn, Texas, you were sleeping with both women at the same time?"

"It wasn't exactly like that."

"What chu' mean it wasn't like that, yes it was. Texas you were using Eva. You had her around to do all your papers, had her cleaning up, doing your laundry and shit, while you were out fucking other women. Then when she fell in love and turned psycho on yo' ass you tried to break it off." He didn't say anything because he knew I was right.

"So, the night Eva came to the room, she must've told Keisha she was pregnant."

"Yep, and when Keisha left my dorm she was upset. I chased behind her and she made a scene in the lobby about how she never wanted to see me again. I calmed her down and drove her home. Next thing I know I was being charged with her murder."

"Why was Eva never arrested?"

"She was arrested but she was released the same day. Her alibi stood. She had been in the library studying. Several people vouched for her time and whereabouts at the time of the murder."

After that incident, I lost it. My world turned upside down. I was so depressed and sad I couldn't function. I couldn't focus on anything. All I kept thinking about was Keisha and our baby. I was so depressed and angry. I would sit in my room for days and not shower or eat. My parents released me from school and I was put in a hospital for ten days."

"What kind of hospital?"

"A mental institution."

"Like a crazy house?"

"Yea, Rae. I lost it. I didn't even realize I was living so I was put on antidepressants. And after six months of intense therapy I started getting better. Rae, Keisha meant everything to me and knowing that she was pregnant at the time of her death just tore me apart. Then one night in a dream I saw her. She was just as clear as me and you talking. Keisha came to me and smiled, but she didn't say anything. She looked so happy. The next day I woke up, got my shit together, and started working out twice as hard. Every time I felt down or depressed I would remember that vision of her and that is what kept me going. I returned to school and worked extra hard and made it to the NFL."

"What about Eva?"

"She left school. And I didn't hear from her until the baby was born."

"So, you weren't there for her doing the pregnancy?"

"Rae, I wasn't even there for myself that year. I was fucked up. Keisha's death broke my heart."

"Why do men think it is okay to play with a woman's feelings? Why do y'all think it is acceptable to toy with our emotions and hearts? That shit isn't cool and it's definitely not cute. White, black, blue, Chinese women are tired of y'all shit."

There was a silence on the phone.

"Raechel, I know. I was young and stupid. I had the big head. I thought I could get any woman I wanted. I used them to get what I wanted then headed straight to my next victim. But I learned a valuable lesson the hard way by losing somebody, I truly loved. After that I made a vow that I'm going to respect women and treat them how I want a man to treat my daughter one day, with loyalty and respect. I blame myself for what happened to Keisha. Because I put her in harm's way by messing with her, knowing how crazy Eva is."

"But, you didn't know Eva was going to do what she did."

There was a silence.

"Yes, I did. Eva had told me if she couldn't have me then nobody could. Raechel, listen to me. That girl is crazy. I want you to go to the house, look on top of my closet in the red shoe box, and get that gun outta there."

I gasped. "Texas, I'm not touching a gun. Are you cra—"

He interrupted me in mid-sentence. "Baby, you don't understand. This woman is dangerous. At least carry it until the police get her. I wouldn't be able to live with myself if something happened to you."

"Texas, nothing is going to happen to me. I'm going to get a restraining order against Eva. Besides, God will protect me."

"Yeah, that's the same thing Keisha said."

Chapter 16

Sasha and I got up the next morning and went to church. I needed it because I felt like something was about to happen. At the end of service when they asked if anyone needed extra prayer to come to the front, I did. I prayed that the Lord would protect me and keep me from danger. I also prayed for Texas and for Eva as well. I really didn't understand what was fully going on with her but I prayed that the Lord would help her see the light. Yet, something in my spirit told me things were about to get worse.

I was still kinda pissed at Texas, because I couldn't appreciate the fact that he had lied and it bothered me. I was wondering what in the hell else had he lied about. He might have been lying about his feelings for me or lying about being faithful. But then I thought about all the good times we had. The past six months had been total paradise between us. We were not only physically attracted to each other, we were friends. As a matter of fact, I considered him as was one of my best friends. We talked about everything, I had even gotten to the point where I would fart around him and do number two. I used to would never do that around a guy. If I had to fart, I would hold that shit in for dear life, but with him I could be myself I didn't have to pretend. He was the type of man that would do anything for me. I remember one time we had rented a movie. I was too tired to watch it and I fell asleep before the damn movie even started but I woke up toward the end of the movie and I looked at the T.V and the close caption was on. I hated watching a movie with the closed caption on it. I'm a damn good reader but I am not about to watch a movie with closed caption on the bottom.

"Baby," I asked. "Why do you have the closed caption turned on?"

"I didn't want to wake you up."

"Texas, are you saying that you watched the entire movie with closed caption so you wouldn't wake me up?"

"Yes," he said mildly.

I thought that was so sweet. But, he was like that with everything. Several times he had asked me to quit Andrew's Crab and he would give me a weekly allowance, but I would always say, no. I knew Texas had made some mistakes in the past but I was not about to let those mistakes effect our relationship. The good times had definitely outweighed the bad.

Sasha and I walked into the stadium. I could tell she was on cloud nine because she couldn't wait to see Sean. I was still feeling a bit uneasy but church had made me feel a little better. I felt like bishop had a sermon just for me. It was called, *God Is Still In Control.* That sermon was on fire. I almost caught the Holy Spirit. I did cry a lot, but I didn't get to shouting. That has never happened to me. I remember when I was younger, me and Mimi used to laugh at people that caught the Holy Spirit because they would be running around the church dancing and hollering like maniacs. I would ask momma what's wrong with them, and she would say they're happy. I never understood that until I got older. Life can become so hard sometimes. For me, church is a stress reliever where I can go and lay all my problems on the alter and leave them for God to handle.

Sau and I walked in the stadium and I had psyched myself up because I didn't want to seem like a sour puss around her. I hate when people are around you all sad and you're in a happy mood. If you're sad, don't come around me. I had masked my feelings and was pretending to be in a good mood. One of the main reasons for me coming to the game was to see if Eva was going to show up. At first I was going to beat the shit out of that bitch. But after going to church, I changed my mind. Hell, I don't know. I still might beat that bitch's ass. On second thought, I will just wait until the police apprehend her.

This was a very serious game for Tennessee. It was the first playoff game and it was mandatory that they win in order to stay in the playoffs. Sasha and I went to our seats. Right away, I spotted Tex and of course he waved but he didn't smile at me like he normally does.

Sasha had spotted Sean and he waived at her too. They had been spending a lot of time together. Sasha acted like Sean was the bomb. I really hadn't heard her speak too much about him. Like I said, she knows everybody else's business but don't nobody know hers .

Denver was undefeated. On the first play of the game Denver scored then the ball went back to Tennessee and we scored, which put us on the board at seven and seven.

Texas was doing well and had scored the first touchdown. I kept on looking around to see if Eva had come to the game. I was going to have her ass arrested on the spot. During halftime, me and Sasha walked around and got something to eat but I didn't see her. Maybe she hadn't come.

The third quarter started with us up by three, then Denver scored. It was Tennessee's ball but the quarterback threw an interception and Denver scored again. We got the ball back and scored again and now we were one touchdown away from winning. There was a minute and forty-five seconds left in the game. Denver ran the ball first to try to gain some yardage but they only gained a few yards. With twenty-three seconds left in the game, they had to throw the ball. Texas was in the end zone. I knew Texas was going to catch the ball. He was just that good.

The crowd was so silent that one could hear a pin drop. The quarterback threw the ball. The ball flew through the air in slow motion and landed directly in Texas' hand, but another player ran directly into him and he dropped the ball. All the players were huddled around Texas; I couldn't see where he was. Then I looked up at the monitor and saw that he hadn't gotten up. I saw the team doctors rush to where he was on the field. They started clearing people off the field.

I looked at the monitor and Texas was still laying flat on his back. When they showed the replay, I saw as he was catching the ball the player from the other team ran directly into him and they butted heads. The way the impact hit Texas it seemed like he took the most crucial hit. Next thing I know, I saw the stretchers. Texas was unconscious.

I jumped out my seat and ran to the sideline with Sau following me. By the time I made it to the sideline they were carrying Texas off the field. Security wouldn't let anybody near him but I looked from afar and noticed a lady running with the paramedics to get him to the hospital. It was Eva.

Chapter 17

Sasha and I arrived at the hospital but the hospital staff wasn't giving out his room number, and they told us only immediate relatives were allowed to see him. I begged the nurses to let me in to see him. I told them I was his fiancé.

"Ma'am, his fiancé is in the room with him right now," one of the nurses told me.

"What?" I asked confused. Eva must have told the nurses that she was his fiancé and not to allow anyone in the room, which is why I couldn't see him. I asked the nurse could she at least tell me his prognosis. She said that he had suffered a concussion and was in a coma but that was all the information she could give me.

I was so distraught. All I could do was cry. I waited for hours in hopes that they would let me see him. The doctors kept coming back saying they were running tests and that we needed to go home. I went home and prayed. I couldn't eat, sleep, or do anything.

I called the hospital and this time I was told that they couldn't give me any information because of his celebrity status. I finally fell asleep. When I woke up I picked up the phone to dial Texas' number and the phone just rang and rang. I had forgotten all about the accident. I had fallen asleep in my clothes. I looked in the mirror and my eyes were swollen from the crying I had been doing all night.

I looked awful I showered and went to my first class. I had a break in between classes I was going to run up to the hospital after my first class. I went to class and had forgotten we had a test. I didn't even study; everything on the test looked foreign to me. I knew I was going to fail that bitch. I couldn't even focus on the test; thoughts of Texas consumed my mind.

As soon as class was over I went to the hospital. I walked up to the critical care unit. I didn't exactly know what room he was in, but then I saw one of his teammates coming out of a room, so I just walked in the direction he was coming from in the critical care unit. I looked in every room; determined to see him. A nurse walked pass and I gave her a fake smile and kept walking like I knew where I was going. The very next room was Texas' room. I looked in and saw his mother sitting by his bedside, and his father in a chair on the other side near the window. I walked in the room and there was Texas laying in the bed sleep. Tears gushed from my eyes. His mother and father looked up as I walked in the room.

"Hellooo, how are you doing, Mr. and Mrs. Reynolds?" I winced as I swept tears from my eyes.

"Young lady, what are you doing here and how did you find this room?" his mother asked in a less than pleasant tone.

"I'm coming to see my fiancé, and the nurse gave me this room number," I lied.

"Fiancé?" She looked at my hand.

"Yes, fiancé." I showed her my ring. "Texas didn't tell you? We've been engaged for a month now."

She looked at her husband. "John, did you know anything about this?"

"Well, yes. He mentioned it to me; he was going to tell you at Christmas."

"Why in the hell did he tell you and not me?"

Texas' dad looked at her. "Elizabeth, shut the hell up. This is not the time or the place to discuss this. Our son is in a coma for Christ's sake. The only thing I'm concerned with is my son getting better."

She looked at her husband and fumed. "Yes, you're right, honey. Raechel, can I speak with you in the hallway?"

We stepped outside the room and I looked at her. "I'm sorry, Mrs. Reynolds, that Texas hadn't told you about the engagement. Like your husband said, Texas and I decided we would tell you at Christmas. Texas and I have been dating seriously for six months, and we are in love. I know that we got off on the wrong note, and I really want to get to know you better. I believe that once you get to know me, you'll see how much I love your son and how I want the best for him." Tears flowed from my eyes. "I am so hurt because of what he is going through right now. I want to be here for him." I paused. "I can't imagine not being by his side when he wakes up."

She walked over to me and got extremely close to my face. "Look, sweetie, I don't know what you think you may have had with my son, but it's not real. My son will not marry your little broke ass. I know you're just hanging around for his money. Next thing I know you'll be talking about you're pregnant. That's how you li'l gold diggers work."

I couldn't believe the things she was saying to me.

"You are just another fuck to him. And I know if my son was awake he would not have your ass anywhere around here." Then she summoned the nurse.

"Excuse me, ma'am, can you please not have any more visitors come to this room. My son is in critical condition and needs peace and quiet. If one more fan is allowed near this room, I'll have your job," she seethed.

While she was screaming at the nurse, Eva walked into the room carrying a bouquet of flowers. She walked in and laid her head on Texas' chest. I saw her through the window pane in the door. She looked at me and gave me the most evil grin. I took one last look at Texas and I left. I didn't want to cause a scene while he was in the hospital. I knew when he woke up things would be back to normal.

Texas remained in a coma for a week. That week was the longest week of my life. Not being able to see or hear his voice was killing me softly. Sean kept me updated on his status.

I was in class one day when I received a text from Sasha saying Texas was awake. I got up and walked out the class, got in my car, and headed to the hospital.

I called Sasha back. "Sau, did you get my text?"

"Yes."

"Sean said Texas was awake, but that he had suffered some memory loss."

"Is he okay? How is he doing?" I asked anxiously. I had a million questions.

"Sean said he seemed to be doing fine. He said when he left the hospital that Texas was up and walking around. He's being released from the hospital today."

I was so thankful, a sigh of relief came over me. I was so nervous driving to the hospital. I sat at a red light and glanced at the bracelet he had given me when we first met. I couldn't wait to see his smile. I was so lost in thought. The light had turned green, the car behind me blew the horn for me to go.

I arrived at the hospital. I got out the car and caught the elevator. I knew Texas was probably wondering where I was and why I wasn't there. I would tell him everything that had happened but right now I just needed to see his face. I walked up to room 254. I saw Eva and his mom right by the bed. Eva was feeding him and his mom was fluffing his pillows. I entered the room and my face lit up. I was so relieved to see him. I walked in and they were stunned.

"What are you doing here?" his mother asked.

I didn't even respond. I walked straight to Texas and dared one of them bitches to get in my way. I knew I could whoop Eva's ass, but that momma if she had gotten in my face I was going to knock the shit out of her and not think twice about it. My nerves were shot. I hadn't eaten nor slept in a week and I was not about to put up with anymore shit from either of them bitches.

"Hello, my sweet angel." I gave him a hug.

"Hey." He gave me a warm smile and I rubbed my hand gently across his face.

"Baby, how are you?"

"I'm okay. I feel fine, baby." I turned around and looked at his mother and Eva.

"Excuse me, do you mind if we have some time alone?"

"He needs me here at all times," his mother, Elizabeth, persisted.

"Ma, please can you get out, and, Eva, I don't even know why you're here. I've asked you to leave several times. He looked at both of them… "Bye."

"Eva, there is someone waiting for you outside." As soon as I said that the cop knocked on the door.

"Excuse me, are you Eva Hunter?"

"Yes," she hesitated.

"You are under arrest for assault."

"Assault?" Her eyes bulged.

"Yes, remember the Andrew's Crab incident? Did you think I had forgotten?" She was so shocked when they put the handcuffs on her.

"Raechel, you are going to pay for this!" she screamed.

"I'll be waiting."

I focused my attention back on Texas. "Baby, I miss you so much."

"I miss you too."

I kissed his lips. His kiss was cold and dry. He had been laid up in the hospital for days. What more could I expect.

"Texas, I'm so thankful that you are okay. I'm sorry I wasn't here when you woke up but your mother made it so difficult for me that I just decided to go home and pray for your recovery." I hugged him again.

"Baby, you did right. It was best you went home. I know my momma can be difficult. I've convinced them to fly back home today. My father has to get back to work. My mother wanted to stay longer but I asked my father to please make sure he takes her."

He smiled and that was the first time I had seen that sparkle in his eyes.

"As a matter of fact, I believe their flight leaves in a couple of hours."

"When are you going to be released?" I asked.

"Today? Are you sure, baby?"

"Yes, I'm sure. I feel so much better." He started getting up to go to the bathroom and I rushed to assist him.

"Raechel, I'm okay," he assured me.

"Baby, let me help you."

"I said, I'm okay. I got it!" he yelled.

I didn't say anything because I knew he was going through a lot with the accident and I didn't want him to get upset.

He came out the bathroom. "Where are my clothes?"

"Well, baby, when you came here you were in your uniform, but I bought you a change of clothes. I left them in the car."

"Well, go get them," he spat.

I ran down to get his clothes. When I came back up he asked, "Where did you go?"

"I told you I was going to get your clothes."

"Where they at?" he asked in an irritated tone.

"Right here." I handed him the bag with the change of clothes.

The doctor came in to give him the release papers. He signed them and I followed the doctor outside the room. "Dr. Clayborn, is Texas going to be okay? Are you sure he's okay to be released?"

"Yes, he is okay to leave." The doctor paused for a moment. "In my professional career I have never seen a recovery so miraculous. His recovery has been amazing. When I first saw him I thought that he would be here for a while. Then suddenly he was better. He was like a new person. He just needs to take it easy, but he should be okay in another week or so. He may still have some memory lapses, but everything should be back to normal soon."

I helped him get dressed and we took the elevator down with his parents.

"Son, are you sure you don't need us to stay?" his father asked him.

"Nah, Pops, I'm good."

I went to pull the car around, while he told his parents goodbye. I offered to take them to the airport, but they had rented a car and needed to return it.

I got out the car to tell his parents, bye. His mother walked away. His father gave me a hug.

"Raechel, I'm sorry about my wife," he paused. "You know she's really not a bad person. There is a reason why she is the way she is."

"That's okay, I understand."

He put both of his hands on my shoulder and looked me in my eyes. "Raechel, promise me you will take care of my son."

"I promise."

He handed me his card. "Please, call me if there is any trouble. Let me get your number also." He programmed my number in his phone. "Daughter-in-law," he said as he saved my number in his Blackberry. He gave me a warm hug.

Texas hugged his parents again and told them bye then got in on the driver's side.

"Baby, you can't drive. You just got out the hospital."

"I'm straight."

"Come on, baby; let me drive. The doctor said you shouldn't be driving for a couple days."

"Look, Raechel, I told you I was straight. I don't need you babying me. I can't deal with that shit right now. If I wanted to be babied, I woulda stayed in the mutherfuckin' hospital."

We got in the car. He turned the radio up extremely loud. I turned it down; he turned it back up.

"Baby, can you please turn that down?" He ignored me.

We got on Old Hickory, the two-lane highway, which leads to his house in Brentwood. We were behind this car that was going slow.

Texas started riding on the car's bumper and honking his horn in hopes that the car would speed up. He was trying to pass the car, but he couldn't because there was too much traffic coming in the other lane.

"Texas, baby, calm down." I was still nervous from the wreck I was in, and he was driving very erratic.

"Shut up. I'm driving, not you."

We finally got to the intersection that was four lanes and pulled up next to the car. The driver shot us a bird.

"Mutherfucker!" Texas screamed; he became furious. He mashed the gas and followed the car to the next red light. When we stopped at the light, Texas put the car in park.

"Baby, what are you doing?"

He got out the car.

"Texas, please, baby, no." I tried to stop him from getting out the car, but he didn't listen to a word I said. He popped open the trunk and pulled out a crow bar and tapped on the guy's window. There was a middle-aged white man driving the car with a pair of bifocals on.

"Get out the car, muthafucka," Texas shouted at the man. The poor man just sat in his car looking straight ahead with both hands on the steering wheel shaking like a leaf. As soon as the light changed, the man sped off. All I could see was smoke. I'm sure he was scared for his life the way Texas had acted. I thought he was actually going to harm the man if he had gotten out the car. When he got back in the car I didn't say one word. He had already yelled at me and I didn't want to fight. We didn't talk at all on the rest of the ride home.

We arrived at the house and went to the bedroom. He was acting strange but I guess he was trying to prove to me that he was feeling better, plus I knew he was feeling guilty for making the Tyrants lose the biggest game of the season. I didn't want to add to him feeling inadequate. I just wanted him to take it slow, since he had just had a serious accident.

I got in the shower. When I came out, I still had my towel wrapped around me. Texas was sitting on the edge of the bed.

"Come here, Rae, let me look at you."

I took off my towel. He admired my body as if he had never seen me before. He touched me all over and pulled me between his legs while sitting on the edge of the bed. He started kissing me on my stomach.

"No, Texas, baby you know about the promise we made."

"What promise?" he asked while placing gentle kisses on my stomach.

"Remember, we promised we wouldn't have sex until we were married?"

He raised his head and pulled me closer. "Raechel, are you fuckin' somebody else?" he yelled.

"No, Texas, where did you get an idea like that?"

"You are my future wife. And you don't want us to make love? You musta been fuckin' somebody while I was laid up in the hospital."

"Texas, that's not true." He shoved me out of the way and went and stood near the dresser. There was an uncomfortable silence. I walked up behind him and rubbed his back.

"Texas, I have not been with anyone but you. And we made a promise, but if you want us to make love, we can." At that point, I'd do anything to make him feel better.

"Yes, I want us to make love." He kissed me. "I missed you, baby." He turned me around and tied a scarf around my eyes.

I tensed. "What you are doing?"

"Shhhh," he whispered in my ear as his lips grazed my ear lobe. He laid me back on the bed and tied my hands to the bed post. Then he kissed my lips and began to slowly kiss every facet of my five-six frame. His tongue entered into my pussy. He licked it so gently and sucked on my clitoris. He would pause and then slowly began to kiss my inner thighs. He sucked until I felt an intense surge flow throughout my body. The sensation was so deep that my entire body froze until the feeling flowed out of my pussy as Texas savored my sweet nectar. I was so weak but that didn't stop him from thrusting his penis inside me vigorously, all while my hands were tied. I wanted so badly to hold him. but I couldn't. I felt myself about to cum again.

"Baby, I'm cummin."

"Me too," he screamed.

Our love both came down at once and he collapsed on top of me. We woke up two hours later. My hands were still tied to the bed post.

"Texas, please untie me." He did and the two of us laughed. I got up to use the bathroom. When I got back in the bed I couldn't sleep. My mind was consumed with all types of thoughts. Like what if I'm pregnant because I had stopped taking my birth control pills. Plus, I felt dirty because Texas and I had sex. I was ashamed about us making love. I got up and took a long, hot shower; I didn't know why I was having those feelings. I assumed it was because I had broken my promise. I wasn't going to beat myself up about it, because I can't cry over spilled milk. I looked over at Texas; he was sound asleep

Chapter 18

It was hump day. I stayed on campus on Mondays and Wednesdays because I had two early morning classes on both days. I didn't want to drive from Texas' house in Brentwood trying to make it to my early morning classes on time. I don't know what happened to my sleep patterns after I got to college. In high school I had to be at school at seven o'clock and I was up bright and early ready for school. Since I got to college I couldn't get up for an eight o'clock class to save my life. I have two alarms, plus I tell my mom to call and wake me up. My sleep patterns are all jacked up.

I had a busy day ahead. Wren and I had to finish up our senior project presentation and I had plans to meet Texas later for dinner. This would be the first time since Texas got out the hospital that we were going out.

Texas had been acting strange and he had become argumentative. He normally would never argue with me about anything. He didn't call me as often as he used to. At night, we don't cuddle anymore. Instead, he turns his back on me and goes to sleep. We used to always go to sleep holding each other's hands. Now he barely kisses me goodnight.

The pain medication the doctor prescribed him, he has been poppin' like its candy. He acts like he has to have the pills to function. When I asked him about it he told me he was in a lot of pain and that was the reason he was taking so many. And he has been forgetting things. For instance, the other day he locked himself out of the house and he called me to come let him in, but he always kept a spare key hid on the porch. There has been a lot of tension between us. Texas has not been the same. I hope it's just a little phase he's going through. I'm going to talk to him tonight and let him know I'm worried about him, and I think he needs to lay off the pain pills.

I met up with Wren at about five o'clock. I was rushing because I stayed after class for a conference with my organic professor.

Wren and I were grading papers and working on a molecule experiment when Texas called and told me he had made our dinner reservations for seven o'clock. That put me in a bind because I wasn't done with my work study duties. But I desperately wanted to meet

Texas and be on time because I didn't want to upset him. I begged Wren to finish up the molecule experiment and asked him to call me with the results. I had to run home and change clothes because I wanted to look my best when Texas saw me.

I arrived at the restaurant a few minutes late. When I walked inside the restaurant, I saw Texas sitting at one of the tables talking on the phone. I walked around the table and leaned down to give him a hug. He didn't reach his arms up to hug me back, nor did he greet me. I sat down and he shot me a look so nasty it could've burned a hole in me.

"Why in the fuck you late?" he snapped.

Damn, he was already in a foul mood; I took a few deep breaths and tried to remain calm hoping he would eventually chill.

"Baby, I'm sorry. I got stuck in traffic." I sighed, while taking off my jacket.

He looked at his watch. "You wasn't stuck in no muthafuckin' traffic." He turned his attention to the flat panel television that was over the bar. I didn't want to get off on the wrong note; I was going to do everything in my power to keep from arguing, so I bit my tongue and grabbed his hand.

"I miss you, baby." He rolled his eyes and jerked his hand back and grabbed the menu. I put my hands back in my lap and slowly exhaled. "Tex, we need to talk." He didn't acknowledge one word I said. He kept his eyes glued to the television.

"Did you hear me?"

"Well, talk," he snapped.

A churning stirred in the pit of my stomach. I desperately wanted to say the right thing. I wanted to get through to him.

"Baby, I know you're upset about that football injury, but that's the past and you can't change what happened in the past. You walking around being mad at the world ain't gon' solve it, so let's put that terrible accident behind us and move on."

"Look, I'm cool; don't worry about me. You the one with the problem."

"What?" I was shocked by his comment. "How is this about me?"

"Because I told you to be here at seven and here you come waltzing yo' ass up in here thirty minutes later."

"Hold on, Texas. I know you ain't still on that. I told you I was stuck in traffic," I replied softly trying not to cause a scene.

"You wasn't stuck in no traffic. Yo' ass was somewhere fuckin' off."

"What are you talking about?"

"You know what the fuck 'um talkin' about."

"No, I don't know what you're talking about; tell me." He threw me for a loop.

"The nigga you said you was studying with." He spat, he was getting loud and people started to stare.

"Texas, you know, Wren?"

"Nah, I don't know the nigga; I ain't never met him."

"Well, you've heard me talking about him. He's just like my play brother."

"Shut that shit up. You know I don't believe in that play brother bullshit. Every time I hear a bitch talking about a nigga being her play brother, she's either fucked 'em or she still fuckin' 'em. So you can go on with that shit."

"You know what? Fuck it," I said under my breath. I grabbed my purse and my keys. I'd had enough. I wasn't gon' sit there and let him continue to embarrass me. I got up.

"Sit down," he grunted through his teeth.

I sat back down. "I don't know what the deal is with you, but I came here to have a good time." I fumed.

"Man, fuck that." The waitress came and asked if we were ready to order. I hadn't even looked at the menu, because as soon as I sat down Texas started in on me.

"Yea, I'm ready," he told the server.

"Texas, I haven't had time to look at the menu." I grabbed my menu and began to glance through the entrée options.

"You need to pick something. I've been sitting here for thirty minutes waiting on yo' ass."

"Do you have any pasta dishes?" I asked the server.

"Yes, ma'am," replied the server.

"I would like chicken pasta with garlic sauce and a glass of your house red wine." We both sat at the table silent.

I was contemplating apologizing, and then I decided against it because I hadn't done anything. I don't know where Texas' insecurities had come from. He had never been the jealous type. During dinner he rarely looked at me. The entire time he kept his eyes glued to ESPN. I decided to say something to try to spark a conversation.

"So how was your day?" He didn't respond. When our meals came I took a few bites of my pasta dish but my appetite was ruined. I was disturbed because Texas was acting so insensitive.

I noticed my phone vibrating on the table; it was Wren. I didn't want to answer because I didn't want it to cause an argument. So I pushed the ignore button and sent Wren to voicemail.

"Ahhh, you didn't wanna answer in front of me. What the fuck you tryin' to hide?"

"I'm not hiding anything. Wren was probably calling about the results of our experiment, but I'ma call him back later." No sooner than I said that, my phone was buzzing again. It was Wren.

"Answer the phone," Texas seethed.

"Baby, it's not that serious, I'll call Wren back."

"Answer the goddamn phone," he screamed. He reached to pick up the phone. He saw Wren's name flashing on the screen. Wham! He pitched the phone smack dab at the rim of my nose. My nose stung with pain. I grabbed my nose as blood sprouted out like a water fountain. He knocked everything off the table. Food, plates and glasses went crashing to the floor. A quiet hush filled the room. I could feel my nose swelling; blood filled up my hand and trickled onto my clothes. I was covered in Alfredo sauce and red wine.

"When I tell you to do somethin', do it goddamit!" His voice echoed off the walls and his nostrils flared like a raging bull. "Do you understand me?" I gently nodded my head as tears blurred my eyes. He pulled two one hundred dollar bills out and slammed them on the table. I was in total shock. The weight of stares laid heavily on me as I tried to make sense of what had just occurred. With my head low, I grabbed my handbag and slowly preceded to the exit. As I approached the door, an older white lady, probably in her mid-sixties, approached me.

"Sweetheart, are you okay?"

"Yes, ma'am." My voice trembled as tears streamed down my face.

She touched my shoulder. "Sweetheart, leave now… it's not worth it."

I rolled my eyes so hard at her, I didn't ask for her advice. She doesn't understand. I'm engaged to Texas Reynolds, NFL superstar wide receiver for the Tennessee Tyrants. My baby is stressed; he's having some problems right now. At least that's what I kept telling myself. I should've been on time. It's my fault he got angry.

I walked out the door and got into my truck. I sat there for two hours trying to make sense of what had just occurred. I was so upset. I made an excuse for everything that Texas had done. Even though he was dead wrong, I somehow found a way to blame myself for his faults. I was determined from that day forward to do everything I could to keep him happy. I didn't want to lose what I had. Texas was the best thing that ever happened to me and I know that he loves me.

On the drive home, I thought about what had happened. I don't know what had set him off, but he just wasn't the same. Everything about him was different. Starting with the way he looked at me. When he used to look at me, it would ignite a fire in my soul, but it's not like that anymore. I'm losing him and I don't know what to do.

I went back on campus, and cleaned myself up. A hump had formed in the center of my nose from where he hit me. I made an icepack and sat it on my nose to try to ease the swelling. My entire face had swollen up. My eyes were puffy and my nose was swollen I looked like the man from that movie "The Mask." I took two Tylenol PMs and cried myself to sleep. I was awakened around ten-thirty by my roommate knocking on the door. I crawled to the end of my bed and opened the door.

"Rae, you have company," she said.

"What?" Texas walked from behind the wall. I leaned my head against the headboard and he walked into my room.

When he walked in I turned my head because I was too embarrassed to look at him.

He sat on the edge of the bed. "Baby, let me see." He tried to turn my face toward him but I wouldn't turn around. He finally grabbed my chin and turned my face to him. "Oh, baby," he gasped. "I'm so sorry." He wrapped his arms around me, "Baby, I'm sorry, baby." I leaned on his chest and cried in his arms.

"Texas, why did you do it?"

"Raechel, I promise I didn't mean to hit you with that phone. It was an accident, I swear, baby... it was an accident. I promise it won't happen again.".

I believed him. He had never raised his hands towards me. But that still didn't justify why he got mad and shot off.

"But what about the other stuff you did. Why you get so upset about Wren calling me?" I sniffed and wiped tears from my eyes.

"Baby, I don't know what came over me. It's just I got mad when you didn't answer the phone. I thought you was trying to hide something."

"You know Wren is my study partner and friend, and yet you made assumptions that we were sleeping together or that we may have slept together in the past, which is total bull. I don't even look at Wren like that nor am I remotely attracted to him in any way," I sighed while sitting and leaning back on the headboard. "Besides, I'm in love with you. I don't even think about another man."

"Raechel, I'm sorry. It's just that I love you so much and sometimes I let my emotions take control of me." His words seemed so sincere that I couldn't help but forgive him.

He laid his head on my stomach and grabbed me around my waist. He placed gentle kisses between my thighs.

"Texas, no." I pushed him off me.

"Why not?" he said while still trying to pull up my skirt.

"We agreed we would wait to have sex."

"Man, come on, baby. You've already broken your promise." He pulled my thong off and devoured my sweetness while caressing my breasts; I came instantly. Then I climbed on top of him and rode him until I came again. I got up and took a shower. After we had sex, I started to become consumed with feelings of guilt and shame. But this time I felt worse and couldn't understand why. When I got out the shower, I looked at myself in the mirror, trying to understand the feelings I was having. I climbed back into bed and laid on top of Texas. He kissed me on my forehead.

I lifted my head up and looked him in the face. Texas was so handsome. It was so hard for me to stay mad at him. I noticed a scar over his right eyebrow.

"Where did that scar come from?"

"What scar?" he asked touching his face.

"Right over your eyebrow." I placed my finger on the scar.

"Oh, that. I got it when I was a kid. I fell off a skateboard."

"Uhm, I never noticed it." I rubbed his chest. "I notice something different about you every day." I kissed him on his lips.

"Baby, I'm really sorry. I promise it won't happen again."

I laid my head down on his chest, and within minutes he had fallen to sleep. But I couldn't sleep. I remained awake, wondering why I was feeling so guilty.

Chapter 19

Since the incident in the restaurant, Texas had been treating me like a princess. We drove to Memphis for the weekend so he could finally meet my mother. When she met him, they seemed to hit it off well. The three of us went to dinner and then we went by my grandparents' house so that I could introduce them to Texas.

♣

Texas and I made it back to Nashville Sunday afternoon. I was anxious to call my mother to get her real opinion of Texas.

"Hey, Mom; I'm home."

"Aw, y'all made it back already?" My mom always insists that I call her as soon as I get off the road to make sure I made it safely.

"Yeah, Momma, it's only a three-hour drive."

"Where are you?" she asked.

"I'm over Texas' house." My mother wasn't as talkative as she normally is. "So, what did you think about Texas?"

She hesitated. "He seems okay."

I could hear some apprehension in her voice so I walked outside just in case Texas was eaves dropping.

"That's all…he's okay?" I asked.

"I mean, he seems nice but I just don't think he's the man God has chosen to be your husband." Her response totally took me by surprise.

"But, Momma, we're engaged."

"Raechel, it's just something about that boy I didn't like."

"What chu' mean?" I asked.

"I don't know. It was something about his eyes, and his demeanor that just didn't sit well with me. Rae, I'm sorry but I just didn't like him."

"Momma, how can you say that? Texas is good to me, he comes from a good family, he has good morals and—"

She cut me off in mid-sentence. "Raechel, I still didn't like him."

I mean how could she say that? Texas was the best thing that ever happened to me. I quickly got off the phone with her because she was starting to piss me off.

"Well, that's too bad because he is going to be your son-in-law."

I slammed down the phone. I thought about the visit Texas and I made to Memphis. I tried to think of what could have possibly happened for her to say that she didn't like him. I couldn't think of anything. I thought just the opposite, that he and my mother hit it off.

♣

I woke up the following morning with the things my momma said about Texas weighing heavily on me. I had hung up the phone in her face, and I felt bad. I tried to call her to apologize but she didn't answer the phone, so I left a message on her voicemail. I resented what she had said about Texas but it was hard for me to ignore her words because nine times out of ten my mother is always right. I just hope she's wrong this time.

I looked around the house; Texas was gone. I called him and he answered on the first ring.

"Hey, baby." I purred. "Where are you?"

"I left early; I had a few errands to run. Everything okay?" he asked.

"Yea, I was just worried when I woke up and didn't see you. You never leave without giving me a kiss."

"I'm sorry. I didn't wanna to wake you," he said.

"Okay, well I'm getting ready for class, so I'll call you later." We hung up and I got dressed. It was nippy outside so I dressed in jeans and my Kenneth Cole thigh-high boots. I had a long day ahead of me with classes back to back.

I was done with all my classes at three o'clock. I looked at my phone. I had eight missed calls, and they all were from Texas. I became worried. I hoped he was okay. I immediately called him back.

"Hello," he answered.

"Hey, baby." I was relieved when I heard his voice.

"Rae, why haven't you answered the damn phone?" he screamed.

"Texas, I'm sorry. I've been in class all day. Is everything okay?" I asked frantically.

"Hell, 'nah," he shouted.

"What's the matter?" I asked worriedly.

"Nothin' now. You musta been hanging with yo' homeboy, Wren, again?"

"Texas, what are you talking about?"

"Listen, when I call you answer the fuckin' phone," he yelled in my ear so loud I had to pull my cell phone away from my ear.

"Texas, you know I have classes all day on Friday. I can't answer while I'm in class."

Click.

"Hello...hello." I looked at the phone. The call had ended; he had hung the phone up in my face. I called him back several times but his phone went straight to voicemail. I drove to his house and got ready for work but he wasn't there. I continued calling to the point where his voicemail was not allowing any more messages. Nothing pissed me off more than when somebody hangs up the phone in my face. For a moment, I imagined how my mother felt when I hung up on her. Finally, I said to myself, "Forget it." I stopped calling and went to work. I tried to ease my mind of the fact he hadn't answered the phone.

♣

My shift ended and I still hadn't heard from Texas. I was on my way home when Cece called.

"Hey, girl, what's up?" I answered.

"Girl, nothin, chillin. C'mon, bitch, let's get out."

"Get out and do what?"

"I don't know. Let's go get on some drinks, maybe we can go downtown. It's whatever, I just need to get out."

"Aiight cool, but you gotta come get me."

I was tired and my feet hurt, but I did want to go out and relieve some stress.

"I'll come get you."

"Okay, that's what's up. I'm on my way home. Give me time to shower and change."

"Cool, I'll call you when I'm outside."

I love hanging out with Cece; she cool as hell. She isn't one of those friends that was all in your business, and she keeps her comments and opinions to herself, unless you ask her.

I went to my apartment and showered. After I got out the shower I noticed I had a missed called from Texas, but I didn't call him back. I was not about to argue with him. I made plans to go out with Cece and get my mind off the conversation with my mom and everything else that had been going on in my life. I put on a sexy Michael Kors wrap around dress that went up in around my neck, and tied in the back. I was putting on my makeup when Cece called.

"Hey, girl."

"Chick, I'm finishing up my make-up and I'll be ready," I told her.

"Well, I'm outside. I see your man walking up to your apartment," she told me.

"What…are you serious?"

"As a heart attack," she replied.

I walked to the door and as soon as I opened it, Texas was standing in the doorway.

"Why haven't you answered the phone?"

"Look," I said mildly. "I've called you several times and you didn't answer, and let's not forget, you're the one who hung up in my face," I snapped. As I was talking to him I was looking around for my keys because I was about to bounce. I was not going to let Texas, or anyone for that matter, ruin my evening. He walked to where I was standing near the kitchen table. He sat down and pulled me in between his legs.

"Listen, I got mad when you didn't answer yo' phone. You know I don't like that," he commented.

A light sigh escaped me. "Texas, I called you back when I could."

"I know, baby. I was being an asshole." He wrapped his arms around my waist and leaned his head on my stomach. "You forgive me?"

"Yea, I guess so." I rubbed his head. Then I gathered my purse and jacket and started walking towards the door.

"Hold up, where you going?"

"Me and Cece fixin' to go have a few drinks."

He grabbed my arm and pushed me against the door. "I don't want you to go nowhere," he whispered and caressed my breasts. They hardened as he massaged them through my silk dress. He stroked his hands up and down my body as he planted soft, subtle kisses on my neck.

"C'mon, let's go in the room," he spoke softly. He was making me so wet. My mind kept telling me, no, but my body was telling me, yes. I was getting wrapped up in the moment until I heard Cece blowing the horn.

"No, baby, I gotta go. Cece is waiting on me."

In that instant his whole demeanor changed and I realized he was the type of person who always gotta be in control. He rubbed his hand under my skirt and felt my lace thongs.

"What's this shit you got on?"

"Baby, these my panties," I replied but I was confused by his question.

"These ain't no goddamn panties, bitch; these thongs." He pulled the side of my thongs up and twisted it around his hand. He pulled them so tight they started cutting into my coochie.

I pushed his hand out the way.

"Then you got this tight ass dress on wit' ya' titties and shit hangin' all out. You must wanna get out so you can show ya' ass to some nigga!"

What? I know this nigga ain't trippin.' He had pissed me off. I tried to move his hand from under my dress. He clutched my ass and palmed it so tight he left a bruise. I tried to squirm out of his arms, but he had me pinned to the wall and I couldn't move.

"C'mon, Texas, stop. I have to go," I said, moving his hand trying to get him off me.

His sturdy arms gripped me with more vigor. "Come on, gimme this pussy." He forcefully pulled up my dress and continued to knead my ass like it was pizza dough.

"No, Texas." I pushed him off of me. His body didn't bulge but he took his hands off me. "I told you, I have to go. Cecily is waiting on me!" I turned and walked toward the door.

"Aye, get yo' ass back here!" he yelled.

"What?" I snapped.

"I said, you ain't going nowhere. Get yo' ass back here!" He grabbed my arm.

I yanked my arm away. "Bye!" I shouted, and slammed the door in his face. *He got me fucked up.* I walked down the stairs and straightened my dress. I heard him coming down the stairs behind me but I didn't turn around. As I was walking to the car I heard him yell.

"Rae, you better come back here."

I kept on stepping, pretending not to hear him. Suddenly I felt a tug on my dress. I turned around and he was pulling on my dress.

"Texas, stop it!" I struggled to get away from him but he jerked really hard on my dress and slung me down. I heard my dress tear. As I was lying on the ground he viciously pulled and tugged on my dress until it came clean up off of me. A mantle of embarrassment and shock fell upon me. I was lying in the parking lot of the Ford Complex in a pair of red thongs and no bra. I was speechless.

"Bitch, I told you that you ain't going no fuckin' where! Gimme them gatdamn keys," he spat angrily while standing over me with balled up fists.

Fear closed in on me. I held my breath and covered my face because I was sure he was about to hit me. He put his hand down when he noticed people standing around staring.

He snatched my purse out my hand and emptied all the contents onto the pavement. I scrambled through the contents of my purse and quickly handed him the keys. The thought entered my mind to throw them but I quickly rejected it because I didn't want him to hit me. There was no telling what else he might do.

"Hoe, fuck you! The next time I tell you to come here, bring yo' mutherfuckin' ass here... you hear me!" he screamed. "You just wanna get out with them hoes so you can fuck around." He ranted like a mad man.

He got in his car and sped out the drive way. Cece jumped out of her car and helped me gather everything that had spilled out my purse. I slowly got up and wrapped the shrivels of my torn dress around my waist. I picked my jacket up and put it on.

"Are you okay?" Cece asked.

I was speechless. Tears rolled down my face like rain. Cece helped me up the stairs.

"Rae, are you going to press charges on him?"

I looked at her, shocked she would even say something like that. "Girl, no; for what?"

She shot me a surprised expression. "Rae, are you serious? That nigga just humiliated you in front of everybody, pushed you down, stripped your ass naked, and you're not gonna press charges, girl?"

"No, girl, I'm cool," I mumbled as I hobbled up the stairs.

"Girl, I'm fixin' to call the police."

"No, Cece... don't," I begged.

"Rae, I'm not trying to get in your business but you need to leave that nigga alone."

"Nah, girl," I said sadly. "It's my fault. I shouldn't have worn that dress. Plus, I think he was high. When he be on them pills it make him aggressive like that. He didn't mean nothing by that. He was just mad 'cause I didn't answer the phone. And I didn't make the situation no better when I told him we was going out."

I walked to my room and put on my robe.

Cece followed behind me. "Pills? What type of pills? The nigga poppin' pills, you really need to leave him. You know how them pills be fucking with people minds. Just because you didn't answer the phone that still don't give him a reason to act like that, pulling off your dress and causing a scene. And you know how these State people gossip."

I laid back on the bed because what did she know, she wasn't in my shoes. Everything she was saying was going in one ear and coming out the other. Texas is having some problems right now and that's why he was acting like that. I just have to figure out a way to make things better, because I love him so much.

"Girl, I'm straight." I said that to give her the hint that I needed to be alone.

"Well, chick, I'm fixin' to go. Is it anything else you need?"

"No, I just need to be by myself right now."

"Okay, bye." She gave me a hug. Before letting me go she said, "Girl, you need to think about what I said."

Chapter 20

The next morning was Saturday; I was still in shock about what had happened the previous night. I had laid in my bed all night replaying the events over in my head. I was so disturbed about me and Texas' relationship. It was spiraling out of control right before my eyes, and there was nothing I could do about it. I had started to question our love.

Maybe my momma was right, maybe Texas wasn't the man I was supposed to spend the rest of my life with. The violent, temperamental side he had been showing me I couldn't deal with. The way he had acted the previous night was scary. I felt like Tina Turner at the mercy of Ike. I'm not trying to live a life like that. I wanna give him the benefit of the doubt, that those pills are causing the dramatic change in his behavior. He hasn't been on them for long. I'm going to talk to him about not taking them anymore. And if he says he can't stop, we'll try to get him into a rehab. I picked up the phone to call him but when I looked at the screen he was already calling me.

"Hey, baby, we need to talk," Texas said.

"About what?"

"About everything." He paused. "Let me take you to lunch."

"Texas, you humiliated me last night."

He sighed into the phone. "Raechel, I know, and I'm so sorry. Let me make it up to you." I gave in to his pleas and agreed to have lunch with him.

When he came and picked me up, I asked, "Where are we going?"

"It's a surprise." He took me to a boutique on West End called *615*. When we walked in the store, Texas went and sat down in one of the comfy chairs strategically placed throughout the boutique. "Baby, get whatever you want," he told me.

"How much can I spend?"

"We can buy the entire store if that's what you want."

I picked up everything I could get my hands on. I got me two pairs of Citizen of Humanity jeans, four badass Cavalli dresses, five pair of Gucci shoes, and a slew of little designer shirts, skirts, and accessories.

The store was crowded because that night was the Mary J. Blige concert and chicks were trying to find them a hot outfit.

All eyes were glued on me and Texas. Chicks were looking at Texas trying to get his attention but he wasn't giving them any eye contact. That was one of the things that I liked about him; he was always into me. And when we stepped, out we were like Will and Jada because we were truly a good-looking couple. After I got my share of outfits, Texas and I left and went to lunch at Southstreet.

"Texas, thank you for taking me shopping, baby."

"Anything for my princess." He grabbed my hand from across the table. "Raechel, I'm sorry about last night. I've been under a lot of stress lately with me blowing the season, and this medicine they got me on got me trippin'. I can't think straight, and I can't remember a damn thing," he said in such a forgiving tone.

"Baby, that's what I wanna talk to you about. Texas, how often are you taking them painkillers?"

He was silent. "Every day."

"How often?" I asked again, staring into his eyes trying to pick up on if he was lying.

"Just a couple times a day. Raechel, baby, I be in pain. I have to take these pills. You don't understand."

"I know. But, baby, them pills got you acting crazy as hell. I mean do you even remember what you did last night?"

"No, I don't."

"Texas, you stripped me naked in front of the Ford Complex. I was humiliated."

"What? Rae, I'm so sorry. All I remember is bits and pieces of the night. I don't even remember doing that shit. All I remember is when we was inside of the apartment."

"You don't remember calling me outta my name, calling me bitches and hoes in front of my apartment?"

"Nah, I don't."

"Well, you did and that's why you gotta let them pills go."

"Yeah, you right, I'm not taking them again."

I placed my other hand on top of his. "Texas, you didn't blow the season, baby. You busted your ass for that team this year and you did a hell of a job. Why do you think they're increasing your contract? I'll tell you why; it's because they don't want to let you go. You're just going through a little storm. It will be over soon," I told him as I lightly kneaded his hands. "Baby, maybe you need to tell the doctor that you've been having side effects from the medicine."

"Yeah, I will." He yawned.

"Come on, let's go. You look tired."

"Yeah, I am. I couldn't sleep last night for thinking about your ass."

I gave him a little smile and we left the restaurant.

♣

Cece called. "What's up, girl? Listen, I got tickets to the Mary J. Blige concert."

"Oooh, I wanna go," I squealed.

"Chick, why do you think I called you?"

"How did you get tickets? That concert sold out the first week."

"Girl, Cali gave them to me. You know he the one bringing Mary to Nashville."

"Ah, forreal?" I said with excitement.

"Wait, Rae, here's the killer," Cece paused. "He got us a limo, and he got us some VIP passes so we can meet Mary."

"Girl, you are lyin'? You mean we gon' meet Mary J. Blige?"

"Yes, girl!"

"Broad, hold up. Did he just get you a VIP pass or did he get passes for all of us?"

"Didn't you hear me? He got us four VIP passes. I got the passes in my hand right now."

"Ahhhh," I screamed. "Girl, I can't believe I'ma meet the legendary Mary J. Girl, that Cali nigga put it down. Broad, you need to gon' get with him."

She got quiet. "Girl, you know I can't leave Daddy Rich. I mean, Cali cool and all, but Daddy Rich got my heart."

At that point, I changed the subject because I know how it is when somebody has your heart. Even though they may be the scum of the earth, but if you're in love with them then it ain't nothing you can do about it. But that Cali is a top of the line dude. He fine, swagged up, plus he got that paper, and he ain't got a million shorties running around Nashville.

"I told everybody to be ready by six o'clock cause we gon' have dinner at the *Palm* first then we'll head on over to the concert."

"Alright, girl, I'll be ready."

I love me some Mary J Blige. She just don't know how many times I have put on her album when I was going through some bullshit with a nigga, and how she has gotten me through. I prefer the old Mary. Now the new Mary is the bomb, but that old Mary when she was going through, those are the classics.

♣

When I came out my apartment and climbed in the limo, the purple haze immediately tickled my nose as I situated myself in my seat. Cece and Sau were sippin' on Grey Goose and cranberry and taking shots of Patron.

"What up, biatches?" I squealed, hyped and excited about our evening.

"What's up, foxy?" Mimi responded as she took a long pull from the blunt in her hand.

I looked at everybody's outfit. We were all fly as hell. I knew we would be the baddest bitches up in the concert. One thing I love about my crew is all of us are cute and have a good sense of style. Whenever we hang out together you had better bring your A game or else you'd be the one falling off, because my entire crew is five star chicks.

"Damn, y'all look good," I commented.

Sasha said, "Chick, you do too."

I looked at Cece's Chloe canvas handbag. "Cece, I like your purse."

"Yeah, courtesy of my little friend."

My little friend usually meant a guy that she was dating that felt like sponsoring a broad, and didn't have any spending limits on his pockets.

"Sau, gon', diva. Are those Louboutins?" I commented on Sasha's shoes.

"Nah, these Gucci?"

"That's what up."

"Well, girl, you know how I do it." She giggled and we high-fived.

Sasha is a label whore. If it ain't designer, she won't be caught dead in it. She doesn't brag on her shit but if you got out of line and tried to insinuate she was in bootleg, she wouldn't hesitate to let you know how much her shit cost, where it came from, and who bought it…. don't play. Her and Cece are always competing on who has the latest Gucci bag or the latest shoes. Sasha's parents keep her laced, and niggas keep Cece tight. It used to be a time Sasha would always have on the baddest gear. Not anymore, because Cece done stepped her game up and got niggas lacing her too. She can roll neck and neck with Sasha in the latest designer wear and fashions. And I'm right behind them, because ever since Texas Reynolds has been on my team, he has moved me straight up outta Express and Macy's into high end boutiques and signature stores like Bottega Veneta, Prada, and Kate Spade. Now Mimi, she don't half step either. Her gear ain't just top of the line, but what sets her apart is her face. Mimi's face is so unique that if you see her, you'll definitely look at her twice because her beauty is so striking. We arrived at the concert; it was jam packed. Nash Vegas was out in full effect. Texas called just as we were about to pull up at the concert.

I answered. "What's up, baby?"

"Hey. What are you doing? I've been sleep," he said in a groggy tone.

"I'm out."

"Where you at?"

"I'm at the Mary J. Blige Concert."

"What concert? You didn't tell me you were going to a mutherfuckin' concert."

I hesitated. I couldn't believe his tone. "I know. I didn't find out until tonight. Cece won a pair of tickets on the radio," I lied. I didn't want him knowing a dude gave us the tickets. That would have sent him through the roof.

"Mmm-hmm," he murmured in an unexcited tone. "What chu' doing after the concert?"

"I'ma probably go to the after party at Blu Diamond." There was a pregnant pause. "Hello?"

Click! He hung the phone up. I didn't bother calling him back. I was with my girls. I didn't want them to see me calling back and arguing with him on the phone. Plus, I didn't need them in my business. I'm sure Cece had told them about the incident at my apartment.

The concert was off the chain. Mary J. sang all of her old hits as well as a lot of songs from her new CD. We had a blast. After the concert, we met Mary J. She was so cool and down to earth. I don't usually do autographs but I was straight jocking her. I had brought "My Life" CD and asked her to sign it. The girls each bought a CD and got her to autograph theirs as well, and she took some pictures with us. We walked back to the limo. We had hooked up with Wren and some of our other homies from school that we saw at the show. We were all standing outside the Municipal Auditorium, joking, laughing, and cracking on people as they left when Texas called me again.

"Hello, what's up?"

"Hey, baby what are you doing now?" His demeanor had totally changed from earlier. Lately he had been having such extreme mood swings. One minute he would be all calm and sweet and the next he would become a raging bull.

"Nothing, just chilling," I said in a dry tone. I was still pissed because he had hung the phone up in my face earlier.

"Who them niggas I hear talking in the background?"

"Oh, they're some friends of ours from school."

"Which one is tryin' to holla at you?"

"Neither one of them. We just met up with them after the concert. Where are you?"

"Looking dead at your ass." My eyes skated across the parking lot. I looked across the street and spotted his truck. My heart dropped. I prayed that he wasn't about to start no shit.

"Were you at the concert?" I asked.

"Nah, I came to get you."

"Texas, I'm going to the after party. I told you that." A wave of anxiety struck me. I was highly pissed now, but I tried not to let it come across in my voice, because I didn't want to argue.

"You must want to go so you can fuck off."

"Here you go with that again, Texas. I thought we talked about this earlier. You know how much I love you. You know I ain't cheating. Baby, you are who I'm with, we're going to get married. Remember?"

"Then come get in the car and let's go home."

"No. I've already told the girls I was going to the after party."

"Aiight. I see the shit you on, take ya' hot ass on. But when you done, bring me all that shit I bought today. And get one of them broke muthafuckas to take ya' ass on shopping sprees and trips to Hawaii." He hung up in my face again. I didn't understand where that comment came from. My phone rang again and of course it was him calling back.

"Yeah," I answered in an irritated tone.

"Baby, I'm sorry for hanging up in your face. I'm just trippin," he said in a mild, sweet voice.

"Texas, I don't know what is wrong with you but if you hang up in my face again, don't worry about calling me back."

"Raechel, come and talk to me for a second."

"We're talking right now." I spat irritably.

"Please…come sit in the car for a few minutes," he pleaded. "I just wanna talk."

"Okay, but only for a few minutes because we're about to leave." I walked over to his Range Rover, opened the door and got in. The smell of alcohol flooded the air in the vehicle. His eyes were bloodshot; I could tell he was drunk and high.

"What's this li'l skimpy ass shit you got on?" he barked.

I rolled my eyes. "This is one of the outfits you bought me today. If you didn't like it, why did you buy it?"

"Shut up." He pushed me upside the head almost snapping my neck. "I didn't buy that shit for you to wear out wit' no other nigga."

"Fuck you," I screamed. "Don't put yo' hands on me no more!" I grabbed the door handle. He was about to start some shit, and tonight I wasn't up for it. But before I could get out the car he locked the doors, put the truck in gear and sped off the parking lot almost running over two people.

"Texas, stop the car," I insisted. He didn't respond. He got on I-65 South and accelerated to one hundred and twenty miles per hour. My heart pounded wildly. *Oh, my God!* I held onto the door handle to brace myself.

"Texas, please stop the car," I cried. He didn't acknowledge my pleas. My stomach did somersaults as he dodged in and out of traffic, riding on people's bumpers. I prayed that we would be seen by the police but there wasn't a cop in sight. We came to a four-way stop and he drove straight through it. We went around a winding road and he accelerated even faster, driving on both sides of the road. We ended up at Percy Priest Lake. He was driving so fast; he was headed directly into the lake.

"Stoooooop," I screamed and closed my eyes.

"We 'bout to die!" He laughed wickedly.

"Aaaaaaahhh," I screamed. My life flashed before me.

He slammed on the brakes right before we reached the embankment of the lake. My heart was thumping so fast I lost all sense of my bodily functions. I was so scared I had peed on myself. Terror immobilized my breaths. I sat motionless in a state of shock. Sweat rolled from my armpits down my side. I felt the heaviness of his gaze on the side of my face. I gradually turned to look at him. An evil smirk adorned his face.

"I told you I wanted to talk," he barred through his teeth.

I swallowed hard. "O..oo..kay." My voice quivered. I tried to conceal my fear and pretend like everything was normal, but I knew deep down this nigga was crazy as a Betsy Bug.

"I love you, Raechel." I was quiet as a church mouse; my pulse was pumping like a freight train. He began to talk to himself.

"Stop it, stop it," he screamed. "Shut up, nigga," he shouted. He frantically moved his hands over his face and head, like he was trying to clear his thoughts. He repeatedly blinked his eyes and then he began to mumble to himself. His words were jumbled and inaudible. I wanted desperately to get out and run but I knew he would catch me. Besides, it was pitch-black and there wasn't a soul in sight.

"Get out the car," he said quietly. I was too terrified to move. "Get out of the car," he commanded in a threatening tone.

"Texas, I'm not about to get out. Please take me home," I pleaded. I pulled out my cell phone and dialed Sasha's phone number.

"Gimme that mutherfuckin' phone!" I refused and we began to tussle over the phone. He easily pried the phone from my hands and threw it out the window into the lake.

"What is wrong with you?" I cried.

"Get out, since you wanna go fuck off, maybe you can suck some nigga dick for a ride!"

"Texas, I'm not getting out."

"Bitch, get out my fuckin' truck," he screamed. I refused. He got out the truck, ran to my side, and opened the door.

"Please, Texas….Noooo," I screamed. He pulled me out the truck, dragging me into the gravel.

"Bitch, I said get the fuck out." He got in the truck, and drove off blowing dust and smoke in my face. I was sprawled out on the cold gravel. My knees and legs were scuffed up. I slowly rose to my feet and dusted off my legs and clothes. I couldn't believe that he had left me in the middle of nowhere. My legs were shivering from the cold, and from the wetness of when I had peed on myself. I started walking. With each step I made; the heel of my stilettos sank into the loose gravel of the embankment. My warm tears turned cold as they dried on my face. I was headed in the direction of the highway, when I heard his truck pull back around. He pulled up on the side of me and rolled down the window.

"Raaa-chel, you've been a bad monkey, haven't you?" I kept walking, not looking in his direction while he drove slowly beside me.

"Say it," he barked. I slowed my pace.

"Say what?"

"Say that you have been a bad monkey."

"Fuck you, I'm not saying shit."

He jumped out of the truck, wrapped his hand round my neck, and slammed me against the side of the truck knocking the wind out of me. He put his body so close to mine. His breath reeked of alcohol.

"Now, hoe, say it!" he barred through his teeth.

"I've been a bad monkey," I softly whispered.

"Say it louder," he ordered and tighten his grip around my neck.

"I've been a bad monkey." I squeezed out of my crushed vocal cords.

"Louder," he screamed.

"I've been a bad monkey," I yelled as tears streamed down my cheeks. He finally unleashed his grip I fell to the ground coughing and gagging.

"Get in!"

I was hesitant to get in, but I was afraid to defy any of his commands. I wanted to walk off but I prayed that if God got me home safe and sound that would be the last time I saw Texas Reynolds. I opened the door to get in and he pulled off slowly. He looked at me with a wicked grin. I attempted to get in again and he pulled up again and started laughing hysterically. After doing this several times, he finally allowed me to get in the truck. I was freezing cold and he rolled down the windows, and turned up the music as loud as it could go while speeding down I-65.

I sat silently, praying that I made it back to campus safely as the wind beat the side of my face. When he got off the interstate near campus a sigh of relief came upon me. He parked in front of the campus apartments and gave me a guiltless look as if nothing had happened. I unbuckled my seat belt to get out the vehicle. Then he grabbed my hand, my heart stopped.

"Rae, you ain't gon' give me a kiss?"

I slowly leaned over and gave him a peck on the lips. He grabbed me by the back of my head and forced his tongue in my mouth. *Ugh.* I played along until I got out the car. I got out the car and told him, "Texas, don't ever call me again."

I ran, as fast I could. He saw the campus police so he didn't try to chase me. I got to my apartment and broke down. I didn't understand what had happened to my Texas, but I knew after tonight, it was over.

Chapter 21

I haven't spoken with Texas in two weeks. He has tried to contact me, but I will not answer any of his calls. After I broke up with him, I sank into a deep depression.

I miss him so much, but I can't be with someone that is mentally unstable. I keep trying to convince myself that the coma is what caused the paranoia. Something got shook up in his head and that's the reason he's been acting so crazy. Texas would never treat me the way he has been treating me if he was in his right mind. Before that football accident, Texas would always treat me like a queen. I'm so confused. Maybe it's the pills, but the Texas I fell in love with is not the same person and it's tearing me apart.

I remember before the accident he had started having outlandish nightmares, and he complained about headaches. But his behavior was never irrational. I don't know what it is but I keep feeling that something bad is going to happen to him.

I didn't have anyone to talk to. I couldn't talk to Sau, Cece, or Mimi. They were done with Texas. After that incident at the concert, they had deemed Texas crazy as hell. They demanded that I leave him alone. They didn't know all of the details of that night, but they knew it wasn't good. The way he balled out of the parking lot almost hitting two people scared them to death. They stayed outside of the concert for nearly two hours waiting for me to return. I didn't blame them. I would have probably felt the same way if a guy had taken off with one of them.

One thing about our friendship, we try to help each other out with relationship issues. We don't necessarily tell each other what to do, but we try to give the soundest advice as possible and we are honest with each other. I could appreciate that. I have other girlfriends that will be going through pure hell with a nigga but they would make it seem as if they were having the best time of their life, all the while living pure hell. That shit never worked for me. I sometimes need to talk to access the situation and get things straightened out. Maybe picking up the phone to dial one of them wasn't so bad after all.

I called Sasha. There was music blasting in the back ground. "Hey, chick, where are you?"

"On my way to meet Cecily."

"Where y'all goin?"

"Fridays, for a few drinks. Wanna come?"

"Yea...I guess so. I ain't got shit else to do."

"Rae, you got to promise one thing. You can't come around with that crying and looking all crazy."

"Okay." I laughed. I knew it would be hard to mask my emotions inside but I was so tired of sitting in the house.

I had thrown myself into studying for the MCAT, the medical school entrance exam. I had picked up extra shifts at Andrew's Crab to buy me a car. Since Texas and I had broken up, I didn't get a chance to get the car he promised me. And I had spent part of the money I had saved. I would either drive Wren's car or catch a ride to work with Tangerine.

We arrived at the restaurant. I didn't have an appetite. I had already lost seven pounds but I forced myself to eat because I knew I would be drinking. Cece and Sasha were having small talk, laughing, and enjoying each other's company. My mind kept going back to Texas' face. I couldn't help it; my eyes watered. They finally stopped chattering and they both looked at me. Cece wrapped her arm around me and comforted me. I laid my head on her shoulder and cried so hard I stopped breathing for a second. You know that cry you would get when your momma would pop you in the back as hard as she could when you were being bad and it was hard to catch your breath, that's how I cried. Good thing we were in the back of the restaurant where no one could see the spectacle I was creating.

Sasha looked at me. She was less comforting. Sasha is that friend that didn't want to see you down. She didn't believe in feeling sorry for yourself or taking too much time getting over a relationship that wasn't worth it. But she did understand my pain this time and grabbed my hand.

"Rae, it's going to be okay; calm down. There are plenty of good men out there."

"No, it's not, Sasha. Stop lying. Black men are fucked up, and I'm tired of their shit!" A glob of snot ran down my nose. I blew my nose and wiped my eyes. "It's either a nigga is crazy, got self-esteem issues, two or three kids, married but cheating, or they have some type of sexual issue. Whether it's they're gay or addicted to porn; they are just all fucked up."

"Listen, Rae, I refuse to let you sit here and bash black men. That's bullshit." She looked at me with a stern look. "Now I'm sorry things didn't work out with you and Texas, but that's life. This is not the first time your heart has been broken and it won't be the last. Black women are one of the main contributing factors as to why black men behave the way they do. We allow these niggas to treat us any kind of way. We believe muthafuckas are too good for us. Niggas fuck up, cheat, beat us, and what do our ignorant asses do? Take them back. How in the hell do you expect for a man to treat you with any respect and he has just disrespected you, and you are totally aware of the disrespect. Then just because he apologizes, agrees to sex you up or flaunt you with gifts, we think it's all good. That's bull. Black women have made it too easy for men. We fuck on the first night, move in and shack with niggas, but then we want a ring. Why the hell buy the cow if the milk is free? Chick, you betta wipe your face. It's plenty of good, black men out here. You have to just find the one that's right for you. When a relationship doesn't work out, take the lessons from the relationship—the good and the bad. But whatever you do, don't let that nigga keep you down for long because life is too short. Before you know it, you'll be forty, single, with no kids, and never been married. I'm not trying to be like that."

"Yea, you're right. It's just hard."

"I know it is," Sasha agreed. "Yeah, I'm just glad it's you this time and not me. Hell, my heart is getting broke every other month." They laughed and gave each other high-fives. "Chick, that heartbreak shit is for the birds."

Cece gave me a wary stare. "Rae, are you in love, I mean really in love with Texas or is it just his money and fame?"

I didn't respond, because deep inside I knew words could not describe how I felt about Texas Reynolds. I played if off and pretended like I was pondering over the question she asked.

Sasha took me back to my apartment. We sat in the car for a moment. She looked at me. "Rae, I wasn't trying to be hard on you. I just don't want you to be sad and I definitely don't want you to give up on love."

"Yeah, I know it's just so hard because I never got any closure. Texas' behavior went from normal to fanatical in a matter of weeks."

"Sasha, I love Texas." We were both silent for a moment; she looked at me.

"Rae, I know. I can see it in your eyes."

"Sau, I feel so sorry for him." I exhaled. "I have never believed in leaving someone when they're down. What type of human would I be? It's just not in me. Yeah, it's been good, all good but, Sau, you know I'm not the type that's all about money, fame, and fortune. Yeah, that shit played a part, but it doesn't define the whole relationship." I paused, and smiled, reminiscing.

"Hell, I love my baby's swag, his style, all that, but that's not all. It's much more than that. It's the way he makes me feel. Texas made me a better person. He cares about me. He understands me, and you know I can be difficult to understand sometimes. But for a person to truly understand you is a good thing. The way you think, the way you act, who you are, understand when you are up, or down. They sympathize with you and give you the freedom to be who you are; that's some real shit. And that is why I love him so much, because he believes in me and I believe in him." I looked her directly in the eyes. "I can't just leave him. Not right now. I've gotta help him get better."

Sasha sighed. "Rae, I'm not going to tell you what to do because it's not me or my situation, but remember this nigga has been acting crazy as hell. The night he kidnapped you at the concert was scary. We didn't know what was going on. She sighed. "Okay, you said he was drunk and that his medication caused him to act like that. But what if it's not his medication? What if this guy is really psycho? I mean, really nuts? And remember you said he's been put in a crazy house before. Remember, chick, you haven't even been with Texas a full year. I mean, how well do you know him?"

We were both silent for a moment. I was thinking about her last statement.

"Okay, maybe you're right. Maybe I don't know him that well, but, Sasha, I have to be absolutely, positively, one hundred percent sure that this man is not the one for me." I sighed. "If not, cool. I can accept that, but for now I have got to see what's going on with him; why has he gone from being the perfect gentleman to a crazed lunatic in a matter of weeks. Something is not right, and I'm not going to stop until I find the answers."

Sau gave me a worried gaze.

"Rae, just be careful. I have a feeling things are gonna get a tad bit ugly."

"Well, that's a chance I'll have to take."

Chapter 22

I laid in bed. I just couldn't sleep. I was tossing and turning. All I could think about was Texas. I'm in love and I can't help it. I picked up the phone and dialed his number but he didn't answer. I called again and still no answer. I've got to go see him; the blood in my veins is running warm. I won't be satisfied until I am in the presence of Texas Reynolds. I got up out my bed at two o'clock in the morning and drove to his house.

On my way over there, the thought to turn around occurred to me more than once, but I kept driving. I kept telling myself, "Rae, this is dumb as hell; why are you driving to this man's house at two o'clock in the morning, and in Wren's raggedy ass car that didn't have any heat. It was freezing cold outside and I had to stop and get gas. I just had to talk to Texas I needed to see his face. I missed him so much. I didn't even care about the crazy shit that he had been doing, I just needed for Texas Reynolds to touch me, even if it was just for one night. Love will make you do some crazy things.

When I arrived at the house I noticed Texas' car was in the driveway, which was odd because he always parked his car in the garage. I called him again while sitting in the car but he didn't answer. I still had my key to his house. I debated if I should go in. *Rae, just go in.* I could always pretend like I had left something really important in the house. That could be my reason for coming over at this hour.

I walked in the house. It was pitch black. I heard noises coming from the bedroom. I crept down the hallway. The closer I got to the bedroom, the louder the noises got. I pushed open the bedroom door and my heart literally stopped beating. Eva was on top of Texas riding his dick like the urban cowboy and Mimi was coming out the bathroom butt ass naked.

I stood there for about a minute. At first I was a bit dazed, and it hadn't registered in my brain what my eyes were seeing. My ears started to burn and I became very hot, I mean heated.

"Huh," a heavy sigh escaped Mimi's mouth, and then everything began to register. They were having a threesome. At that point I didn't see nothing but red. I snatched Eva off Texas.

"Bitch, get off me," she screamed. I lost it; I hammered her in the face. I was so angry; I was releasing all my frustrations on her.

"Get the fuck out my house!" Texas screamed and snatched me off her. Mimi had run into the bathroom and locked the door.

I banged on the bathroom door. "Mimi, open the goddamn door, bitch! You a nothin' ass bitch. How the fuck you gon' do some shit like this and you my fuckin' cousin?" I couldn't believe it. She had stooped so low as to sleep with my ex and to top it all off she was partaking in a threesome with his baby momma.

"Rae, get out of my house before I call the police," Texas yelled.

I stared at him with fire in my eyes, and my heart racing. I took a moment to catch my breath. "How could you?" My voice trembled. It took everything in me to hold back my tears. "What the fuck is your problem? How long you been fucking these bitches? You probably been sleeping with them the whole time. And Eva, you are one sick fuck. All of you are sick." Mimi was still in the bathroom and Eva was sitting on the bed holding her nose. He didn't respond. He was standing there completely void of any emotion.

"How could you, Texas?" I smacked him across the face.

He grabbed my hands and pushed me out the door.

"Don't put your hands on me again," he warned. "You need to get the fuck out my crib."

"Yeah, you're right; I do need to leave." I got in his face and smacked the shit out of him again. I pounded him in the chest hard as I could. I lost it. "You need to tell me why in the hell you are fucking my cousin!" I pounded him in his chest. He stepped back. "How could you do this to me?" He grabbed me and tried to force me out the door.

"Get your hands off me," I screamed. He man handled me and shoved me toward the door.

"Raechel, get out of my house."

I turned around. "I'll leave your house. I hate I ever met you! If I see your ass layin' on the side of the road I won't stop to help you." I turned around and began to walk out the door. "You can have them hoes." That is when Mimi peaked her head from around the corner.

"Who you calling a hoe? It ain't my fault you couldn't keep your man." She slung her hair around and pranced around like she was a runway model. "My bad he wanted to upgrade." When she said that, I rushed toward her because I was about to deck her ass, but Texas jumped in front of her to protect her.

"Raechel, I said you need to leave my house." I looked at Mimi and looked at Texas. I didn't say one word. I turned around and walked out the door. As I was walking out the door, I was shoved from behind. I tripped and fell. Eva pushed me. She jumped on top of me and we started tussling in the grass. I pulled her hair; she pulled mine. We rumbled in the grass until the cops broke us up.

They handcuffed us both. I was breathing hard. My hair was all over my head and mud was everywhere. There were two white cops that had arrived.

"Ma'am what is going on?" One of the officers asked.

"I walked in on these bitches."

"Wait a minute, ma'am. You need to watch your language, the officer warned me.

I calmed down and explained to them everything that had taken place. I also told them that this was the second time that Eva and I had had a run-in. I explained to the cop that I was leaving until I was attacked from behind. For some reason, the cops sympathized with me.

"Well, I understand why you're so upset," one of the officers told me. They made me promise to leave and not come back and they would not take me downtown. I know they probably didn't want to do the paper work. However, they did issue me and Eva a citation. They told Eva if she was anywhere near me again that she would have to serve some time.

They took the handcuffs off me and let me get in my car. They told Texas he could do whatever in the privacy of his home but that they had gotten complaints from the neighbors, and that he needed to keep it down. Then they asked him for his autograph.

As I walked to the car, tears filled my eyes. I couldn't hold them in any longer. When I got inside the car, I fell apart. I was crying uncontrollably. I couldn't cope with what had just taken place. I drove off and pulled over on the side of the road. I sat there for what seemed like hours and cried, and cried. The only reason I left was because a cop pulled over to see if I was okay. He advised me to leave and that I shouldn't be on the side of the road.

On my way home, daylight had begun to break. I walked in my apartment and laid down in my clothes and went to sleep. When I woke up it was ten o'clock. I had several missed calls. Wren had called and texted as well as Sasha. I didn't have one call from Texas.

I looked at the clock and laid back down and went to sleep. I only had two classes today; I was going to miss them. I was mentally and physically drained. I turned off my phone. I would wake up and then go back to sleep. I woke up around five and ran. I worked out so hard my legs were shaking when I was done. I came back to my room, and cried myself to sleep. For the next two weeks I repeated my same pattern. I got up, went to class, came home and turned my phone off, and cried myself to sleep. I didn't talk to anyone. Sasha and Cece had been calling for days. I would either tell them I was sleep or I just wouldn't answer the phone. Wren had been covering for me all week in work study and with our organic experiment. I just couldn't find the will to do anything. I was devastated, My heart was broken.

♣

It's the end of the semester and I'm going home Thursday for Thanksgiving, which is a relief for me. I needed to get home and get away from everything. I'm sort of looking forward to it. I'm sitting in my apartment bored as hell. Campus is empty, and everyone has left for the holiday. I can't leave until Thursday. I'm riding home with Sasha. She wanted to spend an extra day with Sean before the break. She is in love and I'm happy for her. I would have been gone because Wren let me keep his car since Texas took back his Range Rover But just like Wren's car doesn't have any air, it doesn't have any heat either. I worked out late and I found it difficult to go to sleep.

I came back to my room; that is when it all started again. The tears started to roll down my face, the tears of expectancy. I tried to psyche myself out today telling myself I would not cry tonight, but I could not help it. It's like deja vu. I knew Texas and I wouldn't last. It was too good to be true. I was so stupid for opening up my heart. I wish I had never met Texas Reynolds.

Chapter 23

I got back to Nashville after Thanksgiving. I felt a lot better. I only had a few more weeks to go and it would be time to go home for Christmas. I had fun in Memphis and couldn't wait to get back home for the holidays. I was still hurt about Texas, but each day it was getting better and better. I was gradually getting over him.

I had so much school work to get caught up on. All projects and papers were due. Since Wren had been looking out for me at work study it was my time to pay him back. We had to finish our senior project that was due first thing Monday morning so we worked all day to get our assignment completed.

"Aye, big homey, let's go out for some drinks; my treat," I offered Wren.

"That's what's up. Where we going?"

"I don't know; you decide."

Wren picked me up in his hooptie. For the past week we had been sharing it because his Escalade was in the shop. We decided on Sunset Grill. It's one of the few places where the kitchen stays open pass midnight and that serves alcohol. It was a lovely night out in Hillsboro Village. Wren and I sat outside on the patio. The heated lamps were on emitting a warm and cozy vibe. While Wren was talking to me about the latest freak joint he was hitting, he stopped mid-sentence. "There go yo' boy," he said.

I looked up and saw Texas' black Lamborghini roll pass. He slowed down as he passed us, but when he noticed me looking he sped down the street. My phone rang. I glanced at the screen. Restricted flashed on the screen. I don't answer Restricted calls, so every time he called, I sent him to voicemail. He called about twenty times. I eventually turned my phone off and continued to enjoy my evening with Wren.

Wren and I were having such a great time. He took me to the Opryland Hotel and we toured the Conservatory. The hotel has a greenhouse inside along with waterfalls and high end restaurants. As we walked inside, it was like touring a tropical rainforest. The sound of the waterfalls singing, the Christmas decorations, and little children laughing and running around made me forget all about seeing Texas.

We walked around and looked at the Christmas lights. We talked for hours and had the best time. Wren is truly one of my best friends and hanging out with him had made me feel a hundred percent better.

I woke up the next morning and laid in the bed with my eyes closed, thinking about everything I had been going through. I thought about the great time Wren and I had. I hadn't laughed like that in so long. I love Wren like a brother. That is the type of guy I would do anything for. I'm one of those people that if you're down with me and got my best interest then, hey, I'm down with you, and Wren that is my nigga it don't get no bigger. I put my phone on the charger I had it in the bed with me because I had told Wren to call me when he made it to the house, but when I looked at it I didn't have any missed calls. Plus, I needed to see what time he was gon' bring me the car.

I looked around my apartment. It was a mess. I got out the bed and started cleaning up. I turned on the television. The news was on, so I turned down the volume and put on my Jay Z "Blueprint 3" CD. I was folding clothes when I looked up at the TV. The caption read *Man Burned Alive.* I turned off my radio and turned up the volume on the television. The reporter mentioned an African-American male in his early twenties was found burned alive in his car, after his vehicle crashed into a telephone pole. They say that alcohol may have played a factor. For some reason it made me think about Wren, so I called Carlos, Wren's roommate.

"Los, is Wren there?"

"Nah, he ain't here, Rae."

"Did he come home last night?"

"I don't know; let me check his room."

My heart started racing as I waited on him to return to the phone.

"His bed hasn't been slept in. He musta stayed at his girl's crib. Hold up, I thought he was with you last night."

"He was. I told him to call me when he got home, but he didn't." I nervously bit the inside of my jaw. "Well, as soon as you here from 'em, tell him to call me."

"Okay."

I went about my day. Wren and I was supposed to meet at the library at one-thirty to get our presentation together. When I got there, he wasn't there. I called his phone several times then I dialed Carlos again. He answered on the first ring.

"Hello."

"Hey, Los. What up? Have you heard from Wren yet?"

He sniffled and sighed deeply. "Rae, I got some bad news." His voice trembled.

"What?" My breaths stilled as I anticipated his reply.

"Wren was killed last night."

A heavy sigh escaped me. "Noooo!" I screamed. "Carlos, tell me you lyin'. Please, tell me you lyin'," I begged as tears rushed from my eyelids.

"I'm sorry, Rae…he's gone. Wren is dead."

I put the phone down.

"Ahhhhhhhh," I screamed. My ear piercing screech penetrated every soul in that library. "Nooooo, no, no. Not Wren. It can't be. Not Wren." Tears flowed from my eyes. With every breath I took, it felt like a ton of bricks was sitting on my chest. Thank goodness two of my sorority sisters were in the library and saw me having a fit. Because in any other case, the librarians would have called the police and they probably would have admitted me to the crazy house.

My two soros helped me calm down, and drove me back to my apartment. That is one thing about sororities that I love. Soros develop an automatic sisterhood with each other, and they are always there when another soro needs them, especially when it is fifty-eight chicks on a line. They took me back to my room. They had to almost carry me up the stairs; I was too through. My world was crumbling down. I couldn't take it. I called my momma to come to Nashville. I'm a strong black woman, always have been, always will be but sometimes life gets so crazy and messy that there is only one person that can make it better, and that was my momma. When I call my mother that means it's serious. Sometimes in this world, the only person you need, got to have, is your momma, and I had to have mine before I lost my mind.

My mother arrived the next day. She stayed with me for five days. Wren's funeral was that Saturday and my Momma had to be back at work. She had used her last vacation days to come and be with me, but I needed her so badly.

Mom left right after Wren's funeral. I didn't want her to leave but I knew she had to be back at work the next day. She would have taken off another week but I couldn't have her doing that. As soon as she left, I became nauseated and started throwing up. I was sick as a dog. I took two valiums my mom had given me before she left, and I went to sleep.

The next day I had to be back in class. My professor knew why I had been out. It was all around campus about Wren's death, and the school had a memorial service for him. My organic professor allowed me to turn in me and Wren's assignment late. I turned in the work and she gave me a B and Wren an A. Even though he could not see it, he would have been proud.

♣

When I got from class the next day, there was a tall, dark-skinned brother with dreads standing in front of my apartment.

"May I help you?" I asked.

"Yes, I'm looking for Raechel Jones."

"I'm Raechel Jones," I said apprehensively.

"Hi, Miss Jones." He pulled out a badge. "I'm Detective Kendall Stevens. I need to ask you some questions about the death of Wren Staples."

"Oo..kay." *Damn, what does he wanna know about Wren*? We walked inside my apartment. I set my book bag and keys on the table.

"Have a seat." I pointed him to the living room chair.

"Thank you." I leaned up against the counter in the kitchen.

"Miss Jones, were you with Wren on the night of his death?"

"Yeah, Wren and I had spent the entire day together." I explained to him in detail everything that Wren and I had done that day up until the minute he dropped me off. After I answered his questions, I asked him. "Why are you asking me all of these questions?"

"Miss Jones, your friend, Wren Staples' death, was not accidental."

"What are you saying?"

"I'm saying, he was murdered."

"Murdered?" A deep chill covered me. I was so taken aback; I had to have a seat.

"Yes, murdered. It appears that someone cut the brake lines, so when he went to mash on the brakes, his car wouldn't stop, which caused the fatal crash."

"But who, and why, would someone want to kill Wren?"

"That's what I'm trying to find out. Do you know if Wren had any enemies?"

"Nah, nobody that I know of. I mean everybody liked him. He was known all over campus, and he was cool with everybody." The detective jotted down what I was saying. "I don't understand why someone would want to kill him."

"Miss Jones, did Wren ever deal in drugs?"

I was silent for a moment. I debated whether or not to tell the truth. Wren was the weed man. He had been selling weed since his freshman year.

The detective looked at me. "Remember, any information you provide may help us apprehend his killer."

I decided to tell the detective what I knew, because I definitely wanted Wren's killer to be caught. "Yes, he did sell weed, but he was real low key. He didn't deal with no local cats. He basically had the same customers." I paused trying to think if Wren had ever been reckless with his drug business. "He wasn't the flashy type. He went to class every day and very few people on campus knew he sold weed."

"Do you know if he dealt with any other drugs…. crack, cocaine, ecstasy?"

"No, not to my knowledge. All I ever knew him to deal with was marijuana."

The cop looked at me. "Well, thank you for your time, Miss Jones." He stood up and handed me his card. "If there is anything else you think of, give me a call."

"Okay."

A few days later, while I was sitting in class, I started daydreaming about Wren. I thought about the night he died. I just couldn't believe that Wren's death was drug related. He was smart about handling his business, and if he felt like somebody was after him, he would've mentioned it. Then I shifted my thoughts to Texas and how he just flipped the script. He really pulled a whammy on me. He's nothing like the person I thought he was. But then I smiled to myself, I'm glad his true colors came out before I married him. I would've made the biggest mistake of my life if I had married him. My life has been full of drama lately- my best friend's death, the shit that I had to put up with from Texas, catching him in a threesome, the fight with that crazy ass baby momma, Eva. I thought about her idle threats and how she had acted on the night I caught her and Mimi in bed with Texas.

Then it dawned on me. I was in the car with Wren the night he died. Maybe I was supposed to die that night; maybe the brake cord was cut for me. I had been driving Wren's car all week. Oh shit, what if that was Eva driving Texas' car that night; maybe she had something to do with Wren's death. I immediately walked out of class and dialed Detective Stevens but he didn't answer, so I caught a cab down to the police station. Luckily, he was there. I told him about Eva's threats directed at me, and that I had been driving Wren's car all week. I also told him the story about what happened when Texas and Eva were in college. Detective Stevens told me he would check it out and would get back with me in a couple of days.

On my way home, I told the cab driver to take the scenic route, mainly to think. I noticed all of the Christmas lights and decorations everywhere throughout the city. I hadn't even taken the time to soak up the Christmas season because of everything that had been going on in my life. It was already December fifteenth and Christmas was just a week away, and I hadn't done any Christmas shopping. Sasha had left me the keys to her apartment and her truck; she was spending her Christmas in Miami with Sean. I was a little jealous because Sasha and Sean's relationship was like heaven on earth, and me and Texas' relationship had crumbled to pieces.

My plans were to stay in Nashville and work so I could make some extra money for Christmas, and I'd be heading to Memphis the following week just in time for Christmas.

Chapter 24

It was the last day of classes and I was glad to be finished. Campus was empty because most of the students were gone home. All students had until Saturday to be off campus because that's the day they were closing campus. Sasha and Cece had already left but I wasn't going to leave until Christmas Eve. I stayed on campus that Friday night. I had to be out the apartment by noon the next day. My plans were to stay in and relax, because I was going to work all day Saturday and Sunday so I could have some extra money to buy Christmas gifts for my family and friends. I went to the liquor store and bought two bottles of Relax Riesling.

I walked into my apartment. It was so peaceful and quiet with all of my suitemates gone. My apartment is facing the street. It was a warm night out so I opened the patio door and sat outside on the terrace and drank my wine. I wrote in my journal and reflected on everything that had been going on. I cried again. My heart ached terribly for the loss of my friend. I was fucked up. I was at the end of my first bottle of Riesling when it started to get nippy. I got up and stumbled to the inside. I locked all the doors and ran myself a nice, hot bath. I turned on 92Q, the Quiet Storm, dimmed the lights and drank more of the wine that I'd brought in the bathroom with me. I lit a few candles and soaked in the tub.

I sat in the tub so long the water started to get cold so I ran some more hot water. I repeated this cycle until I dozed off and went to sleep. I thought I was dreaming when I felt someone push my head under the water. I frantically fought my way to the surface. I scratched and clawed at the person's face but I was quickly dunked back down in the water. Water flooded my nostrils and stung my eyes. I struggled for air as I pushed my head from under the water. "Hu..hu…hu…hu," I heaved in and out trying to get air into my lungs, but I was I was quickly submerged again. This time for good, the warm water filled my chest cavity. *Oh, my God!* I kicked and scraped the air like I was climbing an imaginary beanstalk. My heart pounded as the water tore into my lungs. My hands collapsed into the water as my consciousness slowly slipped away. I guess the person thought I was unconscious, because he loosened his grip, my survival instinct kicked in. I burst out the water. "Ahhhhh!" I screamed and grabbed his shirt, and pulled him into the tub, catching him off guard. I quickly grabbed the shower curtain to pull myself out the tub, but the entire shower rod fell on top of me and him. I climbed out the tub, but he had hold of my ankle. Wham! I broke the wine bottle on top of his head; he stumbled back dizzily and then took off running. I collapsed face down on the cold tile heaving up phlegm and water. "Oh, Jesus…Oh, Jesus!" I cried. I grabbed my phone off the sink. Still coughing and panting like a dog, I dialed 911.

The campus police was there in seconds, followed by metro police and Detective Stevens. They walked around the apartment and checked for fingerprints. Then, one of the officers came into the bedroom and told me that the patio door had been pried open with a crowbar or some similar object.

I sat on the edge of the bed in a daze. "Raechel, what happened?" Detective Stevens voice pulled me out of my trance. I was still shocked and stunned. My thoughts were scattered but I tried to put the pieces together and explain to him what had occurred.

"Did you get a look at the person's face?"

"No… they had on a mask," I whispered in a daze. "Th..th...they took me off guard so I didn't see anything."

"Who do you think it could have been?"

"I don't know," I mumbled as hot tears burned my eyes. "I'm so scared." I wiped snot and tears from my eyes with my hand. Detective Stevens handed me a tissue.

"Why is all this shit happening to me? Why is somebody trying to kill me?" I cried. "I don't know what the fuck to do."

"Do you have any friends or relatives you can stay with?" One of the campus police asked.

"No," I sobbed. "All my friends are gone home for the holidays." I did have the key to Sasha's apartment, but I just couldn't fathom staying there by myself that night.

"Ms. Jones, you can stay at my place for the night," offered Detective Stevens. My eyes widened. He threw me for a loop. "First, I need to go by the Precinct and finish up some paper work, and I need to get a statement from you."

"Kay." I gently nodded my head. "Thaaank you." A wave of relief came over me. I packed my bag and left with Detective Stevens. First, we went back to the station where he asked me a few more questions about what occurred at the apartment. I made a statement about what had happened, then we went to his house.

When we first arrived at his house I was a little shocked. It was in Belle Meade, a very historic part of Nashville where homes range from the lower five-hundred thousands to a million dollars. I saw a Porsche truck and a BMW 5 Series parked in the drive way. The inside of the home was plush. It had a state-of-the-art sound system and all his furniture was Moroccan. The only way I knew it was Moroccan was because Sasha's parents had the same type of furniture. It was just strange that a cop could be living so lavish on his salary. But I dared not ask any questions. I was just happy to have somewhere to lay my head. I sat on the edge of the couch, replaying the night's events in my head.

"Raechel, are you okay?" I shook my head.

He sat down beside me. "Look, everything will be okay. I promise." When he spoke those words a flood of memories came back. That is what Texas would always say to me. But look at all of the shit that has happened to me.

Detective Stevens got up and took off his guns that were in the holster on his side. My gaze rose up his statuesque frame. That is when I noticed how attractive he was; he had almond-shaped eyes and a smooth, peanut butter complexion. What really caught my attention were his dreads; they gave him that edge. Dreads were never my thing but on him they did him justice. He had some pulled back with a tie and some hanging down in the back. It was evident from the ripples I saw in his arms that he worked out; he without a doubt had sex appeal

"Ms. Jones, you're welcome to sleep in my guest room."

"No, I can sleep on the couch… thank you though."

"Alright, if you insist." He elicited a half smile.

"There is one thing," I paused. "Detective, will you stay here until I fall asleep?"

He paused for a moment. "If you promise to stop calling me Detective." He smirked and walked toward the stairs.

"Okay. Where is the bathroom?" I asked

"On the door to your right." His voice faded as he ran up the stairs. I went in the bathroom and changed into my night gown. I put on a t-shirt over it so it wouldn't be too revealing. Then I sat on the toilet and peed. While I was on the toilet, I broke down. I cried so hard my stomach hurt. Why would somebody want to kill me? I didn't know what to think. Maybe it was Texas. Maybe he had really lost it. Then I thought about Eva. That bitch had made several threats that she was going to kill me. Either way, I was scared shitless, and whoever it was they weren't playing. They had already proven that they were worthy of taking a life because my friend, Wren, was gone. But I know one thing, they won't catch me slipping again. First thing in the morning, I'm going to go get strapped. I'ma get a gun, Taser, mace, whatever I can find. The next time they run up on me I'ma be ready for sure. I heard Detective Stevens come back down stairs. He knocked on the door.

"You aiight?"

"Yeah," I muttered with a congested nose. I wiped my eyes and started fanning my face with my hand in an attempt to dry my tears. I looked at myself in the mirror. My eyes were bloodshot red from crying. I washed my face and tried to get myself together. When I opened the bathroom door, he was standing right in front of the door. When I walked out, he wrapped his huge arms around me giving me the most heartfelt embrace. I closed my eyes and laid my head on his chest and cried for another five minutes.

"It's okay, baby." He rubbed his hands down my back consoling me. He reminded me so much of Texas. I felt so safe in his arms.

"I'm sorry, Detective. I mean, Ken." I wiped the tears from my eyes.

"Nah, you're cool. I understand."

I could tell he felt sorry for me. I'm sure he sees women crying all the time. I noticed he had placed a couple of blankets and a pillow on the couch. He removed the throw pillows from the couch.

"Miss. Jones–"

I interrupted. "Please, call me Rae."

"Well, Rae, where are you from?"

"Memphis."

"What about you?"

"Atlanta."

"What brought you to Nashville?"

"My ex-wife," he said while shaking out the blanket to place over the couch.

"Oh, so you were married?"

"Yeah, we gotta divorce."

"Forreal, what happened?"

"It was my fault, well I'ma say it was both our faults, I worked too much and she started cheating." He tucked the blanket into the folds of the couch.

"Damn, I'm sorry," I said.

His eyes wandered off." She's gone now."

"Have you gotten over it, I mean do you miss her?"

"Nope. I haven't gotten over it, and yea, I miss her, but that's life. People are in your life for a reason, a season, or a lifetime. She was just in my life for a reason."

His words made me reflect on my situation. What was Texas' purpose in my life? It definitely was not a lifetime, because my future with him is over. After everything I had been through I was starting to wish I never met him.

"What about you? Have you gotten over Texas?"

His voiced pulled me from my thoughts. "Nah, I still think about him every day."

"When was the last time you seen him?"

"The same day Wren died." I frowned and rolled my eyes as I thought back to Texas and Eva licking and sucking all over each other.

"Damn, was it that bad?"

"What?"

"Well, you frowned all up when I asked you that question."

"I walked in on him, with his baby momma and my cousin in a ménage a trios'."

"Daaamn, forreal? What did you do when you saw them?"

"Well, me and his baby momma got into it, and we was cuffed and issued citations."

He paused. "Raechel, why didn't you mention that to me?" I was silent.

"I don't know. Probably because I didn't want to think about it. I tried to put that shit in the back of my mind. Plus, I was embarrassed." My mind lingered.

"Embarrassed about what?"

I sighed. "I don't know. I guess the fact that he had gone back to his baby momma and I caught him in bed with her and my cousin. Besides, I really didn't think it mattered. Did you ever look into what I told you about Eva?"

"Yes, as a matter of fact I did. I'm still working on it. I'ma pay her a visit real soon."

I fluffed the pillow he had given me in preparation to lay down.

"Oh, and, Rae, everything matters when somebody trying to kill you."

I marinated on his comment. "Yeah, you're right," I whispered in a daze. I got under the covers; he stayed downstairs with me until I drifted off to sleep.

Chapter 25

I got up early the next morning and went to a local gun shop and tried to purchase a gun. They wouldn't let me get one because my ID still had my Memphis address on it. So I purchased a Swiss army pocket knife and bought me some mace. After that I got ready for work. I was still shook by what had happened the previous night, but I felt a little bit better since I had purchased some weapons. I was gonna be ready for whoever or whatever rolled up on me. On my way to work I got a call from Mimi but I sent her straight to voicemail. I was through with her ass. It was nothing she could say or do to restore the bond we once had.

We were busy as hell at work. Everybody was in the Christmas spirit and people were tipping good. After work I went to a Christmas party my job was having. I was kind of excited because I knew it would help keep my mind off of things. Before I walked in the party I checked my phone somebody had called me like twenty times from a private number.

The Christmas Party was at the club house in Nashboro Village. Christmas Parties are always fun to me. Seems like everybody gets drunk as hell and end up doing stuff they are embarrassed about the next day. I didn't drink at all because I had to drive back to Bellevue and I wanted to be alert. The party was live; we played dirty Santa with gag gifts. I got stuck with a white dildo. I was having a good time when I noticed my phone vibrating: Someone had been blowing my phone up all day from a private number. So I decided to answer it.

"Hello."

"Hello," the person whispered and hung up, but called right back.

"Hello," I answered.

"Rae."

"Who is this?"

"It's Mimi."

I could barely hear her, so I walked outside on the balcony away from the noise of the party. "What chu' want?" I snapped.

"Rae, we need to talk."

"Baby girl, we ain't got shit to talk about. Bye."

"Rae, please don't hang up, listen to me, please," she whispered. "We can discuss that later. Raechel, can you come and get me? I have something to tell you," she slurred.

"Come and get you? Hell, nah, I can't come and get you, not after the shit you did, I'm through with you, Mimi."

"Pleeease, Rae," she begged. "I'm in trouble."

"Well, sorry I can't do nothin' for ya. And you can quit calling my phone." *Click! I can't believe she waits to call me when she is drunk and high to apologize. She has some nerves.*

I thought about what I'd just done. *Despite everything she's done to me, what if she really needs me?* I thought about it, but it was too late. I had no idea where she was or where she was calling from. I went back inside to the party and stayed for another hour before leaving. By the time I left the party, I had forgotten all about Mimi's phone call.

♣

It was Tuesday and my day off so I went Christmas shopping. I shopped for hours. As I was walking out of the mall, it felt as if someone was following me. I looked around and although I didn't see anyone in particular, I removed my pocket knife from inside my purse and placed it inside the pocket of my jacket. Then as I put my bags into the trunk of the car I was suddenly struck in the back of the head and knocked unconscious for a couple of seconds. When I came to, Eva was on top of me pounding me in the face. I struggled and managed to reach in my pocket, I pulled out my knife and jabbed her in the arm. She stumbled and fell, then she got up and tried to take off running, but the mall security caught up to her before she could get away. Thank God, the mall had beefed up security since it was the holidays.

With shaking hands, I dialed Detective Stevens who arrived on the scene shortly after the police arrived. I watched as she went ballistic in the back of the police car. She was kicking on the back of the seats and banging her head against the windows. She was acting so crazy I almost felt sorry for her.

I was giving my statement about what happened to one of the police officers when I heard another police yell, "She's having a seizure."

Detective Stevens, along with the police who was taking my statement, rushed over to the police car. I followed behind them. Eva was in the back of the police car shaking violently and foaming at the mouth. Her eyes rolled to the back of her head. I thought she was about to die. At that moment I said a silent prayer for her. I couldn't stand another person dying, even if she was my enemy.

The next day, Detective Stevens called and told me Eva had been admitted to a local hospital for psychiatric evaluation. They found traces of Adderall and cocaine in her system. I asked him what Adderall was. He said it is a drug that causes an increase in heart rate. It's an upper, and when mixed with a dangerous drug like cocaine it can be a deadly combination, which caused Eva to have a seizure.

"Eva is lucky to be alive," he told me. "We also have evidence that proves she was the person that assaulted you in your apartment."

"How do you know?"

"Because her prints matched the ones found at the crime scene."

"Oh, my God, Ken; she may be responsible for killing Wren. I told you she was crazy."

"I know, Rae. I'm still working on it, these things take time. Just be thankful, she's been put away and can no longer cause harm to you or anybody else."

Chapter 26

I hadn't heard from Mimi since the night of the Christmas party. I had a funny feeling so I decided to give her a call, but every time I called her, the voicemail picked up.

I went to work. For some reason, I was so drained. I started getting sharp pains in the pit of my stomach. It felt like someone was stabbing me with a pitchfork. *Maybe I'm about to come on my period.* I worked a few hours, but the pain had me so broke down, I could barely walk. I told my manager I was sick and needed to go home. I transferred all my tables to Tangerine and left.

On my drive home, I broke out into a cold sweat. My stomach started doing cartwheels. I pulled over to the side of the road and started throwing up like it was Christmas. I pulled over twice before I made it back to Sasha's house. I took two Advil and laid down.

The next morning I wasn't feeling any better so I called Tangerine to see if she could pick up my shift.

"Hello," she answered.

"Tangie, this Rae," I grunted while kneeling over the commode.

"What's up, girl?"

"Can you work for me today?" I asked weakly.

"Yeah, why? What's wrong with you?"

"Girl, I'm so sick. I've been throwing up all day. I think I got a virus."

"Either that or you pregnant."

"Pregnant?" I paused for a few heartbeats; the thought of pregnancy never entered my mind. I tried to bring to mind my last period but I couldn't remember. "Shiiiit, I hope I'm not pregnant. Girl, I'ma call you back."

I rushed to Walgreens to purchase a pregnancy test. I kept trying to remember the last time Texas and I had sex but I couldn't recall. I had been under so much stress that I had forgotten all about my period. *That's it, stress.* I kept telling myself that was the reason for my nausea and missed periods. But ever since the first time I had started on my period, I had never missed one. My period comes around like clockwork. It may change the times of month it shows up, but it definitely comes once a month. And I hadn't missed one since, except for the time I was pregnant. I didn't even want think about that. *Please, God above don't let me be pregnant. I can't have another abortion.*

I purchased two tests and rushed home to take the test. I went to the bathroom and peed on the sticks. While I was waiting for the results I kept repeating my prayer. *Please, God don't let me be pregnant.* What am I gonna do if the results are positive? I started throwing up again. When I finished my bout of sickness, I checked both tests. One revealed a plus sign the other was blue, they both were positive.

"Fuck! Fuck! Fuck!" I screamed. I sat on the cold bathroom floor with my head in my hands. I was too through. *Are you kidding me… how in the hell did this happen? What am I going to do?* I sat on the bathroom floor for almost an hour thinking about what a fucked up situation I was in. Remembering the abortion I had two years prior, it was an awful experience. I had vowed that I would never have another one, not thinking I would be pregnant again two years later by a lunatic.

I called Tangerine back. "Well, bitch you jinxed me," I remarked in a depressing tone. What made me call Tangerine back, I don't know. Maybe it was because I knew Tangi wouldn't ask any of those probing questions that my other friends were sure to ask. Like, how did I let something like this happen, didn't we use protection? Then maybe I trusted Tangerine because sometimes people like Tangerine are the least judgmental, not to mention that she had been pregnant six times.

"How did I let this happen?" I asked myself out loud. "Girl, what am I gon' do?" I asked Tangerine.

"Drink a Sprite and eat some crackers. That should help settle your stomach." I wasn't asking her for a remedy for my symptoms, I wanted her to tell me what to do.

"Are you going to keep it?" she asked bluntly.

"I don't know."

"Why?"

I sighed. "Tangi, the father and I are not together. We've been having problems, plus I'm not ready for a baby right now."

"Don't your man play professional football?"

"Yes."

"Bitch, you crazy. It couldn't be me. I'd gladly drop that shorty off. Don't you know if you have that baby, you'll be set for life?"

At that point I knew I had to get off the phone with Tangerine, because she was on some other shit. If she thinks I would consider having a baby for financial gain she's crazy. There are so many other ways to gain financial stability, like working hard, going to school, and accomplishing the goals that I have set for myself. I just don't know if I want to do that with a child right now.

The next morning when I woke up, I felt a little better but it didn't take long for my ritual to start up again. Standing over the toilet, I was confused about what I was going to do. I went back to bed and slept all day. I was glad that I didn't have to be at work until that evening.

I was well rested; it felt like I had slept for hours. As I was getting ready for work I studied myself in the mirror. I looked awful, I had bags under my eyes, my skin was dry, and I had lost a substantial amount of weight. My butt and titties had shriveled up like old peaches. My appetite hadn't been the same since Texas and I broke up, and since Wren's death I don't remember eating a full course meal. Now, the little food I have been eating has been coming right back up.

On my drive to work I turned up my radio, hoping to drown out thoughts about what I was going to do about my pregnancy, but it didn't help because that's all I could think about. I didn't want to tell anyone because I wasn't for certain if I was going to keep the baby. I glanced down and noticed the phone ringing.

"Hello," I answered on edge.

"Hello," the voice on the other end responded.

"Who is this?"

"It's Dr. Reynolds."

"Oh, hi, Dr. Reynolds. How are you?" *Why in the hell is he calling me?*

"I'm good, what about you?" he asked.

"I'm okay."

"Raechel, I'm calling because I'm trying to get in touch with my son"

I paused for a moment. "Uh-mmm, Dr. Reynolds, I haven't spoken with Texas in about a month."

"A month, What! Is everything okay?"

"No, not really," I sighed. "Texas and I broke up. The engagement is off." I was shocked that Dr. Reynolds didn't know about it.

"What do you mean, it's off? Raechel, what happened?"

"Well things weren't working out."

"Look, Raechel, I may be an old man but I'm hip to the game. Tell me what happened. My son loves you. What's going on?"

I hesitated. I really didn't want to tell him me and Texas' personal business. "Dr. Reynolds, I don't know what happened myself." I took a deep breath. "Right after Texas got out of the hospital, things started to change. From that day he was a different person; he was not the man I fell in love with."

"What do you mean by different? Tell me what's going on with my son. I don't understand." he asked with worry.

"First, I thought he was depressed about blowing the season. He was tore up about that then he started smoking and taking prescription pills. But not only that, he became violent and abusive. Dr. Reynolds, Texas started hitting me."

"What?" he snapped. "Raechel, I don't believe that. That doesn't sound at all like my son!" I could tell he was shocked by this news.

Once I started talking, I told him everything that had happened, starting with the evening he tore off my dress, to the terrifying night of the concert.

"Raechel, I don't understand."

"I don't either. He just changed." I was baffled myself just thinking back on the past weeks he just did a complete three sixty." My eyes watered "I don't know what is going on."

"Normally, I wouldn't believe you because I know my son and what you've just told me doesn't sound anything like him. I didn't raise him to put his hands on women and I never have known him to act in such a manner." The tone in his voice sounded like he was quite disturbed and cautious at the same time about the things I revealed to him about Texas. I couldn't blame him because I wouldn't have believed me either had I not been the woman who went through it.

"Dr. Reynolds, I know it's hard for you to believe, but everything I've told you is true. Texas has done all of those things and more." Thinking back on all the shit he had put me through had made me heated. "I don't know why you're trying to keep him on a pedestal. You need to knock him off that pedestal because the nigga is not an angel.

As a matter of fact, he's trifling, abusive, a cheater, and some more shit."

"Raechel...Raechel... calm down."

I hated to go there but Dr. Reynolds was about to make me cuss his ass out. My ass is pregnant and my patience is short.

"What I was saying before you interrupted me, is that I know things are a bit strange. Texas was supposed to go see his mother but he hasn't, which is why I called to see if you could tell me what was going on."

This time it was my turn to be puzzled. "Dr. Reynolds, what are you talking about?"

"Raechel, my wife is in Tennessee."

"Really?" I replied confused.

"Yes, she's an inpatient at Tennessee Mental Institution in Cane Creek, Tennessee."

"Is she okay?" I couldn't believe what Dr. Reynolds was saying. Texas' mother, in a mental institution?

"According to her doctor she's not doing good. Since I couldn't make it there, I was depending on Texas to go and check on her to make sure she was okay."

"Why is she there?"

"Rae, my wife has a mental illness. She has suffered from the disorder for many years."

"Oh, forreal?"

"Yes, there is a history of mental illness that runs in my wife's family. My wife is bipolar and schizophrenic. Her father was schizophrenic and committed suicide when he was thirty-three years old. Two of her brothers had to be institutionalized, and her sister killed both her little girls, and then killed herself."

"Oh, my God." I swallowed hard, totally stunned.

"A couple of years after the fire, my wife shut down and she was institutionalized for three years," he said solemnly.

"That's awful. I'm so sorry to hear that, Dr. Reynolds."

"Every now and then, when she gets stressed, she stops taking her medicine. She'll have an episode, and has to be institutionalized, but as soon as she sees Texas she immediately starts to get better. You see, Raechel, Texas is our pride and joy. That's why it's shocking to me that

I haven't heard from him and that he hasn't gone to see her. He assured me that he would visit her every day."

"Dr. Reynolds, let me ask you this. Is schizophrenia hereditary? Do you think Texas may have some mental illness traits?"

"It is very hereditary. That's why I'm so concerned about what you're telling me. I pray that my son is not as crazy as his momma."

"Huh?"

"Well, Raechel, I'm just being honest. My wife is crazy as hell, but when you love somebody you have to except everything about them."

At that point, I broke down because everything started to make sense. Maybe Texas was crazy just like his whole family, and just to think I'm pregnant with his baby. I don't want a baby by a fucking psychopath.

I sobbed uncontrollably.

"Raechel, are you okay?"

"Yes, it's just that I don't know what to do." I sniffled hard and wiped the tears from my eyes.

"Do about what?"

"Nothing, I'll be okay?" I replied with a stuffy nose.

"Raechel, is there something else going on that I should know about?" he asked with sincerity in his voice.

"Dr. Reynolds, I'm pregnant," I blurted out.

"Pregnant? You mean I'm going to have another grandchild?"

I was silent. "I don't know."

"Please, don't tell me you're considering what I think I hear in your voice."

"Dr. Reynolds, I can't bring a baby into this world and me and the father are not together. I'm not trying to raise a child by myself."

"Raechel, you won't ever have to worry about anything financially."

"It's not that. I want to be married to my child's father. I want us to raise this baby together under one roof. I just want the old Texas back. I want my man back, but I know that's wishful thinking 'cause it's over."

"Raechel, before you make a decision about the baby, he at least should be told that you're pregnant." Warm tears blurred my eyes. I had to pull to the side of the road.

"Please, Raechel; let him know. Besides, whatever choice you make you shouldn't go through it by yourself. Please call me, Raechel, as soon as you hear from Texas and I'll call you if I contact him first."

"Okay," I replied uneasily, because I wasn't sure I was ready to speak to Texas.

"Raechel, please let him know that his mother needs him. I'll be in Nashville in a few days. I have some loose ends I need to tie up here and then I will be on my way. But, Raechel, please talk to him about my grandson."

"What grandson?"

"The one you're carrying."

Chapter 27

I thought about what Dr. Reynolds said. I really did want to keep the baby. The timing is off but I laid down and got pregnant. And in my heart the right thing to do is be responsible and have the baby. It's just Texas. I don't know if I want to have a baby by someone who is mentally unbalanced. Then his momma is crazy too. That mental illness shit is hereditary. I don't want my baby coming out crazy, and as for that shit he did with Mimi, I can't ever forgive him for sleeping with her. Even though he and I had broken up he knew how close we were, and he knew that she is my cousin. Before I found out I was pregnant I didn't care if I ever saw his ass again. But things have changed, I have a more serious issue on my hand, and that is this baby.

I took a deep breath before dialing his number. I let the phone ring once then I hung up. *What the hell.* I might as well call him because whatever I decide to do I will need his support regardless. After I was done dialing his number, I put the phone to my ear.

"Hello," he answered.

"Hey."

"Heyyy…Raechel…" he stuttered like he couldn't believe it was me. "How are you?"

"I'm good," I said indifferently "What about you?" The sound of his voice was annoying to me.

"I'm not doing so well. I miss you, Raechel; I really need to talk to you."

"Yeah, I need to talk to you too."

"Can you meet me in half an hour?"

"Where?"

"Meet me at Café Java."

I literally drug myself out of bed. I was nauseous. But I knew I had a lot of things I needed to discuss with Texas. I was still unsure about this baby. I had always vowed I would be married when I had my first child, and I didn't want my child to grow up without a father like I did. Things between Texas and me is fucked up. I don't ever see me getting back with him. But an abortion I just didn't want to go through with it. I had already had one abortion by David, and it was a horrible experience to me. I just don't think I can do it again.

I stopped and picked up a Sprite to settle my stomach before I drove over to Café Java. I sat in the parking lot and waited for Texas to arrive. After sitting there for ten minutes, I was about to leave, when I noticed him pull in. When he walked over to my car, I stared at him for a minute out the window. He didn't even look the same to me. He needed a haircut and a shave. *Is this the man I fell in love with?* I opened the door and got out. He hugged me. I barely hugged him back. He had a foul order; he smelled like he hadn't showered in days.

"Raechel, I miss you so much." I rolled my eyes at him and we proceeded into the restaurant.

We were seated beside a man that was handicap. He was basically a vegetable. He looked to be about my age and he was confined to a wheel chair. His parents were feeding him. I immediately became overwhelmed with sadness and started crying. Texas tried to calm me down but for some reason I was so torn up about this man. I know the only reason I'm so emotional is because I'm pregnant.

"Raechel, please, baby, everything is okay."

"It's not okay, Texas. We need to be thankful for our legs, arms, and the fact that we can see. There are so many people that are not as fortunate as us." He was looking at me from across the table pretending like he was interested in what I was saying, but I could look in his eyes and could tell he wasn't listening. He was just trying to get back in good with me. I cried for another ten minutes then finally calmed down. We both sat at the table in silence.

"Texas, your father has been trying to reach you for several days. He said that he has left messages on your phone and you haven't returned any of his calls. He's concerned about you and your mother. He says you haven't gone to see her."

"Yeah, I know. I finally got in touch with him yesterday."

That's strange. Dr. Reynolds promised he would call me as soon as he spoke to Texas.

"You know how busy my pops is, he's a hard person to keep in touch with. And I've been up there to see my momma every day."

"How is she?"

"She's doing fine. She's been in and out of it but the doctor says she doing better. She should be released in a few days. She's coming home with me for Christmas."

"Mmm-humm," I murmured and nodded my head.

"Rae," he grabbed my hand." Enough about my family. I want to talk about us."

"What about us?"

"Raechel, I'm so sorry."

I let out a deep sigh. I really didn't want to get into that whole Mimi, baby momma shit. As far as I was concerned it was over between us. I just needed to tell him about the pregnancy. My eyes wandered around the restaurant.

"Texas, please; I don't want to get into that."

"Nah, Raechel. I'm sorry forreal. I've been goin' through so much these past few weeks. I know I've been trippin'. I've had so much shit on my mind and I know I've fucked up big time but—"

"Look, I don't want to talk about that," I seethed in a low voice. "We are both grown. You know exactly what you did. I don't want to hear that I made a mistake shit because that's bull. Next, you're going to tell me she slipped and fell and landed on your dick. Nah, boo, I don't think so. You can save that one for somebody that wants to hear it."

The waitress approached the table slowly; like she could tell I was furious. I think she may have overheard a little of the conversation, but at this point, I didn't care.

"What would you like to order, sir?"

"Water, please and a bowl of the soup of the day."

She turned her attention to me. "And you, ma'am?"

"A Sprite and I would like the soup as well." Since I had been pregnant, my temper was out of hand. I had been snapping on people left and right.

The waitress brought our entrées. I took two spoons of soup and felt my stomach turn. I sprinted to the bathroom holding my mouth. I couldn't make it to the toilet so I used the garbage can. When I was done, I leaned over the faucet heaving and trying to catch my breath. Tiny sweat beads had formed on my nose. I splashed cold water on my face and slowly walked back to the table and sat down.

"You aiight?"

I nodded. "Yes."

He handed me the Sprite. "Here, drink your Sprite."

I gulped the Sprite down like I had been stranded in a desert. I was trying to get the awful taste out my mouth.

"Texas, I need to talk to you about something important."

"What is it?" he asked and grabbed my hand. I jerked it back.

"I'm pregnant." He glared at me expressionless for about thirty seconds. "Did you hear me? I'm pregnant."

"Yea, I heard ya, but I don't know what you telling me for."

I shot him a ferocious stare. "What tha fuck you mean? I'm telling you because you're the father."

"Nah, it ain't mine. I can't have kids. I'm sterile," he chuckled.

I looked at him, totally blown away by his remark. "Did you forget you already have a child? You couldn't possibly be sterile. You a stupid muthafucka!" He put his hands on his head and started blinking his eyes and twitching his jaws the same way he was doing on the night of the concert."

"You know what, just forget it." I threw my hands up in the air. "Forget I even mentioned a baby." At that point I knew I was not going to have that baby. I stood up and grabbed my keys. "Dude, you crazy forreal! I tried to give you the benefit of the doubt. But I realize you are a complete, fuckin', nut case. I'm so glad I left yo' crazy, deranged ass. I'd rather have a baby by a dog than to have a baby by yo' retarded ass."

"Shut up, shut up," he hissed, and slammed his fists on the table, startling me. "Bitch, I'ma fuckin' kill you! You gon' hate the day you ever met me."

As soon as he said that the room started spinning and I sat back down.

"Fuck you, nigga, you ain't gon' do shit to me muthafucka!" The more I ranted the more my head swirled. "I ain't scared of you, they gon' lock yo' crazy ass up!"

The features on his face became distorted. I was zoning in and out. I saw his lips moving, but I couldn't hear anything.

He mouthed, "Bitch, I'ma, chop yo' ass up and feed you to my shark piece by piece - you funky bitch!"

My eyelids were heavy. I kept fighting the sleep. I went in and out of consciousness and my vision was hazy.

The waitress mouthed, "Ma'am, are you okay?" Her lips were the size of balloons and her eye sockets were black and sunk into her skull.

My eyes rolled into the back of my head, and I blacked out for a second.

"Yes ma'am, she's pregnant." Texas replied just as cheerful as a child on Christmas Day. In a dazed stupor I glared at the waitress, I tried to speak but couldn't get any words out. *No, no help me!*

Texas helped me up and escorted me toward the door. I couldn't feel my feet. I was leaning on him as we walked out the door, with my feet dragging the floor.

When we got outside the restaurant, I remember falling to the ground. He picked me up and laid me across his arms and whispered in my ear, "Raaae-chel... You've been a very bad, bad, girl." He scoffed, "Now it's time for your punishment." He sniggled and proceeded towards his truck.

"Sir, is everything okay?" I heard someone ask.

Texas quickly answered. "Yes sir, she's fine. This is my wife. She's pregnant and she's not feeling well."

He put me into the truck. My head lazily fell forward. The last thing I remember is whispering, "Take me home."

I heard the sound of the car crank.

"I'ma take you home alright." He cackled.

Chapter 28

I opened my eyes. There was blackness all around me. At first I thought I was dreaming until I felt the tape covering my mouth. *Oh, God, where am I!* I tried to move my hands. They were tied above my head, and my feet were bound together. I moved my head around trying to take a glimpse of my surroundings but there was only darkness. Then a sharp pain shot from my stomach all the way to my asshole. "Ummm," I moaned. *Where in the fuck are my clothes?* I was laying butt ass naked on my back.

I tried to recall the events that led me to my current situation but I kept drawing a blank. *God, please help. Where am I? Lord, please help me to remember.* My heart rate increased, and my breathing became shallow. I was about to have a panic attack. *Ok, Rae, breathe.* I inhaled deeply and let out a long sigh. I repeated this step for about five cycles. I attempted to recall the last thing I remembered. I steadied my breathing and focused on my thoughts. Bits and pieces of my most recent memories started to resurface. I started playing this cat and mouse game in my head, then his faced appeared. *I was with Texas. The baby. I was telling him about the baby.*

I heard a door open. A cool breeze swept over me, sending a chill over me. A light came on; my eyes squinted from the brightness. Then I heard his footsteps slowly approaching me. The next thing I know, he was towering over me with the look of hell in his eyes. Fear swallowed me and a thick lump formed in my throat. My heart thumped like I had just ran a marathon. I became hot and started sweating profusely, and the cramps in my stomach were getting stronger.

He pulled up a seat and moved the hair from my face.

"What up, Rae? I bet you wondering why I got you here."

I swallowed hard and wondered what the hell he was about to do to me. He grabbed a handful of my hair and twisted it around his hand and snatched my head close to him.

"Ummph," I whimpered, terrified and in pain from the pressure he was putting on my skull.

"Well, hoe, you 'bout to find out."

What are you talking about? I started pulling and jerking on the chains that bound me. *Texas, please don't hurt me. This muthafucka is crazy as hell. I can't believe this is the person I fell in love with, the person I wanted to spend the rest of my life with. How could this be? This can't be Texas.*

"Yeah, li'l momma, I been waiting on this shit a long time. Now it's finally 'bout to go down." He took a puff from the cigarette he was smoking. "Bitch, I'ma cut yo' fuckin' throat and watch yo' ass squirm around like a sprayed cockroach." He pulled from the cigarette and then slowly blew the smoke in my face. "Along with the rest of dem sorry, low-life muthafuckas."

Please, somebody help me. My sobs were loud. Tears and snot was running down my face.

He leaned down and whispered in my ear. "But for the next three days you gon' wish like a muthafucka somebody had already stepped on you and squished yo' ass." He chuckled. "Bitch, after I get finish with yo' ass, you gon' be begging me to kill you."

I glanced into his spacey, sunken eyes; he pulled some pliers out of his pocket. *Oh, God.* My eyes widened. I thought he was about to hit me in the head with them, but instead he walked to the edge of the bed and grabbed my foot.

"This is to make sure you don't try no dumb shit."

"Ohh, God! Nooo! He grabbed my foot. *Let me go, you sick muthafucka!* I pulled and jerked on the handcuffs like a wild animal. He grabbed my right foot and then he took the pliers and crunched down on my big toe. He pulled and tugged on my toenail and then yanked it off my skin.

Aaahh! A bolt of pain shot through my body like lightening. My heart pounded rapidly and I felt my chest caving in, and I couldn't catch my breath. Then he went to the second toenail and yanked it off. My body convulsed like I was in an electric chair. My breaths were thin. I inhaled repeatedly but I couldn't catch my breath. Tears rained heavily down the side of my face.

He grabbed my foot again but it slipped from his hand; it was so bloody. He sat on the edge of the bed and put my feet under his arm and removed every toenail from my right foot. *God, please take me right now.* Then he grabbed the left. I said a silent prayer to God. *Heavenly Father, please take me now, I surrender.*

The next morning I woke up to agonizing pain. I had already pissed on myself and my stomach was rumbling. I felt myself having to shit but I was trying to hold it, because just the thought of me using it on myself was unbearable. I clinched my ass cheeks together tighter than a clam in a bucket, praying he would let me go to the bathroom.

The door opened. He walked over to me and snatched the tape off my mouth. That pain was nothing compared to what I had already endured. He unlocked the cuffs that bound my wrist.

"Bitch, get up so you can take a bath." I slowly sat up. I tried to stand up but I immediately hit the floor, my feet were swollen and my legs were like jelly. I laid out on the side of the bed, my eyes met his muddy boots.

"Look at cha now, bitch. I see you ain't talking shit no more. Get up, bitch." *Wham!* he kicked me dead in the stomach, right then my bowels released. I laid on the floor doubled over in pain.

"Bitch, did you shit on my floor?"

He kicked me again. "Uggh!"

"Yeah, skank bitch. Look at cha' now! Where all them muthafuckas that was gon; lock me up, huh?" He barked and kicked me again. He grabbed my arm and drug me into the bathroom, and laid me on the cold tile. "Now clean yo' shitty ass up. Bitch, you stank." He cocked up a big glob of spit. *Puh* and shot it dead in my face and walked out the room. I climbed into the tub and sat limply as water poured over my body like rain. I closed my eyes and pondered on what a fucked up situation I was in. I was so numb, I couldn't even cry. I kept telling myself *Raechel, you gotta get out of here.* I knew I had to channel all the negative energy around me into positive energy and focus on getting out, because if not I was going to end up dead.

After I cleaned myself up, I noticed the different photographs on the wall. They were all family photos, but the faces had been blacked out or the frames were broken. One picture in particular looked like it was a photo of Texas and his mother. Her head was cut off and *Die, Bitch Die!* was scribbled in red ink. I started trying to find a way out. The door was locked and the windows had been nailed shut. There was a lamp that I could use to break the window but I was on the second floor.

I would risk jumping two stories to my freedom but I would probably break a limb, and I wouldn't make it that far because of my feet. The pains in my stomach flared up again so I laid down, wondering how I was going to escape.

I was asleep when he walked in the room. He came and slapped me on my ass. "Aiight, bend yo' ass over the edge of the bed and spread dem cheeks."

I slowly sat up still in a daze, still unclear what he wanted me to do.

"Bitch, hurry up. I ain't got all day," he yelled.

I slowly leaned over the edge of the bed with my ass facing him. "Tex, please don't," I muttered.

"Please don't what? Hoe, you betta spread dem cheeks and get ready to take this dick." He took out his limp dick and slapped it on my ass, and ran it up and down my crack. I felt it stiffen as he searched for my hole. "And you better act like you like this dick; moan and shit." He rammed his dick in my ass so hard. I whimpered softly as tears flowed down my face.

"Ugggh," he moaned as he plunged in and outta my ass, tearing into my asshole. He took the handle of his gun and plopped me in the back of the head. "Moan, bitch!" he snarled.

"Um, um," I moaned weakly and grabbed the bed sheet to brace myself.

"Yea, bitch, gimme this ass. I'ma get all this shit until I kill yo' ass."

The pain was agonizing. He took both his hands and grabbed me by my waist and pumped in and outta my ass like he was pumping a well. His fat dick ripped my asshole apart. I knew he was about to cum when he gripped my waist tighter and started slamming his dick in and outta me.

"Ugggrrrhhhh," he groaned and leashed his dirty load inside of me, then he collapsed his sweaty body on top of me. When he got finished, I limply fell to the floor.

"Why are you doing this to me?" I whispered weakly.

"Do what? You did this to yoself. You just got with the wrong nigga. Now I gotta do you like I did yo' homeboy, Wren." He mocked in a girly voice, and chuckled. My eyes widened.

"You killed Wren?" My heart sank and tears filled my eyes.

"What chu think? Yeah I killed him and I ain't finished. Before it's all done everybody will be dead." He zoned off into a deep trance.

"Texas, what are you talking about?" I sobbed uncontrollably.

"My peoples…my family," he scoffed.

"Are you going to kill your parents too? Why, why?" I cried. "Why are you taking innocent lives?"

"Shut up. Shut up," he screamed and rammed the semi-glock into my nostrils. "You don't know shit, bitch!" He spat. "You don't know shit about me! Yes, I'ma kill them, I'ma torcher them, then I'ma gut them fuckers from limb to limb! From limb to fuckin' limb," he raged.

He snatched the photos off the walls, ramming his fists into the frames, shattering the already broken frames even more.

"Limb to limb," he screamed as spit and snot flew from his nose.

He ranted and raved until he was out of breath. He stood over me panting like a dog, sweat dripping from his face. He whispered, "Yes, bitch, I'ma kill my piece of shit ass daddy and my crazy ass momma then I'ma blow yo' fuckin' brains out." He snickered. Blood trickled down my nose. I was paralyzed in fear. I was scared to take my next breath. "But first I gotta get me some more of that ass." He squeezed my already sore right breast and left out the room.

I was at a loss, how did I end up in this shit? I became so angry I rammed my fist into the wall almost breaking my knuckles. I laid on the bed consumed with anger and sadness and cried myself to sleep.

I saw angels surrounding me I knew I was I heaven. Then I saw Mimi. We were young again playing hide-n- seek at my grandmother's house. I was counting one, two, three…When I was finished I ran to find Mimi. I searched everywhere for her but couldn't find her, and I became worried. I went in my grandmother's bedroom and Wren said, "Rae, she's in there," and pointed at the closet. When I opened the closet door, Mimi's pale body tumbled out, she was dead. I screamed and woke out my dream I couldn't go back to sleep.

The next day Texas walked into the room. He pulled me out the bed by my hair.

"Suck this dick, bitch," he demanded. Tears filled the wells of my eyes, but I noticed he hadn't locked the door. I got up and hobbled toward him, my feet still sore and swollen. "Bitch, dance. Get a nigga hard and get that ugly ass frown off yo' face, bitch. Look sexy, and

smile, hoe, before I pump this led in yo' fuckin' brain. Dance, bitch!"
he barked.

"It's hard for me to dance with these cuffs on."

He took his keys out his pocket and unlocked the cuffs. They fell to
the floor; I rubbed my wrists.

"Bitch, try some stupid shit if you want to and I'ma rock yo' ass to
sleep," he warned.

I jiggled my ass in his face and played with my pussy, he leered at
me as he started massaging his dick.

"Ummm, yeah," he moaned.

I looked at his dick; it was hard as a rock. He leaned back in the
chair and massaged his dick.

"Now, come over here and suck this dick,"

"Okay, baby." I got on my knees and eyed his nasty ass dick. I went
to my happy place because I was about to throw up at the site of that
shit. I wrapped my lips around his dick. I put it all in my mouth.
"Mmmm," I moaned. I took my tongue out and ran it down the shaft of
his dick. He laid back in the chair and got comfortable. I licked my
tongue around the head, then I slid my hot mouth onto his eleven
inches.

"Mmmmm," he moaned. His phone rang. "Gotdamnit." he barked
and picked up the phone. "Keep going, bitch." His whole demeanor
changed. "Hey, Pops. How you doin'?"

I heard his dad on the other end. "Hey, Son. What's going on?"

"Ah, nothing; just hanging out with Rae."

"Oh, I'm glad to hear that. I was calling to tell you what time my
flight will be arriving."

"Aiight. What time?"

"Three p.m."

While he was talking I noticed the cuffs on the floor. I slid them
closer to me along with his keys.

"Okay. I'll pick you up from the airport about three o'clock. We can
go to Cane Creek to get Mom and then we're going to come back to my
house because I have a special evening planned."

"Sounds good. I can't wait to see you, son."

"Man, I can't wait to see you either, Pops. It's gonna be a nice
Christmas."

"Yeah, I got a feeling it's gonna be unforgettable. "I love you, Son."
I love you too, Pops. Later." He turned and leered at me. "Bitch, keep going."

"Yeah, that's what I'm talkin' 'bout. Suck that dick, now lick all over them balls."

I gently took my tongue out and licked around his balls. When I saw him close his eyes and relax, I went for the kill. I opened my mouth wide and stuffed all his dick down my throat. I almost choked as I deep throated his dick. I took it out and did it again. Slob dribbled down the side of my mouth. I suctioned my lips on the head making a popping sound as I released. His dick started to throb. He was about to cum. I stroked one hand up and down his shaft as I gently massaged his balls with the other. I gripped his dick and opened my mouth like jaws. I chomped down on his meat like an angry piranha, and squeezed and twisted his nut sack like I was juicing a lemon. I tried to rip that shit off.

"Ahhhhhh!" he roared in agony. He grabbed his dick and bowed over in pain. "Bitch….oohhhh, shit…ohhh, bitch…I'ma kill you," he stuttered.

I quickly took the handcuffs and locked his ankle onto the chair. I grabbed the keys off the floor.

Pee-une, Pee-une. Gun shots rang out like it was New Year's. I knew I was dead, dashing out the door. I rushed down the stairs, missing a step, and tumbled to the bottom tweaking my ankle. But my will to survive ignored the pain. I looked back, he was in the door way stuck, trying to pull that chair through, but at the same time aiming that glock dead at me. I scurried to my feet, and ran out the door not looking back. I ran like my life depended on it. I hit the keyless remote on the Lamborghini and sped out the drive way. The icy surface caused me to spin into a donut. My heart stopped. I fish-tailed and sped out the subdivision and did not stop until I was at the Metro Police Station.

I sat in the car panting harshly. A wave of relief rushed over me. I was safe. I leaned my head on the headrest and smiled. "Thank you, Jesus, I made it." I was butt ass naked. I looked in the car but there wasn't anything for me to put on. I didn't have any money, no purse, no ID, nothing. I sat in the car and watched the snow flurries as they melted on the windshield and thought about my next move.

I went to my on-campus apartment and snuck in. I took a quick shower and found me some clothes. I went through all my handbags and scraped up thirteen dollars and headed to the police station. I got out the car. A frigid wind attacked my body as I hobbled in the police station. My ankle had started to throb so I was walking with a slight limp as I shifted all my weight to the other leg.

When I got to the front desk, a white man greeted me, with a head that was too small for his body.

"May I help you?" he asked.

"Yes is Detective Ken Stevens here?"

"No. Detective Stevens is on vacation. He won't be back until after the New Year."

"Well, I want to press charges against someone."

"Okay, wait just a minute."

I wrote out my statement telling everything that was done to me. After I filed my complaint, an officer walked in the room, it was the same officer that had come to Texas' house when me and Eva got to fighting.

"It's you again."

"What do you mean by "It's you again?" I began to explain, my story. I told them everything. How Texas had raped me and had plans to kill his parents.

"So you tell me you have been at Mr. Reynolds house for three days?" The officer asked.

"Yes, and he would've killed me if I hadn't gotten away." A chill came over me as I recapped my past three days.

"Now, Miss Jones." His southern accent was so aggravating. "In a past affidavit it states that you and Mr. Reynolds have had a previous altercation, and you were not allowed to be anywhere near his house."

"I know. Did you hear what I was fuckin' saying? He kidnapped me." I motioned my hands in the air.

"Watch your language, young lady," he warned. "Where did he kidnap you from?"

"From a restaurant...Café Java."

"So you agreed to meet him at the restaurant and then he kidnapped you?" he asked suspiciously.

"Yes, he carried me to his truck."

"Were there other patrons in the restaurant?"

"Yes."

"These patrons didn't think it was strange that he was carrying you out the restaurant?"

"Look, I don't know. I told you he drugged me. I was out of it," I snapped.

"Well, we didn't get any reports of a kidnapping, nothing suspicious at a Café Java."

"Miss Jones, have you ever done any drugs?"

"Naw, I don't do drugs," I replied, irritable. "I mean, damn you interrogating me like I'm the criminal. I'm here to report a crime. Where is Detective Stevens?"

"I told you, he's on vacation!" the first policeman repeated.

"Well, I need to speak to somebody that will listen to me. It's obvious y'all are not listening." I huffed and rolled my eyes.

"Miss Jones, wait right here." They returned with the captain.

I repeated my story for the third time but he still didn't give a fuck. He eyed me suspiciously.

"Miss. Jones, there is a procedure we take in handling domestic violence cases."

"This is not domestic violence," I interrupted.

"Wait just a minute." he held up a finger. "I let you speak; now it's my turn." I sighed with an annoyed expression.

"You showed up here. You and Mr. Reynolds have had a prior altercation. Your feet are hurt no denying that, but you may very well have done that yourself. I'm sorry, it's just not enough evidence for us to issue a warrant for Mr. Reynolds' arrest. It's really nothing we can do."

"Nothin' you can do? What the fuck you mean? He tried to kill me and he's still allowed to roam the streets? Look at my feet; he pulled off my toenails one by one. He raped me, beat me, and it's nothing you can do?" I screamed.

"Like I stated before, we can perform the rape diagnostic for you, but right now we don't have enough evidence to issue a warrant for his arrest."

I asked impatiently, "What about his parents? He's going to kill them. He's crazy."

"When is this supposed to take place?" the Captain asked.

"He told me he's going to do it tomorrow. His parents are visiting him for Christmas and he's going to kill them." The unconvinced officers eyed each other like I was crazy.

"Miss Jones, do you have any proof, any documentation of these alleged threats? Any tape recordings made by Mr. Reynolds?"

"No. Can you at least call the mental institution and tell them not to release her?"

"No, Miss Jones, that's her son. We have no right to deny a person visitation to their family member. Right now it's your word against his and it's nothing we can do about it."

"This is unfucking believable."

"Miss Jones, watch your language."

I was getting nowhere with them. "Let me get this straight." I ran my finger through my hair and massaged my temples. I told you this dude is a stark, raging, lunatic. He has already killed before. He killed my best friend, Wren. He tried to kill me. He is going to kill his mother and his father, and y'all ain't gon' do shit about it!" I screamed.

"Now, Miss Jones, you calm down before you are locked up and have to spend your Christmas in here. Now you wouldn't like that would you?"

"Man, fuck that. I bet if I was a white bitch that rolled up in here screaming rape, y'all a be done sent the President, National Guard, and so' mo' folks. But because I'm black, y'all standing around like something stuck up y'all ass….prejudice muthafuckas."

He slammed his hand on the desk. "Okay, that's it, lock her up!"

They put me in a holding cell. My adrenaline was pumping and my heart was racing. I was so fuckin' mad them bastards weren't listening to me. I paced the floor until I finally calmed down. I laid on the hard mattress and tried to relax my body. A stabbing pain pierced my abdomen. My adrenaline had been pumping nonstop. I had ignored my injuries up until now, but now that I steadied my brain, everything started to throb, from my stiff ankle to my ripped asshole. I was pissed that I was locked up, but truthfully I wouldn't wanna be any other place. I knew I was safe, and I didn't have to worry about Texas coming and slitting my throat.

I had trouble sleeping though. So many thoughts bombarded my brain. I was scared for my life. The first thing I'ma do when I get out is get the fuck outta Nashville. I couldn't believe it. I was in jail, and I hadn't even done shit. I looked around the cell and reflected on my current situation and was like how in the fuck did I end up here. It was Texas, Texas fuckin' Reynolds. My goal is to get as far away from that nigga as I can. I thought about everything that had taken place. I questioned myself. How could I have been so stupid and naïve? How could I miss how crazy this dude was? Why didn't see it?

I thought back to when we first met. He was perfect. I reflected on the entire relationship, and I tried to capture the moment things started to go wrong. I knew after he got out the hospital things went downhill, but how come I didn't see it before then? I thought back on all the good times we had. Our vacation in Maui when he proposed. How excited I was to get back and tell my friends and family about our engagement. Then it hit me like a ton of bricks. That was the turning point. Right after we got back from that trip was when he choked me in the bed. The next day I spoke with Ma'Sadie. Her voice came back to me clear as day. *Three people are going to die.* I replayed the conversation over in my head. How could I have forgotten it. *Oh, my God.* Threes. Death happens in threes. I sat up and covered my mouth. He had already killed Wren. What next? His momma and daddy. He really is going to kill them. *Oh, God help me, please don't let them people die. They don't deserve to die.* I had to warn Texas' parents, because I believed in my heart that they were next to die.

The next morning, I woke up to the guard yelling my name. "Jones, Jones," he screamed. "Let's go." He escorted me to the front desk. It was the same white officer from the previous day.

"Miss Jones, you are released on your own recognizance." They made me sign some release forms. I skimmed through the papers and signed my name. They had issued me another citation for disorderly conduct.

"Sir, can you give me Detective Stevens' phone number?" He looked in the rolodex and wrote his number down. I grabbed the small slip of paper and ran out the door.

"Thanks." I smiled and headed to the car. As I cranked up the car, the engine roared while I let the car warm up. I got on the interstate and headed to 440 East. I had to warn Elizabeth and her husband about Texas. I couldn't live with myself if I didn't.

Chapter 29

While I was on my way to Cane Creek, I called Dr. Reynolds several times, but he didn't answer.

"Dr. Reynolds, hey this is Raechel. Call me as soon as you get this message."

My entire body hurt but nothing was going to stop me. I had to let this lady know that her son was crazy and he was going to kill her and her husband. When I got off on the Cane Creek exit, the snow really started to come down. It was hard for me to see the entire road because it was white. I pulled off the exit slowly, trying not to slide. The snow was beautiful, but I hate it because we never get snow like this. I knew it was going to stick, and that's what I was afraid of, because most people down south can't drive in snow and I know I'm one of them people.

I desperately needed to get to Cane Creek fast and make it back to Nashville before the roads got bad. As I neared the facility, a queasiness rumbled in the pit of my stomach. I looked around the parking lot; it was empty. As soon as I got out the car, a brisk wind smacked my face. I wrapped my scarf around my neck because my throat was getting sore and every time my throat is aggravated, I get laryngitis.

I walked to the receptionist desk. There was a fat, white woman with a pair of reading glasses on that were too small for her face sitting behind the desk.

"May I help you?"

"Yes, I'm here to visit Elizabeth Reynolds."

"Are you a relative?"

"No, I'm a friend of the family. Her husband, Dr. Reynolds, put me on her visitation list."

"May I see some identification?"

As she was checking my identification I asked, "Is there something wrong with your phone lines?"

"Yes, they're down. A tree fell and hit one of the towers. The phone company is working now to get the lines repaired."

When she finished checking my identification, she said, "Okay, Miss Jones, have a seat; we'll take you back shortly."

"How long is it going to be before I can see her?" I asked impatiently.

"I said it will be a few minutes," she snapped.

I rolled my eyes and went and sat down. But I was so nervous I jumped right back up and started pacing the floor. I called Texas' dad again, but he didn't answer. I had been waiting for thirty minutes when I decided to ask, "Has Mrs. Reynolds had any other visitors?"

"No, you are the first person that has come to visit her since her arrival three weeks ago."

"Her son hasn't come to visit?" I asked

"No... no one has been to see her." I paced the floor consumed with anticipation, constantly checking my cell phone to see if anyone had called. The time was ticking. It was two-thirty. I had to get back to see this lady before Texas came to pick her up. The time was winding down and I still hadn't been taken back to see Mrs. Reynolds.

I was so anxious. I asked the receptionist, "How long is it going to be. I've been waiting thirty minutes." She caught my attitude and gave me a nasty glance. "Look, I apologize but I really need to talk to Elizabeth. It's very important, and I need to make it back to Nashville before the roads get bad."

"Wait just a minute; let me check." She slowly hobbled to the back. *Bitch, hurry up. People's lives are at stake.*

"Well, I spoke with the nurse. Mrs. Reynolds just had an episode.

"An episode? What do you mean?"

"Well, she tried to escape." She claims that her son is trying to kill her.

"What?" *Oh, my God, she knows he is trying to kill her.*

"Ms. Jones, you must understand that many of our patients are severely mentally unstable. Mrs. Reynolds has been coming here for years, and every time she always claims that her son is trying to kill her. But her husband says that she loves her son. This just shows you how unstable her mind is."

"What causes her break downs?"

"Oftentimes it is stress, or if something traumatic happens to her it can cause a relapse, especially if she isn't taking her medication properly." She picked up her diagnostic report. "Her reports say that the episode that caused her to be here this time was brought on by stress.

Her husband states when he found his wife she said she was following the birds. She said the birds would take her to Texas. She was found about a hundred miles from their Houston home, near the Mexican border."

I sat down. I felt sorry for Mrs. Reynolds. I didn't know what I would say when I went in to visit her. I looked outside. The snow was coming down even harder. Time was running out. I needed to get back there and see her soon. It was almost three o'clock. I waited about twenty more minutes and then a man in a white pair of scrubs told me she was stable.

He escorted me to her room. I walked in; she was staring out the window watching the snow fall.

"Elizabeth," my voice echoed off the walls. She didn't budge. I looked at the man in the uniform, to let him know he could leave. "I'll be okay."

As soon as the nurse walked out the room, Mrs. Reynolds ran to the glass panel in the door to make sure the nurse was down the hall.

"Where is Texas?" she asked

"Elizabeth, I need to talk to you."

"Are you going to take me to him?"

I stumbled for words. "No, Elizabeth." She got her shoes from under the bed, and grabbed her suitcase.

"Mrs. Reynolds, no. I'm not coming to get you." I closed her suitcase. "Mrs. Reynolds I can't take you," I insisted.

"Please, you have to." Her eyes watered. I touched her shoulder. "I can't stay here," she mumbled. "He's going to kill me."

I wrapped my arms around her. "No, Elizabeth; no one is going to kill you. Everything is going to be okay." Her sniffles stopped and she raised her head and looked at me. "But he's going to kill Texas first."

A chill came over me. Tears poured from her eyes. I placed both of my hands on her shoulders. "Elizabeth, what are you talking about?" I sat in the chair across from her so that I could look her directly in the eyes. She sat silently for a minute with her arms folded rocking back and forth in her chair.

"Texas was a very sickly child. He was born with a rare form of stomach cancer. He couldn't hold any food on his stomach and had to be fed through a tube. By the time he was three he had already had seven stomach surgeries. Several times we thought he wasn't going to make it. The doctors had told us he wouldn't live pass five years of age. But I refused to believe those doctors. Nothing was going to take my son from me." She walked to the window and stared outside as the snow fell gracefully to the ground. "We sought out the best treatment for him. We took him to a treatment center in Canada, and the cancer finally went into remission when he was exactly five years of age. He hasn't had any problems since. But in the back of my mind I always thought the cancer would come back or there would be some complications, so I was overprotective of Texas.

I loved my children the same. But I showed Texas more attention because of the cancer." There was a pregnant pause. "And Phoenix hated me for it."

I stopped her. "Elizabeth… who is Phoenix?"

"Phoenix, that's my other son. He's Texas' twin."

"Texas has a twin?"

Our gazes locked. "Yes, a very evil twin."

I took a deep swallow.

"I felt them fighting in my womb. Phoenix was always jealous of Texas. I tried to show him as much love and attention as Texas, but Texas' illness was so demanding. At first Phoenix was outgoing and he was very smart, but at about four years of age he started to withdraw and became very temperamental and violent. He was disruptive in school so I took him out and home schooled him along with Texas. While home schooling he became even more withdrawn, so John and I put him in therapy.

But things just got worse. One day, while Texas was eating a bowl of cereal, I heard a loud scream. I ran to see what was going on. Blood was gushing from Texas' mouth. At first I thought he lost a tooth. But when I looked in his mouth there was a piece of glass jabbed in his jaw. Phoenix had put broken glass in Texas' cereal."

I gasped, and covered my mouth. "Oh, my God."

"Soon after that incident, Phoenix was diagnosed as being schizophrenic with multiple personalities. He was placed in an institution. He stayed away for several months. We would go up and visit him on the weekends. When he got better they released him but advised us to put him in a program where we lived. Things were back to normal. Phoenix and Texas were happy and getting along, and my life had started to come together, at least I thought."

"What happened?"

"Then from out of nowhere Phoenix became consumed with fire and started to burn anything he got his hands on. He developed an alter ego named Dameon."

"Was he still in therapy?"

"Yes, he was in therapy. The psychiatrist told us not to worry, that it was just his way of releasing his anger. One night I was awakened by the smell of smoke. The house was on fire." She teared up. "The fire started in the room with Texas and our daughter, Lake. Texas slept in the room with Lake all the time. We woke up and tried to get the children out of the house. Texas made it out of the house but Phoenix and Lake were still inside. The fire was so bad; I knew that they were both dead. My husband ran back into the house to try and save Phoenix and Lake." Tears streamed down her face and she sobbed.

"Elizabeth, it's okay," I consoled her.

"Those moments were the most agonizing moments of my life. When I looked around, Texas had ran back into the house to try and help his father." She paused and took a deep breath. "I about died. My entire family was stuck in that burning house. The fire department arrived and went in to try and rescue them."

A sharp pain jolted in my stomach, but I ignored it as I listened to her story.

"My husband was burned on over seventy percent of his body. Texas had severe smoke inhalation and was in a coma for three months." Her voice trembled. "My daughter was burned alive." She hung her head low and sobbed. My eyes welled up from seeing the pain she was in.

"Elizabeth, I'm so sorry." I hugged her. "What about Phoenix?"

Her tears stopped. "He wasn't even in the house. He had made it out of the house and was hiding in the back seat of our van. When I saw him, I knew he had caused the fire. I remember it like it was yesterday. Phoenix, oh, Phoenix, I cried. Tell me you didn't do this. Please tell mommy you didn't do this. He looked at me with the most horrifying stare and smiled. He said, 'Yes, I did it and I'll do it again.'"

I gasped.

"He wasn't remorseful, not one bit. I was so afraid of him. I didn't know what to do. My husband and son were fighting for their lives, my daughter was dead, and one of my children had caused all of this pain. While John was in the hospital, I took Phoenix to an institution in Washington State for children with severe mental disorders. I signed over the parental rights.

I was so tired of everything he had put us through. He was my son and I loved him, but he was very troubled and I knew in my heart he wouldn't stop until he hurt someone else. I also knew he would never get better. I put him behind us, and I focused on Texas and my husband, and trying to nurse them both back to health. When my husband was in the hospital I told him that Phoenix and our daughter had both been killed in the fire.

Texas almost died. His lungs collapsed after the fire and he was in critical condition for three months. When Texas woke-up he had to re-learn how to walk, talk, everything. He had no memory before the fire, and he had no memory of his brother. And that's the way we kept it. We told him about his sister. He vaguely remembers her but he has no memories of Phoenix. Our life became normal again and we moved to Houston, raised Texas, and lived a happy life—until one day he appeared on my doorstep."

"Who?" I swallowed.

"Phoenix."

"What?"

"He told me if I didn't tell him where Texas was he would kill me. I begged him not to hurt Texas. I told him I would do anything if he would not hurt my Texas. He demanded that I give him money."

"Elizabeth, how long has this been going on?" I asked frantically.

"For ten years."

"So he has been blackmailing and threatening you for ten years?"

"Yes, he said as long as I gave him money he would leave us alone."

"Elizabeth, why didn't you go to the police?"

"Because he said if I ever went to the police he would hunt Texas down and kill him. I didn't tell my husband or Texas because I had kept that secret hidden for so long, and John thought Phoenix had been killed in the fire. My husband would have never forgiven me for that lie."

"Elizabeth, I'm so sorry." I handed her some tissue as more tears streamed down her face.

"Are Texas and Phoenix identical or fraternal twins?"

She wiped the tears from her face and blew her nose.

"They're identical. I mean they look exactly alike." She blew her nose. "The only difference is Phoenix has a small scar over his eyebrow."

Her words were inaudible because her hand was covering her mouth. "What did you say?"

"Phoenix has a small scar over his right eyebrow. You can barely see it, you can tell it's cut away."

I was confused. "No, Elizabeth, you must be mistaken; Texas is the one with that scar because I noticed it a few weeks ago." Her gaze met mine.

"No, Raechel, Phoenix has that scar because that was the only thing that was burned on him. During the fire, a piece of lent fell on his eyebrow and burned him, so hair doesn't grow in that area of his eyebrow."

My breath stilled, and my body went numb. I couldn't hear anything but Elizabeth's voice echoing in the background and the constant pounding of my heart. I replayed the past months in my head like the scenes from a movie. I put two and two together; everything became crystal clear. The mood swings, the violence, the smoking, the cheating, even the way he touched me, it just wasn't the same. An intense chill came over me as my ears opened back up and reality set in. I heard Elizabeth calling my name. She was standing in front of me.

"Raechel, Raechel are you okay?"

I was in a daze. My eyes locked with hers. "Elizabeth, I've been sleeping with the enemy."

"What are you talking about?"

"Texas. I mean Phoenix has a scar right over his eye. We were lying in bed one night and I noticed it." The blood in my veins ran hot. "If I was with Phoenix, then where is Texas?" I jumped up and grabbed my coat and keys.

"Oh, my God; he killed Texas!" she screamed. I heard her holler and scream as I ran through the double doors of the hospital. I couldn't stop to console her. I had to get back to Nashville and go to the police as soon as possible. I called Dr. Reynolds again. Thank God he answered the phone.

"Dr. Reynolds, this is Raechel. Are you with Texas?"

"No, I just got off the plane. I'm on my way to baggage claim to retrieve my luggage. He should be waiting on me outside."

"Dr. Reynolds, please don't go to that car."

"What, what are you talking about?" he stuttered.

"Texas is not who you think he is." My heart raced frantically as I tried to catch my breath. "Dr. Reynolds, I have a question, did you have twin boys?"

He was silent. "Yes, Texas had a twin brother that was killed in a fire as well as his sister, our only daughter."

"Did they find the remains of your son and daughter?"

"They found some of the remains of my daughter, but both were so badly burned that they couldn't recognize them. Why are you asking all of these questions?"

As he was talking I was running out of the hospital to my car. "Dr. Reynolds, your son is still alive."

"Who?"

"Phoenix."

"No, Raechel. You're mistaken. Phoenix was killed in that fire twenty years ago." he assured me.

"Dr. Reynolds, Phoenix is in Nashville and has been impersonating Texas. He kidnapped me and held me hostage for three days. He told me he was going to kill you and Elizabeth. He has already killed a friend of mine, Wren Staples."

"Young lady, I don't know what kind of sick joke this is but my son is dead," he snapped.

"Dr. Reynolds, shut up and listen!" I swallowed hard to coat my raw throat. "I can't speak loud because my voice is leaving." I cranked up the Lamborghini. I was out of breath; white air escaped my mouth as I sped out the driveway.

"After the fire, your wife put Phoenix away in an institution in Washington State." I swallowed to catch my breath. "She kept it hidden from you. Apparently he was released when he was eighteen, and ever since then he's been extorting money from your wife and threatening to kill you, her and Texas for years."

"Wait a minute, Raechel. Did Elizabeth tell you all of this?"

"Yes."

"Raechel, I told you my wife is crazy. She's delusional. She's always making up stories, Besides, I have the death certificates of both my son and daughter."

"Dr. Reynolds, ever since Texas' accident there has been some apparent changes with him. He was just different. At first I thought it was the medication, then I noticed drastic changes in his moods and mannerisms. Like certain things he would say and do that Texas would have never done. He had mood swings, and he became very paranoid. After he kidnapped me, he beat and raped me. I knew something was terribly wrong with him."

"He raped you? Raechel, you're lying. I just don't believe this is true."

"Dr. Reynolds, please think back. After the fire, where were you?" After every other word I had to swallow because my throat was raw and my voice was giving away."

"I was in the hospital. I was out of it for months."

"While you were in the hospital is when Elizabeth had Phoenix admitted to the institution. She must have had a false death certificate made up for Phoenix." I swallowed hard. "Just think about it, Dr. Reynolds. Texas normally calls you every day. You didn't hear from him until the other day." There was no response from Dr. Reynolds.

"My God, Raechel! If what you're saying is true, do you think he's done something to Texas?" His voice quivered.

"Dr. Reynolds, please go to the police. I'm on my way back to Nashville. Call me after you have spoken with the police."

The snow was coming down harder and harder. I jumped on interstate 40-East headed back to Nashville. I dialed 911 and explained everything. I told them I had reason to believe that Phoenix Reynolds, Texas Reynolds' estranged brother had done something to him. They acted like I was crazy and they made me repeat the story several times. They said they would send a car to Texas' house but I would have to come in and file a report when I got to the city.

Where could he be? Tears filled my eyelids but I calmed myself down. I felt like Texas was still alive. *Where is he, Lord? Please guide me.* As I drove, I replayed everything in my head about where Texas could be. Then I remembered what Ma'Sadie had told me. 'There will be a battle between good and evil, but the good will prevail if you follow your heart,' and she kept saying she saw water. I meditated on it. *Water, water, the lake; he's at Hillsbury Farm, which would explain the mud on Phoenix' shoes.*

I called Ken but he didn't answer the phone. I left a message. "Ken, this is Raechel. I'm in trouble; please meet me at Hillsbury Farm. It's right pass the Concord Road Exit. Texas Reynolds has a twin named Phoenix Reynolds who's living in Nashville. I think he's responsible for the death of Wren Staples, and he may be responsible for other deaths. Detective, this is a life or death matter. Please call me as soon as you get this message."

I replayed everything in my head, starting with the first day I noticed a difference in Texas. How could I be so stupid when everything about him was different? Then it dawned on me. Oh, my God. I'm pregnant. I kept trying to think back to the last time Texas and I had sex, but I couldn't remember. I know it was over two months ago. I'm pregnant with Phoenix's baby. Tears poured from my eyes like rain, and another sharp pain pierced my side. I kept driving, tears rolled down my face. All I could think about was Texas.

I prayed, "Please, God in heaven, don't let Texas be dead."

Chapter 30

I passed the Concord Road exit and got off on Hillsbury Highway. It was Christmas Eve and I hadn't seen a car for miles. As I drove down the lonely road, my heart pounded with every second. I finally made it to Hillsbury Farm.

I killed the lights; it was pitch black as I slowly crept down the gravel highway up to the cabin. I pulled the car behind an abandoned barn and inhaled a deep breath. *God, please protect me.* I put the pocket knife and phone into my coat pocket and quietly got out the car. Slam! A gust of wind slammed the car door. My heart damn near jumped outta my chest. *Fuck! That scared the shit outta me.* I gained my composure and headed towards the cabin. With every step I took, my heart thumped. Anxiety consumed me as my feet lightly crushed the freshly fallen snow. Another sharp pain surged through my abdomen.

"Ohhh," I shrieked and fell face forward into the snow. I laid there paralyzed in pain for a minute. "Huh, huh, huh." I swallowed hard to coat my raw throat. "Mmmm," I moaned, then I noticed a light coming from the cabin. I ignored the pain in my stomach and stumbled to my feet. I made it to the back of the cabin. I closed my eyes and sat down on the side of the cabin to catch my breath. *I can do all things through Christ Jesus that strengths me.* I tiptoed to the lighted window and my heart stopped—it was Texas.

Warm tears streamed from my eyes. "Oh, my God, it can't be."

My heart melted. "Thank you, Jesus," I whispered. "My baby is alive." I was so thankful. He was tied to a chair and his eyes were covered with a scarf. His arms were tied behind the chair and his feet were tied to the legs of the chair. I ran to the front door. My hands quivered as I tried to find the right key. There were about ten keys on Texas' key chain. Each time I inserted a key the lock didn't click. Nervously, I tried all of them until the last one that I stuck in the lock opened the door.

I ran into the house, pulled the scarf from around his eyes, and took the tape off his mouth.

"Rae," he wept.

I hardly recognized him.

"Is…is it really you?" he asked.

I hugged him and kissed him all over his face. He was badly beaten, and he was skin and bones.

"Yes, baby it's me," I cried.

"Rae, hurry up and untie me before he comes back." I heard a car door slam. "Baby, go…go," he demanded. "He's coming!"

"No, Texas. I'm not leaving without you." Sweat beads covered my face; my heart thumped so fast I could feel it in my knees.

"Raechel, please; go now!" he screamed.

My hands trembled as I tried to free Texas. I sniffed in the snot that was running out of my nose. I took the pocket knife and cut one of the ropes that bound his wrist. Then suddenly, *Whack!* I was struck in the back of my head. I blacked out for a few seconds.

"Uhhhh," I moaned and stumbled to my feet and attempted to run.

Phoenix grabbed the back of my shirt and slammed me on the ground. My head hit the floor and the knife fell from my hand. He kicked me in my side repeatedly. I struggled to reach for the knife. He halted my attempt by crushing my hand with his boot. He stomped my hand like he was trying to kill a spider.

"Ahhhh," I screamed as I heard my bones crack. He pounced on top of me and struck me in my nose so hard, blood flew out my mouth. I grabbed the knife with my other hand and jabbed him in his shoulder. Blood splattered across my face.

"Bitch!" he seethed and grabbed his shoulder and fell backwards. I staggered to my feet and ran upstairs.

"Run, Rae, go!" Texas screamed.

"Shut up." He smacked Texas across the nose with the butt of his gun.

When I got to the top of the stairs it was pitch black. I ran into one of the bedrooms and hid in the closet. My heart was beating faster than a speeding train. I closed my mouth and breathed slowly through my nose to steady myself. An awful stench pierced my nose. I leaned back and a cold hand fell on me. I pulled out my cell phone to get some light. I almost passed out when I saw Mimi's lifeless body. I covered my mouth with my hand to help control my sobs while crocodile tears rolled down my face. I dialed 911 but I hung up when I heard him coming up the stairs.

"Raae-chel, you've been a bad monkeeee…now I'ma have tooo…kill you!" he scoffed and laughed hysterically.

I could see him coming into the bedroom through the shudders in the closet. As he slowly walked around the bedroom, my phone vibrated. *Buzz Buzz.* I pressed the button and it beeped. I swallowed hard. Fear arrested my breaths.

Phoenix walked directly in front of the closet and stopped. My heart pounded out my chest. I closed my eyes. *I'm dead.* But instead of opening the closet he turned and walked out the room. I sighed gently and dialed 911.

"911. What's your emergency?" the operator asked.

"Help me," I whispered. "Hello?" I looked at the phone; it was dead. *Fuck!*

I slowly opened the closet door and quietly walked out the room. As I entered the hallway I looked around but I didn't see him. Then I saw his shadow coming from behind me. I attempted to take off running but he snatched me by my hair and yanked me backward. I tumbled to the floor. He picked me up by my hair and bashed my head into the wall. I attempted to take off again, but he grabbed my leg and dragged me back to where he was.

"Get off me, you crazy muthafucka!" I pounded him in the face with all my might. "Get the fuck off me! Ahhhhhh!" I kicked and screamed trying to squirm away but he got on top of me. I bit his arm. I tried to rip off a chunk of his skin. He jumped off of me.

"Ahhhh!" he screamed. "Bitch, I'ma kill you."

I crawled away; then I ran down the stairs with him right on my tail. He pushed me from behind and I tumbled down the stairs. I heard my leg snap and I knew it was broken.

"God, help me," I begged. As I crawled across the floor on my elbows, he jumped on top of me again. I pounded him with my fists. I used every ounce of my strength trying to fight him.

"Help, somebody help me, please! Get off me, sick muthafucka!"

He grabbed my head and began ramming it into the hardwood floor. *Whack! Whack!* He hit me so hard in the face, blood gushed from my nose and splattered across the white walls. My face and mouth filled with blood and saliva. I stopped screaming because I was choking and coughing up blood. He struck me repeatedly in the face until I was unconscious.

I woke up disoriented, naked and tied to a chair with my legs spread eagle. At first I couldn't see because my eyes were so swollen. I forced them open just wide enough to look across the room. I saw Texas, and my heart stopped. I took a moment to study him, but my vision was hazy. I wept.

"Texas, I tried to save you."

"I know." He cried and I cried.

"Baby, I'm so sorry," I responded through tears and sobs. This was it for us.

"Shut the fuck up!" Phoenix screamed. There was immediate silence, except for my sniffling. He was standing by the fireplace shuffling the logs in the fire with the poker.

I raised my head and my eyes skated the room. Through my blurry vision I saw a can of gasoline and a gun on the table.

"That's yo' problem, nigga. You talk too fuckin' much. And you think you know every gatdamn thing, but actually you don't know shit. You ain't smart, nigga, you dumb. I was able to come in and take your life right from under yo' nose." He laughed. "Now who the smart one? Not to mention I fucked this bitch plenty times in the ass and some mo' shit."

Phoenix stuck the poker in the fireplace and let it get piping hot, then he came over and rammed it dead in my pussy.

"Ahhhhhhhh!" I screamed in agony. I felt like somebody was pouring hot lava inside me.

"Yeah bitch, that's for biting my dick off. Did you think I was gon' let yo' ass get away with that shit! Huh, Huh?" He seethed, and rammed it in me even harder. Blood trickled from between my legs.

"Stop, you crazy muthafucka!" Texas screamed.

He pulled the poker from between my legs and whacked Texas on the side of the face leaving a gigantic gash. Blood gushed from his head.

"Now it's my time to talk and you listen." He lit a cigarette. "Y'all left me to die. I lived on the streets like a fuckin' stray dog. Doing whatever I had to survive, while you sorry, low-lifes was living like royalty. But not no more. Y'all gon' pay for what y'all did to me. The hell that y'all left me in is fixin' to be the hell y'all about to see." He picked up the can of gasoline.

"I've been trying to destroy you for years. I started to come and kill you, and them worthless pieces of shit you call Mom and Dad. I was just gon' wipe all of y'all out. But that shit just wouldn't do me justice. Y'all muthafuckas gotta suffer! Plus, why not take advantage of the good life since you Mr. Big Shot NFL playa." He puffed on his cigarette. "Shit, I figured I might as well just kill you, and live as big baller Texas Reynolds. Ya, heard me?" He sneered.

"And after I kill ya' mammy and pappy, I'ma really be paid, cuz I'ma get all that insurance doe. Oooh," he scoffed and rubbed his hands together.

"When I saw yo' raggedy ass was in the hospital, I knew my life was about to change. It was the perfect time for me to kidnap you and take over your life. Awww, before I forget, you remember that bitch, Keisha Greenlee? She died a slow death. I killed her and yo' baby. And you know the fun part about that whole thing? The whole time she thought I was you." He bowled over in laughter.

Texas sat there motionless, except for the tears that flowed from his face. It was fucked up that Keisha died thinking Texas was the one that was killing her.

He paused with an evil smirk on his face. "Hummm, look at how history repeats itself. Now I'm going to do the same thing to this bitch." He laughed wickedly.

My heart pounded as he walked toward me. He got close to my face and yanked me by my hair.

"That ain't my baby you dumb fucking slut, I'm sterile. That's what happens to little boys that have to live on the streets and that's in and out of jail getting raped by grown ass fuckin' men. They become sterile. Say it," he screamed.

I softly said, "Sterile."

Then he smacked me in the mouth. "I thought you had died in that car crash. I wish you had. 'Cause yo' stankin' ass gettin' on my nerves. I shoulda killed yo' ass a long time ago. And you fucked up my plans to have that nigga's bitch ass momma and daddy come to this house."

"That's yo' momma and daddy too." Texas screamed. He punched Texas in the face. "Them old shriveled up prunes ain't my fuckin' momma and daddy." Then Phoenix took the cigarette he was smoking and put it out on Texas' hand.

"Muthafucka!" Texas yelled.

Phoenix whispered in his ear. "The poison I've been giving you eats your guts slowly. That's right; it's a slow grind." He laughed. "And it's almost time."

Texas was in total awe. Texas jerked and yanked on the ties that bound his wrists together. It was useless; the knot wouldn't budge.

"Mom and Dad always loved you more. First it was baby sista, then you, and then it will be Raechel. Everything that was taken from me, I'm going to take from you."

He opened the can of gasoline and poured it over the house. Then he doused my body with gasoline. The strong vapors intoxicated me and made me sick to my stomach. Hot vomit shot from my mouth and all over him.

"Bitch!" He smacked me across the face with the can. In my peripheral I noticed Texas maneuvering his arms. Then I saw a shadow outside of the window. Phoenix pulled out the matches in his pocket just as Detective Stevens kicked open the door.

"Drop it, Phoenix." His 44 was aimed directly at Phoenix's dome.

"Are you kidding me?" Phoenix laughed. "Ahhh," he cracked up. "Nigga, please. You must think I'ma damn fool. Even if I don't drop this match, you fire that bullet and the heat from it gon' ignite a fire anyway. That's what I want; for y'all to burn up in a blaze of glory."

Phoenix turned the radio up extremely loud. The sounds of Li'l Wayne's "6 Foot 7 Foot" roared from the surround sound. Phoenix bobbed his head and mimicked the lyrics to the song. "I lost my mind. It's somewhere out there stranded. I think you stand under me if you don't understand me." He chuckled wildly. Then he stopped. The look of the devil was on his face. He lit the match.

"See you in hell, muthafuckas!" He dropped the match; flames swiftly encircled the living room. "Burn, baby burn!" he screamed and watched in amazement as the fire danced around the room.

I held my breath and tried to free my hands. The thick smoke clouded the room. Detective Stevens slowly put down his gun.

"Phoenix, I'm not trying to hurt you. See, I'm going to put down my gun." Detective Stevens slowly put down his gun. Then he eased toward Phoenix and grabbed him by the neck, and the two men began to fight.

I saw Texas free his hands while they were fighting, then he rushed over to where I was and untied me.

"Run, Raechel!" he screamed. But I couldn't. My leg was broken.

"Ugh," I groaned as I crawled toward the door on my elbows trying to stay free of the smoke. Phoenix had knocked Detective Stevens out.

I turned around. Texas tackled Phoenix. Phoenix picked up a chair and threw it at Texas, but Texas ducked, and then gripped Phoenix by the neck. They tussled and fell to the ground as they were choking each other. Texas was trying his best to choke the shit out of Phoenix. He finally knocked Phoenix out. I was crawling out the door. Texas stopped to try to help Detective Stevens get up.

Phoenix suddenly stormed out of the kitchen with a knife in his hands. I turned around and screamed.

"Texas, look out!"

Swoosh! Texas ducked. Phoenix barely missed his head. The knife landed in the wall. Phoenix punched Texas in the face and knocked him down. He hovered over Texas and pounded him in the face. The flames licked up the walls and thick smoke clouded the house. I crawled back coughing and hacking from the smoke. I yanked the knife out of the wall

"Ugh…Ugh…Ugh." I repeatedly rammed the knife into Phoenix's back. He collapsed on top of Texas.

Texas gagged and got up. The two of us grabbed Detective Stevens. We couldn't stay a second longer in that house.

"Ruunn, Raechel, Ruun!" Texas yelled.

My leg was broken, but I got a bolt of energy from somewhere. Moments after we got outside the house, there was a loud explosion, flames spouted from every angle of the house. Texas and I held each other.

"Without you there is no me," Texas said softly in my ear.

"And no me without you," I whispered, before collapsing in the snow.

Chapter 31

I woke up and stared at the ceiling. An antiseptic smell tickled my nose as my eyes skated my surroundings. It didn't take me long to realize I was in a hospital. My left eye was swollen shut and I could barely see out of my right eye. Pain and soreness struck every angle of my body. I was startled by the man sitting beside me until I realized it was Texas.

"It's okay, baby." He rubbed my head. "It's me, sweetheart."

My mind was blank. I couldn't comprehend why I was laying in a hospital bed, but one thing I knew for sure, without any shadow of a doubt, I loved the man that was sitting next to me. I closed my eyes and thanked God for his very existence. During my prayer I saw another face. My heart raced, my breaths became thin. I squeezed Texas' hand.

"Nurse! Nurse!" Texas shouted and ran into the hall way.

The nurse rushed in and upped my oxygen level. I inhaled the air and watched the monitor as my heart rate slowly decreased.

"It's okay, sweetheart. You just had another panic attack," the nurse said.

Bits and pieces of my memory started to come back, but the clearer the images in my mind got the more emotional I became. Tears blurred my eyes. I couldn't get any words out.

"Baby, it's okay. Please, calm down," Texas pleaded. "You're going to be okay." He grabbed my hand and kissed it. I weakly squeezed his hand back. "Trust me, everything is going to be okay."

The nurse checked my vital signs "Are you in pain, sweetie?" she asked.

"Yhhh," I tried to speak.

"Shhh, Raechel. Don't try to talk. Your jaw has been wired shut. It was fractured in three places," Texas told me.

She whispered something to Texas and then walked out the room.

"Raechel." Texas grabbed my hand again. "We lost the baby."

At first I was thrown off by his comment then I remembered I was pregnant. My memory was still scattered. The recent events were like a puzzle, and I was still trying to put the pieces together.

"You had a miscarriage."

I was sad that I had lost my baby, but maybe it was God who took the baby. Maybe he knew that my body just couldn't take all the pressure it had been under.

"I'm sorry, sweetheart." Texas wept with tears in the corner of his eyes.

I sighed deeply. I asked him for a pen. He looked around and came back with a Sharpie. I wrote, *No me* in his hand.

"And no me without you," he said.

I laid back and closed my eyes but terror shook me. Phoenix's face reappeared and my heart almost exploded in my chest. I tried to sit up in the bed. I wrote *Phoenix?*

"Baby, you have nothing to be afraid of; he was killed in the fire." He rubbed my head.

I laid back and reflected on the past forty-eight hours. I started squeezing Texas' hand as the events became clearer in my mind. Then suddenly an image of Mimi appeared. I looked at Texas.

"Mimi," I wrote.

He looked at me and shook his head. "Raechel, Mimi is dead." I remembered her lifeless body and my heart broke.

No, nooo. I tried to scream but nothing would come out. Tears poured from my eyes. I couldn't breathe.

"Nurse!" Texas yelled again. She rushed back in and checked my vitals again. This time she called the doctor to come and assist. They injected my veins with some poison and my heart rate slowly decreased. I kept seeing Mimi's lifeless body in that closet. I remembered how rude I was to Mimi; she just couldn't be dead. Tears streamed down my face until I fell asleep.

♣

Mimi's funeral was on New Year's Day. Our family was devastated. It was particularly sad because it had to be a closed casket funeral. Phoenix had raped and sodomized Mimi's body until she was unrecognizable. Mimi's death really fucked me up, mainly because I had treated her so bad. Now that I look back, I realize that when Mimi called me to come get her, Phoenix had kidnapped her. But I let my anger and resentment keep me from saving my cousin's life. I didn't tell anyone about that phone call because I felt responsible for Mimi's death, a secret that I knew would hunt me until the day I died.

Texas and I got married but we didn't tell anyone because we're going to have a huge wedding at the end of the summer.

I had to sit out of school this semester because physically I just couldn't make it. I had three cracked ribs, a fractured jaw line, and four broken fingers along with a bunch of scrapes and burns. We don't know if I'll be able to have children because my uterus was damaged when Phoenix jabbed me with the poker. My plans are to finish school in the fall and graduate next spring. Both Texas and I are in therapy. Texas is in a twelve-step program for post-traumatic stress disorder. He can't sleep at night and whenever he's awake he's irritable and on edge, so our psychiatrist suggested a twelve-step program to help him cope with the trauma he has faced.

I had been so traumatized by what I had gone through, I couldn't function with everyday life. The doctor put me on a high dosage antidepressant. I was so spaced out I couldn't even complete simple tasks like bathing and cooking, so I stopped taking it and decided to face my fears instead of trying to mask them with pills.

We purchased a new home with a state-of-the-art security system. This house has more cameras than Fort Knox, and we have a gun in every room. Texas has become obsessed with guns. Even with therapy, and the high dosage sleeping pills he's taking, he absolutely cannot sleep unless he has a gun under his pillow and one on the nightstand right beside our bed.

Texas' parents are doing fine. Mrs. Reynolds was released from the hospital, and is at home in Houston. She apologized for the way she had treated me, and she credits me for saving her and her family's life. I told her it wasn't me, it was the good Lord that deserved all the credit. She and I talk every day.

Texas has gotten sole custody of his daughter. Eva has some severe mental problems. She served eight months for assaulting me, not in jail but a mental institution.

We discovered that Phoenix was responsible for more than a dozen deaths. He apparently had been killing random people; anyone that got in his way.

Phoenix Reynolds took a lot from me. My life is slowly getting back to normal. I have my good days and my bad days. One thing for sure is I'm so thankful for my husband. Without him I don't know how I would have made it. I haven't gotten over Phoenix Reynolds. Even though I know he's dead, he haunts me in my dreams. I still ask Texas to keep the lights on until I fall asleep.

Chapter 32

I looked at myself in the mirror and tears welled up in my eyes. The anguish and the pain I had faced in the past year stared back at me. My once beautiful body was now covered in burn marks, cuts, and scrapes.

This scar on my neck, I hate it. It seems like it's the first thing people notice when they look at me, but I try not to let it bother me. I'm so thankful my face did not scar. I only have a small mark on the side of my face from where I had reconstructive surgery on my jaw line. The scars on my body, I can hide, but if my face was fucked up, I don't know what I would do. But anyway, I'm not focusing on the scars or burn marks today, because today is Valentine's Day. Me and my baby are celebrating the love we have for one another.

Texas and I have decided what happened in the past is over. We can't change the past. What we are focusing on now is our future together. I told him that I would, as long as he continues to go to counseling. He has just completed a twelve-step program, so that's a start. I had the cast removed from my leg that I had been toting around for two months. So tonight is going to be special, because I have a little surprise in store for my baby. Ever since the cast was removed, I've been practicing this striptease that I'm going to perform for him tonight. I even got my girl, Tangerine, who dances at Platinum Paradise, to come over and teach me some of her sexy stripper moves. After my boo gets a peek of me winding and gyrating my ass, he'll be ready to plunge all eleven inches of his beefy dick inside me. I'm so excited; this is the first time in months we've had a romantic evening, and I'm hoping the special night I have planned helps spark some of the magic we once shared. I'm doing everything in my power to make sure this evening goes as planned.

Texas and I have been through so much. From the baby momma drama to the mental and physical abuse. But I feel this relationship is worth fighting for. My girls are always asking how I can still go on, considering everything I've been through. I tell them because of love. If you truly love somebody, you'll accept the good, the bad, and the ugly. You'll do anything to make them happy. Plus, I can't do without the lifestyle Texas has accustomed me to. See he's a professional football player, been in the league almost ten years and he is still good; I'm talkin' ESPN sports highlights every Sunday. So from since the first day I met him money ain't never been a problem. We live in a two million dollar home in the Governor's Club at Brentwood. We have a beach home in Charleston, South Carolina, and we own a cottage in Aspen. If you ever lay eyes on him, you would know God himself sent one of his angels down in the form of a man. Standing six five and two hundred and forty pounds with a rich mahogany skin tone and major swag, that's killin' Jay-Z, LeBron and Obama put together, everything about my man is top notch. If you had the chance to receive some of his good lovin', you'll be saying the same shit. Because a man like Texas Reynolds, you'll do almost anything to keep.

Anyway, tonight I have everything laid out. First, we're having dinner at Ruth's Chris Steak House, and afterwards I reserved us the master suite at Loews Vanderbilt Hotel, which is right next door. That's when I'ma surprise my boo with my dance, and after that it's gonna go down.

We arrived at dinner and Texas was just as excited as I was. We both missed the closeness that we once shared and it seems as if we are beginning to bond again.

"Rae, you know I love you," Texas said and grabbed my hand and kissed it, "Without you there is no me."

"And no me without you." I smiled and planted a soft kiss on his juicy lips.

Our entrées were served. We held hands as I led us in a silent prayer. Then I picked up my knife to cut a bite of my filet but quickly dropped it back down on the plate. My fingers went numb. Texas' gaze caught my anxiety. It was the nerves in my hand, they had been badly fractured.

"Babe, you okay?" he asked

"Yeah, Bay." I winced and flashed him a smile faker than a three-dollar bill. I played it off, grabbed my glass with my other hand, and took a sip of champagne. Truth was the nerves were so fractured in my right hand that I would often times have severe nerve spasms that would paralyze my hand for a few seconds, sometimes minutes. But I acted like it was nothing because I'm not going to let anything ruin this evening– no thoughts, no memories, nothing from the past.

After feasting on a delicious dinner of salad, filet mignon, asparagus spears, and a bottle of Perrier Jouet Fleur, we were good and toasted when we left the restaurant. I blindfolded Texas and we walked next door to the Loews Vanderbilt.

"Baby, where we goin'?" Texas kept trying to make me tell him what my plans were.

"Tex, I told you, it's a surprise. You're just gonna have to wait and see." I smiled and grabbed his hand and led him to the elevator.

He was grinning from ear to ear. "Baby, c'mon tell me where we going," he pleaded and pulled me close to him.

"Texas, be patient! Why you think you always gotta know everything?" As soon as the elevator doors opened, I grabbed his hand and led him up to the penthouse suite.

"Relax, baby, I got this."

When I entered the room, I was blown away. It was laid out. The hotel staff had really surprised me. Candles were lit around the room emitting a sweet fragrance. Red rose petals had been placed on the bed in the shape of a heart. The fireplace was lit, with the logs making the room warm and cozy. The curtains were pulled back displaying an intoxicating view of the city. Everything was perfect just as I'd planned.

I removed the blindfold and right away, his eyes lit up like stars against a midnight sky.

"Ahhh, baby, this is so nice."

He picked me up and swung me around then he quickly put me down. "Hold on, baby, let me take this burner out." He pulled his gun from underneath his shirt and placed it underneath the pillow. He wrapped his arms around my waist and picked me up from the ground. He held me for a minute and kissed me before gently laying me down on the bed. His lips touched mine and he snaked his tongue into my mouth. We greedily kissed each other like our lives depended on it. My body unwound as he planted soft, delicate kisses on my neck. A mild tingle rushed through me. My back arched as he slid his slick tongue down my neck, he unleashed my firm titties from my low cut dress and sucked on each of my puffy nipples like a melting ice cream cone.

"Oooooh, baaaaby," I murmured. "Let me feel that dick." I unbuttoned his pants, but before I could pull out his dick, he had dug his fingers into my creamy wetness. "Mmmm," I moaned in ecstasy as I slowly rotated my hips and sucked his fingers inside me.

"Damn, baby you so wet," he whispered. He tried to take off my thong, but couldn't get it over my phat ass.

He smacked me on the ass. "Take that shit off," he insisted and gently gripped me on one of my ass cheeks. He stood up and quickly undressed. His thick pole poked through the slit in his boxers. I pulled down his boxers and slowly stroked my hand down the shaft of his thick, juicy, slab and watched as a small amount of precum oozed out.

My mouth watered. *Mmmm, ain't nothing in the world better than a fat, vein-poppin' dick.* Then I remembered my dance. *Damn! Damn! Damn!* I couldn't wait to slide my simmering pussy on his eleven inches and swallow every inch of him inside me. But I had to be patient first; I really wanted to do my dance that I had worked so hard on. I reluctantly got up to go get in the shower. Texas sat up and grabbed my hand.

"Hold on, mama…where you going?"

"Baby, I'm about to take a shower." I teasingly smiled at him.

"A shower?" He shook his head. "Nah, ma." He pulled me close and nuzzled his head into my belly, softly kissing me on exposed skin. "You can take a shower later."

"No, baby, I'm about to take a shower now." I leaned down and playfully kissed him on the lips. "Plus, I don't wanna ruin the surprise I got for you."

"Dang, Rae, you gon' leave me hanging like this." We both looked down at his swollen head.

A slight smirk adorned my lips. "Baby, be patient; I'ma take care of that later." *Believe me, boo, I wanna tackle that big muthafucka right now.*

He grabbed my wrist. "Man, c'mon on; quit playin'. Lemme get some right fast." He softly kissed me on the stomach.

"No, Tex. If we do it now it'll ruin the surprise I have planned for you." I tried to pull away but his grip around my wrist was so tight. "Boy, let me go." I giggled and he finally unleashed his grip but not before slapping me on my ass.

"Ouch!" I screamed and playfully punched him in the arm, and sashayed off to the shower.

We both got in the shower and bathed each other like we always do. Texas continued trying to make love to me but I wouldn't let him. I wanted to do my dance first. I had worked so hard on this dance I had the ideal song, "Adore You" by Prince, and had the perfect lingerie outfit that accentuated my nice, round ass and slim waistline.

Texas got out the shower first, and I stayed in. I let the warm water stream down my body as I reflected on memories from the past and hoped for a better relationship in the future. After I got out the shower and dried off, Texas peeked in the door as I had my leg on the toilet lathering it with lotion.

"Ooooh, look at that ass," he teased while grabbing onto his hardness.

"Shut the door, boy."

We laughed.

"Hey, baby. I gotta go get something out the car. I'll be right back."

"What you gotta get outta the car. Your pajamas and everything is in the suitcase I brought here earlier."

"Well, I gotta get my phone and some other stuff."

What other stuff? "'Kay. When you come back, I'll be ready," I replied anxiously.

"You betta. If not, I'ma catch a case, cause ya' ass gon' get raped."

We both laughed.

He shut the door and I finished getting ready for my striptease debut. I'm so excited. Everything is going as planned and Texas seems like he's getting back to himself.

The steam from the shower had fogged up the mirror. I took my hand and ran it across the glass. Water bubbles cascaded the mirror and it fogged back up. I opened the door to let some steam out, and then flossed and brushed my teeth. I washed my face with my Shiseido skin care line and some of the cleanser got in my eye.

"Damn!" My eye started stinging. I splashed it with cold water and held a towel to it until it stopped watering.

While I had the towel to my eye, I was retracing my dance moves in my head. When I put the towel down and looked in the mirror, my heart skipped a beat. Texas was standing right behind me. I grabbed my chest.

"Baby, you scared the shit outta me!" I let out a sigh of relief. "I didn't know you were standing behind me." I smiled at him through the reflection in the mirror but the stone cold expression on his face didn't budge.

"I see you found the pajamas I packed for you." He didn't respond. I looked in his eyes. They were different. I sensed something was wrong.

I turned around. "Baby, what's the ma—"

His iron fist met the side of my jaw, crushing my reconstructed jaw line. *What the fuck!*

He grabbed a chunk of my hair and rammed my head directly into the mirror. Glass shattered everywhere, blood gushed from my forehead, and a tidal wave of pain and terror exploded in my head.

God, please, no this can't be happening again. I stumbled back woozily. Grabbing the towel rack to steady myself, I swung at him but missed. His fist landed directly on the rim of my nose. *Plop!* I fell into the tub. The back of my head collided with the concrete wall, and my eyes rolled into their sockets. I blacked out.

"Uhhhh," I moaned, with my mouth hanging open. My eyes fluttered opened, and the grim fate of my reality began to crystallize. My blurry eyes met his. *Nooooo!*

He stood over me celebrating the present state I was in. "Ple….stop," I muttered, as my jaw dangled on its hinges and blood flowed into my mouth.

"Bitch, I'ma kill you!" he snarled through clinched teeth. He snatched me out the tub by my hair, and drug my body through crumpled shards of broken glass into the bedroom. I stumbled to my feet and swung at him. My ring scratched the side of his face. He slugged me in the temple and I collapsed on the bed. He jumped on top of me. His knuckles pounded my face repeatedly. "You, bitch!" He grabbed my neck and started choking me. I tried to fight him off but it was just like hitting a concrete wall.

"I… can't… bre…" My eyes watered as his hands locked around my neck like the jaws of a pit-bull. I tugged and scratched at his hands, trying to pry them off my neck, but the more I pulled, the tighter he squeezed.

"Die, bitch, die!" He seethed and jolted his arms back and forth like he was trying to rip my neck off. I looked up at him and saw pure evil in his eyes. Veins pulsed outta his head as he choked the life out of me. I knew he wasn't going to stop until I was dead.

I stretched my hand across the bed to grab the gun that was under the pillow, but I couldn't reach it. I heard Texas banging on the door.

"Raechel!" he screamed. "Raaaaechel!"

"Noooo....please...noooo. Texaaaas, help me!"

Sweat from Phoenix's forehead dripped on my face as my lungs desperately struggled for air. I kicked and squirmed as he tightened his grip with all his power. I faded in and out of consciousness. I reached for the gun again, but I didn't feel it. My eyes connected with his I caught a glance of death. At that very second I felt the tip of the gun. I nestled the gun into the palm of my hand and aimed it at him. He immediately loosened his grip and went for the gun. We recklessly tussled over the gun and fell to the floor.

"Ugghhh," I grunted as he landed on top of me, knocking the wind from my lungs, but my grip on the gun was secure. He squeezed my throat with one hand, and he reached for the gun with the other. Suddenly my fingers began to tingle then they went numb. With no trouble the gun was pulled from my hand. My heart stopped.

Boom! Boom! Two shots rang out. His body collapsed on top of me. Texas ran over and quickly pulled him off me, and wrapped his arms around me. I cried in his arms. I looked at Texas wondering where he had gotten the other gun.

"I went to the car to get my other gun. I wouldn't have been able to sleep," he told me.

I looked over at Phoenix laying in a pool of blood. I closed my eyes and laid my head on Texas' chest. *Death number three.*

Texas rubbed my head. "It's finally over."

THE END